GOLD CITY

BY
M. T. Meyer

Words Matter Publishing
P.O. Box 531
Salem, Il 62881
www.wordsmatterpublishing.com

This is a work of fiction. All characters, with the obvious exceptions of Winfield Scott Hancock, George Armstrong Custer, Frank and Jesse James are fictional. All details, incidents, and places are used fictitiously or are products of the author's creative process.

ISBN 13: 978-1-947072-43-5
ISBN 10: 1-947072-43-9

Library of Congress Catalog Card Number: 2018930167

AUTHOR'S NOTE

The details of Hancock's coming to Fort Larned, and the activities surrounding the forts and the Indian situations are a matter of public record. Custer is certainly well known for his exploits and well documented. The James brothers are quite well documented as well. All of the aforementioned can be researched in depth with the click of a mouse. However, in researching the James brothers, I came to feel deeply for them as individuals as they had to endure great adversity in their lives due to the greed of others. I have taken extreme liberty with them in this book, and I know that authors must be very careful with characters that actually existed.

No, Frank, to my knowledge, was never interested in becoming a doctor. His stepfather was in truth a doctor who was torturously hanged for trying to protect his family. Frank and Jesse had a younger brother who was killed, and their mother injured when representatives from the railroad who was determined to have their property dynamited their house. Throughout history, more has been written about Jesse than his brother Frank. I chose to delve into the man that Frank 'could have been' if only he'd had someone take a keen interest in him. I thought it made for a unique twist in the story and might get others to look into the lives of these men to whom history has given a bad rap. It is true that Frank was highly intelligent, known to quote Shakespeare during robberies, and held early dreams of becoming a teacher. He was aggravatingly slow according to some, but what most men would call a 'deadeye.' He was deadly with a gun but slow on the draw. Jesse was like an angry rattlesnake, deadly from any range, angle, or speed. He was a youth when he rode with Quantrill and learned early in life that sometimes life just is not fair.

We may never know the entire truth about these men, but their legends live on. They refused to become victims. They rallied and rebelled and would go down in history as some of the most prolific bank and train robbers in the West. To some they were outlaws, to others, they were just brothers fighting for their lives as the law had proven to be as crooked as a sidewinder. On either side of the law, they learned that *sometimes, blood is all that saves us.*

Acknowledgements and Thanks

First of all, thanks to my Creator for giving me the gift of creativity and love for the written word. A special thank you to my wonderful family: my parents, who thought that ten years is long enough to craft a story worthy of the ages yet still believed in me; my sisters who were my sounding boards and my cheerleaders throughout the process; and my son, who is my reason for being.

A special thanks go to author Brian Moreland for his wisdom, insight, and encouragement that helped me realize my wildest dreams.

My dear friend Russell Beatty who helped me wade through the final drafts and craft the finished product, thank you! You and Greta mean the world to me.

And I cannot forget a very special friend, Dean Smith, for all her encouragement and for providing such wonderful hospitality, which helped me accomplish the finishing touches of this story.

I thank all of my dear friends for having faith in me, and all of my fans that will read this novel and hopefully stay with me for years to come.

M. T. Meyer

Foreword to Gold City

Legends, they say, are made up of truth and myth. The characters may be real but tend to be larger than life, their heroism, their bravery, inflated almost to positions of deities by the common man who struggles to fathom the true human spirit that abides within us all yet is demonstrated and displayed by so few.

The American West is full of legends, great and small, and some of us find ourselves longing to enter that portal of history, if only for a short time, to be witness to the vastness, the glory, the passion, of a time that is no more. In the heart of every man and woman beats the heart of a pioneer, whether it beats for music, language, technology, history, or science, it rests there, waiting, hoping, dreaming.

The day of the American West has come and gone, the days where life was hard, tomorrow not promised, and hope as fleeting as the western wind.

It is a new west we live in, where the same themes still apply, but in a more urban environment. History has a way of repeating itself, and in today's battleground and frontier, we still root for the hero, that individual who can face adversity, rise above it, and conquer it with grace, grit, and strength.

I hope that this book proves that our heroes don't always have to be 'cowboys.' I hope you enjoy, and God bless.

M. T. Meyer

Synopsis

The war of Rebellion is over. The great expansion to the west has begun. It is a frontier, not of just land, but of heart and spirit. Only the strongest survive. This is the saga of a town of individuals who refused to give up, their struggles chronicled, their joy and despair a written word.

There is the doctor, new to the town, a man with a secret and a price on his head. Travers Gage has come west after the War Between the States to rebuild his life. Running from a reputation he never wanted, and the memory of a young girl whose heart he broke, he struggles to find his footing among a town newly sprung up on the Kansas plains. A doctor forced to pick up a gun; he faces an inner battle that could destroy him. Can he overcome his past, and can he get to the bottom of the mysteriously missing men of the town without losing his own life in the process?

There is the sheriff, a man who knows his best days are behind him. Erasmus Tate and his wife Louella are the voice of reason for the town. Aged and tried, they know that life can turn on a dime. An unlikely pair, they are the glue that keeps the town strong. But will Ras take one too many chances wearing that badge?

There is the blacksmith, a freed slave, who along with his wife seek validation in a white world. Clayton and Sarah Moss never expected their lives to be easy now that they were free. Nor did they ever expect to find a friend in Travers Gage, a Southerner. Clayton knows the moment he meets the doctor that he will never find another like him, and Sarah learns that sometimes, trusting your heart is the only freedom you have.

There is the madam whose heart is bigger than the west itself. Flora McDonough never dreamed she would end up in a place like Gold City. All she had ever known was hardship. But Gold City was her fresh start and a chance at true love for the very first time. Would she find it with the new schoolteacher, or would her heart get broken yet again?

There is the wife whose husband may be the devil himself. Jim and Maggie Bowers are the richest couple in the territory. Unfortunately, money can't buy love. Both harbor a deep secret that could be the other's undoing, and no one is willing to spill their guts as the price could be higher than either wants to pay.

There is the friend who chooses to be only that. Laura Murphy has found her place in Gold City. Fiercely independent, she owns the boarding house in town. One of the first to meet Travers Gage, she knows there is something about him that this town needs, and it is not just his medical services.

There is the tomboy who captures the soul of a warrior. Sally Sharpe knew the journey out west for her father's health would be an adventure. She just never expected to lose her heart and soul to an Army scout that had red skin. Can their love survive prejudice and fear?

A town, new and on the verge of legend. The place — Gold City

PROLOGUE

The crash of thunder in the distance shook the earth with such force that his horse sidestepped even in mid-stride. At any moment the bottom was literally going to fall out of the heavens as Travers raced into the darkness of the night—to save *her*. His heart twisted at the thought of what she must be going through at this very moment. He had tried so hard to keep her from this, to keep her safe: to make her his. Time and distance had changed things between them. Death had changed things between them. Their relationship was strained at best. Things had been said, awful things that could not be taken back, no matter how true they were. Hurtful things. On both sides. But he owed her. He felt fear rise up like bile in his throat threatening to choke him: fear of what he would find and fear of the blackness of the night that he raced headfirst into. He had to trust Cirrus. His faithful stallion had never failed him before. He prayed he wouldn't this time, for he needed his instincts in this world that seemed to be made of pitch, lighted briefly by the sharp, jagged electric light that caught his breath every time it touched the earth. Out here it was a fearsome thing, both beautiful and extremely dangerous. He willed his heart to still and his breath to return to normal after the last strike, knowing he could not stop until he reached his destination. He had to get there, reach her in time.

PART I

Journey's End

ONE

Somewhere in the branches of the tree above, a bird sang its sweet song, undisturbed by the activity, or lack of it, going on below. It should have been a beautiful spring day, the sun was shining, the birds were singing, but a heaviness draped the land. The air was still tinged with the faint hint of sulfur and death, and the music from the creature in the tree sounded a bit out of place. Perhaps he sang for the purpose of lifting the spirits of the country around him because he knew that nature had drooped its head. The land was too quiet by far with no one out in the fields that had long ago seen a fervor of activity. For the most part, the country was barren, the landscape dotted with abandoned shelled out homes, leaving the world to appear like a ghost town. Even the grass did not appear to be in line with the season. It was April, a time of new beginnings in all things, especially rebirth in the very essentials of life. Yet the grass looked as dead as the scores of men lying beneath the once fertile earth. Men that had once walked this land, their backs stiffened with pride, resolve, and honor. Honor, above all else, had led those men to their deaths. Well, honorable men stopped bullets just as well as the rakes and dregs of society. Four hard years of war had proven that.

A breeze rustled the branches, and for a second the bird hushed its song, only to begin again when the leaves stopped their dance. The man lounging beneath the tree, his back propped against its trunk, knew all about those dead men. He had helped put many of them in their graves. He had been trying to rest here in the shade of the tree, but rest was not finding him. Every time his eyes closed, he saw rows upon rows of dead men, some staring into his eyes accusingly. He was weary of life. Running from a past, he could not escape. He had often wished to be counted among those who haunted his dreams at night, but it was not meant to be. The ironic tragedy of it all was that he was a surgeon, a man trained to save lives, not take them. The last four years he had been guilty of both, and the knowledge of it was like gall in his throat. The man's eyes opened to the dismal scenery around him, the brown grass, and the empty landscape. It looked like fall of the year. The striking silver-gray eyes missed nothing as they peered from beneath the lowered brim of his black Stetson. Most people never got close enough to notice the ring of dark blue that bled to a lighter blue when he was amused. He'd been told on a number of occasions that he had the strangest eyes. They appeared as molten steel when his ire was raised and many a man had seen that fire firsthand. He was a hard man, the last few years had seen to that. His dark, rugged features gave little indication of the man who lay beneath. He was not overly tall, nor heavily muscled, but he was lean and compact, hard where it counted. His carriage was one of authority. He was an educated man, a surgeon no less, and he'd had his own clinic before the war. Four years he had practiced medicine, before the madness, before the country had ripped itself apart in a senseless, drunken revelry for blood. Travers Gage had always considered himself a man of honor and morals. The war had left him without both, stripping him of his integrity, causing him to wonder if he had stepped a few rungs lower into hell. The good doctor had been a prominent citizen of a small town just west of Lynchburg, Virginia, called Fellowship, and as the only doctor in town, he had enjoyed a good clientele. Fellowship was a small town, but he had done well for himself. The son of a merchant who had believed slavery was wrong, he had found himself at a crossroads when the first shot was fired on Fort Sumter in Charleston Harbor. Townsfolk had come knocking on his door in the night, his neighbor out front leading the pack.

"We're going to sign up for the Army of the Confederacy. You with us?"

They had been met with silence. The murmurs had started then. He was known to shelter runaway slaves. Everyone in town knew his view of slavery, yet he had not made the abolition of it his life's work. His refusal to go with them had soon produced an angry mob who threatened bodily harm, but no one had wanted to be the one accused of killing the town's only doctor.

And so, Fellowship had lost practically every man of fighting age overnight to the call to arms. It had been like watching an exodus, he recalled. Some of the men were mounted on workhorses. Most were piled into the backs of wagons, waving their hats gallantly to the women and children who lined the streets, tearful, yet cheering their men on. Less than a quarter of those men would return home.

For weeks Travers had sat on his hands, listening to the cock and bull fly back and forth. He knew, just as most reasonable men did that the South was in for it. But he also knew that the North was in for a big surprise. The Southern states were full of scrappers who would not go down without a fight. Bull Run had proven that. Just as Travers had feared, the war had only begun.

And like all men who had believed in preserving a dream that had previously been bought with the precious price of blood, he had joined the Union Army, hoping to restore what radicals and fanatics seemed bent on destroying.

Travers Gage shook himself, rose and stretched his arms to the sun. He was leaving the unpleasant memories behind. West, he was headed. That was where he would make his life now.

Away from the pain.

He walked over to the two horses tied nearby, checked their cinches, and secured the packs on the packhorse. He was tired of riding, but he wasn't going to stop here. The memories were still too fresh. He was headed further West, maybe Kansas or Kentucky. He would know when he got there if the place was a fit.

The clothes he wore were not his standard attire. He had always been partial to the finer styles of clothing, satin or silk vests with tailored jackets. But for this trip, he had chosen to dress as inconspicuously as possible. The country was rife with thieves these days. Soldiers returning home from the war who found there was nothing to go home to had turned to thievery and often murder, their minds warped by the ravages of what they had seen. To the untrained eye, he appeared as much a saddle bum as the next man, his jacket ripped and dirty, his pants threadbare and worn. His hat, his one vanity, was black and new. Some character headed west in the hopes of making a living making and selling the things called it a 'Stetson.' Travers liked the look and feel of the thing, and it wore well. He had not thought twice about buying it from the man, it was so well made. More than likely, anyone who happened across Travers would assume he had lifted it from someone else. There was three days growth of his beard and that only intensified the color of his eyes. His hair was dark and fine with a few sun-streaked highlights scattered throughout. His boots were the ones he had worn throughout the war and were in desperate need of a polish.

He swung himself into the saddle and paused, thinking about which course to take. Finally, he decided to get moving. His horse, Cirrus, had miraculously survived the war but Travers knew he was just as weary as his master from the miles he had logged. Travers often stopped to allow the horse to rest and so far he seemed to be holding up fine. The pack horse was new. He had bought him from some old friends back in Virginia, probably the only friends he had left in the world. They had been sympathetic to his needs, and he had supplied them with much needed federal cash. Everyone was in need. Everywhere he went he came across groups of people headed west, or so they said, and they never failed to beg for money or something to eat. Food and money were both in short supply in the region, and Travers had hated to turn a deaf ear to the plight of others, but he could not afford to endanger his own life, and that was exactly what he would do if he offered food or money to the other stragglers he came cross.

He shifted in the saddle as the horse plodded on towards an uncertain destination. There was no hurry. He hated leaving the only place he had ever called home. Virginia. It had once been a lush, green wonderland of perpetual beauty. Years of war had turned it into a wasteland, and he was loath to stay and watch its further destruction by the vultures circling, hoping to cash in on the carnage leftovers from the war. He'd had enough of war and its glorious intrigues. He was leaving, and he was never coming back. That saddened him to no end, but he would not dwell on it now. He had a long way to go. Putting a light spur to Cirrus, he and the horses renewed their journey.

He stopped at sundown and made camp. He had found a sheltered spot where a large oak had fallen across another, yet still provided a good view of the stars. After the horses were brushed down, fed and watered, and hobbled nearby, he set about building a small fire for making coffee and cooking some beans and bacon. He was running low on supplies and knew there was a town up ahead a few miles. Boone's Mill, he believed it was. He had passed through there before the war on his way to treat a patient who refused to have any other doctor look at him. He had certainly been a grouchy old cuss. The man's name escaped him at the moment. No matter. He would stop there to stock up again. The only supplies he had brought with him he had gotten from the people he had gotten the packhorse from, a family who had lived just down the road from him, the Giles'. Travers knew he would not be welcome in any of the stores around Lynchburg or Fellowship, so he avoided the towns as much as possible. He no longer belonged there; they had seen to it that he got that message plain as day, and he would not force his presence on anyone.

He lay back against his saddle holding a fresh cup of coffee. The beans smelled good, and he could not wait to chow down on the bacon that was now sizzling on a stick over the low fire. The temperature had dropped significantly with the setting of the sun and Travers was glad that he had made the coffee now after he had considered foregoing the fire, knowing it was a safe bet not to attract attention to himself. Spooning the beans onto a plate and taking the bacon from over the fire he settled back and before long had devoured the little meal. He had not realized just how hungry he was until he smelled the food cooking over the fire and in minutes the food was gone. He should be grateful for this little bit of sustenance, he thought. Some folks didn't have even this to eat. He had survived the war on less. He gave a silent prayer of thanks, for the food and for seeing the end of the fighting.

Cleaning his plate and stuffing it back into his saddlebag, he relaxed once again onto his saddle. It was a clear night, however cold it was, and Travers was enjoying the view above him. The stars were magnificent tonight. They looked close enough to touch, and he found his thoughts straying to Maggie.

"Do you think my mother's up there? One of those spar-klin' lights?" She had asked hopefully, looking at the twinkling stars overhead. Travers had taken her rail-thin little body into his arms and held her close.

"I know she is, Maggie. She's up there looking down, watch-ing over you and your little brother. No matter how alone you feel, she will always be close by."

Maggie had thrown her arms around him, clinging tightly as if he were the last lifeline to safety from a sinking ship. He had held her for a long time. That was before the fight, before the accusations. A serious shudder wracked his body, and he forced the picture, the thoughts of Maggie from his mind. She was the past, a past he was leaving behind. All of it. Besides, she was gone now, and he would never see her again. He didn't even know if she was still alive if she had survived the war. The thought of Maggie dead caused an ache in the pit of his stom-ach. He comforted himself with the thought that she just had to be out there somewhere.

Damn. Now he would have difficulty sleeping tonight. It wouldn't be the first time. The last couple years he had seemed to sleepwalk, never seeming to sleep, only to dream, nightmarish dreams, with the war, the general, and Maggie all jumbled to-gether in one long, terrifying dream sequence. He would awaken to find his bedroll soaked with sweat. The few times he had been lucky enough to sleep in a real bed, he would wake to find the covers flung about as if he had wrestled all night.

In a sense he had.

The last year Travers had finally broken down and used lau-danum at night to help him sleep. It had helped to some extent. But the memories haunted him by day now, and he could not seem to find peace. His face appeared drawn in the flicker of the firelight, his eyes clouded with memories he'd just as soon forget. He was going to forget . . . start over.

If only he could.

Tossing out the last grains of coffee in his cup, he put it away and lay down hoping for sleep, his eyes on the glittered velvet above him. Maggie's image rose before him, and he filed it away, saving that memory for another time. He couldn't handle anymore. He needed rest tonight. He had a long road ahead of him, and he needed to be sharp in the morning. With a sigh, he pulled his hat over his face and closed his eyes determinedly. He laid there, his eyes closed, listening to the sound of the wind in the tree above him and the occasional chirp of crickets.

He awoke to brilliant sunlight hovering just on the horizon. It sat on the little valley like a golden beam and Travers took it as a good sign. Surprisingly, he had gotten a decent night's sleep. The dreams, if they came, he could not recall, and Travers was grateful. Refreshed, he packed up, saddled his horse and broke camp. Riding at a leisurely pace gave him time to think, about the past, his uncertain future. He didn't like to think. Thinking only brought pain, so he concentrated on the rhythm of the horse and the landscape as he went further west. After an hour or so of travel, he noticed that the grass was greener here, an oasis it seemed as if it had escaped the ravages of war. A promising sign if Travers had ever seen one. He had known that west was the best possible route. Now it was being confirmed. Kicking Cirrus into a gallop, he headed towards that brighter future.

———◆———

As he suspected, the town came into view just after two hours of riding. He almost stumbled onto the dilapidated sign that read 'Boone's Mill, Virginia.' It was not a large place by any means. Not even half the size of Fellowship. A few grizzled old men sat in front of the barbershop shooting the breeze. They eyed him up and down as he rode by, none of them giving him so much as a nod good day. Children played in a lot beside what Travers assumed was the Schoolhouse. Few people were on the street this lazy day in April, and that was good. That suited Travers just fine. He was in no hurry to be around people. He would just as soon avoid them if possible, but he needed supplies and get them he must. He headed straight for the general store and dismounting, tied the horses securely before going inside. He had to stop a second to let his eyes adjust to the dimmer light.

He slid his hat off his head and let it hang from his neck, running his lean fingers through his hair. His eyes scanned the store, seeing only the clerk helping an elderly lady with some bolts of cloth. He strolled down the aisles looking for the things he had come for, tins of food, toiletries, and bullets for his guns. He had quite a stack on the counter by the time he was ready to pay up. The clerk was finishing up with the lady, so he continued looking around the store while they concluded their business.

The store clerk was keeping his eye on the stranger. He had noticed him the moment he walked in. He knew the sort, straggler from the looks of him, headed west to escape the aftermath of the war and the wolves poised to consume the leavings. He had also noticed the growing pile on the counter and hoped the man knew what he was about. There was a sign on the door and the counter.

ABSOLUTELY NO CREDIT

Over the last few months, he'd had to introduce the shotgun he kept hidden behind the counter to several stragglers such as the man he was now watching. Too many folks had come through with not a penny to their name, expecting to rob him blind or wanting a handout. The fools. They had done it to themselves, their uppity views about state's rights and their own sovereign nation. He had no sympathy for them.

The little old lady left, and he turned his full attention to the stranger. At closer glance, he could see there was something different about this one. His carriage was that of one who had educated himself, and his hands were well manicured, an oddity out here for sure. He appeared to have little other than the clothes on his back. Looking pointedly at the pile on the counter, he said to the stranger who had just walked up. "No credit allowed, mister. No exceptions."

Travers had been in the middle of withdrawing a wad of federal currency from inside his shirt when the storekeeper's words stopped him cold. Pinning the man with his steel blue eyes, he told him "I can read, mister."

The man grunted and began adding up the bill. Travers waited for the total before removing the roll of bills from his shirt. The storekeeper tried to hide his surprise, wondering where a Southerner had come across a wad like that. The look the stranger was giving him told him to mind his own business, so he decided to do just that. Sooner or later though, someone would relieve the man of his stash. After counting out the bills, Travers had the man wrap his purchases into two bundles to fit in his saddlebags. The storekeeper gave a grunt but didn't argue, ready to be rid of the stranger. His kind always meant trouble. In a few minutes, Travers was on his way, not wanting to spend further time in this town. He had noticed the looks from the men as he passed. This was not a very welcoming bunch. That was fine. He preferred his own company anyway. Kicking his horse into a canter, he and the packhorse made for the freedom of the prairie.

TWO

Two months passed. The farther west he went, the greener the land grew. He took his time, enjoying the scenery, the newness. His few stops into the towns for supplies had been uneventful, and he had even spent the night in a hotel in south Missouri. That night in a fresh, soft bed had done wonders for him. He had slept like the dead. No nightmares to keep him busy or leave him exhausted afterward. He had felt a peace come over him and he knew he was headed to a brighter future. He had to be. He rode until dusk every day, occasionally stopping to rest and water the horses. By the time he stopped to make camp each night, they had covered twenty miles or so. Sometime during the journey, he had crossed into Kansas he believed. The land had begun to flatten out, and in the distance, he could make out herds of cattle. He had given them a wide berth not wanting to draw the attention of any living creature at the moment. He had found a huge sprawling Sycamore under which he made camp, and the horses grazed nearby.

He heard them before he saw them, their voices carrying, coming to him faintly on the breeze. He reached and settled his gun belt beside him. Pulling his hat low over his eyes he reached for his coffee cup and took a sip, watching them as they rode into view. A sandy lot for sure. Just his luck. He had seen their kind once too often: stragglers, turncoats, yellowbellies who found war didn't sit well with their breed. These men might have seen war and maybe not. But they were the same breed he was familiar with: coyotes, with mean, hungry eyes that snapped and snarled at anything that stood between them and what they wanted.

He stilled himself mentally, preparing. They appeared to be up to no good and in minutes he was certain of that fact. They fanned out around him keeping mounted, their eyes taking in everything to make sure he was alone. Their leader seemed to be the slender one with greasy hair because he did all the talking.

"Howdy mister. You from some outfit around here? You don't look like no cowpoke."

"Just passing through."

Greasy hair grinned exposing rotten teeth.

"Where ya' headed?" he wanted to know. Travers eased back

in his saddle, his cup of coffee held in his left hand, his right hand resting on his thigh within easy reach of his gun which lay holstered on the ground beside him.

"West," he told them, his voice even, his eyes taking them all in. There were three of them, and he ticked off their positions in his head.

"Well, hell, you already there, mister. Kansas here, it be cattle country. Me, Lars, and Finch here got us a mind to start our own spread. Gonna rustle us up some cattle. Could use some help. You int'rested?" he asked, spitting a stream of foamy brown tobacco juice.

"No."

The man apparently didn't like that answer. He frowned, his horse dancing slightly away, sensing the tension. He looked Travers over good for a second time.

"That there gun of yorn' says you got grit. I know a well-used piece when I see one," the man challenged.

"I'm no hired gun," Travers said, looking Greasy Hair in the eye.

"That a fact? And I guess that there satchel by yore' bedroll ain't for carryin' money either, is it?" the man sneered.

"No."

The man was getting irritated now. Travers was not giving him what he wanted, just sitting there cool as a cucumber. It chaffed Greasy Hair's hide. He made to move forward, but his horse danced away skittishly.

"What say I take a look see? I've a mind—"

"—the size of a peanut, apparently," Travers said flatly, taking another sip of coffee. At those words, the man jerked himself up straight in his saddle, his face burning fire red, the subdued chuckles of his companions ringing in his ears.

"Now look here, mister, yore not being very neighborly," His face was twisted angrily, his fist raised slightly.

"I'm not your neighbor," Travers deadpanned, "and curiosity has gotten many a man killed. Careful, that nose of yours is about to enter uncharted territory. You'd best rein it back in and be on your way."

The trio looked at Travers, then at each other. The one called Finch eased forward and muttered to the other two. He was ready to leave, and from the looks of it, he was leaving whether his two companions chose to or not. With a sigh, he turned his horse away and left the other two bickering before Travers. The pack didn't appear to be too hungry for trouble or knew trouble for what it was: the man sitting so casually in front of them. Travers knew a measure of satisfaction when they muttered to each other for a few moments more before turning back to

Travers. Greasy Hair glared in his direction once more, muttered something under his breath, before cursing and then as one they turned and followed Finch who was by now well on his way.

Travers got up and followed them for a few minutes on foot to make sure they weren't thinking of doubling back to ambush him. Apparently, one round was going to do it for them. According to Greasy hair, they had other fish to fry and considered he was not worth the effort. Back at camp, he eased back to his position by the fire, propped against his saddle. It was his first encounter out here with such riffraff, and he was sure it would not be the last. Next time he might have to fire that gun.

He stared into his coffee cup, his thoughts on a little boy and little girl he had wronged years before. It seemed like yesterday.

They had walked into his life soon after he had finished his first-year practicing medicine. He had just closed up his office one night when he saw the two of them watching him from the road. He waved goodbye to them, but they scampered away like frightened rabbits. He thought he recognized them as the Pritchard children. They were poor, the father having died years before and the mother scraping together what she could, sewing in the little town of Fellowship. Travers hadn't given them another thought until that day that Maggie had made herself at home on the porch of his clinic, where many of his customers often sat on sunny days. Old man Hayes was sitting out there about to have his ear chatted off when Travers walked out to his rescue. Maggie was squatted down examining Hayes' grotesquely swollen ingrown toenail.

"Yup, that nail gotta come off'n there, Mister. If'n it don't that toe gonna rot right off yore foot." She rose and put her hands on her hips, telling him matter of factly, "Yup, get that nail off an' soak that toe in pickle juice. All that pizen' dry right up."

The look on Hayes' face was comical. Travers didn't even try to suppress a grin.

"What's this now? A lady doctor trying to take over my practice?"

Maggie cocked her head at him.

"I was just trying to tell 'im what he needs to do 'bout that toe. Pizen's gonna get 'im if'n he don't git tat nail off."

"That so? Well, maybe Mr. Hayes would like a second opinion. Step inside, sir, and let me get a good look at that thing."

Old man Hayes had gladly shuffled inside to avoid the little chatter bug. Never having children of his own, they tended to make him extremely nervous. Maggie just followed right along as if she had done so before and belonged there. Travers started to say something to her but thought better of it. He was going to have to lance that toe, and it was not going to be a pretty sight. Hayes began to fidget something awful at the merest touch and at Maggie's presence, and Travers finally had to tell her, "If you want to stay you're going to have to be quiet, all right?" Maggie clammed up instantly and took up a position right beside him where she could get a good look. Travers soaped the foot good and rinsed it with whiskey. Drying it, he gingerly picked the swollen flesh around the nail bed with a needle. A huge glob of dark, bloody, yellow-green puss shot forth onto the cloth Travers held ready.

"Gorsh! That looks like that 'mater worm I squished in the garden last week!"

Maggie's eyes were huge, her mouth open in a little 'o.' Travers looked up at Hayes who was looking at Maggie as if she were a tomato worm herself. He couldn't help it. He started to shake with silent laughter. Hayes noticed and gave a disgruntled 'humph' but said nothing. After that, she and her brother were constants in his life, hanging around the clinic. He knew they needed money, so he had struck a deal with them. He agreed to let them stick around during the day, but only if they worked for him. Maggie kept the place clean and tidy, and her little brother Rance kept him supplied with stove wood and such. For their efforts, they got paid a combined total of a dollar a week. They had beamed with pride when he had given them their first dollar, running home to show their mother that they had a real job and that they weren't just harassing the doctor and his patients.

That was a lifetime ago. A different place, a different time, he thought, shaking himself mentally. A new life waited for him somewhere out west, and he meant to find it. Tomorrow he would seek it. Tonight, he wanted only to sleep as peacefully as he had the last few nights. It was a luxury for him. Since the war, he'd had few decent night's sleep, and tonight he couldn't wait for the Sandman.

He was to be disappointed. The dreams came almost the moment his eyes closed. The sweat beaded on his head and he clenched his jaw against the searing pain. He saw red everywhere he looked. He could smell the smoke and see the fire. The screams, dear God the screams . . .

Sometimes blood is all that saves us.

With a jerk he came awake, sitting up on his bedroll, his breathing coming out in ragged gasps. He fought for control, and it was several moments before his breathing got back to normal. He lay back on his bed with his arm across his eyes and finally gave in to despair, his body shaking with sobs. He had thought he had it beat.

Instead, he felt beaten. . .

————◆————

When the sun rose the next morning, he did not greet it with a smile. The journey that had begun to look promising now no longer did. The lack of sleep and the return of that old, nagging ache and itch, his wonderful souvenirs of war, only served to dampen his spirits. Wearily he climbed onto Cirrus and headed due west.

————◆————

He traveled for weeks before he stumbled upon a scene to behold. The sun was setting low in the sky as he topped a hill and the view before him was breathtaking. It looked like an oil painting on canvas, with reds and golds playing for prominence creating a dreamlike look on the town before him. He sat there a moment to drink in the view, thinking how lovely a sight and that it looked like a little slice of heaven on earth. A place that just from appearances, he would love to call home. In his experience, however, looks could be very deceiving. He saw no sign to indicate the name of the place, and he thought that couldn't be good. Perhaps he was hallucinating. If he was, it was a powerful experience. He had never seen a lovelier sight. The town looked brushed with gold dust and was nestled in a little valley along an ambling creek that traveled for some ways. It was indeed a welcome sight. He was weary and hungry, and so thirsty for a sip of whiskey that his throat ached. Putting the spurs gently to Cirrus he headed down the hill, hoping that this would be it, the place he had been looking for. If not . . . he didn't want to think about that. Cirrus had thrown a shoe a ways back and that had to be fixed regardless.

Travers felt the tension ease out of him as he made his way through the town. He observed the bustling activity of the town as he ambled by. Some of the folks cast a curious glance or two his way before going back about their business. They seemed unconcerned that a stranger was among them. A few even waved hello and offered a smile. That pleased him. He tipped his hat in kind and noted the reception he was getting was a good one, in stark contrast to some of the other places he had ventured into. It appeared to be a town just recently sprung up, and everyone was too busy to give a stranger in their midst the time of day. New construction appeared here and there giving credence to his suspicions.

He came to a stop in front of a large building that had a shingle out front identifying itself as the blacksmith's. He studied on that for a moment thinking that the place looked more like a house than a blacksmith shop. The flower beds on either side of the front door spoke of a woman's touch, and he was about to turn away when he heard the muted clanging of striking iron. He followed the sound to the back of the place and found what he was looking for. The man was busy with a piece of iron and didn't look up as Travers approached him. Not wanting to disturb the man, he dismounted and waited patiently for the man to finish his task, looking around the place as he did so.

Travers was impressed. It was a well thought out space, compact and well organized. There was no wasted space, and his tools were the best in the business. He turned back to study the man laboring over the iron. He was a large black man, tall, his arms and shoulders thick with muscle. His shirtsleeves were rolled to the elbows, and his pants were tucked into boots that contained the largest feet Travers had ever seen. He appeared to be in his mid-thirties with just a hint of gray showing at his temples. He struck the iron with authority and Travers could see that this man knew his business. He was no stranger to work, and Travers wondered how he had come across his training as a smithy. The man finished his hammering and placed the iron to the side, his arm rising to swipe at his brow, removing the sheen of sweat the heat of the fire had elicited. He seemed to suddenly become aware of Travers and wiping his hands on a cloth, came forward to greet his customer.

"Something I can do for you, sir?" His voice was even, respectful, and a little wary. Travers threw him a curve by extending his hand.

"Travers Gage. My horse needs some shoe work. Seems you're the man for the job."

The smithy shook the extended hand, visibly surprised at the gesture. Even out west, it was hard to find a man who shook hands with a Negro. The war had seen many a displaced Southerner head west, and they carried their pride and prejudice with them, wrapping themselves in it like the rebel flag draped over their shoulders, and if he wasn't mistaken, this man before him was from the South as well.

"Clayton Moss. You new in town?" Clayton asked casually as he moved to examine the horse, taking care to stroke the animal, speaking soothingly to it before examining its feet. Travers propped a booted foot on the lower rail of a makeshift stall, his arm resting upon the top rail.

"Just passing through."

Clayton finished with the horse and moved to face the stranger.

"You a long way from home." It was not a question, but an observation. Travers met the man's steady gaze.

"Virginia, actually. Just west of Lynchburg, little town called

Fellowship."

The big black man crossed his massive arms across his chest, giving the stranger a good look. "That's a federal bridle you got on that stallion." It was an observation. A probing one, to be sure. Travers knew that the big man was sizing him up and while ordinarily, that would have rankled him to no end, he felt no angst towards the man for doing so. Given the same circumstances, he would probably be a little wary himself. No, the blacksmith didn't worry him, but other people did.

"Yes, sir," Travers admitted, "that's the one I was given when I enlisted."

Clayton studied him closely, then shook his head, a smile creeping across his lips before exposing gleaming white teeth. His eyes went from the horse to Travers as he released a pent-up chuckle at last.

"A Virginian fightin' for the North. . . I bet you caught hell."

Travers gave a low grunt, before grimacing at the man.

"That's putting it mildly, friend."

Clayton eased over to the stall and leaned against the rickety partition, causing it to squeak and groan under their combined weights. The big man didn't move, but Travers wasn't so sure that the thing would hold the two of them and eased gingerly away to rub his horse's neck. He knew the blacksmith was not finished with his questions.

"I see you carrying around a medical satchel. You a doctor?"

"Doctor, surgeon, sawbones. . . I've done it all, seen it all . . ." his voice broke off, remembering some of the horrors he had actually seen. His eyes closed against the memory. Clayton noticed. He liked this man. There was something about him that he felt fit right in with this town. He was no liar, that was for sure. Clayton could spot those a mile away. This man was honest and forthright, and Lord knew they could certainly use a doctor. But he sensed something in Travers Gage, a trouble that went way beyond the war.

"You headed anywhere in particular?"

Travers sighed heavily.

"Haven't really given it much thought," he admitted. Travers looked out at the activity going on up and down the streets. Clayton noticed the lost look in his eyes and pondered softly, "Perhaps you're one of those who come out here looking for somethin' that somehow got lost somewhere down the line."

That weighed heavily on Travers, and he studied on that for a moment before admitting, "Perhaps."

"Got a mind to settle down? This town sho' could use the likes of you. We growin' by leaps and bounds every week. All those wagon trains headed west, lots a folks lose in'trest in going on once they find a town after crossin' those plains."

Travers could well understand that, but he had found Kansas a breath of fresh air compared to where he had come from. There was something about the land out here that spoke of freedom, room to breathe. And this little valley called to him, its beauty a thing of wonder.

"I don't know, doesn't seem like such a bad idea," he admitted with the least bit of caution. Clayton was watching him closely, and at Travers' comment, he broke into a huge smile.

"Tell you what. You get acquainted with the place while I look after your horse. There's a nice hotel with a big dining hall. They got good food, though I'm partial to Sarah's. That's my wife." He gave Travers one of those 'you know what I mean' looks before continuing.

"All the businesses, 'cept the saloon and cathouse are on this end of town. They's on the other end. Hotel down on the corner to the left. General store down the street to the right, gots whatever you need."

Travers looked around him again. Coming to stand before the black man, at last, he extended his hand again.

"Mr. Moss, it's been a pleasure talking to you. I think I will take a look around."

"Take your time, sir," he called as Travers headed out the door. A thought stopped him at the door, and he turned to find Clayton Moss grinning like an idiot.

"By the way, what's the name of this place? The town, I mean."

"Ain't got one. Next town meeting, though, we gonna vote on it. You being a doctor, you'd have some pull if you chose to stay." Clayton wasn't making this easy on him. He wanted him to stay, that was for sure, but the rest of the town might not. It was time to find out.

Outside, Travers stopped at the front of the place, his eyes taking in the small town hustle and bustle. This wasn't just some little cow town, though he was sure it had seen its share of cattle and cowboys. This was a planned place from the looks of it, and he liked what he saw. A group of folks had come together to build something out here, a future for themselves. And they were succeeding. He liked the place at first sight. It had strong storefronts and fresh paint and was well laid out. There appeared to be not a speck of trash or rubbish anywhere, and Travers was genuinely impressed. Cautious by nature, he reined in that urge to throw caution to the wind and do what his heart demanded. After all, the last town he had been part of had practically thrown him out. He knew he had better take a look around first.

Ambling along the boardwalk, he found the butcher shop

next-door to the smithy. The smells coming from within testified to fresh cuts of meat. Beyond the butcher shop was the general store: a huge one at that. Travers stepped inside, pushing his hat back to hang from his neck, running his fingers through his hair to shake out a bit of the dust, and was immediately impressed. A few folks were about, and they each greeted him cordially, no suspicion or fear in their eyes. An attractive blonde-haired woman was chatting with the clerk, her face seeming to glow as she smiled at something the clerk said. The clerk turned his attention to the newcomer, nodding in greeting before resuming his conversation with the woman. Travers returned the greeting before turning his attention to the contents of the store. His eyes, however, returned frequently to the man and woman chatting at the counter, their conversation reaching his ears. He didn't really mean to listen, but theirs was so animated that it was hard not to hear.

"I tell you, Pete, I can't get over how many people this town has seen in the last few months. Two years ago, this was nothing but a cattle crossing. I'm so glad we founded a city council. Just look how much we've grown," the blonde said to the clerk. The man nodded.

"Yep, we've come a long way, but we've still got a long way to go. Sheriff Tate says we'll be incorporated if we can ever decide on a name. You given any thought to that? You know we're supposed to vote on that next week."

"No, I haven't," the woman admitted. "I've no idea what would really suit this town. What about you?"

The clerk shrugged. "I don't know, Laura. I've never been any good at naming things."

About that time, Travers spotted some medical journals stacked near the counter where they were talking. Curiosity got the better of him, and he strode purposely to them, not caring that their attention was now on him. Hungrily he pored over the latest edition, realizing that he hadn't seen nor read any of these volumes.

The man and woman exchanged looks. As one they eased over to where Travers stood at the end of the counter, absorbed in the contents of the journals. They didn't want to seem rude and interrupt, but now their curiosity was getting the better of them. The woman took in the man's dusty attire, noting the gun, which he wore with authority. The hunger in his eyes as he pored over the journals told her all she needed to know. Never one to be shy, she turned to address the stranger.

"New in town?"

Travers turned his head, barely, to acknowledge her, though his eyes never left the book.

"Just rode in."

"From the way you're devouring that book, I guess it's safe to assume you're a doctor?"

Travers looked up then, finding two pairs of eyes glued to him. He found the same hunger written there as he had found in Clayton Moss's.

"I am, actually. Dr. Travers Gage," he said extending his hand to each of them in turn. The two of them seemed to have been holding their breath and released it upon his confirmation. They beamed at him, each pumping his hand joyously in greeting. The woman introduced herself as Laura Murphy and the clerk as Pete Barton. They had each come here a few years ago before there was anything resembling a town. A few buildings here and there, they said, until the cattle drives began to frequent the place. From there it had grown considerably and especially in the last year.

"Yessir, we've seen lots of folks come an' go. But the wagon trains headed west, and all the folks burnt out from the war . . . well, somebody always stays. Get tired of traveling. Can't say I blame them. We got a choice spot here. Plenty of water and shade. We're practically an oasis, I'd say, in a desert of plains. Ain't had much trouble with the injuns, neither." Pete, the clerk, was a talker for certain. Amiable and informative. Travers knew he would never be in the dark in this town as long as Pete was around. The thought made him smile.

Laura Murphy gave this Travers Gage the once over. He was quietly listening to Pete as he rambled on about the town, nodding in response to the one-sided conversation. He definitely seemed to be curious about the place, and she was bursting to ask him. As soon as Pete stopped speaking, she steered the conversation to a more personal nature: him.

"So, you headed anywhere in particular?" Laura asked, her eyes dancing.

Travers chuckled despite himself, shaking his head. Laura's eyes rounded, and she colored a bit in the cheeks, thinking maybe she was a little too forward.

"I'm sorry. It really is none of my business I suppose," she told him hurriedly. Pete just stood there with a grin on his face, waiting for a reply. Before they got one, however, Pete piped up.

"You gotta' forgive us, doc. This town's in need of your services. We'd just about hog-tie ya' if we thought you'd stay."

At that, Travers laughed out loud. Laura found it a pleasant sound and looked at Pete who was chuckling a bit himself, his chest heaving. She smiled nervously waiting to see what the stranger's response would be. It was fast in coming.

"I don't suppose you'd get that smithy of yours to do the

dirty work for you, now would you? I get the impression he'd be more than willing to take on the responsibility." His teeth flashed as he recalled the grin on Moss's face as he had left the blacksmith's shop. Seeing his merriment, Pete and Laura burst into laughter as well, realizing they weren't the only ones trying to recruit the good doctor.

"So, you've met Clayton. He's a sharp one. Got a good eye. I'll bet you got an earful from him as well."

Travers nodded.

"I take it that you folks are in desperate straits for a doctor."

"Yes," Laura told him, a disgusted look crossing her face. "There's a doctor over in Nicholsville, but he's a certified drunk. Most folks just suffer rather than let that old codger get ahold of them."

Travers winced visibly, the thought of letting a man under the influence of alcohol work on him caused an ache in his insides. His eyes shuttered, but not before his two new pals noticed. The two of them exchanged looks again, but Travers knew it was for an entirely different reason. They figured that they had pulled off the impossible by playing on his sympathies and were sure he would stay now. And they were right, but for an entirely different reason than they suspected. Experience could often be a bitter pill to swallow.

Travers knew he had no other choice. The place had pulled to him before he had ever dismounted in front of Clayton's. He had known it as sure as the sun was shining and the need of these people had confirmed it. He was home. He released a breath and placed the medical journal he had been devouring on the counter along with another one before turning to Laura and Pete.

"Looks like you folks do have a serious problem on your hands. I'd never put myself in that sort of situation either. I guess that settles it. I'll be staying. For a while, at least."

Laura Murphy clapped her hands in an agitated little rush, softly as not to disturb the other customers in the store, her smile was stretched from ear to ear as was Pete's. The clerk came around the counter to grasp Travers about the shoulders.

"Thanks, doc. You won't regret it, I promise you."

"Why, this is just grand!" Laura gushed. "Have you a place to stay? I've got just the thing. I run a boarding house just down the street. Oh, my," Laura realized suddenly, "we didn't even ask if you had family or anything."

Travers assured her that he was definitely alone in the world. To his amazement, Laura Murphy linked arms with him and corrected him.

"Well, you're not alone anymore. You've got me, and Pete

and Clayton, and this entire town. We'll be your family." She said it with such genuine inflection that Travers felt an uncomfortable lump form in his throat. He forced himself to return her smile, realizing that he had not had reason to do so in a very long time. Never one to be unsure of himself, he found himself awkwardly rubbing the back of his neck now, merely nodding his agreement to Laura's proposal, her generosity of heart touching him like never before. He found he could really start to like this place. He arranged with Pete to hold the medical journals for him and suggested to Laura that they take a look at her rooms for rent. She smiled brightly, glad that he would consider her place first over the hotel.

Walking the short distance to the boardinghouse, they were the recipient of several curious looks. Laura made no comment to anyone as she was wrapped up in trying to get information about the new doctor. He had no family, was from Virginia, had fought in the war, though he had never said which side she assumed it was for the South, and that was all he would reveal. He was a quiet one, for sure, never giving too much away.

Travers had given Laura little to go on, and he knew she was curious, but he was hesitant to reveal too much about himself just yet. He wanted to try the place on for size to see if it was going to be a good fit before he got too chummy with anyone. That way, if it backfired on him, he could leave the place with no regrets.

He settled on a room overlooking the street on the second floor. It was of a size and suitable to his needs, which were few. He hadn't much in the way of personal possessions save a few changes of clothing in his saddlebags, his medical satchel, and the medical journals he had just purchased from the general store. His collection back home had been destroyed. No matter. He was going to start fresh. He would rebuild his medical library and his practice from scratch, the way he had done it years before.

In talking with Laura, he learned that there was space available, that was suitable for a clinic, and she offered to show it to him the following day. It was getting late and Travers, weary from travel, was eager to sleep in a bed again. Not that he had minded sleeping out in the open under the stars, it was just that a bed offered a sense of comfort that the cold hard ground couldn't. Years of war had seen fit to accustom him to little to no luxury. Now, he had found a place to hang his hat, and he was going to enjoy a featherbed.

After paying for the room a month in advance, he excused himself to go fetch his horse and give Clayton Moss the good news while Laura tidied up the room a bit, dusting and putting fresh sheets on the bed and water in the basin.

The blacksmith knew from the look on the doctor's face what his decision was before he even said a word. They just grinned at each other for a moment before pumping each other's hands gladly. Each of them realized that this was the beginning of a new friendship, a treasure that some would never know due to prejudice and fear. It was their loss, however, and these two men's gain.

"So, what's the verdict on old Cirrus here? Got him fixed up?" the doctor asked.

Clayton nodded his massive head. "He's all set. Mighty fine animal you've got there. Had him long?"

"Well, since before the war. A year or so, I guess. He managed to make it through somehow. He's a real trooper. Sometimes seems like he's the only friend I've got."

Clayton heard the loneliness in the doctor's voice and informed him, "Well, sir, we've a remedy for that around here. All it takes is one dose of Sara's cookin' and a little muscadine wine to ease the ache and yore good to go. You be here at seven sharp. I've done told her to expect company, so I don't wanna' hear no 'buts' about it," he said when he saw Travers about to object.

Travers just shook his head at the big man, a grin stealing over his face.

"Now just how in the world can you predict so much about me, a man you've known all of an hour or so? How do you know I'm not some jakeleg up to no good? I could be some riffraff out to fleece this town and make a fool of you all."

The big man looked him up and down, nodding his agreement. "Could be, but we both know you ain't."

The blasted man was so sure of himself that it irritated Travers just a bit to be that readable. How on earth did he do it? Not wanting to hazard a guess at the moment, he agreed to have dinner with the man and his wife. He paid his bill and led his horses to the stable nearby where he got them settled and took his saddlebags up to his room where he unpacked. Yes, sir, he thought. Things were certainly beginning to look up. Laura had seen to it that he had warm water for his bath. There was an old porcelain tub that she said was his to keep in his room, so he really felt like he had died and gone to Heaven.

Travers stripped off his dusty clothes and climbed into the tub, sinking into the warmth awaiting him. He closed his eyes and released a sigh of pleasure. He couldn't remember the last time he'd had a real tub bath. Weeks certainly, perhaps a month or two. The water rose to mid-chest, relaxing what little tension he had left in his travel weary body. For several minutes he sat there with his eyes closed in bliss, savoring the feeling, the knowledge that finally he was going to be perfectly clean again. He had a strange feeling bubble up from somewhere deep inside him, and it began to spread throughout his being. It elicited a laugh that he could not contain. Try as he might, he could not. A chuckle became a belly shaker, and he reared his head back and let it come, not caring who heard. He was happy. For the first time in years, he had reason to have hope, reason to live. These people needed him as much as he needed them. It was good. It was all finally good.

Downstairs, Laura had heard that laughter and had smiled to herself. She knew the joy of finding one's self and it sounded like that is exactly what was going on with the new doctor. She liked the man. Felt good about twisting his arm to stay. He seemed more than some backwoods doctor to her. He struck her as a man of culture, refined by money, education. She wondered about his background, his life before the war. It was strange how curiosity could eat at a person. She had never been one to be overly nosy, but she found her thoughts returning to the man upstairs. He had told her upon his return that he had been invited to have supper with Clayton and his wife, so she would not need to include him in the evening meal she always offered her other tenants. There were four besides the doctor, and she always made sure there was food throughout the day, though she served meals only at breakfast and supper. Most everyone else chose to eat their midday meal at the hotel or do without as they worked. She didn't mind. It freed her to do other things during the day, the washing, the cleaning, relaxing when she could. Fridays were spent with Flora, the town's gorgeous madam and her best friend in the world. Flora had arrived last year, and she and Laura had known an instant kinship. Laura couldn't help the smile that crossed her face at the thought of Flora. She wondered what the redhead would think of their new doctor. Lord help him when they did meet.

She was just putting an apple pie in the oven for dessert after the evening meal when he walked into the kitchen. She nearly dropped the pie. Catching it, she managed to shove it on the rack and close the door, hoping he hadn't noticed her reaction. She was stunned. She had thought him attractive before, but clean, mercy, he was a sight to behold. He had shaved and combed his overly long hair back, but it fell haphazardly about his face giving him the appearance of a rake. His suit was black and tailored to his form perfectly though its cut revealed it to be a few years old. The jacket was long with a square cut tail, and he wore it open over a red and black brocade vest and white starched shirt. He had yet to put on a tie, so the collar was still open down to his vest revealing a bit of the dark curly hair that she knew must cover the rest of his body. She also noticed that he had shined his boots to a high polish.

He was a striking man, no ifs, ands, or buts about it. Being a woman, she admired a good-looking man as much as any woman would, but she found that the doctor was different. He should have caused her to have butterflies inside. He didn't. Her heart should have leaped into her throat. It didn't. What he did cause was a warm feeling when he came towards her and put a question to her that she never would have guessed he would ask her.

"Laura, what's your opinion. Should I get rid of the vest and not wear a tie, or should I wear the vest and tie? I don't want to make them uncomfortable in any way or put them on the spot by overdressing for dinner. The last thing that I want to do is offend them."

Laura batted her lashes a moment before answering.

"No tie, I think. The jacket may be a bit too much as well. You're a good man, Travers Gage. Not many folks would have considered the feelings of others on such a simple occasion as dinner."

A thick dark brow was raised at that. "I don't want to do anything that would make them think that I think less of them. Clayton Moss strikes me as an exceptional man, and I figure his wife is the same. I just wish I had something to give my hostess."

Laura knew just the thing. She held up her hand and left the room for a second before returning with a bouquet of freshly cut flowers. They were beautiful, a mix of purple verbena, goldenrod, and blush pink roses. She dried the stems off before wrapping them up in a sheet of newspaper and handed them to Travers.

"These should do just fine." She offered a smile as well.

"They are perfect, but I wouldn't want to take your flowers. Where on earth did you find such blooms out here?"

"They're from my flower garden out back. I've got vegetables too."

Travers gave her a look of admiration. Laura, he predicted, would be a surefire friend. He thanked her and, deciding to doff the jacket, removed it, and ran it back upstairs to his room before taking his leave, wishing Laura a good evening as he left.

⸱────⸱────⸱

Clayton answered the door before he got through knocking, so eagerly was he waiting for the doc. His wife was there as well, Clayton having ushered her to the door to admit their guest. The big black man was pumping his hand in greeting, nudging Sarah forward to meet the new doctor. Travers shook her hand graciously and presented her with the flowers, and to his horror, he saw tears spring to her eyes. He looked to Clayton for help, and the big man just gaped for a moment as well. Uncertain what he had done wrong, Travers groped for an excuse, an explanation.

"I'm sorry, it was such short notice I wasn't sure what to bring for a hostess gift. Laura thought they might be appropriate . . ." His voice trailed off as a solitary tear made its way down Sarah Moss' cheek. She shook her head at him, her voice soft as rain falling softly as a spring shower. "They're lovely, Dr. Gage. I just can't remember receiving such a gift before from anyone other than my husband. Thank you. I'll go put them in some water."

She swished out of the room with a rustle of petticoats. Clayton watched her go. When she was out of sight, he told Travers, "You've just made a friend for life. That woman has had it rough. She's real quiet, keeps to herself. Scared, mostly, of bein' rejected now that she's free."

Travers shook his head. It shouldn't be that way, but it was. A shame that folks couldn't respect each other, but he knew the battle that Sarah Moss fought. He had lived with the fear and prejudice all his life. The war brought it home as never before.

Clayton Moss saw the look that crossed Travers' face. He knew what was going on in his mind. The fact that this man had seen fit to honor his wife with a bouquet of flowers swelled his chest to the point of bursting. He had never seen his wife at such a loss for words before. She may be quiet in public, but she had never lacked for words at home. Travers next words stunned him even more.

"Well, sir Moss, you promised me the best meal this side of the Mississippi. I'm here to collect, seeing as how you twisted my arm and all." Travers gave the man a wicked wink. Sarah chose to return then and announce that dinner was being served. The three of them entered a large dining room and seated themselves around a large square table that Clayton said he made himself. Travers was doubly impressed with the man's abilities. The furniture looked like something that belonged in a grand mansion back home in Virginia. The top was solid mahogany, smooth with rounded edges, the sole detail being a hand carved medallion in the center in which the fresh bouquet of flowers now sat. The legs were ornately carved to match the medallion. The blacksmith had polished it to a high shine, giving it a mirror effect.

As Sarah brought the last of the food in, Travers' eyes roamed, taking in his surroundings.

It wasn't a showplace. It was a home, and he automatically felt welcome. Sarah was a tidy housekeeper, and everything had its place. All of the furniture had been made by Clayton he found out as they prepared to dig into the wonderful smelling fare that Sarah had prepared.

Clayton turned to Travers and asked him to say grace. Travers was taken aback for an instant, before muttering that maybe his host should do the honors. He passed the buck, knowing that he was definitely not in the best of shape to be doing such things at the moment. God had not figured into his life in some time. Not by choice, mind you, but by necessity. During the war, he had seen many a man kneel to pray before going into battle, and he had wondered at the lucidity of those men. What on earth were they expecting of Him? To walk into a hail of bullets and not be scratched? It was madness to believe that one could be invincible in such a maelstrom thing as battle. He guessed if God saw fit to protect those believers once, they had every right to expect Him to time and time again.

He listened to the deep mellow tone of Clayton's voice as he gave thanks for the bounty before them, including in the prayer thanks for having brought Travers into their lives. Sarah was quick to offer an 'amen' when he concluded. He felt a flush rise in his cheeks, and he cleared his throat noisily. The two of them just looked at him and smiled, their teeth gleaming at him.

"Now you jes' dive on in. Don't be shy. We eats around here." Clayton told him as he passed Travers a dish loaded with corn on the cob. There was fried chicken, butterbeans, and squash, as well as southern fried cornbread. In seconds he was enjoying what he thought was surely the best meal of his life. It had been so long since he had eaten any of the dishes Sarah had laid out that he had forgotten what they tasted like. He was having a fine time reacquainting himself. Sarah smiled watching him consume the meal, knowing without a doubt that he was thrilled to his toes with her cooking. When he came up for air, he told her as much.

"Sarah, I do believe that were Clayton not around, I'd abscond with you. You are a marvelous cook!"

She glowed with his praise, her smile stretching even wider if that were possible. She liked this new friend of Clay's. Her husband had told her he was from Virginia and she had been hesitant to meet him, him being from the South and all. But he was a gentleman. Clayton had said so, and he had seemed eager for them to meet. And the fact that he had brought her flowers, why she just didn't know what to think. Her tears had gotten the best of her, embarrassing her, and he had truly seemed embarrassed as well, thinking he had offended her, rushing to offer apologies. She'd never met anyone like him.

They talked about the town and how long it had been there, how long the Moss' had been there, which was little over a year now. The sheriff was a man named Tate, Erasmus Tate. He seemed to be a colorful character if what Clayton said about him was true. Travers would introduce himself to the man tomorrow. The conversation was kept light, steering clear of things like the war and such, though Travers knew they were itching to know what had possessed him to fight for the North. But they didn't press him, and he was grateful for that. He did find out that Clayton was from a plantation in Mississippi. He had been the blacksmith there. His master had liked him so much that after the war began, he had offered him good money to stay on and help with the place. He had stayed for a while before moving on, hoping to find Sarah, who had been sold along with their son, to a neighboring plantation in Alabama. He had found them, luckily.

They had come west and had never looked back. The town had been good to them if slow to accept a black man as a blacksmith. But his work had been of such quality that folks had begun to look beyond color. It was a step, they figured.

The son was not mentioned again, and Travers didn't pry, though he was curious. One thing at a time he thought. Sarah decided at that time to produce their dessert, a lemon meringue pie. Travers nearly groaned aloud, for it was one of his favorites and he let her know it. A taste of it verified that the woman could put the chefs at the most upscale restaurants to shame. He controlled himself and ate just one piece, though she pressed him to eat more. He simply had to refuse, though she gave in graciously. He and Clayton retired to the parlor while she cleared the table. In a few minutes, she appeared with each a steaming hot cup of coffee.

"You've got a hell of a place here, Clayton. You should be mighty proud of yourself. And if I had a wife that could cook like that . . . whew. . ." he said after she had gone to the kitchen to clean up. The big man chuckled.

"She's somethin' else, ain't she? I told you she could cook. Puts the hotel cook to shame."

"I don't know any she *wouldn't* put to shame." Travers agreed.

Clayton took a sip of the coffee, blowing on it before doing so.

"So, you settled in yet? I say that Laura Murphy is a sweet thing. She's been kind to Sarah and me. You done good boarding with her."

Travers leaned back in the rocker that he had taken. "Yes, she is. Got a good feeling about her."

Clayton nodded. "Yup, she's been here 'bout two years.

Don't know a whole lots about her, though. Guess everybody got they secrets."

Travers agreed with a grunt. He knew about secrets and didn't begrudge Laura hers if she had any. He didn't have secrets, though. His were ghosts. Plain and simple. And they walked about with him day and night. He brushed the thought of them away as if shooing a pesky fly. Clayton pretended not to notice, but the furtive movement the doctor had made affirmed what he suspected all along. Yep, the good doc had a past just like everyone else. A past he'd just as soon leave behind.

They made small talk for another hour or so, the three of them, and Travers knew he had never met nicer folks. He thought about what his neighbors back in Virginia would say if they could see him now, sitting and conversing with the Moss' let alone taking dinner with them. The thought brought a smile to his face. Yes, sir, he was home. A short while later, he took his leave of them, thanking them for a wonderful meal and companionship. They promised to have him over again soon, and he smiled his acceptance.

Heading back to the boardinghouse, he caught sight of a flash of red and sapphire blue. They belonged to a woman who was coming out of the place, pausing to speak to Laura as she turned to go. Her hair was a fiery mass of carefully coifed curls, and her gown was the color of gems. Exquisitely low cut, it hugged her like a glove down to mid-thigh before flaring gently to allow movement. There was a tantalizing bit of golden satin petticoat visible, and a golden rose tucked in the valley of her breasts. She looked Travers up and down appreciatively, her green cat eyes roving and lingering before finally reaching his face. He was grinning at her perusal of him. When she spoke, it sounded like Southern molasses, thick and sticky sweet.

"Why Laura, honey, you neglected to mention that he was devastatingly handsome!"

Laura laughed, thinking the redhead's timing couldn't be more perfect. She stepped to the edge of the porch to make the introductions.

"Flora, this is our new doctor, Travers Gage. Travers, meet Flora McDonough. She owns The Velvet Rose."

"Ah, the . . . Gentleman's club. Pleased to meet you, Ms. McDonough." He stepped forward, taking her proffered hand and kissed it lightly. The redhead smiled, her eyes dancing.

"Why, that is exactly what it is, doc, a gentleman's club. We look forward to your first visit. We'll treat you nice. I'll see to it myself."

For the life of him, Travers blushed, and he was glad it was dark, hoping the women hadn't noticed. Ms. McDonough was implying with her eyes just how she would take care of him.

"I'm afraid I'm a busy man, ma'am. I never go off the clock. The only time you'll probably get to see me is if we happen to bump into each other in town."

Flora's lips pursed into a pretty pout. "What a shame."

Travers decided he had better extract himself quickly before they made further eye candy of him. That tub in his room sounded really good about now. He was beginning to feel the need for another dunking and that feather bed was calling his name.

"If you'll excuse me, ladies, I must be going. It's been a long day and tomorrow promises to be as well." He tipped his hat to each of them and went inside, feeling their eyes staring after him.

They stared, even after the door closed behind him.

"Um, um, umm . . . he goes down smooth as Tennessee whiskey. Leaves you all warm inside." She sighed, her head tilted thoughtfully. "A pity though. I was so lookin' forward to gettin' better acquainted."

Laura looked at her friend. "What makes you think you won't be?"

"He's a loner. And got the saddest eyes I've ever seen. Something happened to him. But Lord knows if we'll ever find out what it was."

THREE

The rain of fire had stopped, thankfully, but the smell of burning flesh and sulfur nearly choked him. The haze of smoke was so thick in places that he could barely see the ground in front of him let alone the man beside him. It was treacherous going at best, not knowing if his next step would bring him upon an unexploded shell. He was sweating profusely now; going blindly into the remnants of battle was not good. It was damn right terrifying. The ranks had broken, and it was hand-to-hand now. He swatted at the smoke before him, hoping to clear the air in front of him enough that he could see. A few steps more and he stepped into a clearing. It was like stepping from inside a storm cloud into the actual storm. The rebs were running. They had broken, repulsed at the center where Chamberlain's Maine volunteers had been sent to rest after Little Round Top. Weary and almost out of ammunition, they had still repulsed the Army of Virginia.

As usual, he had been kept in the back of the line. He could ill afford to be lost. There were skirmishes going on in front of him, and he waded into battle, his pistol and sword at the ready. Ahead of him, about one hundred feet or so, he saw one of the commanding officers go down in a hail of gunfire, his body jerking to the tune of three bullets. Travers sprang to his side, but before he could reach him, five rebels made to capture the general.

Sometimes blood is all that saves us.

Travers fired, his bullet striking one confederate between the eyes before taking the back of his head off, blood and gore splattering the man behind him. The other rebs jerked around, spotting the yank that had killed their comrade. Travers felled another one before wading into them with his sword. He became a man possessed, his mission to save a complete stranger. He felt a stabbing pain in his shoulder but kept fighting, and they fell, one by one. Not bothering to look at his handiwork, he grabbed a fallen battle flag and draped it over the unconscious commander. Before he could get him up to carry him to safety, three more rebs were upon him. His sword flashed as he relieved one soldier of his pistol and hand. The man let out a scream, watching the blood gush from the stump where his hand had once been. The two remaining men rushed Travers, knocking him to the ground. He lost his pistol in the fall, but feeling around frantically, he located it and fired it into the belly of the man closest to him. He fell away, and Travers rolled and fired again, the bullet catching the remaining rebel under the chin. A stream of blood gushed from the wound and the man clawed at his neck before turning to stumble away. He got three feet away before falling face first.

Travers looked around. Soldiers from both sides had witnessed the fight. Some were staring in awe and disbelief. He had felled eight of the enemy. All dead in the space of one minute. A couple of men in blue rushed to help him get the general to safety, carrying him back across their own lines to the cheers of their comrades. As Travers headed towards the field hospital leaving the battle behind him, he could hear the taunting cheers of 'Fredericksburg!' No, this was one the South would not soon forget.

Three hours later, Travers was still working on General Sharpe, the man whose life he had been so determined to save. He had gotten the bullets out and had repaired the damage to two of the wounds in his upper body. It was the leg that worried him. He had lost a hell of a lot of blood and Travers was struggling to get the bleeding under control. The arterial vein was lacerated. He had clamped and sewn until the thing looked like a patchwork quilt. Finally, he closed, not knowing what else to do for the man.

He washed his hands and moved on to the other wounded, digging out bullets, and patching up the weary soldiers who filed through the tent. He had set up a separate tent away from the other surgeon, Dr. Morgan. The man was a disgrace to the army and the medical society. He had taken to removing limbs unnecessarily, and Travers had called him on it. Morgan had threatened to have Travers removed from the field entirely, transferred out of their unit. Travers had dared him to, hoping he would so Travers could reveal the atrocities Morgan was inflicting upon his own men.

Travers moved among the more serious of the wounded, evaluating their needs. Then suddenly, he heard a gunshot behind him and turning, found that one of the men had taken his own life, his pain too much to bear. It echoed in his ears like the deafening sound of cannon fire. And getting louder, and louder, and louder. . .

— ◆ —

The noises coming from the doctor's room were getting louder, frantic, strangled, muttered words that Laura couldn't make out. She stood there at the door, her brow furrowed, listening intently. In a moment she was joined by a rumpled Joseph, the bartender at the saloon.

"What the heck is goin' on in there? He demanded, scratching his head. It was his night off, and he was succeeding in getting very little sleep what with all the racket.

"I don't know, but I intend to find out." Laura vanished into her room and fetched the key to Travers' room. Handing the lamp to Joseph, she wrestled with the lock for a minute before the door finally opened for her. Edging it cautiously open, she scanned the room, taking in the tossed bed and broken pitcher on the floor. But there was no Travers. She eased into the room and froze. He was standing behind the door and had a pistol pointed at her head. She didn't move, didn't speak, took in the wild look in his eyes. He was not awake, but apparently in the throes of a violent nightmare.

"Jesus!" Joseph had stepped into the room right behind her obviously and jerked back in alarm. The doctor looked like a wild man, his eyes glazed, but not awake.

"Stop! Don't move!" Laura hissed over her shoulder to the bartender. "He's having a nightmare, that's all," she tried to explain, her eyes never leaving the doctor.

"With a bloody gun pointed at you ma'am, in case you haven't noticed!" His voice was urgent, fearful. She couldn't blame him for being afraid. She was, after all, the one with the gun pointed at her head. She should be trembling with fear, but oddly, she wasn't. She was calm as could be. Strange, but she didn't believe that the doctor would hurt her.

"Ma'am, you best back on out of there. He don't show no sign of coming to himself no time soon," Joseph rasped to her. He was afraid for her, not certain what exactly was going on and wondering why she hadn't already bolted from the room. She shushed him and heard him grunt behind her. She sighed, her eyes still on Travers. He still held the gun pointed at her.

"Travers?"

His left eye twitched the least little bit.

"It's me, Laura."

He didn't move. Neither did the gun.

Laura could feel the tension radiating from his body. He had slept in his clothes apparently. His shirt was not tucked in and was rumpled, his pants unbuttoned halfway, suspenders hooked carelessly over one shoulder. Both shirt and pants were soaked through with sweat. His hair was all over his head, lank and damp with perspiration. He looked like a man who had run a fever all night. He was ill, she thought, but not with a fever. And that worried her. She braved a step forward.

"Travers, it's just a dream. I need you to wake up."

"What the heck are you doin'?" Joseph was a step behind her, his own eyes now looking glazed.

"I'm trying to calm him down. He's got to wake up."

"You go any closer, and he's likely to shoot you!" His voice raised an octave.

A shudder passed over Laura, though she wasn't sure why. She wished Joseph would shut up. He was not helping at all. She wracked her brain to come up with a way to wake Travers up and still keep her head on her shoulders. Then she thought better of it. A confidence came over her that she had never before possessed. Squaring her shoulders, she said, "He won't shoot me."

That elicited a snort from the bartender.

"Well, if he does, the last words you'll hear will be 'I told you so.'"

She took another step into the room, her hand rising slowly to the gun. He batted his eyelids, but the glaze didn't leave them. She began to speak softly, speaking to him as if he were a sick child. It had a calming effect, it seemed, for he began to visibly relax. She pushed the gun down and away but did not try to take it from him. She was not a fool. He could feel threatened and feel the need to protect himself.

"Travers, it's alright. You had a nightmare, but it's over now. I need you to wake up. Come back to me," she pleaded. She raised a hand to brush the hair away from his face. His eyes closed, savoring the contact. He began to mumble incoherently, and she strained to make out what he was saying. It was a jumble of words, but she couldn't understand them. She turned to Joseph and told him to go to the kitchen and brew a cup of coffee for the doctor. He went, but reluctantly, afraid to leave her alone with him. He had only been gone a few seconds when she caught a name on Travers' lips. Maggie. That was all. Just—Maggie. His body had shuddered with the breath that released the name. Then he had seemed to crumble. He sagged, his knees buckling, and Laura caught him between herself and the wall. His eyes flickered open, lucid now, though tired and red-rimmed. She breathed a sigh of relief and gave a silent prayer of thanks. He was coming around.

"Travers? It's Laura. Can you hear me?" She patted his cheek with her free hand, and his eyes finally focused on her.

"Laura?" He looked at her as if seeing her for the first time, then looked down at the gun in his hand. He raised questioning eyes to hers, seeing the worry and fear there. He inhaled sharply, his head flung back, his eyes closed in agony. The pistol fell to the floor, and his hands rose to cover his eyes as he slid along the wall to the floor. Laura knelt beside him.

"It's all right, Travers. It's over. Whatever it was, it's over."

Fear came over him.

"I didn't—hurt you?" His voice was husky with shame. She sought to reassure him.

"No. You didn't hurt me. Just scared us a bit when we couldn't wake you."

That brought a questioning look. "Us?"

She nodded. "Joseph went to get you a cup of coffee. He should be back by now."

Travers groaned. So, his infirmity was witnessed not only by Laura but by Joseph as well. He rested his arms on his raised knees and laid his head upon them. He had a look of defeat about him, Laura thought. She started to say something, but Joseph chose that moment to return. He heaved a visible sigh of relief when he saw that Travers was finally awake.

"Boy, Doc, you sure know how to scare the life out of a body. You alright?"

Travers raised his head and accepted the cup that the bartender offered him. He hoped it was strong. And maybe laced with something. It wasn't. One sip assured him of that. He nodded to the man's inquiry but didn't offer an explanation. He did offer him his thanks for the coffee. The man just shrugged, scratched his head and said he was going back to bed, and left. Travers sipped at the coffee, holding the cup between both hands, his eyes studying its contents, a frown marring his brow. Laura knew he must be feeling awkward after what had happened and sought to put him to ease. Joseph was gone now so they could speak freely.

"That must have been some nightmare. I don't think I've ever seen anyone react so. You scared me, Travers."

He ran a hand distractedly through his hair, sighing.

"Yeah, I'm sorry. I didn't mean to frighten you. Or keep you up all night."

She offered a smile. "Oh, that's all right. I'm usually a night owl, anyway. Besides, my friend needed me."

He wouldn't look at her. Couldn't look at her. He was embarrassed. He couldn't ever remember having such an episode before. Everything had seemed so real, and the voice he had heard had not been Laura's, but Maggie's, her child's voice calling to him, haunting him as he had tried to fight the demons of war. Dear God, he had thought he was free of this, the sleepless nights, the garish nightmares where he was surrounded by death.

She was watching the play of emotions on his face, the shuttered look he had put up to hide what he was thinking, feeling, then the pain as memories assailed him. He was miserable. She could stand it no longer. She wanted to help if she could if he would let her.

"Travers, I don't mean to pry, but maybe it would help if you talked about it. I'm a good listener."

His chest swelled with a sigh, unsure that sharing was such a good idea. She had become a good friend the last week or so that he had been here, but revealing such intimate details of his life that he had rather no one know about, well, that was breaking a rule that he had always lived by. Never reveal too much about yourself because someday it may come back to haunt you. He had a feeling that that was going to happen in his case regardless. His eyes closed, not wanting to admit to himself that he needed help, a crutch, something to help him deal with it. She sensed his reluctance, and knowing that a man often chooses to suffer alone, she began to rise to leave. His hand on her arm stopped her. He pulled her back down so that she sat next to him on the floor, her back against the wall.

They sat in silence for a while, her unsure of her purpose, though she suspected he just needed her there for reassurance. His mouth finally began to work, but nothing came out. He lowered his head again, and when he did, she prodded him, hoping for a response, though she would let it pass if she got none.

"Was it the war, Travers? Is that what haunts you so?"

He looked pale as if he were going to be sick. He nodded.

"I guess you saw plenty that would make any man question his sanity. You're not alone in that."

He agreed with her. He did, but she just didn't know. Should he tell her? Would she understand? There was only one way to find out.

"No, I figure everyone has his ghosts. But I reckon theirs don't still walk around flesh and blood totin' a gun carrying a bullet with my name on it."

Laura frowned. "I don't follow."

"I made some enemies. Some really bad ones back then. They'll be coming for me. I won't know when or where, but they'll come. And when they do, I can't promise that I'll turn the other cheek. I find that mighty hard to do. Not in my nature. I guess it's a good thing I didn't become a preacher."

She smiled, trying to picture Travers as a minister. She couldn't. He just didn't look the part. She accepted what he had said about his past. For his sake, she hoped he was wrong. Taking his hand in hers, they sat in silence once again, finding a comfort in each other's company. Travers smiled at the picture they must make, sitting here on the floor, Laura in her nightgown and robe and he looking like he'd just come off a drunk. Should anyone find them like this, they might think ill of them both. That erased the smile very quickly, for he would never hurt Laura intentionally. He rose shakily to his feet, careful to brace himself against the wall. He pulled Laura up and pulled her into a quick hug.

Only it wasn't so quick. He had meant it to be, but once in her arms, he began to shake. She held him until he stopped, feeling his release, knowing that somehow her being there for him was making a difference. When he had gotten himself under control again, he backed away, his eyes flickering to hers.

"Thank you. For everything."

"But I didn't do anything."

"Yes, you did. You'll never know how much."

FOUR

A month had passed since the doctor's arrival in town. He had been made a member of the town council, seeing as how he was the doctor after all and would have considerable influence in the town and surrounding area. The fact that he had fought for the North in the war and his being a Southerner solidified him as a man of impeccable morals and values in the eyes of the town. His friendship with the blacksmith turned heads, however, for those who applauded his stand against slavery would never admit to fraternizing with what some considered a lower class race. Travers just ignored those.

The town council had been forced to postpone the meeting in which they would choose a name for the town. The mayor had business come up in the neighboring town, so they all agreed to wait until the next scheduled meeting. Everyone was looking forward to it.

Travers and Laura had developed a rapport since the night of his nightmare, and thankfully, he had not experienced anything like it since. They spent a lot of time together, getting the clinic set up, Laura helping him clean the place and liven it up a bit with curtains she made especially for the clinic. Clayton had even made him a shingle to hang out front. Travers could only shake his head at the generosity of these people. He had never witnessed such welcome in a town, and though he knew that they were getting something in return, he couldn't help but think that had he not been a doctor, they would have treated him with the same amount of respect and decency.

The church was already abuzz with folks when Travers and Laura arrived at the meeting. It appeared they were the last to arrive, for as they entered, the mayor called the meeting to order.

"All right, folks. You know why we're here. We've been putting this thing off long enough. The floor is open for suggestions on a name. We'll take all the suggestions, take the top two choices and vote on them. Let's do this orderly folks."

Mayor Parks was a rotund fellow, with a handlebar mustache and round wire-rimmed glasses that sat on a puffy red nose. His hair, or lack of it, was slicked to his head with an oil of some sort that set Travers to sneezing if he got too close to the portly little man. Though sitting at the back of the small gathering, even now he could feel his nose begin to twitch. He rubbed at it in irritation. Laura suppressed a smile. She, of course, thought it was quite humorous that the doctor was allergic to the mayor. Of course, neither one of them had seen fit to mention this little tidbit to the man, but he was ever squinting at the two of them as if he thought they were up to something every time he came near, and Travers shied away. They would have to tell him soon. Poor man. The first time he had been introduced to Travers, he had pumped the doc's hand furiously and clapped him on the back only to have Travers pull away and sneeze uncontrollably. The mayor had stomped off in a huff when Travers had backed away when he offered his hand later in town. Laura sighed. They had to tell the little man so he wouldn't take such offense. It wasn't Travers' fault that he was allergic to the man's hair oil.

Travers nudged her to turn her attention back to the meeting. Several names had been tossed out there for consideration: Walton, Larksburg, even Eden, but none suited. Travers finally got up the courage to suggest the name he had come up with, the name that had struck him the moment he had seen the town: Gold City.

The others just looked at him for a moment, as if chewing that one over in their minds. They began to mumble amongst themselves, and finally, the mayor held up his hand for silence.

"Well, I happen to like that one. Suits the town perfect, I think. I say we vote on it. All in favor of the new name of our town being Gold City say aye." There was a chorus of ayes, and none opposed. It was unanimous. The doctor, a stranger to the place, having been there all of a few weeks, had named the town. Ironic.

Sheriff Tate walked up and greeted the latecomers after the meeting.

"Say, that's a right decent name we got us for the town. You may be of some use to us yet," he chuckled, referring to the fact that Travers had only seen one patient since he had arrived. The town drunk, Amos Dillon had stepped on a nail in the saloon and had gotten an infection. Fortunately, it hadn't developed into blood poison. Travers had patched him up and sent him on his way.

"Well, I'm glad to be of service in any way, Sheriff."

"We're mighty glad to have you, Doc. You come to dinner this Sunday. Louella insists." If Louella insisted, he knew, that settled it. She ruled the Sheriff with an iron thumb. That was one thing he had definitely learned since his arrival. He had met her once and realized she was not the sort of lady one forgets. She was a lovable little thing, a take charge kind of a woman with wispy gray hair that she piled high on her head in a little topknot. He had liked her on sight. He smiled and informed the Sheriff that he would be there with bells on.

———◆———

Dinner with Sheriff and Louella Tate was quite an experience. Erasmus Tate was quite the character. Balding, with thin string hair, and potbellied, he was even more memorable with bowed legs. He looked as if he had forked a saddle from the time he could walk. His mouth was forever fixed in a cross between a smile and a grimace. He could be a hard man when need be, Travers figured, but he had not been braced by any hard cases since Travers had come to town. He kept his guns clean and loaded and seemed to be on top of things about the town. He had gravitated to Travers quite a bit since he had come to town and that had piqued his interest in the man. He seemed to be quite intelligent, though aged, and Travers wondered why the town had chosen to make him sheriff. In looking around the town and the lot who was settling here, the answer came easily enough. He was the only one not in the middle of setting up a homestead, he was of above intelligence, and was a halfway decent shot.

He and Louella behaved like newlyweds, though Travers knew them to have enjoyed many a year together as man and wife. The sheriff didn't say much, mostly because Louella held down her end of the conversation and his too. The tiny woman seemed to have boundless energy. She flitted about the house, readying the table for dinner and stopped every second or so to spit in the numerous spittoons that were scattered about the house. The woman dipped snuff and never failed to hit it square each time she spat. Whenever Tate did open his mouth to say something, however, it was usually pretty humorous or either deadpan. He didn't mince words. Perhaps because he knew if he wanted to get a word in edgewise, he had better make it memorable. The husband and wife were from Charlotte, North Carolina. They had owned a small farm just outside of town and had managed to avoid the war. Tate was the sort who didn't like either side. He hadn't felt that the North had any right dictating to the South how to run their business in their own state, yet he didn't condone slavery either. Either way, he had viewed the war a lost cause, and he and Louella had packed up and come west, hoping to avoid the conflict altogether. He had always been handy with a gun, and when they had settled in the town, the folks had approached him about being sheriff. Louella had not liked the idea at all, but Ras, as folks about town called him, had jumped at the chance. Mostly so he would get a little peace and quiet now and then from all of Louella's chatter. It wasn't that she was a nag, Travers knew that the man would do anything for his wife, but she talked nonstop. He would bet a silver dollar she talked until she fell asleep at night. He bet Ras sighed with relief when her tongue quit wagging. He chuckled to himself, wondering how on earth they ever had relations with her talking all the time.

Travers learned that the town had been the brainchild of the Mayor, Floyd Parks. Parks was from Atlanta, Georgia, and had come west in '63. He had that entrepreneurial spirit that would help to rebuild the nation struggling to come back from years of war. Gold City was his great hope. He had researched the area and found that the government was looking for people of his caliber to settle the area. He had advertised in papers hoping to get people to join his venture. A few had accepted the call to journey west and make a new life for themselves. More had been on wagon trains headed further west but had given up the journey, the trail breaking them, forcing them to settle for the path of least resistance. And that was how Travers Gage had found it, bustling with new construction and lives being lived miles short of a dream. But it *was* a dream for some. It had become a paradise for Travers, as he was finally beginning to settle in and find peace among his new circle of friends. While his own brand of dreams still came, he found he could deal with them better now. They didn't consume him as they once had. He was at ease now, the edge seemingly gone from his existence. It was a good feeling.

＊―――＋―――＊

There is an old saying that 'all good things must come to an end' and for Gold City, it could not have been more accurate. The town was accustomed to traffic, but this was a bit much. People from all over began to come through, prospectors and wagon trains headed to California. Soon, what had once been a trickle became a flood. That flood carried with it the affluent as well as the dregs of society, which unfortunately seemed to like where they had landed. The city was growing, no bones about it, but it was growing with the wrong kind of money and the wrong kind of people.

Jim Bowers was one of those people. Travers detested him on sight, as did most of the townsfolk. He was a braggart, a worthless piece of humanity that most folks hated to see coming. He had blown into town in May, penniless and filthy, proclaiming that he had struck it rich. The how was purely speculation on everyone's part for he wasn't telling. He would just gloat, his slimy grin not a pleasant sight. And just like he proclaimed, he rose from the gutter to a man to be reckoned with overnight it seemed. His riches, however, came with a price and the town was the one paying.

The first man who disappeared was a farmer by the name of Jeb Cooper. The man and his family were new to the area, having only been there a few months. The family stayed in town while Jeb worked the land and built their home. The wife was expecting their second child, the first being only a year and a half. Her time was near, so Jeb had her stay at one of the boarding houses for the less fortunate. It was a rough area of town, but Travers made sure the woman was taken care of. The land the Cooper's had bought was several miles out of town, a rolling stretch of twenty acres. Not large by any means, but enough to support themselves on. Mr. Cooper would come in on the weekends to see to his wife and child before loading up with more supplies and heading back out to their land.

This had been going on for about a month, but one weekend, he didn't show. The man was like clockwork, and Travers knew instantly something was wrong. He paced the front porch all that night waiting for him to roll into town. He never arrived. He told himself that it was possible that he had something come up which held his attention. The second night passed without the man. Now he was worried. The wife, Sonja, was beside herself. She knew something was terribly wrong. Jeb was not a man to ignore an obligation such as his family. He was a responsible person. Together, she and Travers enlisted the aid of Sheriff Tate, and they rode out to the site.

There was no sign of the man. His tent, shovels, ax, everything was gone. It made no sense. It appeared that the man had just up and quit the area. There was evidence of a small frame house that had been begun, but it had been burned, the ashes cold. He had been gone for several days it seemed. Travers and the sheriff scouted around for several hours but found nothing. Whatever had taken place out here, the rain the previous evening had washed away all traces. Travers didn't know what to make of it. He had a creepy feeling come over him that he couldn't shake on the ride home. A queer thing that wouldn't let up. The wife was subdued, understandably in shock. Denial. This just couldn't be right. Not Jeb Cooper.

Back in town, Travers saw the woman to her rooms and headed to Tate's office. Sure enough, Tate was of the same opinion. Something had happened out there, and the *what* they did not know. Time was not on their side, however, for as long as Cooper was missing, the notes on the place would add up. The wife would be held accountable. She had no money of her own. Travers offered his help in keeping the bank off her back for a while until they could locate her husband or find his body. Tate agreed to help as well. There was something afoot here, and both knew it did not bode well for the town. Neither one voiced their opinions aloud, but each was thinking of Jim Bowers. He was a snake. Somehow, Travers knew he was tied up in this. Proving it would be the hard part. Travers had never backed down from a challenge, and he felt this one was going to be a doozy.

He pondered on the situation all day, trying to remember Bowers' schedule. The man didn't have one. Sometimes he disappeared for weeks on end. He came and went as he pleased, never seeming to actually work, but he seemed to have a growing gang around him. He had taken up residence in the hotel, and after his initial arrival he had cleaned himself up, got himself a tailored suit, shave and a haircut, and had surprised a number of people. The man was not bad to look at, but he could be the devil himself for all the women in town cared. They despised him. The coldness in his eyes said there was no soul there, so they steered clear of him, which was just as well. He was not a friendly man by any means. But he was indeed becoming a man of means.

Through the town's grapevine, Travers discovered that Bowers had journeyed to Fort Dodge where he had purchased Jeb Cooper's land. The man had not even been declared dead yet, but the note had been purchased, and he apparently had paid Sonja Cooper a tidy little sum as well. She had refused to speak of it to Travers when he had questioned her about it, but Travers knew she still had misgivings about the man. But with no proof, she had to take the money offered to survive and to support her family. After the baby was born, a son she named Jeb, Jr., she headed back to St. Louis where her sister ran a boarding house. And so, the case of the missing Jeb Cooper seemed to close with her leaving.

<hr>

That afternoon as Laura was setting Travers' lunch out for him in his office at the clinic, she asked out of the blue.

"Travers, who is Maggie?"

His head jerked up, and his eyes narrowed slightly, one seeming to tick at the corner. His mouth went dry.

"Why do you ask?"

She shrugged. "You called her name that night you had the nightmare. Was she your sweetheart?" She teased lightly.

He lowered his eyes, shuttering them and turned his attention back to the journal he had been reading, though his jaw was clenched, and his hands seemed to shake slightly.

"No."

That was it. Just a clipped "no' was all she got. She pressed further.

"Hmm. Sounds . . . complicated."

Travers looked out the window, his hand going to his chin.

"No."

She was dying here. "Aw, come on. Can't you tell me?"

He sighed. "A child."

That raised her eyebrows. She had never considered that maybe he had children. "Yours?"

"No."

Well, it was obvious he was not willing to elaborate on it. He didn't want her to know, whatever the case. And she would be content with that. She was sure though that she would find out sooner or later. She just hated the later part. But patience was a virtue, or so she had been told.

Travers ignored her until she left. She had shaken him by asking about Maggie. *She* was off limits. No one would know about her or her brother and the wrong that he had done them. She was the past. A painful, painful past.

Hurrying through lunch didn't help get his mind off her. He had been doing so well until Laura had said her name. He had felt the blood leave his face and was sure Laura had noticed. Or had she? Maybe not, because she had kept on digging for information, knowing what a private person he was. He shook his head to get his mind on other things. It didn't work. What had begun as a decent day was now ruined.

FIVE

The entire town was abuzz. The stranger was bad news, and everyone was giving him a wide berth after he had pistol-whipped Clayton Moss. The blacksmith was a big man, but the stranger had clubbed him from behind, using one of the man's own irons, rendering him unconscious before proceeding to beat his head to a bloody pulp with his pistol that he seemed to be so proud of. All Clayton had done to deserve that kind of treatment was tell the man no. He had recognized the man and knew him to be trouble and had refused to serve him.

When the men had brought Clayton to his office, Travers' stomach had turned at the sight of him. This whipping was far worse than any the blacksmith had endured as a slave, he knew. Clayton's life back in Mississippi had been a decent one by his own account. He had been lucky to have a master who didn't believe that mistreating his property got more work from them. Now he lay at death's door due to some hard case that had no respect for life whatsoever.

Clayton had become a good friend and the fury Travers was feeling after treating him rose to a dangerous level. He had seen men of stronger constitutions die of such trauma, and that rattled him. He did not want to lose this man. Could not lose him. The hour grew later as he evaluated him, sensing no change in his patient's condition. He was unconscious and had a severe concussion. Unfortunately, his massive frame was more than the small beds in Travers' clinic could handle. Reluctantly, Travers sought the aid of several men lingering outside the place to move him to his own bed where he would be more comfortable, and Sarah could watch him closely. After getting Clayton settled and giving Sarah her instructions, he sought out Sheriff Tate, angry that apparently, the man responsible was still roaming the streets.

Tate and six or seven men were on the steps in front of the jail deep in conversation when he stalked up. When they saw him, all conversation ceased, and everyone looked at Tate with a question in their eyes. The sheriff flicked his hand at them, shooing them away, not wanting them present for this conversation. Travers looked steamed, and from what those men had said, he was going to be boiling before their talk was over. Travers watched them go, talking quietly among themselves.

Tate waited until they were out of earshot before turning to Travers.

"Well, looks like we got us a peck of trouble."

"I'll say. Why hasn't that jackass been arrested?"

The sheriff studied on that a moment, his eyes and mouth drawn into a frown. He didn't want to seem the coward here, but Travers was asking some hard questions.

"It ain't that simple. First of all, the only witness, we got that says he did it is the town drunk. Second of all, that man ain't just some drifter. You don't go lookin' for him lest you got a death wish."

Travers studied Tate, seeing there was much more to the story than the man cared to admit.

"Who is he?"

Tate looked around the town, noticing how empty the streets seemed to be today. The fear coming from the people hiding behind locked doors was a tangible thing. This menace had to be removed quickly, cleanly, justly. And Doc was the man to do it. Looking Travers in the eye, he said,

"Kip Marlowe."

Travers thought for a moment. The name rang a bell, but he couldn't be sure why. Tate saw the confusion.

"He robbed a bank down in Horeb, just south of Wichita, shot and killed seven people there, including two women."

That helped.

"What the hell is he doing out of jail?"

Tate shrugged. "He served four years. They let him out, saying his rights had been violated by denying him a parole hearing."

"I thought the punishment for murder was a public hanging."

Tate nodded, agreeing. "Yep, it is. But he had an uncle that pulled some strings, or so I hear. Anyhow, he's here holed up in Flora's place workin' a girl over as we speak. He won't leave. Flora's a 'feared for that girl's life but feared for her own and the others as well. Flora told Joseph he's been calling your name. Says he's here to wipe your face with the sole of his boot. He's come to call you out, Doc, and he means to kill ya'."

Travers saw red. The town was terrified to come out because some lunatic wanted to prove himself a fast gun. Damn the man! Travers' fists clenched and unclenched. The sorry sap didn't know it, but he had thrown down the gauntlet when he had attacked Clayton. He had gone beyond mean with the viciousness of his attack on that man. He was evil. And evil was not tolerated in this town.

He clenched his jaw so hard his teeth ground painfully.

"We'll just see about that."

Striding back to his office, he strapped on his gun. It was a .44 caliber Remington Army revolver that he had worn during the war. Checking it carefully before easing it back into its holster, he ran his hands down the side of it, getting the feel of it again. It had been a long time since he had worn it. It should have felt foreign to him. It didn't. It felt like a tool that he used with precision, much like his medical instruments. His eyes closed. His stomach churned, dreading the fight that he was going to pick. The people in this town could not afford another Clayton Moss episode. Folks would be packing up and leaving by the droves. The town would die. Travers and these people had worked too hard, fought too hard to build this town, make it safe for families to prosper. Only to have someone like Kip Marlowe come along to disrupt the serenity of their lives? He didn't think so. He would see to it that the trash was taken out personally.

Travers didn't look like a gunfighter as he stepped out onto the boardwalk His pressed white shirt was fastened at the neck with a cravat and tucked into fine wool pants that belonged to a tailored suit. His gray silk brocade vest stood out even more so. His trademark hat was pulled evenly down on his head. He looked out of place, and as he paused there in front of his clinic, he looked down the street where the sheriff stood watching his every move. Giving his hat one last tug, he stepped into the street.

People began to peek from behind their curtains, watching the doc as he passed, fear written on their faces. He didn't notice them, his mind on the task at hand. Down at the saloon, several of the men, one in particular, seeing the gun strapped to his leg and the purpose with which he strode, ventured out of hiding to witness the event no matter how it turned out. It was a curiosity of man, this play of guns, and many a man coming out of hiding to line the streets whispered a prayer that the doc knew his business. It was rumored that he was fast. Tales from the war had finally managed to make their way to Gold City. Now they would get a firsthand glimpse of the man at work.

He came to a stop outside of Flora's place and stood in the middle of the street.

"Marlowe!" he bellowed.

Inside, Marlowe had just given the little redhead the ride of her life. He was washing himself when he heard his name being called.

"What the . . ." Striding naked to the window, he threw open the curtain to see who was waiting for him. Recognizing the man on the street as the esteemed Dr. Gage, the man he had come there to kill, he grinned and saluted him with two fingers before turning to throw his clothes on. He would have preferred to do the calling out, but this time was as good as any, he figured. He was totally relaxed after his session with the whore who lay whimpering on the bed, and so all his attention would be on the good doctor.

When he reached for his shirt hanging from the headboard, the redhead cowered away from him. Seeing it, he grabbed her by the back of the head, jerked her to him and proceeded to kiss her roughly, his tongue thrusting violently into her mouth. He felt himself stirring again. She was bruised and bloody, but she had been a pleasant if feisty, distraction. She struggled against him, trying to break free. He held her close.

"I'll be back, honey, then you an' me gonna have us some more fun." He was cocksure of himself, and it took all the young girl cowering in the bed could do to keep from spitting in his face. Seeing the fire in her eyes, as well as the fear, he gave a nasty laugh. The moment he released her, she rolled into a ball. He finished dressing, strapped on his guns and left. The man on the street would not wait all day.

Flora and Pearl were in the room in seconds, horrified by what they saw. Tandy was covered in dark bruises, and she had bloody bite marks all over her breasts and back. The man was an animal. Flora sent up a silent prayer for Travers to kill the bastard coming out to face him.

Travers had stood there for several minutes before Marlowe finally appeared at the door. He was a tall, lanky fellow and had the look of a coyote about him. He practically slithered down the steps as he came forward to accept the challenge thrown out by Travers. He noted the squinted eyes as they sized him up, looking for a weakness of some sort.

"Well, we meet at last. You know you don't look so tough. I was expecting a little more of a challenge."

Travers' eyes hardened into steel, and the muscle in his jaw clenched.

"You've got a death wish, son."

The outlaw gave a sharp bark of laughter.

"You know, that's pretty funny. Because frankly, I'm afraid yore mistaken. See, I'm here to kill *you*." His body language was cocky as his words. He shifted from one foot to the other as he spoke.

"I'm giving you a chance to leave town. Now. Otherwise, you'll be finding yourself with a severe case of lead poison. You have to the count of three to mount your horse and ride out. Then I'm going to start shooting."

At that, Marlowe's nasty smile disappeared. He began to fidget, his fingers flexing above his gun.

Travers never moved.

"One. . ."

Marlowe's hands began to itch, the palms sweating suddenly, and he felt moisture pop out on his forehead and upper lip.

"Two. . ."

Damn, but the man down the street was too calm by far. He had not counted on his being so arrogant. Well, he would show him! The outlaw reached for his gun, the snarl on his face feral, sinister. The ringing of gunfire sounded too far away, and he blinked, trying to recall why everything around him looked blue. He realized suddenly that he was on the ground looking up at the sky and he couldn't wrap his mind around the how or why. The gun he had shucked lay useless beside him now, just out of reach. A cloud of dust passed before his eyes, and a shadow loomed over him. He blinked up at the figure a few times, tried to speak, to say something. No sound came forth. A blanket of darkness fell, and the man's eyes lost their light.

Travers stood over the man for several seconds, resisting the urge to spit on him. He had made sure that he was the last thing that Marlowe had seen before he passed. The man was scum, no two ways about it, but Travers resisted the ungentlemanly urge to show what he really thought of the dung pile lying at his feet. He looked down the street, seeing men from the town coming towards him, some with their jaws dropped. Excited whispers passed among them, giving the effect of buzzing insects. Women and children began to come into the street as well, all curious to get a look at the body. He didn't notice Jim Bowers standing at the edge of the crowd, a knot between his eyes and his face a thundercloud. The man disappeared back into the saloon.

Travers motioned to Limbaugh, the undertaker.

"He's yours. Best get him off the street."

Limbaugh nodded, motioning for some of the men to help him.

Travers ignored the rumble of comments about the shooting, looking instead at the whorehouse, remembering what the sheriff had said about Marlowe roughing up one of the women. He mounted the steps and went inside, ignoring the more indignant remarks of the proper ladies who had come out to look at his handiwork.

Travers had only been inside once or twice for drinks, never for the other services offered, although he knew that Flora would be more than willing to give him a royal tour of the place. The decor was tastefully done, not bawdy as one would expect in such a place. That was all saved for upstairs he figured.

Downstairs was furnished like any upscale home in town. There were, however, lots of couches and huge palm trees which had apparently been ordered special. No one appeared to be around.

"Hello?" Surely someone was here. After all, the sheriff had said that Marlowe was here with a woman and that Flora was here as well as the other girls. He heard a door shut somewhere upstairs, and in a few moments, Flora appeared, carrying a basin of water. Upon seeing him, she gave a sigh of relief.

"Oh, thank God! Am I glad to see you!"

Travers hung his hat on the coat rack beside the door, running his fingers through his hair as he did so. He got right to the point.

"I heard Marlowe got rough with one of your girls."

Flora nodded. "Yes, Tandy. She's pretty banged up, doc. Think you can take a look at her?"

Travers spread his arms. "That's why I'm here."

The madam smiled, depositing the basin on a table to be emptied later. Travers noticed the pink tinge of the water and the cloths.

"That bad?"

"Afraid so. He did a real number on her. Come on. She's in my quarters," she said as she pulled him towards the stairs. At that comment, he hesitated, raising an eyebrow. She just smiled, tugging his arm.

"Relax, doc. Right now, the only thing on my mind is Tandy. Besides, even if I did manage to get you into bed, you'd be wondering what took you so long getting there."

Travers offered a grin, knowing that she probably spoke the truth. Flora didn't entertain many men. She didn't have to. She left that task to her girls. But she was a beautiful woman, and lots of men wanted what she had to give. To the right man. For some reason, she had decided that that man was Travers, though she was having a hard time convincing him of the fact.

Upstairs, they had to shoo the other girls out of the room, but he asked Flora to stay while he examined the young redhead. She was a mess, and that was for certain. She had a cut lip that would probably need stitches, and bite marks all over her body. Tandy had been sorely misused, the man had left her raw and bleeding with deep, ragged scratch marks scattered randomly across her legs. There was evidence that the scum had used a belt buckle on her as well. Travers felt sick and knew a moment of satisfaction that the man was dead. He wouldn't be able to treat another human being this way.

Tandy was pretty sore already, and it would be worse come morning he was sure. He asked Flora for some of the salve he had given her not long after he got to town for bruising and such and after she fetched it he slathered it on the girl. In the meantime, Flora found the tiniest needle she had and the finest horsehair in the stash that she kept for just such occasions to stitch the girl's lip with. Luckily, the girl had eased off into a laudanum-induced slumber shortly after the doc arrived. Otherwise, the stitching might have taken longer than a few seconds. Having done all he could for her at the moment, he rose to leave. Flora walked him downstairs to the front door.

"Thanks, Travers," she said, linking her arm through his.

"Well, there's not much to be done for bruising except bed rest. And she needs to avoid working for a month or so. She's banged up pretty bad. May take longer."

Flora nodded. "We'll take good care of her, doc. I'll bring her by to see you before she goes back to work just to be sure everything's alright."

"That's a good idea. And I'll warn you now, she may be pretty skittish about getting back into the swing of things."

Flora grimaced at him. "Yes, I know. But it will be her choice. She won't have to do anything she doesn't want to. All of these girls are here on their own free will. I just provide room and board and companionship. They work for themselves, not me. All I ask is that they conduct themselves like ladies outside of this house. I've had enough of madams and pimps to last a lifetime. So have they."

Seeing the rather stunned expression on Travers' face, she laughed.

"Surprised? Well, a lot of people don't know that, so let's keep that our little secret, alright? Wouldn't do to have this town knowing that I've reformed."

"Reformed?"

"Well, of course. I don't still entertain men myself. Why on earth would I? The rent from the girls is more than enough to keep me in style. But I do have to keep up appearances, you know. Being too straight-laced is not good for business."

She took Travers' hat from the hook near the door and handed it to him. Her brow arched as she added, "You know, I'm more than willing to make an exception should a certain gentleman be interested. In any case, you know where to find me." With that, she closed the door on him.

Travers stood there on the porch for a moment, his hat in hand, staring at the closed door. By damn, if he wasn't surprised. He saw Flora in a new light now. She was unlike any other woman he'd ever met. And dang if the thought didn't cross his mind to take her up on her offer sometime. But no, he shook himself. They were friends, and that was how it was going to stay.

Turning to head back to his clinic, it was like stepping onto a stage in a big theater. It seemed the whole town had gathered waiting for him to emerge. Travers felt his face redden slightly as he recalled Flora's parting words and wondered if they had been overheard. Cramming his hat onto his head, he stepped into the crowd.

Sheriff Tate was the first to accost him as he headed to the other end of town.

"That girl alright in there?"

"She will be. Marlowe really did a number on her. She won't be forgetting it anytime soon."

Tate fell into step beside him as they headed through the crowd which parted for them like a wave.

"Which one was it?"

"Tandy, the little redhead."

Tate gave a grunt and nodded. "She'll be all right. That gal's tough as a lighter knot. She came here with Louella and me from Charlotte."

"No kidding?"

"Yep. Louella took a real shine to that girl. She hears about this, she's jes' liable to march up in there and set up shop tendin' her."

Travers laughed at the thought of Louella Tate pulling just such a stunt. Ras was right. She was the sort to do just that. The laugh seemed to ease the tension out of Travers' body that had been there from the moment he had strapped on his gun. Tate sensed the change in him and clapped him heartily on the shoulder.

"That was some mighty fine shooting back there. Don't know as I've ever seen nobody faster."

Travers gave a low grunt.

"Tate, you live long enough, I'm afraid you will."

Travers left him out in the street scratching his head to think on that one as he went into his clinic and shut the door. Unbuckling his gun belt, he hooked it back on the hook on the wall where he kept it and settled himself back at his desk, trying to concentrate on making notes in both Clayton's and Tandy's files. It wasn't working. Marlowe's face kept coming into his line of vision. Somehow, he knew that the gunman would not be the last to come gunning for him. A traitor to his homeland and a fast gun, the war had changed that fact into a certainty. No. Marlowe was only the beginning. Where one skunk roamed, more were sure to follow.

------◆------

It was noon the next day before Travers was able to stop in and check on Clayton. Sarah answered his knock, her white teeth gleaming against her skin.

"Morning, Doc! Finally, reinforcements. Keeping Clayton in bed is a chore in itself."

"He's not up, is he?" Concern clouded his words.

"It ain't from lack of tryin'!" she said as she led the way to the bedroom where the big man was struggling to sit up. Travers rushed to his side, pushing him back down as Sarah tsked, shaking her head at her hardheaded husband.

"Now Clayton, you know I said no sitting or rising for a week solid. That was an awful beating you took, and you have a severe concussion."

Clayton raised his hand to stop the doctor's lecture.

"Doc, a man like me, can't stay abed all day. I got work to do."

Travers folded his arms across his chest, casting his friend a level stare.

"And just who do you think is going to do your work if you fall out dead because you wouldn't listen to your doctor?"

"Doc—" He tried to protest further.

"No! No getting out of this bed until I say so. If I have to tie you down to keep you here, I will."

The gleam in Travers' eye told Clayton that he would do just that, so he sank, unwillingly, into the comfort of his down pillow. His sigh of frustration did not go unnoticed.

Travers chuckled at the baleful look in the man's eyes and offered, "Look at it this way, Clay, you get to be waited on hand and foot by the loveliest woman in town. Who knows what you could persuade her to do for you while you're laid up." That definitely sparked the black man's interest, and his eyes fairly danced as they darted to Sarah who rolled her eyes at the man.

"Lord, Doc, don't be giving him any ideas. He works me to the bone as it is. Sarah, this—Bring me that. You'd think he was a pulin' infant the way he takes on."

That got a glare from her husband and a laugh from the doc. Travers figured he better see to things before the two tied up with him there. He got busy checking his eyes and looked his wounds over good, satisfied that Sarah was doing a good job keeping them clean and told her so. Sarah beamed under the praise and would have blushed if her skin had been lighter. Flustered, she hurried into the kitchen to pour a cup of tea for Travers while he sat and chatted a while with Clayton.

"By the way," Clayton said after they had been alone for twenty minutes or so, "Sheriff Tate came by earlier. Says I don't have to worry about pressing charges against that man what did this to me. Says he's dead."

Travers looked deep into the now empty cup he held, giving

a slight nod as a reply.

"You killed him?"

The nod came again.

"Doc, you did what you had to do. No one faults you there."

Travers looked up at him, the uncertainty written all over his face although he answered,

"I know that."

Clayton snorted. "Then why do you look like a whipped pup?"

Travers sighed, knowing if anyone would understand Clayton would.

"Because, my friend, Kip Marlowe was only the first in a long line, I'm afraid. Word of a fast gun travels fast out here. I never should have called him out."

"Well, it's done. What are you gonna' do about it?"

"Not a whole lot I can do about it. Grit my teeth and bear it, I guess."

"Yep. But you'll be fine. You'll be jes' fine."

With that, Clayton changed the subject, seeing the haunted look come into Travers' eyes. The man's past was coming back to haunt him, and Clayton was sorry for him. He had been forced to make some hard choices in his life, and the consequences were catching up to him. The doctor was a good man and a good friend, the best Clayton had ever had. Yes, he hated that for the man.

They talked a few minutes longer, then Travers rose to leave to tend other business, but he assured Clayton he would be checking up on him to see if he was following doctor's orders only to be shooed out of the room by the grunting blacksmith.

Standing outside in the street, Travers was struck by how normal the town seemed once again. Most of the townspeople looked at him and greeted him with new respect, but they were no longer afraid to go about their business. Some of the men greeted him with such favorable remarks that he was afraid they were ready to make him sheriff. The word was mentioned, but Travers assured them that he had no aspirations to that effect and he sure wasn't about to tell Ras that he wanted his job. Somehow though, he knew Tate would give him his badge on a silver platter if he asked for it, but Travers wasn't of a mind to. He had enough problems just being the doctor here. He grimaced at the thought, thinking he was due for a break.

SIX

Clayton healed as did Tandy and both went right back to work. Travers had expected as much from the blacksmith but was definitely surprised about the little redhead. Three weeks after the incident with Marlowe she and Flora came to the clinic to get a full bill of health. He supposed that Sheriff Tate knew what he was talking about when he said she was a tough knot. She had some steel in her, that was for sure. He admired her for that. He had thought maybe the attack would get her to thinking that maybe she had better find another line of work, for she was a little thing, barely five foot. Probably weighed no more than eighty, ninety pounds at most. Girls that small in her line of work usually didn't last long. Tandy was proving to be the exception.

Clayton, on the other hand, had been a pain in the ass as a patient. A grumpier person Travers had never seen. He had been like a bear with a toothache. Poor Sarah had sighed with relief when Travers had given him the okay to go back to work. Even she was mighty tired of his tirades. Travers had learned little about their son who had died years before. It seemed such a private matter, and he had not felt obliged to ask though the curiosity was there. Friends or no, when and if they wanted him to know about him, they would tell him.

Making his way into the general store, he pulled a list from his vest pocket and finding a basket set about gathering what he required. He had several things to pick up and was only half listening to the conversation between Pete and Clara Walker until he heard Clara say she was going to have to give up babysitting for two of Flora's girls.

"I just don't have time anymore, Pete," she was saying, "Ever since I started baking pies and cakes for the hotel, I'm just so busy, and you know a child needs lots of attention. Babs and Celia are in a pickle, says they don't know what to do now."

Travers wandered over and cleared his throat.

"Mrs. Walker?"

Pete and Clara greeted Travers roundly.

"Well, hello Doc!" Pete grinned from ear to ear, recalling the shooting of that outlaw the month before. Travers had become 'the man' in town in an instant, the instant it took to kill a man.

He had noticed the doctor didn't care much for his celebrity status, ignoring, for the most part, the praise heaped upon him about how incredibly fast he had drawn his gun. Yes, Pete had seen a few fast guns in his day, and Travers was one of them. And he worried about the doc. Anybody that fast had a past. The town really didn't know a lot about the man, he thought. Rumors had surfaced about a fight in the war where he had supposedly taken out several men in one fell swoop. No one really knew the facts except that Travers Gage was fast with a gun. But then, that's all one really needed to know out here. Fast was fast, no matter how you cut it. It just so happened that the fight with Marlowe was the first one of its kind for Gold City.

"I didn't mean to listen in on your conversation, but did you say that you're going to stop babysitting?"

"Yes, I'm afraid so."

Travers jumped at the chance here before him to help a friend.

"I'd like to make a suggestion if that's alright?"

Clara fiddled with her basket of dry goods.

"Why, sure."

"Well, ma'am, Sarah Moss would love the chance to see to those little ones, I believe."

"Sarah Moss?" Clara frowned, not seeming to like the idea.

Pete chimed in. "Yeah. That's a right fine idea, Doc. She lost her boy a few years back, you know, and I hear she's a fine cook."

"And she's wonderful with children," Travers added.

"Well," Clara hedged, "I just don't know if those girls would take too kindly to a Negro looking after their children."

Travers clamped his jaw against the remark he had been about to make, realizing to whom he spoke. Clara Walker was a Southerner, from South Carolina, and she was one of those who lived by the creed that 'white is right.' She was the sort who would always look down her nose at blacks if something or someone didn't prod her otherwise. Travers pinned her with a hard look.

"Mrs. Walker, I hardly think the color of Sarah's skin will be an issue here. Long as the children are cared for properly, those girls would let anyone keep them."

Mrs. Walker gave a low sniff, but Travers noticed it. Now to put the icing on the cake.

"Why don't you put the idea to Sarah yourself, Mrs. Walker? Let her know that you're confident enough in her abilities to have made the suggestion?" Travers kept his face blank, but it was nigh unto difficult.

Clara's eyes bugged, and her face turned red as fire. Why, of all the nerve! She'd never even spoken to the woman before.

Since coming here from South Carolina, she'd had as little contact with the few darkies in this town as possible. A war had been fought over those blasted folks for heaven's sake, and the South had been ruined because of it. Now the good doctor here was all but daring her to approach one about a job. She looked from Travers to Pete, noting they seemed to be holding their breath. Both were waiting for her to say she wouldn't do it, she knew. Well, she would just show them! With a huff, she thrust out her chin.

"Very well, I'll speak to her today. Just don't be surprised when she says no."

Travers smiled as he watched the woman swish out of the store. He and Pete exchanged looks.

"She won't say no," Pete said, grinning.

"I know." Travers grinned, pleased with himself.

<hr>

An hour later, after taking care of other business, Clara found herself in front of the Moss residence. It was a large place. Clayton had taken in the original shop and converted it into a house for his family when they had moved here four years ago. He had built his smithy behind the house, and all the men in the town had raved about his work and the facility. Clayton Moss had done well for himself here in Gold City. He was well known and liked by all. His wife Sarah kept to herself a lot, especially since their son had died. Clara remembered him, a quiet, very polite little boy of about six or seven years old. She had seen him and his mother in Pete's store a few times and had noticed the obvious love the woman had for her child. It had been very apparent that the boy had manners, unlike what Clara had assumed all black children lacked.

She had been thinking. If Pete thought enough of this Moss woman to second the doctor's opinion, well, then that was good enough for her. Gathering her nerve, she marched up to the door and knocked, noticing some well-tended flowerbeds on either side of the door. At least the woman kept her yard presentable, she thought, her sniff not quite having the force it should have. A moment passed before the door opened revealing Sarah in an apron covered in flour. Her eyes widened when she saw who was standing on her doorstep.

"Mrs. Walker, isn't it?"

"Yes."

There was an uncomfortable pause where they just stared at one another, each unsure of what to say. Sarah frowned a bit.

"If you're here to see Clayton, he's out in the shop." Her voice was soft and melodic, surprising Clara. The white woman cleared her throat, suddenly unsure how to go about this.

"No. I'm actually here to see you."

"Me?"

"Yes, I'd like to discuss something with you, if you don't mind."

Sarah wondered what on earth could have brought this woman to her door. In the past, she had always gone out of her way to avoid her kind. Unknowingly, she raised an eyebrow at the woman, but wiped her hands on her apron, and stepping back, invited the woman in.

"Won't you come in?"

Clara hesitated, but the smell of something wonderful from the kitchen drew her in. The room she had entered was large and spacious, simply furnished with few knick-knacks, but it was spotless. Not a speck of dust to be seen. Clara didn't know what she had expected to find, but it wasn't this tidy home. Sarah stood back watching the woman look her fill wondering what was going through her mind when she suddenly remembered.

"Oh, goodness, my pies!"

She disappeared in a flurry of skirts, and Clara followed her into the kitchen where the aroma was like a heady ambrosia. Sarah was removing two golden brown pies from the oven as she entered the room.

"My, those smell divine!" She offered.

Sarah, startled to have been followed, offered a flustered "Thank you."

"What are they?"

"Blackberry."

"Really? Where on earth did you find blackberry bushes around here?" she wondered aloud.

"Behind our house. We have blackberry bushes and a few other varieties."

Clara was awed.

"You don't mean it. I never could get one to grow."

Sarah nodded and offered a smile.

"I know what you mean. We had trouble at first, but one finally rooted and spread."

All Clara could think of to say was "Well, I'll be. . ."

Sarah watched the woman. It seemed she was trying to make an effort here towards something, so Sarah decided to prod her along.

"Would you care for some lemonade? I just squeezed it this morning. It's good and cool."

Cool lemonade? Clara hadn't had cool lemonade since South Carolina. Her mouth watered.

"Why, I'd love some."

Sarah offered another smile, her teeth sparkling white against her face and Clara was suddenly glad she had come. As she watched, the black woman lifted a trap door and disappeared into the floor. If that didn't beat all! In a few seconds, she was back with a gallon jug that appeared frosted over. Pouring two glasses of the wonderful concoction, she handed one to Clara who took it and proceeded to down half of hers in one gulp.

Sarah just stood back, chuckling to herself.

"Why, I believe that is the best lemonade I've ever tasted! And it is cold!"

Sarah nodded. "That's the only way to drink lemonade."

Clara had to agree. "How did you get it so cold?"

Sarah nodded to the trapdoor. "There's a little spring down there that we found when we dug the cellar. It stays cold year round."

"Why, I do declare."

Sarah had been weighing out in her mind what the woman could want with her and decided that she just did not know. Knowing that sooner or later, she would get around to it, she offered the woman some of the freshly baked pie, and she practically salivated.

As she ate, the woman began to talk, about her home in South Carolina and their journey here to Kansas. She rattled on and on, surprising Sarah that she would volunteer so much information about herself. It surprised Clara Walker as well. Why on earth was she sitting here, telling Sarah Moss, a Negro, that her husband had been wounded in the fighting at Fredericksburg, and that they had lost all six of her children to fever? Suddenly, she realized that this woman whom she had avoided for so long could be her best friend. All her life, Clara had been taught that blacks were inferior. She had never associated with them other than to give them orders about the house. She had not come from a rich family, had not married money, but they did well enough to afford a few slaves. She recalled eleven total, all with the mind of a child it had seemed. On looking back, she now realized that that was exactly what they knew was expected of them. It shamed her to think that she had been so blinded by what society had instructed her.

Well, she was here to right that wrong. Turning to Sarah, she got right to the point, knowing that Travers and Pete had been right.

"Sarah, I've got a proposition for you. I don't know if you're aware of it, but I've been keeping Babs' and Celia's little ones while they work during the day. The fact of the matter is this. I've been cooking for the hotel, making desserts, cakes, and pies and such, and with all the new business coming into town, it's keeping me on my toes. I can't look after them properly, any-more. Your name was mentioned as a possible replacement as a sitter. I wanted to offer you the job first."

Sarah was sitting there with her mouth literally hanging open. Of all things, she had suspected, it had not been this.

"What?"

"Oh dear, I think you'd be just right for the job. There's just the two of them. Matilda is three and Harry is nine months. They're really no trouble at all. And the pay is good." Clara gushed as she saw the uncertainty on the black woman's face.

"But—" Clara patted the woman's hand with hers, noting the look of shock on her face.

"You know, I figure you miss having a little one around. I know you lost your son some time ago. I used to see you in the general store with him. Handsome little man, he was. I know what it is like to lose a child. I buried six. But, you have a way about you. I can see it. You've got a lot of love to go around. Besides, maybe, I could come by on occasion to help out when I'm not so busy."

Sarah recognized that the woman was throwing out an offer of friendship in her offhand way. The idea appealed to Sarah. Surprisingly so. The only other women in the town she'd had any serious companionship with were Laura and Louella Tate. Yet, here a dyed in the wool Southern woman was extending an olive branch to her. It was so ridiculously appealing that she wanted to weep with the joy of it. Clara Walker was serious. About the friendship and the babies. Before she accepted, she had to know.

"May I ask who suggested me?"

"Why it was Dr. Gage, and Pete said he thought you'd make a good sitter as well."

Sarah's grin grew even wider. Leave it to Travers to do some-thing so nice for her. He knew about her boy, though he had never pried. Not with her or Clayton. She was going to owe him big for this one.

"Mrs. Walker, I think I will take you up on that offer." Her voice cracked just a bit.

"Call me Clara. And I think we should see the girls this eve-ning to put the idea to them."

The two talked for another hour before Clara had to leave. She turned to Sarah at the door, a look of chagrin on her face.

"You know, I've always lived by a certain code, that was basi-cally forced on me from childhood. I don't take pride in that, especially upon realizing that part of what I'd been taught was a lie. You give credence to that, Mrs. Moss, and I'd be happy to call you friend."

Sarah's eyes welled up; she couldn't help it. The woman was quite teary-eyed herself.

"Clara, I think I'd like that."

Clara took the woman's hand in hers, patting and squeezing it warmly, a smile lighting her face. "Sarah, you won't regret it. I promise you."

SEVEN

Life tumbled along in the little town of Gold City. Anything new happened it was around the town in minutes. Unfortunately, Jim Bowers was still around and that made life in the small town interesting. Two more men had disappeared. Months had passed since the first disappearance, but with two more missing men, Travers' suspicions mounted. Bowers was a certified killer. Smart and lethal as a snake. The how and the why was what had the doc puzzled though. Bowers seemed to be richer than God already, so why would he have reason to kill those men? It was eating him, this not knowing. But one didn't accuse a man of murder without proof. And Travers had none. Not a motive even, except maybe greed. So once again, the town mourned the loss of two men, their bodies never surfacing, though surely dead for neither were the kind to leave their families. Sheriff Tate and Travers were stumped. Each wanted to beat Bowers to a pulp but restrained themselves with the knowledge that sooner or later, the snake would reveal himself.

And other things happened as well. A stranger came to town, not that that was strange in itself for that happened quite frequently, but this man had a way of rubbing the doc the wrong way. It was late August, hot, and Travers was sitting on the porch of the boarding house whittling when he rode in. The stranger looked around him, taking in the few people on the street that day, noticed Travers and reined his horse over to him. He gave his hat a tip.

"Hoyt Grable's the name. Fresh from Kentucky and looking for the blacksmith. Heard he's the best around."

Travers looked the newcomer up and down. He was a dandy for sure. Looked to have money. Lots of it.

"You'll find him in his shop back of that house yonder," Travers told him, pointing out the house. The man stuck out his hand.

"Why thank you Mr. — I don't believe I caught your name."

Travers grinned at the man.

"That's because I never threw it."

The man's hand dropped along with his jaw. He stammered for a few seconds before Travers finally extended his hand which the man pumped furiously.

"Dr. Gage." The man stopped pumping and stepped back. "*The* Dr. Gage?"

Travers leaned back in his chair again, eyeing the stunned expression on the man's face.

"The only one in town," he drawled.

"My, my, my, will wonders never cease." The little man seemed to be in awe of him, but Travers wasn't sure why.

"What's that?" he asked flatly.

"Well, sir, it's just that you're something of a legend in these parts."

Travers shook his head at the man.

"Legends have little truth to them, friend. I figured someone as educated as you would know that."

"So you're saying that you haven't killed fifteen men?" The man looked skeptical.

"Don't recall saying that." Travers busied himself with his whittling again, his chair once again tipping to lean against the wall.

Now the man frowned, looking puzzled.

"So you have killed fifteen men."

What was it with this guy?

"You know, killing's not a sport for me, but sometimes a wild hair gets up my ass," he said, and pausing, dropped the front of the chair to the boardwalk. The legs cracked like a shot before he continued, "and people who should be minding their own business suffer for it."

His eyes bored into the little man who straightened and began to back slowly away from the blue steel of the doctor's eyes.

"My mistake. I'll be finding that blacksmith now." Turning away, he practically dragged his horse across the street. Travers chuckled to himself, half in humor, half in disgust. The nerve of some people. Curiosity was a dangerous thing in these parts. Hoyt Grable was a little too curious, and that bothered Travers. He had mentioned the doc had killed fifteen men. Travers knew that the number was higher than that, due to the war. But not in a gunfight. The man was itching for something, and that would put Travers in a funk for the rest of the day.

——•——•——

Later that afternoon, he paid Clayton a visit and got the gist of what the little man was up to. He was a gambler of sorts, though not with cards. He liked to deal with lives, in a sick sort of way. Apparently, Grable had tried to pick Clayton for information about the doc, but Clayton wouldn't bite. He was too sly for that. He had played dumb about Travers' past, and the man had left in a huff once his business was tended to. But Clayton had learned plenty. The man went about the country in search of killers, fast guns, men with a reputation. Then a challenge was issued. But not in the usual way. He cunningly dangled the idea of besting other famous killers before the one being issued the challenge. Much like a boxing match would be arranged, only this fight was settled with guns.

Travers felt sick inside. He had known it was coming. The string of men to come gunning for him and Hoyt Grable was the one to bring them here in droves. He should have cracked the man's head for him, then maybe, just maybe, he would have the sense enough to clear out of town. Somehow Travers didn't think he was going to be so lucky.

Travers didn't realize it, but luck was on his side that night. Hoyt Grable had settled in for the evening at the bar where Jim Bowers was keeping him supplied with drinks. He knew the little man's reputation and feared he was here to interfere with Dr. Gage. He assumed correctly. The man was loose with his tongue and didn't mind telling Bowers that he had several men who would be more than willing to face the doctor in a duel to the death. Bowers, however, had to bring that possibility to a screeching halt. He had plans for Travers Gage himself and no one, no one, was going to relieve him of that privilege. So he parleyed with the man and laid out his plan, much to Grable's disappointment. But he agreed to stay out of what was apparently a private feud between the wealthiest man around and the doctor who was reportedly swift as lightning. His only regret was that he would not get to see the outcome. The amount of gold coin jingling in his pocket had sealed that deal. He was to never come back to Gold City. If he showed his face, Bowers would kill him.

With that thought in mind, he rode out of town that night, never looking back, thus never seeing the shadowy figure that followed until they were out of earshot of the town. He never even heard the shot that killed him, dead before he hit the ground. His killer relieved him of his gold coin and pocket watch before tossing him up on his horse and riding deeper into the night where he disposed of the body.

Yes, tonight luck was on the good doctor's side.

EIGHT

Winter happened to Gold City. It began as a harsh, biting wind that never seemed to let up, and with it came misery. Fall, it seemed had lasted only a week or so, but during that week a wagon train stopped just short of town, and Travers found a passel of them waiting for him at the clinic one morning. He schooled his features for he could have groaned aloud at the sight of them.

They were all ill . . . deathly so.

One look at them had sent him back for Laura. He would need help. She shoved a cup of coffee in his hand and sent him on his way.

"I'll be over as soon as I can," she called after him. He raised his cup to acknowledge he had heard her without looking back or breaking stride and waded into the sick.

Sure enough, nine of the children and three of the adults were critically ill. Influenza. He bedded down two of the more critical children and stepped next door for the Taylor boy. He and Laura alone would not be able to handle this. He hadn't enough beds. He sent the boy to fetch the sheriff.

By the time Laura arrived, more folks from the wagon train had found their way to the clinic. Travers was scrambling, administering medicine and looking quite harried. He was worried. Worried that they would have to quarantine the town, but in talking to one of the men, found that the entire party was at the clinic. There were twenty-seven of them. All sick, though all were not critical. Yet. Time was of the essence, and he and Laura rolled up their sleeves and dove in. An hour later, the place next door to the clinic was humming with activity. Word had spread. Sheriff Tate had sent for Clayton who had hastily constructed some cots for the place. They were more like tables with sides as there were no mattresses for them, but hay could be placed in them and be covered with blankets to make the patients more comfortable. Louella Tate and Sarah Moss had come along as well and in no time, had arranged a makeshift hospital next door to the clinic. If Travers could have hugged them and kissed them, he would have, but he and Laura were in a state of perpetual motion getting the patients in bed and medicated. Pete had brought blankets and lanterns from the store and two bottles of peppermint whiskey that he made himself. Travers took note of it and breathed a prayer of thanks, knowing it would all be put to good use.

Louella and Sarah had gone back home, each with the sole purpose of boiling chicken for soup. The broth would be in much demand with so many people sick. Word had reached Flora, and she and her girls had cooked for Laura and Travers, knowing that the two of them would need something to keep them going. Steak and potatoes with green peas were on the menu as well as blackberry pie. By the time Laura finally managed a break to sample some of the pie, she thought she'd collapse from exhaustion. Travers was washing up, his eyes taking in the tired woman sneaking a bite of the pie. Flora had set them up to eat in his office, giving them a bit of privacy and rest. For a few minutes, they could at least relax.

Laura was leaned back in her chair, her eyes closed as she chewed the warm pie. Travers noted the way she held herself. She was a strong woman, one who could be depended upon.

"You're in your element, aren't you?"

She opened her eyes, a weary smile crossing her lips.

"What do you mean?"

"I watched you out there. You were calmly in control. You could have been a nurse. Ever thought about it?"

"Not really. I guess I just like keeping busy, feeling useful. Like I have a purpose. Keeps me grounded."

"Well, I'm lucky to have you, Laura. As a nurse and as a friend."

"That's awfully nice of you to say, Travers," Laura said.

"I mean every word of it. You're a fine woman. It's hard to believe no man has snatched you up."

Laura laughed. "No man would have me, Travers. I'm too independent for a man."

"Someday, Laura, you'll find him. Or rather he'll find you."

◆

The next morning brought a rush of newly sick folks. Town folks. The town would have to be closed. Louella Tate, Addie Finch, the schoolteacher and Pete and his wife were among the sick. Flora came to lend her services, and she was a natural at tending the sick. She and Laura worked together like yin and yang and flowed through the sick like angels of mercy. They were godsends, and Travers thanked God for their help.

By nightfall, one of the children from the wagon train and Addie Finch, the school teacher were dead. Their bodies were carried out and promptly buried. Fortunately, the ground had not hardened to the point where grave digging was impossible, or they would have had to winter the bodies in the stable. The mourners did not linger, for the wind cut into them like knives and the illness that had spread so rapidly had them hurrying back to the safety of their homes.

Travers had just returned to the clinic to find that another child from the wagon train and his mother had died. Again, a hasty burial.

Laura was tiring, swaying on her feet. Travers noted and immediately sent her home. In about thirty minutes, Tandy showed up. Laura had sent for her to fill in. Travers just shook his head. These women were from hardy stock. Back home, he had never seen one go out of her way in times of sickness. The lily-white ladies had always had their slaves to do for them. In hindsight, he guessed he owed the town of Fellowship. They had sent him on to better things. He wouldn't look back. This was home, now more so than ever. Illness had a way of bringing people together. In a crazy sort of way, he and Laura had become family. Flora, well, Flora was a different story. She still hankered to get him into bed and let him know it when they were alone, just after Laura left.

They were sipping coffee in the wee hours of the morning, their patients still sleeping. Flora looked as fresh as morning dew, and he supposed it was from experience, her having generally slept during the day and entertained at night.

"You seem to be looking your fill, doctor. Care to go for a full examination?"

That brought a chuckle from him. She was full of sass, provocative to the point of exasperation, and mannered like the brassiest Southern belle he'd ever encountered.

"I think I'll pass. No offense, of course."

"Travers, what is *wrong* with me," she moaned theatrically, "Don't you find me the least little bit attractive?"

"Flora, my dear, you are devastatingly beautiful. Unfortunately, I'm quite sure you're also a hand full. Tangling with you would probably do me in, and I would like to live a bit longer, see the world you know."

She threw a pillow at him, which he caught, his laughter soon joined by hers.

"You're probably right, you know. God didn't make me for the faint of heart." The smile on her face was pure devilish.

"I'm afraid you're right. I'm unwilling to put it to the test, but not necessarily for the reason implied. I like you, Flora. You've got a lot of heart. Sometimes when friends cross that line, it's hard to remain friends. I don't want to lose your friendship."

Flora's lips pouted prettily for a few seconds before she said,

"You're right, of course. I treasure your friendship as well.

More's the pity."

Before the worst had passed, three more people died. Two were from the wagon train, a little girl and her father, and a man from town, one of the mill workers. Overall, Travers felt like they had been lucky. Seven people had died with only two from the town to bury. After two weeks only three children from the wagon train remained as patients, their mothers staying on with them at the clinic. Flora and Laura took turns helping out though they weren't really needed any longer. The children seemed to take to them, so he didn't mind.

They had become close, the three of them. Flora had left him alone since he had politely turned her down. He had known he was doing the right thing in telling her the truth and she had taken it well. Flora and Laura acted like two sisters at times, and he couldn't help but wonder if there was a connection there, but he didn't pry. It wasn't his nature to stick his nose in other people's business. Or so he thought. He had not seen Jim Bowers lately, and that was a man he certainly wanted to get nosy about. The man was a killer, had killed three men from the town or was responsible for their disappearance, and Travers was like a dog with an itch that couldn't be scratched.

The last three days he had walked about the town, looking, watching. Bowers was gone. He usually frequented the saloon, his foreman Sam Bailey lurking nearby, but they were conspicuously absent. Travers had paid Sheriff Tate a visit and voiced his thoughts on the matter. Tate had apparently been watching too because he clearly let on that he was just waiting to hear that another man had gone missing. They sipped coffee in silence, their mind in one accord. Catching a killer.

NINE

They were lining the street again. Men, women, even children. Somebody should tell these folks to get their kids out of harm's way, Travers thought as he stepped off the boardwalk into the street. He had gone inside for his gun, strapped it on and grabbed his hat from the back of his chair, thinking he really should have ignored the man waiting down the street. His name was Case Dillinger, and he had come to town looking for blood. He already had a name as a killer. Rumor had it he had shot a couple of men in the back out in Colorado. Travers figured he had worked his way to Kansas, having worn out his welcome further west. No one could abide a back shooter, except perhaps Jim Bowers, and that had set him to wondering. Had Bowers hired the man to challenge him? The two of them had never even had words, but Travers knew that he watched him. Once, when he had caught him staring, the man had just grinned slowly, evilly. He made Travers' skin crawl. One day, he thought . . . one day.

Case Dillinger studied the man striding down the street to meet him. He had heard of the man Gage before the wire had arrived for him to come take him out. He had as of yet to meet his employer, but no matter. This would not take long at all. The man down the street would be the easiest hundred dollars he had ever made. Gage was supposed to have a reputation from the war. Fifteen men, his ass. Why, Case himself had gunned down twenty-three, counting the ones he had shot from behind.

He had ridden into town, straight for the doctor's clinic, that confident in his abilities to take this man, that he never even considered finding out who his employer was. He swiped at his long greasy hair with his left hand, spitting to the side, his eyes raking over Travers Gage. He sure didn't look like a gunman. A little on the short side, too, he thought as he drew nearer, making Case seem like a giant. Case stood just over six foot, but the doctor was several inches shy of that. Where Case had the look of a drifter, Travers looked like a businessman, all spit, and polish. Case almost laughed aloud.

"My, my, folks. Looks like we've got us a bit from the Bible playin' out here. Another David and Goliath. I think we can all guess who's Goliath."

There was a nervous titter of laughter. Travers had reached the man, stopping just short at a reasonable firing range. He made deliberate work of rolling up his sleeves, taking in the man's disheveled appearance before commenting.

"I guess that makes me David. So you're a learned man are you, Mr. Dillinger? A man who can quote the Bible? If you recall, the Bible says that Goliath was roughly ten feet tall. You, sir, are a tad shy of that."

The laughter swelled at that, and the man's face reddened. His eyes darted at the crowd which was now laughing at him. He'd show them. Just as soon as he finished with Gage, he would wreak his own havoc with them. A sneer fixed itself on his lips. The doctor was speaking again.

"Do you recall the story, Mr. Dillinger? Or is it a mere memory of something your mother used to tell you about to put the fear of God in you?"

Dillinger turned three shades of a motley purple. Travers had hit it right on the head. His mother had told him stories from the Bible when he was just a child, but he never had paid her much mind. He found himself suddenly trying to recall the story, but he could not for the life of him remember it fully. He itched to get this over with suddenly.

"Quit all this Bible talk, I'm here to kill you, Doctor. I've been promised a hundred for you."

"Is that so?" Travers found that mighty interesting, his drawl carried to the man standing in the shadow of the hotel porch. His eyes locked on the black ones of Jim Bowers who raised innocent brows at his perceptive gaze. Travers turned back to the man down the street.

"By all means, let's get this show on the road."

The crowd held their breath. The man, Dillinger's foot, moved a fraction of an inch just before he went for his gun. He never cleared leather. He stood there, his eyes full of shock as he blinked, trying to see past the smoke of the gun that had done him in. He fell as Travers walked up to him. Travers looked down at him, offering the end of the story.

"You should have paid a little more attention to your mother, son. See David killed Goliath, then he chopped off his head with the giant's own sword. But, I'll forgo that pleasure. No need to thank me. And by the way, thanks for the heads up about the killer among us. I've known it all along."

The man's eyes closed, and his chest heaved a final time. Travers stood looking at him for several long minutes before he turned and pinned Bowers with a challenging stare. Then he walked over to him, stopping just inches from the man.

"You're getting sloppy, Bowers. Next time the poor unlucky

devil may actually know your name."

"I don't know what you're talking about. I've never seen that man before in my life." He was calm, Travers had to hand him that. He truly acted the fine upstanding citizen.

Travers wasn't fooled. He let the man know it.

"I'm no fool, Bowers. I know what you've been doing, and one of these days I'm going to prove it. I know you watch me. You know that I'm too smart to let these little things get by me. To you, they're just insignificant men standing in your way. Well, they have families, responsibilities. They're citizens of this town. And everyone here knows that you have somehow had a hand in their disappearance. You watch your back, Bowers. Someday, when you look over your shoulder, I'll be there. You can send for all the killers you want. You won't win. This town won't let you. Your money is covered in blood, and soon it will no longer be any good in this town. The only reason you're still here is we've no proof. But we'll get it. Then maybe you and me will settle up."

Bowers had studied the doctor's face as he spoke. The man was so confident. It was almost laughable. True, the doctor was a smart man, maybe too smart. He would be trouble, no doubt about it. He would have to take extra precaution. No mistakes. "Dr. Gage, you must have me confused with someone else. I have harmed no one from this town. I did take it upon myself to purchase the land from the unfortunate wives of those men for a tidy sum, of course. That hardly makes me responsible for their disappearances. Besides, it is possible that they're not dead at all. We've found no bodies. Perhaps they've simply run off." The look he gave Travers made his skin crawl.

"Oh, you and I both know that's not what happened. One day, Bowers. One day . . ."

He turned and walked away.

TEN

Christmas came and went in Gold City, and it saw the worst snow the country had seen in years. Laura and Flora kept things lively. They had planned a huge dance, but unfortunately, it had to be canceled. A blizzard had rolled in forcing everyone to stay inside. They seemed to be buried in snow, the world white about them. Travers and Laura fared well enough as they had Joseph, along with Jack and Shamish O'Neal, the two brothers who ran the mill to keep them company. The two brothers had come to town shortly after Travers and had established a lumber and gristmill for the town. Business was booming. They were from Ireland and loved to sing. Sometimes it could be a little much for Travers, but he endured it. He had never known anyone who found such joy in life. He could understand their love of working with their hands though, for it was something he loved as well.

Jack was the eldest, and they had come to America after their parents had died. The government in Ireland had taken everything they owned. They had arrived penniless and starving. They had been taken in by an Irish family in New York but had found the place to be too crowded for them. They longed for the wide-open spaces where they could feel the wind on their faces, the freedom of the prairie where they could build their own future with their own hands beholden to no one. And they had. They employed several men from the town, having lost one to the influenza outbreak that first winter. Life was good in Gold City even if the weather was harsh.

The years passed swiftly, and Travers fit in quite nicely into the little town. The first two were productive, more people coming through, some staying, some moving on. Life was good and moved in a steady rhythm. Until the army came to town.

In 1867, General Winfield Scott Hancock came to Fort Larned and set up his command there in an effort to route the Indians who had begun to raid along the Santa Fe Trail. Gold City had been fortunate, being in the western portion of the state, but the Cheyenne and several other tribes had begun to roam the area, raiding homesteads and nearby Fort Wallace. It was a trying time, for the cavalry was now a constant presence, and that was not always a good thing. Hancock had survived the conflict between the North and the South and had high hopes of squashing the uprisings in the West. There was land to be had, and it was his job to see that the path was clear for those headed for the further plains of Nebraska and Wyoming. Wagon trains were coming through weekly now, some having been hit by the raiding parties. Travers stayed busy. If he wasn't patching up folks from the trains, he was patching up soldiers.

He had the occasion to meet Hancock and his commanding officer, a George Armstrong Custer on one of their forays into town. Hancock had been winged by an arrow and had lost a significant amount of blood before seeking medical attention. Travers had not been impressed with the fair-haired Custer. Hancock, on the other hand, he had met briefly before on the eve of a battle at Gettysburg, Pennsylvania. He had struck him as a good man, though they'd had little to say to one another since Travers was at that moment working on an injured soldier's leg. The soldier had been one of Hancock's staff, and the general had merely come to check on him. He was surprised that Hancock remembered meeting him, for it had been a few years and such a brief encounter, but he had called him by name when they walked into his office. The general had stepped forward and shook his hand as if they were old friends.

"Dr. Gage, it's good to know we have such a capable doctor in the area. I thought this damned bleeding would stop, but all this riding seems to encourage the flow. But we must soldier on, doc. With the Cheyenne getting bolder, I'm certain we'll be requiring your services from time to time." He seemed to pause and consider before adding, "It is a small world, is it not, to find you out west?"

"General Hancock, small world it is, sir," Travers had replied. He promptly set about to patch up Hancock as the general continued.

"This is George Custer. He served under McClellan during the war. He'll be in charge of routing these red devils from the area. Has quite a knack for it, too. I see great things for him."

The blonde man had stepped forward and shook hands with Travers, and the doctor had disliked him instantly, a fact that had not escaped the man sporting the almost white hair he was so famous for. The Indians had already taken to calling him Yellow Hair. He had not said anything to the effect that he knew of Travers' opinion of him until they had bumped into one another at the saloon one evening.

"So, the high and mighty doctor thinks I'm not up to the task of routing these insurgents. I had no problem with the insurgents from your neck of the woods a few years back." He had meant to get Travers' attention and get it he did.

"I don't recall saying anything of the kind. However, if the shoe fits. . ."

Custer had snapped to and stood so close to the doctor he could smell his mustache wax. "Why, you blue-bellied Southerner. I ought to just take you to task now for insolence."

Travers didn't give the man so much as an inch. "I'm not part of your cavalry, colonel. I do hope you exhibit better manners when dealing with your adversaries. I hear the chiefs don't take kindly to threats. Neither do I. Keep your distance and we'll get along just fine."

Custer had studied him thoughtfully, noting the steely look in his eye and knowing it for what it was. This man was not to be pushed. Custer had backed off reluctantly, though he itched to slap the man. This would not look good in the eyes of his men, his backing down from a slur. With a muttered curse, he turned on his heel and left.

He had asked Hancock about Gage later, and the general had been frank.

"You are to leave that man alone. He is hell on wheels with a gun, but most of all we need him. He's a fine surgeon. He fought for the North, went against his own countrymen to preserve our nation. He was at Gettysburg with us, with the 7th from West Virginia. That should tell you all you need to know about him. You won't find a better man, George. Leave him be."

Travers had not known about that conversation, but whatever had transpired, Custer had left him alone. He still saw him from a distance when the column rode into town for supplies and such. The soldiers had become a rowdy bunch and were prone to shoot up the town. Flora's place had become a hothouse of activity, and she had resorted to calling herself Starr to the paying public in hopes of keeping her personal life separate. He didn't blame her. If he could hide, he would too. Travers had had to pull a few men off of her on occasion. The fools didn't know how to take no for an answer. He had made a point to stay nearby lest she should need him, and Flora was grateful. It had brought a closeness to them that had never been there before, and he knew that she depended on him as well as the rest of the town. It made him feel full of purpose.

Spring, when it finally came, was wet. And Travers hated to travel in wet weather. But it could not be helped. He had to attend the medical conference. It had been too long since he had gone, and he desperately needed to go. Weather had slowed the mail out here, and he had received only three of the journals that he so prized. They were full of information that he knew was vital to treating his patients and often arrived too late to help. He sent a wire to a longtime friend in Boston letting him know he would be in the area for the conference and when he would arrive. Then, after speaking with Laura, Sheriff Tate, and Clayton, he hopped the stage to the neighboring town, Nicholsville. It was a stop on the way to Fort Dodge. There he would board the train to Springfield where he would change trains for the final leg of his trip.

The trip was long and uneventful. No one held them up, no Indians to fight off. He grew quite bored. By the time he had reached Boston, he had read the one book he had brought along three times over. He could have quoted it from memory or given a lecture on the various types of parasites found in the human body and the treatment of them. It was really quite disgusting, he thought, but entirely possible for those things to actually climb aboard and thrive without its' host knowing.

Boston was as he remembered it, but growing quickly. His friend, Thomas Allen, met him at the train station.

"My God, it's good to see you Trav. It's been too long." Thomas came forward to grasp his friend's hand. The two of them had gone to medical school together years ago and had become close. They had bumped into one another during the war a few times but had not seen each other since. Travers' wire had been a pleasant surprise for he had not known whether or not his friend had survived the war.

They hugged like brothers, and as they walked to his carriage, Thomas filled him in on things. He had been with General Sharpe at the Wilderness. The man must be traveling under a lucky star. His leg had healed almost completely, well enough to sit his horse on the battlefield. Travers shook his head, recalling how badly the man was injured at Gettysburg and how he had fought to save his leg, his life, actually. Thomas studied his friend, recalling himself the tales he had heard about his friend.

"Seems a long time ago, doesn't it? All the killing, the senseless waste of life."

"Seems like only yesterday." Travers' voice held a bit of sarcasm. Speaking from experience, he knew that Thomas probably wouldn't understand the life he had been living out in Kansas. He knew the man must be itching for details, but he wasn't hungering to give them. Kansas was still a wilderness compared to the eastern part of the country, and the lawlessness there was a way of life just as the South had their slavery.

Thomas was born and raised in the city. He wouldn't understand the reasons behind Travers' decision to live there. Another friend of his might, however, but that was neither here nor there. That one was probably off in some exotic locale drumming up a story for his father's newspaper. But Thomas was a city slicker, and he knew all of the fine dining establishments, one of which he promptly took Travers to. The moment they were seated Thomas asked him about Frank.

"I know the two of you were close. I was just wondering if you had heard from him. Was a shame he had to leave when he did. Wonder where he is now. Reckon' he fought for the South. Don't recall seeing his name on any of the casualty lists, though."

"I don't know where he is. He did fight for the South for a while, or so I heard. Last I heard he was riding with Quantrill." He was referring to the murderous William Quantrill who had raided and all but demolished Lawrence, Kansas.

"Quantrill?" Thomas was frowning. "That can't be good. He bought it in '65 and old Bill Anderson went down in '64. Not many of them left alive." He leaned back in his chair, a cheroot held loosely between his fingers. He offered one to Travers who refused it. Instead, he took a sip of his brandy. The place was crowded, making Travers uncomfortable. He was used to more space, fewer people. Once he had considered moving here. What had possessed him to do that? He was already homesick.

"So what have you been doing for yourself, Thomas? Are you in private practice?"

"No, I'm working at the hospital. Surgery. There's a few of us, but we stay busy."

"I guess you've married that little blonde you were so in love with back then."

Thomas sighed. "Alas, no. She married a banker two weeks after I left to go to war."

That was a surprise. Travers had figured him to be madly in love with the woman. Apparently no, or he wouldn't have let her get away.

"What about you? You married yet?" Thomas took a sip of his whiskey. His friend seemed to be doing fine for himself. He was dressed in a black tailored suit, his white shirt boiled and starched under a brocade vest. The women must love him, he thought. He had always been a tad jealous of the man. Jealous of his looks, his talent with his hands, his innate sense that he had when it came to medicine.

"No, not married. Not really looking in that direction. I've got my hands full with the clinic."

"Well, a wife could help you out at that clinic. Help you pass the time when things get slow." An amused smile spread across Thomas' face.

"I've got a nurse. Two, actually."

Two! You've got two nurses at a clinic in the middle of nowhere?" Thomas was incredulous. "Why, you dog, you! No wonder you haven't a 'need' for a wife!"

Travers grimaced, realizing that his friend was assuming far too much.

"They're not actually trained nurses. They're two friends of mine who have helped me out more than once. Laura owns the boarding house where I live, and Flora is the town madam." He should have kept quiet because he figured he'd just dug himself a hole. From the expression on Thomas' face, one would think he'd just said he was having the time of his life out in Kansas having his way with any woman he chose.

"Ah-ha! I knew it! I bet you can't keep them off of you. Are they beautiful? I bet they're crying in their cups with you gone."

"You've got it all wrong, friend. I've not been intimate with either of them. But they both are incredibly beautiful, to answer your question."

"Let me get this straight. You're not married, have two lovely lady friends who you claim you have had no relations with. Man, what do you do for fun out there?"

Travers laughed. Thomas was too much. The man must be hard up for a woman to want to know all about his sex life.

"We shovel snow in the winter and birth babies in the fall," Travers said jokingly, though it was a half-truth. Last fall, there had been six babies born in August and September alone. Thomas joined in the laughter. It was good to see his old friend again. They spoke of Thomas' work at the hospital, and he agreed to take Travers on a tour of it after the conference. They had been doing a study on, of all things, parasites. It was an interesting if disgusting, subject and Travers knew it was something he really should know more about. Tapeworms and pinworms could very well be responsible for several of the illnesses in the children back home.

They spoke of trivial things over dinner, and Thomas turned the topic to a string of killings they'd had in the area. It seemed the sheriff was stumped. Travers couldn't help but think about Jim Bowers and let Thomas know they were having problems in Gold City as well.

"I take it you've no love for the man," Thomas correctly assumed.

"He's a snake. But he's smart. There have been five men disappear to date. No bodies, no blood, nothing to prove that they're even dead. But in my gut, I know it, and so does the sheriff. These were men with families. I know that there are men who abandoned their families, but my gut tells me these didn't. They are dead. He knows that I know. He hired a man to kill me just to get me out of the way. He knows I won't let it go."

"Sounds like a rough character. You sure he's responsible?"

"If he didn't do the deed himself, he had it done. He surrounds himself with an army of cutthroats."

"And what happened to the man he hired to kill you?" Thomas asked.

"We met. Briefly. Name of Dillinger. Ever heard of him?"

Thomas sat forward.

"Case Dillinger?" The cheroot hovered over the man's plate, the ash falling unheeded into his garlic potatoes.

"That's the one."

"Dillinger was a killer all right. He was from upper state New York. He was in trouble from the time he could walk, I figure. Stayed in trouble with the law through his teens, mostly minor stuff. At nineteen, he shot a man over some woman. His life pretty much went to hell from there. His less than stellar extra-curricular activities were fodder for all the papers here bouts. And you killed him?"

"He likened it to David and Goliath. Of course, I passed on the chopping off of his head, which I'm sure he was thankful for since I'd already taken his life. He told me he had been offered a hundred dollars to take me out."

"Whew. People paying to have you killed. You must have really ticked the man off." Thomas settled back in his chair, ignoring his plate now. The conversation was way too stimulating to miss. The man he called his friend apparently led an eventful life. He had aged, thought Thomas. Travers had never been a loud person, and now there was a way about him that demanded respect. He almost longed to pay his friend a visit out in Kansas, but he knew that wasn't the life for him. Travers was speaking.

"Well, he's in for a rude awakening. I know he's guilty and I plan on proving it, one way or another." The doctor took another sip of his brandy and sighed, knowing he had his work cut out for him.

✦

The conference was long and informative, and Travers soaked in every word. There were surprisingly no women present. Travers had heard women were being admitted to the college of medicine now. He applauded their efforts, though he knew that most men frowned on women trying to step into such a daunting field. The war had opened his eyes to the fact that women were just as capable, perhaps more so than men at performing such tasks as treating the wounded, calming those who were panicking from pain and fright.

Thomas had insisted he stay at his house while he was in town and Travers had agreed, knowing Thomas as he did, he knew the man loved to hear about how wild the West truly was.

Before leaving, he'd had to tell about every outlaw, every gun-fight, and every Indian raid he knew about. He spoke of it with such reverence that Thomas knew his friend had truly found his place in life. They touched base with several old school chums and went to a local pub before Travers had to take his leave of them for his journey home. He was actually looking forward to it, he found, longing for his one-room upstairs at the boarding house, for Laura, Clayton, Flora, and Sheriff Tate. His true friends. Heck, he was even anxious to get back to see what Bowers had pulled in his absence. With a final goodbye to his old friends, he boarded the train that would take him all the way to Springfield, Illinois before he would have to change trains. He settled himself down with a book he had purchased at the conference and found his thoughts straying to home.

PART II

HOUSE OF CARDS

ELEVEN

Travers was standing on the boardwalk, his dark suit coated with a fine layer of dust from his long journey. He sat his travel case down and squatted quickly a time or two to ease the cramping in his legs. Removing his hat, he slapped it a time or two against his leg, raking his fingers through his hair before he replaced the hat. Inhaling deeply of the fresh air, he ignored the dust that assailed him. Home. He breathed it in, feeling his entire body relax in the fact that his traveling days were over for a while. The sun rested low on the horizon casting the clouds in a wonder of reds and golds. It was late evening, and most folks were taking their evening meal, so few people were on the street to greet him. Sheriff Tate happened along at that moment doing his rounds and clasped hands with him on sight.

"Doc, we've really missed ya'. Louella still has supper on the table. Won't you go grab a bite? I know you prob'ly ain't had a decent meal since you left."

Travers laughed. Eating seemed to be all he had done since he had been gone. Thomas apparently thought he wasn't being fed out here and he had seen to it that Travers ate three square meals a day, the evening always seven courses.

"Ras, I'm afraid I'll have to disappoint you. All I really desire right now is a walk to stretch my legs and a bath, followed by perhaps a good long nap."

"A'right. Don't say I didn't offer, now. Gotta catch up on things. Cain't say that I like you being gone so long. Makes a person a mite jumpy. 'Sides, Louella'll want a see that yore still in one piece."

Travers laughed. "You tell Louella I will see her for Sunday dinner as always."

Sheriff Tate tipped his hat and sauntered on off on his rounds, heading straight for the other end of town. Travers watched him for a moment, then stretched tiredly, before picking up his train case and headed home. Laura would have a pie of some sort to tide him over until morning if he should want something to eat.

He had only taken a few steps when he heard his name being called. The voice was soft, feminine, questioning, and stopped him in his tracks. A hand hesitantly touched the back of his arm.

He turned and stared. Stunned. He was looking into the bluest eyes he had ever seen.
Oh, God.
Maggie . . .

TWELVE

It was her. Plain as day. She was standing there smiling at him as though it were perfectly natural. It wasn't. He had never in his wildest dreams imagined this happening. This wasn't Maggie, not the thirteen-year-old child who had been a constant in his life until the day her mother died. This was Maggie, the woman. The eyes gave her away. He knew without even asking.

"Maggie . . ."

It was more statement than a question, and it was breathed softly, reverently.

Her eyes twinkled, and her smile grew.

"Yes! How did you know? It's been so long, I didn't think you would remember."

Travers shook himself mentally, a warning going off in his head. He needed to tread carefully here.

"The eyes," was all he could manage. He was dumbstruck.

He let his eyes feast on the beauty before him. Her hair, ebony and shiny, was piled up under a bonnet, but he knew that the frizz she had suffered as a child was gone now. Her skin was like the finest porcelain, and she carried herself erect, not slouched as in childhood. Her voice was soft, cultured, no longer showing the slightest hint of backwoods twang that had both tickled and irritated him to no end.

"Yes, I guess my eyes are the only thing about me that hasn't changed," she agreed, laughing softly.

He continued to stare, and Maggie grew uncomfortable under his perusal.

"Is something wrong, Travers?" Her brow was knit slightly.

"No! No, not at all," he hurried to assure her. "It's just—well, Maggie. You're a sight to behold."

Maggie flushed slightly, and Travers knew she must get that frequently from men. Men left speechless from her beauty. Her lids fluttered low, her lashes looking like giant feathered fans and he felt the sudden urge to run his thumb along their edges to feel their softness.

"Why, thank you, Dr. Gage. That is certainly a compliment coming from you."

He took her gloved hand and pressed a kiss to it.

"My, it's been a long time," he said quietly.

"Yes, it has."

In a split second, he could feel her slipping away, the memories of years before coming between the two of them.

"Let me buy you dinner. We can catch up."

Maggie hedged, looking around. She wasn't certain that was a good idea. It was getting late. But this was Travers, a friend whom she had not seen in years. Besides, she had not eaten yet, and her escort seemed to not be available.

"Alright."

He offered his arm and together they walked to the hotel where he left her briefly to stow his train case safely behind the front counter. He took a moment to gather his thoughts. Maggie was here. Dear God. He wasn't prepared for this. He had finally stopped dreaming about her at night. Now, it was as if she had suddenly stepped from his dreams. He felt a panic he had not known in a long time. His hands were shaking. He had noticed it when he had put his case away when he had taken her hand in his and kissed it. And at the very thought of going back out and having dinner with her. He closed his eyes, opened them in hopes that he was waking from a dream. No dream. She was really here, and she was waiting for him. He shook himself mentally, regaining his composure once again.

He found her right where he had left her. She was looking out the window pensively, gnawing at her bottom lip. Vintage Maggie. A slight frown marred her brow, and he studied her for a moment. She was dressed in blue, her dress the height of fashion with its' bustle, an item which had replaced the hoop and crinoline that many a woman had been glad to get rid of. She had removed her bonnet, and he found that her hair shimmered in the light of the crystal chandelier as if it had been streaked with fairy dust. This Maggie was cultured, refined, and he found he could not take his eyes off of her. This girl had meant a lot to him as a child. Now she was a woman grown coming back into his life, and he felt the attraction instantly and fought it. She took his breath away.

She turned slightly and spotted him watching her. She smiled hesitantly. He went to her and offered his arm once more, and they entered the dining hall where he seated her away from the bulk of the diners. He felt the need for privacy for this reunion. They both ordered a steak with potatoes and vegetables, and after the waiter left, each hesitated to be the first to speak. There was an awkward silence for several moments. Finally, each could stand it no longer, and both attempted to speak at the same time.

"Maggie—"

"Travers—"

They smiled at one another, embarrassed. Travers tried to

relax, but his body felt tight as a bowstring. His collar seemed to have grown tighter suddenly, choking him.

"Maggie, it's good to see you."

She met his eyes and said, "It's good to see you, too, Travers."

They had broken the ice and Travers found himself hungry to know about her life since she had left Virginia.

"Tell me about yourself. What have you been doing these last several years? It appears you've been quite busy."

"Well, there's really not much to tell. You know most of it; that we went to live with my aunt and uncle in Georgia. My uncle worked at a bank in Columbus. My Aunt Netta had Rance and I both privately tutored. I think she was rather ashamed of us though she would never admit it."

"This was your father's sister, right?"

"Yes. It was difficult at first. After all, I was a bit of a ragamuffin. But Aunt Netta saw to it that I was finished properly."

"Yes. Yes, she did," he agreed softly, whole-heartedly. He couldn't take his eyes off of her.

"And Rance. Where is he?" he asked, trying to keep his thoughts from straying into places they shouldn't go.

"He's here as well, down at the saloon, I'm afraid." She let out an exasperated sigh.

Travers nodded but didn't say anything. He fidgeted with his napkin, trying to find the words. He decided to jump in head-first.

"Maggie, about your mother—"

"Travers," she interjected, "it's ancient history. I forgave you long ago for that." She reached out and touched his hand briefly. The very contact seemed to startle her, and she pulled back.

"I'm so sorry, Maggie. I would have moved heaven and earth to save her. You know that."

"I do. I just needed someone to blame, Travers. I'm the one who should be apologizing for the horrible things I said to you that day. I had no right."

She wore a pained look, and he sensed she had dreaded this conversation just as he had.

"Time for a fresh start," he told her hopefully. "Friends?"

"Friends," she agreed, smiling brightly at him, thinking him even more handsome than before. He had changed very little, she thought. He seemed harder around the edges, but he was still her Travers. Her Travers? She had to stop that right now. He was speaking, and she forced her thoughts aside, embarrassed.

"So, what brings you to Gold City?" he asked and took a sip of the tea the waiter had just delivered to their table.

Maggie seemed to squirm a bit in her seat before she answered.

"Marriage."

The teacup froze in mid-air, the liquid in Travers' mouth suddenly seeming to have turned to glue. He lowered his eyes and carefully returned the cup of tea to its saucer, though it rattled loudly on contact, perhaps because his hand shook so violently.

"Marriage?" he managed to ask through the constriction of his throat.

She nodded, a smile lighting her face.

"And who, may I ask, is the lucky guy?"

"Jim Bowers."

There was a rock in the pit of his stomach. He knew it because he had felt it crash into the bottom just now. The thought of retching was not unpleasant at the moment. His face, fortunately, gave nothing away as to the shock of hearing such news. How on earth had Bowers kept this one a secret, he wondered? Is that where he disappeared to all the time? Was he back in Georgia wooing Maggie? Did he know of their connection? Did she? He carefully schooled his features before asking, "Is that a fact?"

"Yes," she said, beaming suddenly. "We met back in Georgia. He was an associate of my uncle's."

He tried not to look at her as he toyed with the rim of his teacup, running his finger along its edge, back and forth. He trod carefully into deeper waters.

"How long have you known Mr. Bowers?" he asked, struggling to sound casually interested.

"A little over a year. Why do you ask?"

"Just curious. He's lived here for a little over two years. I'm surprised he's not mentioned you, that's all."

"Well, it was something of a whirlwind courtship. Uncle Charles brought him home for dinner one night, and we have been friends ever since. That's important, you know."

"Ah, but do you love him?" He could have kicked himself, but there it was. He had to know.

"Why, Dr. Gage! I hardly think that *that* is any of your business," she answered indignantly.

His question had flustered her. She pinkened, and Travers knew it couldn't be from anger.

"I think it is my business. I've known you for a long time, Maggie. You're my friend. I only want the best for you."

Her eyes darkened before she responded, pinning him with her eyes.

"It's true, we were friends a long time ago, Travers, but you've been out of my life since I was a child. I respect that you care enough to be concerned for my well-being, but in answer to your question, yes, I do love him," she said and seemed to straighten in the chair.

The waiter chose that moment to bring their food, and each clamped their mouth shut waiting for him to leave. When he did, Maggie picked up her knife and fork and attacked the meat, sawing on it, wishing it was Travers instead. Ohhh, she could just spit, she thought angrily, trying her best to control her temper. After seven years of absence, here he was trying to tell her what was best for her. Of all the nerve!

Travers knew the telltale signs. She was put out with him. The clenched jaw and fake smile she flashed him didn't fool him one bit. He caught her eyeing the knife almost lovingly and couldn't resist.

"Thinking of carving out my liver with that?"

Her eyes flew to his, and she grinned slowly, sweetly.

"No, just your tongue."

He couldn't help it. He laughed. Loudly.

"Maggie, you haven't changed much at all. Under all that nefarious beauty, you are still little Maggie."

Blue eyes clashed with pale ice, and she answered calmly, "That may be, but I'm a lady alright, in manner and indeed. And you will respect that I have a mind of my own and I have chosen to marry Jim Bowers."

That brought a sigh from him. He had to make her see, make her understand.

"Maggie, he's trouble, in a big way."

She put down her utensils and leaned back in her chair, folding her hands properly in her lap. The look she shot him was mulish, but her raised eyebrow let him know he could proceed, with caution.

"I know he's a rich man, Maggie, but he's not well received around here. Folks talk. There's been a lot of things happen that we think points back to him. Men from this town, good men, have disappeared. He ends up with their land. He came here with barely a penny to his name. Suddenly, he's the richest man around. How did he get that way, Maggie? Do you know? No one around here seems to." He flourished his fork around the room to indicate the other diners still lingering about. He saw they had attracted a good deal of attention, but at this point didn't care. Looking back at her, he saw she was frowning, her eyes lowered, shielded so he couldn't read them. He returned the fork to the table and steepled his fingers, his elbows resting on the arms of his chair.

"Look. I don't mean to hurt you, but everyone around here despises him. He's not the type of man you want to be involved with, Maggie. Trust me," he implored.

Maggie had heard every word. She had wanted to scream at him to stop, but she hadn't. She had let him say his piece. She knew Jim to be a rags to riches story, and she believed he had come by his fortune fairly. The people of the town were just jealous. That was all, jealous. She took a deep breath and looked Travers in the eye.

"That is enough. I know that this is quite a shock for you. It has been for me as well. I never thought to see you again, Travers. I am not a child to go willy-nilly into anything without thinking it through. I have accepted his marriage proposal and would appreciate it if you would refrain from making further comments concerning my fiancé."

Travers sat there at a loss for words. She seemed to be blinded by this man. He shook his head and looked at her.

"You're making a terrible mistake."

The look she gave him said the subject was closed.

"It's my mistake to make, isn't it?"

With that, she finished her tea and pushed back her chair before he could attend her. She pulled on her gloves and without looking at him, said,

"I would like to say this has been a pleasant reunion. However," she paused sadly before adding, "It is good to see you again."

With that, she swept from the room and up the grand staircase.

He followed her only to the foyer, watching her disappear from his life again. So she was staying here. He returned to his unfinished meal though he only pushed it around on his plate as he pondered what to do. He ran his hand across his face as if to remove a cobweb of thoughts. He had failed to find out when the marriage was to take place, he realized. He considered finding her room but knew that wasn't the proper thing to do. He would have to catch her about town tomorrow and find out. That is if she would even speak to him again. He had certainly blown it this night. After seven years, he could have at least held his tongue for a night. Hell, he should have just laid it out on the table for her to whack off with that knife she had expressed such a desire to use on him.

This was going to throw things off kilter with Bowers. He would really have to tread carefully now. And he would have to talk to Ras. He paid for their meal and picked up his train case at the desk before crossing the street to the boarding house he called home. He was going to have a hard time falling asleep this night after all. Maggie was back in his life.

Damnation. Damn, Damn, Damn.

She watched him from her window, noting the clenched jaw even at this distance and in the fading light. She let out her breath slowly. It had been a difficult evening. She had been shocked to find him here. It had been a long time. Too long. She had thought about him every day in the past seven years. She had imagined him just as she knew he would be. Steady. A gentleman. Handsome. Unchanged. The love of her life. . . His good looks still devastated her though she had covered well. She had fought the urge to throw caution to the wind and say to hell with marrying Jim Bowers.

She wanted Travers.

Always had.

She had never dreamed their paths would cross again. She had committed to Jim, thinking, knowing in her heart that she was doing the right thing. He would be good to her. He had money, power, and was building them a home, would have it ready by the time they married in the summer. She would be content to play housewife to him. He treated her like a queen already, so it bothered her to even consider that the things Travers had said might be true. The setting sun cast a golden glow over the room, and she settled into the rocking chair to think. She had to think. . . .

She would be there all night.

True to form, Travers grabbed a bottle of whiskey on his way up the stairs, barely acknowledging Laura who came out of the kitchen only to watch him ascend the stairs two at a time. She let him go, thinking perhaps the trip had been harder than he expected. Morning would be soon enough to welcome him home.

He tossed and turned all night, finally giving up on sleep. He sat propped against the headboard and considered wildly for a second taking Flora up on her standing offer of a romp in the sack. He knew in his gut that Flora had nothing that would quench the fire inside of him tonight, no matter how beautiful she was. He watched the lamp burn out and wondered if Maggie was having the same trouble he was.

THIRTEEN

Laura was humming gaily to herself as she put breakfast on the table the following morning. Travers could hear her all the way upstairs. He smiled, knowing she was glad he was back. He entered the dining room just as she was bringing in a plate of bacon, which she promptly sat on the table and grabbed him in a big hug.

"Oh, it's good to have you back!" She squealed when he squeezed her tightly in return.

"I'm glad to be back! I hope I won't be taking another trip like that for a long time."

He released her, and she swiped at a few loose tendrils of hair that had already escaped her bun. Laura was so very pretty, he thought, though so different from Maggie. Laura had an inner beauty that he had come to appreciate. He'd had no chance to get to know Maggie as a woman, to see how she compared. She had been a sweet child, wildly precocious, and entertaining. Now, she seemed so changed. And he had to get her off his mind.

Laura was looking her fill, as well. Something was wrong with him, though he was doing his best to cover it. He had been up all night. She knew. She had heard him rattling around in his room into the wee hours of the morning. Patience had kept her from going to him. If he wanted her to know what was troubling him, he would tell her.

"So, what have I missed since I've been gone?" he asked as he poured himself a cup of coffee and seated himself at the table where he began to fill his plate. Laura sat across from him and passed him the syrup for his biscuit he was opening up.

"Well, let's see. Stan Farley was found hung out on his farm the day after you left. I guess you know who's responsible for that. That murderin' sack of trash had the nerve to suggest it was suicide. Can you believe that?" She gave an unladylike snort.

"I was afraid he'd pull something while I was gone. What has Sheriff Tate said about it?"

"Not much. He's been unusually quiet about it. I think he knows more than he lets on. Maybe he's got evidence this time."

"Maybe. I'll check in with him later. Anybody been needing my services?"

"No. But there are some new folks in town. Some folks from a wagon train gave it up and decided to settle here. A family of seven from South Carolina. All five of the children are boys. Good Lord, that woman must have nerves of steel. We're looking into getting a new school teacher. Folk have been antsy, wanting their kids schooled. Ras has wired to Chicago for one. I forget the name."

Travers nodded as he ate, and Laura talked on.

"And Jim Bowers brought his bride to be and set her up at the hotel. A Margaret Pritchard. Beautiful woman. How on earth he managed a woman like her is beyond me. Her brother's a little strange, though. Hear he fancies himself a writer and painter. Go figure."

Laura didn't notice Travers go still and taut. She was busy sopping her biscuit in a pool of gravy. That was a good thing, he thought because if she had, she'd question him about it and he didn't want to talk about his relationship with Maggie just now. Didn't know if he'd ever want anyone to know. He knew though, sooner or later they were bound to bump into one another again, and Laura would only have to take one look at the two of them before she put two and two together.

He was considering the possibilities, but Joseph settled the matter for him as he chose to arrive at that moment for breakfast. Laura rose and poured him a cup of coffee and Travers decided it was a good time to make his exit. As he walked out the door, she called after him that she would bring his lunch to the clinic and they would talk before she waved goodbye. With that thought in mind, he stepped into the sunlight that was already blinding.

FOURTEEN

She was coming out of the general store when he saw her. Dressed in pale yellow with a straw bonnet secured with matching yellow ribbon, he thought she rivaled the brightness of the sun. His heart seemed to have stopped so he inhaled quickly and forced himself to move towards her. She turned and saw him, and a slight frown marred her face before she smiled hesitantly at him. When he stood before her, he paused trying to find the words to make up for last night. His eyes traveled the length of her, noting the tiny pink flowers that dotted her dress and the spray of flowers lining the inside of her bonnet. It made for a startling contrast to her black hair and intensified the brilliance of her eyes.

"Good morning, Travers." Her voice was low, hesitant. He could well understand her reaction. He had acted badly last night.

"Maggie," he said and tipped his hat to her. "Look, about last night. I didn't mean to upset you. I apologize for my, bluntness, for lack of a better term. I didn't mean for our—reunion—to be so uncomfortable."

She was searching his face earnestly, hoping he was speaking the truth. She so desired to be able to spend time with him, even if it would only be as friends. She had missed him terribly over the years, and now that he was back in her life, she hoped to remain friends. She smiled, and the force of it nearly knocked him off his feet.

"Travers, forget it. We're friends, and friends forgive one another, right?"

He could only nod in response and tried to take his eyes off of her, actually finding it quite difficult.

"I meant to ask you last night. When exactly is the wedding?" he asked lightly, casually.

"Two months from now. June fifteenth. Jim is still working on the house, and he wants it to be complete when he carries his bride over the threshold, or so he says," her eyes crinkled, and the smile deepened.

He cleared his throat.

"I hear it's a veritable mansion. Have you been out to see it?"

"No, we thought we should wait until after the wedding." She was getting uncomfortable with this turn of conversation. He realized and thankfully changed the subject.

"So, where is Rance? I have yet to see him."

She looked back through the open door of the general store and said,

"Well, you're in luck. Here he comes now."

A man of average height with dark brown, thick wavy hair had just settled up with Pete inside and was making his way towards them. His clothes were clean, but rumpled looking as if they had been slept in. He had the look of a scholar about him. Stopping next to Maggie, he said, without bothering to look at her, his attention on his package, "They were out of some of the colors I needed. The clerk says it'll be two weeks before they'll be in."

Maggie looked at Travers.

"He's talking about paints. Rance dabbles a bit in painting and writes a little as well. Dime novels, of all things." That last remark was accented with a rolling of her eyes.

Travers studied the man before him. The boy had grown into a man and had changed quite a bit in his looks. He had not aged as well as Maggie, his eyes already showing fine lines as if he spent a lot of time reading. He looked at least five years older than Maggie although Travers knew him to be two years younger.

"Rance?" he said and extended his hand.

Rance had flushed at Maggie's remark about dime novels and turned to give the man Maggie was conversing with a once over. He looked familiar. Taking the hand, he shook it, but Travers saw the blank expression.

"Travers Gage. It's been a' while."

"Dr. Travers Gage? From Virginia?"

Travers nodded. Rance chuckled, then turned pensive.

"Huh. Maggie's childhood flame. Imagine that. Looks like you accepted Bowers' proposal a little too quickly, now doesn't it?" He said to Maggie, who colored hotly at the barb. She turned aside pretending to admire the items displayed in the store window. She saw nothing, however, except rage at her brother. She fought the unladylike urge to kick him in the shin. Fortunately for him, he moved away, leaving the two of them standing there on the sidewalk. She had been fighting a losing battle where he was concerned. Travers watched the play of emotions on her face and knew she was glad her brother chose to wander off.

"He's changed," he offered.

"Yes, and it wasn't for the better, I'm afraid."

"What happened?"

"I don't really know. But ever since our mother died, he's distanced himself from me. We're not close anymore. I miss that."

"Well, people do change. Look at you."

She gave a wave of her hand, and they began to walk along the boardwalk, slowly, and they were attracting attention, though neither one of them noticed. They were too caught up in each other to think about how it must look, the two of them moseying along at a snail's pace.

"But I changed for the better, I'd like to think. Rance just . . . I don't know what happened. Uncle Charles demanded a lot of him when it came to his studies. Maybe he thought that was the only way he could succeed in the world. But he shut me out in the process." She sighed heavily.

They stepped off the walk and crossed to the clinic where Travers unlocked the door and led her inside. She removed her bonnet and looked around in awe. She went to the table where his instruments were laid out and touched them reverently, a smile lighting her face. She had always admired the way he kept them cleaned and organized, reflecting on the man that he was. She inhaled the old familiar scent of the solution he used to cleanse his hands and closed her eyes, remembering just how he did it in her mind's eye.

He watched her, his eyes eating her up. He had never imagined her like this. She was always the child he had let down. His head bowed, and he told her gruffly, "I hurt you. You must have hated me."

Her head whipped around and in the silence that fell before them, she studied him with piercing eyes before answering,

"No, Travers. I never hated you. You meant too much to me for me to hate you."

"You were so young, just a child. I tried to make you understand that it wouldn't be right. You were scared and all alone suddenly, and I—"

She came closer and placed her finger to his lips.

"Shhh," she told him softly. "I was wrong in putting you in that position. You did nothing wrong. I never should have lied to my aunt and uncle. They tanned my hide for it later." She smiled now, remembering her aunt's expression of horror and the fury on her uncle's face. She had been so foolish. And all for the love of this man. Apparently, it had pained him all this time. She tried to pass it off as ancient history. He wouldn't let it go.

"Maggie, you don't know how many times I wanted to reassure you that things would be alright. I tried to do the right thing for *you*, and for Rance. I hope you honestly believe that I didn't intentionally let your mother die."

"Oh, Travers. I do know that. I was angry with you and lashed out. I wanted to hurt you. I was such a child, and I made a complete fool of myself."

"I worried about you and your brother, you know. I waited

to hear from you, but I never did."

"I know. Aunt Netta confessed that she had burned my letters to you. I guess I figured that it was better that way. You didn't need your life complicated by a thirteen—year—old girl who had thrown herself at your feet professing her love for you one minute, then accusing you of rape the next."

"And I thought it best to stay away. I knew you were terrified of moving away to live with relatives you'd never even met before, but if I thought for one moment that it wasn't the best thing for you, I never would have let you go."

"You were right, as always." She touched his face. Couldn't help it. He stepped away from the feeling it evoked, and she dropped her hand, having felt it too. Fortunately, the door opened at that moment and Laura walked in carrying a basket with his lunch inside. She took in the two of them standing awkwardly there, noting the stiffness in Travers' body. The dark haired woman seemed to be searching his face but quickly turned to face her. It was Bowers' intended, and the two of them seemed to be more than well acquainted. Suddenly, Laura had a really bad feeling.

"Why, hello. You're Margaret Pritchard, aren't you? I don't believe we've met. I'm Laura," she said, coming forward to shake her hand.

The woman shook her hand, then turned nervous eyes towards Travers, as if unsure what she should do next. Laura studied her for a moment, thinking she was, even more, striking up close. She had only seen her from a distance before today, but Flora had chanced to meet her in the general store. Apparently, Bowers had informed his fiancé that she was the town's madam and that she was to steer clear of her. The Pritchard woman had coolly rebuffed her.

Travers cleared his throat nervously at that point and came forward to take the basket from Laura.

"I thank you for lunch, Laura. It certainly smells good." Another awkward silence fell. He was clearly not going to strike up a conversation, let alone explain Miss Pritchard's presence in his clinic.

Laura knew there was something here she was missing. They both looked guilty as sin, and they each seemed reluctant to speak lest they draw her into the conversation. She decided to take her leave.

"I guess I'd better be getting back. I'll see you back at the house tonight?" Her eyes challenged Travers', who moved uncomfortably at her words.

"Tonight," he agreed, knowing that Maggie was watching the two of them nervously.

Laura backed towards the door, addressing Maggie as she went.

"It was a pleasure to meet you, Miss Pritchard. I hope I'll be seeing more of you."

Maggie nodded in assent and watched the woman go out the door. When she was gone, she turned to Travers and said, "I didn't realize you were married. Oh, what must she think of me?" she gasped softly, her eyes rounded, her hand going to cover her mouth.

Travers took a step towards her and grasped her by the arms. How could he explain?

"Maggie, Laura is not my wife. I'm not married. But in answer to your question, I'm sure she's probably busting a gut right now wondering what on earth we're doing in here alone." He sighed heavily. Yes, he could just see her now. She probably went back to the house and attacked the dishes, scrubbing vigorously at some innocent plate, wondering what in the world he was thinking associating with the woman engaged to Jim Bowers.

Maggie gave a grateful sigh.

"Well, I sure don't want folks around here to think that you are anything less than a proper gentleman. I would never try to hurt you like that, Travers."

"I know. But maybe I'd better escort you back to your hotel now. I'm sure we've set the tongues a'waggin' enough for one day."

Maggie gathered her bonnet and purse, taking care to replace the bonnet, which she tied swiftly, before turning for the door. Travers gave her his arm, and they walked to the hotel together in silence. In the lobby, she was loath to see him leave, not wanting their encounter to end so quickly. Travers seemed to hesitate as well.

"So, I guess Bowers will be getting wind of this. He'll be paying me a visit, I'm sure."

"Oh, don't worry about him, Travers. He's really a big pussycat. I can handle him. Besides, you and I are old friends. He has no say over who I associate with."

Travers grunted to himself, thinking that she was more naive than he thought, but he chose to say nothing at the moment about that. Bowers would keep her under lock and key when he found out that the two of them were old acquaintances. If the man had paid to have him killed once, Travers could damn well count on it that the man would do so again, now with a certainty. "I'll remember you said that."

"Perhaps we could have lunch sometime?"

"Perhaps. I must be going. Word travels fast around here." He didn't want folks thinking the worst of her. She nodded and watched him stride out the door and down the street. He went back to his clinic and shut the door. Maggie sighed, wishing they could go back to that time in Virginia when things were so much simpler and uncomplicated. She wanted to spend time with Travers, to know about his life, to share hers. Going up the stairs, she knew in her gut that her boast to Travers about remaining friends was in all probability impossible. Jim would not like it one bit. He was extremely jealous of her.

Strange, she thought, that he had never mentioned Travers to her. Maybe he already knew there was a connection there. If so, why would he not tell her about Travers? It was odd for him to never have mentioned the doctor when he had mentioned everyone else in town. He had spoken as if he wanted to fit in here so badly, but they were determined to push him out. So far, the town was nothing like he had described it and Maggie was glad, for she had actually been dreading coming here. Knowing Travers was here changed everything. She only hoped she could keep the peace between those two.

FIFTEEN

Travers had worked at his clinic the rest of the day, hoping to avoid Maggie. He didn't trust himself to keep his mouth shut with her about Bowers, and he didn't want to turn her against him. Not just yet, anyway. Besides, he had a lot of thinking to do where she was concerned. He had been mesmerized by her instantly, and that could not be a good thing, he was thinking. Not with their history. It wouldn't be right. Would it? Of course not. She was no longer a child, that was for sure, and the attraction was total. Any man in his right mind would want her, and he was sure she'd had her choice of men. But Bowers? What on earth had attracted her to him? His money? Sure, he could be called attractive by the fairer sex, he guessed, but none of the women around here seemed to want anything to do with him. In hindsight, though, that surprised him because lots of women were attracted to that sort of man, one who had power, money, and a little mystery about him. But Bowers was not one to frequent the town these days. Before Travers had left for his trip to Boston, he couldn't recall seeing the man for several weeks. And shouldn't he be playing escort to his fiancé? It was a puzzle, indeed.

He was going to be grilled when he got home, he figured. Laura was too keen for her own good. He should go ahead and tell her the truth, get things out in the open. Laura was family, after all. As close to family as he was likely ever to get. Marriage didn't appeal to him, nor apparently to Laura. But he did long to have someone to grow old with. He envied Clayton and Sarah. They seemed to be genuinely happy. Just before he left on his trip, Clayton had searched him out to thank him personally for what he had done for Sarah concerning the children she had started keeping. He had held his hat before him, and profusely told Travers how she had seemed to come alive before his eyes. Travers had waved away the thanks, saying that he was glad to be of help. It had been worth it.

His thoughts were interrupted by the object of his thoughts. Sarah poked her head in the door of his office.

"Afternoon, Doc. Good to see you made it back in one piece." Her smile gleamed as she moved on into the room. "I saw Laura just now and invited her to supper tonight as well. I told her that you would be dining at our place this evening."

Travers opened his mouth to speak, but she interrupted.

"Ah—uh—un. I won't even hear yore excuses. I told Clay I was gone' do this before you ever left' for that trip and I ain't takin' no for an answer. I owe you for what you did for me. Besides, I kinda' think I'd like to hear 'bout that big city Boston." Her hand had flown to her hips, and she postured adamantly.

He grinned, knowing he really didn't want to argue with her since she *was* the best cook around and with Laura coming along as well, the conversation would be a lively one. He shrugged his shoulders, expressing defeat.

"I guess I have to, then. A beautiful woman demanding my presence, with a talent in the culinary arts that no chef in Boston could ever hope to match. You just leave me with no other choice. What time, pray tell, should I be there?"

She clucked her tongue at him.

"Oh, you just bad. Seven sharp. You not there at seven, we gone' eat it up from you."

Travers laughed, knowing she would hold dinner no matter what until he got there. She was too much a lady not to.

"Then I shall see you at seven o'clock, madam." He gave her a salute, which she received and took her leave. Travers watched her go, thinking she was such a fine woman. Clayton and his wife made such a fine contribution to this town. He shook his head, thinking, what would the good citizens of Fellowship think if they could see him now.

◆——————◆——————◆

Dinner that night was a rousing affair. Laura busied herself helping Sarah, and the two of them chatted like old friends. They both seemed to have the urge to be doing something at all times. He guessed that was just the way some folks were. Clayton had slapped him on the back, glad to have his friend home. He had poured the two of them a brandy while they waited for dinner to be served. The black man filled him in about the man found hanging on his farm.

"Sheriff Tate came by one day, said Farley hadn't been seen in town for a few days. You know he always come in ever' other day to see to Tillie, his mother. She's in bad shape, you know, can't get around by herself. She gots a colored lady stay with her to help out. When Stan didn't come to check on her, she sent for the sheriff. Tate decides to go look for him and came by to get me. We found him hung from the beam of the barn he was abuilding."

"Do you think it was suicide, Clay?" Travers asked. The black man shook his head.

"No. His hands weren't tied, but he had marks 'round his wrists. He had been tied up all right, but whoever done it, they took the rope off after he was daid." He had encircled his wrist with the fingers of his other hand, showing Travers, literally, how the man was tied.

Travers found that interesting. Whoever had done in Farley had not been too smart. Anybody who used rope knew that it chaffed the skin if resistance was demonstrated. Bowers probably had not overseen that one himself. He had left it to one of his goons, one who, obviously was not too bright. But it was a lead, now. One he intended to follow up on. He would seek Tate out, and they would figure out how to do just that. And maybe, just maybe, they would reveal Bowers to be the murderer he was before Maggie married him.

About that time, Laura and Sarah called them to the table to eat, and the subject was dropped. Sarah had outdone herself. There was turkey, dumplings, and squash dressing, with giblet gravy for the turkey. Freshly baked rolls slathered with butter were piled high in a cloth covered-basket. He almost licked his lips. As they seated themselves, he offered his thoughts on the spread before him.

"Sarah, I do declare. I'm gonna get big as a house, you keep feeding' me this way. One has only to look at Clayton to know that is a fact."

Sarah laughed. "I like to watch a man eat. Means he works for a-livin'."

Travers grunted, adding, "Now I know that *that* is not always the case. I've seen many a man who eats like a horse but wouldn't do a day's work if their life depended on it."

Laura agreed. "That is a fact." She raised her glass to that one.

They gave thanks and dove in, chatting as they ate. Clayton was on his second plate when Sarah brought it up.

"Have the two of you met the Pritchard woman who's here to marry that Bowers fella'?"

Laura paused in her chewing, looking at Travers, who chose to remain silent. She swallowed and said,

"I met her this morning, actually, however briefly," she said as she pinned Travers with a look. "She seems to be nice."

"I met her in the store earlier," offered Sarah. "She seems to be a quiet one. Her brother is, too. Although he got quite upset with Pete about some paints."

Travers knew Laura was watching him, waiting for him to say something. He finally told them, "I met her this morning. She's a lovely young lady."

"Hardly the type I'd have imagined for Jim Bowers, though, don't you think?"

Clayton was getting into the conversation now. "Find out

anything about her?

Where's she from?"

Travers shifted in his chair uncomfortably. "Georgia, I do believe she said."

"Well, she is very pretty. Though what she sees in Bowers is beyond me," Sarah said with a roll of her eyes. She thankfully changed the subject then to the little ones she had been keeping. She thanked Travers for what he had done and told him that she also had him to thank for helping her make a new friend in Clara Walker. The two of them had found so much in common it was surprising even to them. Travers was thrilled it had worked out even better than he had planned. Sarah seemed happier than ever, and Clayton had told him he had made a friend for life in her. He believed it.

They talked long into the evening, and Laura and Sarah cleared the table, leaving the men to their vices. The two of them eased onto the porch, savoring a brandy. Travers leaned against the railing looking down the street, his eyes going to the saloon and Flora's before settling on the hotel. He scanned the upstairs for lights but didn't know which one was hers.

Clayton watched his friend, followed his eyes and presumed where his thoughts were. He had seen Travers and the Pritchard woman together today and figured there was more there than met the eye. There was an intimacy there of old friends. He guessed aloud.

"Old ghosts?"

Travers sighed heavily, knowing exactly what Clayton was talking about. There was no point in denying it, but he wouldn't reveal everything.

"Yeah. . ." The word seemed to be dragged from him.

Clayton swished his brandy in the snifter several times before offering, "Only you can banish them. Tread carefully, friend. You can't shoot this one. I wouldn't advise it, anyway."

Travers gave a nervous laugh.

"No, I think not."

Laura came out then and suggested that they head home. She and Travers thanked the couple for a lovely evening and took their leave.

The walk home was silent, Laura with her arms crossed, looking everywhere but at Travers. They walked leisurely, Travers thinking hard about what to tell Laura about Maggie. Should he let her bring it up? What should he tell her? All of it? The truth? Did he want her to know the whole story? Would she understand? He only knew that he was in a predicament. Maggie was back, and he knew that, somehow, his life would never be the same.

When they entered the parlor, Travers went straight to the liquor cabinet where he pulled out two glasses and a bottle of scotch. Laura watched him in silence as he poured them each a substantial amount. She seated herself on the couch and sipped her drink, turning the conversation to the evening with the Mosses.

"They really are such wonderful people, don't you agree?"

"They're the best. I couldn't ask for better friends, except, maybe you."

Laura's brow raised. "Oh?"

He moved to take a seat beside her on the couch. His brow knit in thought. He needed to tell somebody. Why not Laura? She was like his sister.

"You're like my own family, Laura. I couldn't keep anything from you if I wanted to."

Laura knew what he was referring to. She didn't want him to feel obliged to tell her anything. He owed her no explanation where the woman was concerned. She was leery, though, for Travers seemed to know the woman far too well for her presence to be a good thing.

"You don't have to tell me anything, Travers, if you don't want to. I'm concerned, that's all. You two seem to be acquainted and the fact that she's Bowers' fiancé, well, even you have to admit that could spell trouble."

"You have *nooo* idea," he offered quietly before taking a gulp of his drink. He rose to stand by the fireplace, his arm resting on the mantle. He stared at nothing in particular, seeing the past rise before him in a wave. Silence fell, and he waited, but she kept silent, and he realized she was not going to pry. He would have to be the one to break the ice.

He gave a sigh and stepped into the murky waters of the past.

"It's Maggie."

"Maggie? The one from your dream?" she asked.

"Yes."

Her lips formed into a little 'oh' and she eyed him gravely. It was apparently not a reunion to be celebrated. Bowers had never really had serious reason to battle Travers, but he possibly did now.

"She was a child when you last saw her, right? Must have been a shock to see her all grown up."

"You can certainly say that again. I had never imagined what she would look like as a woman, simply because I never thought I'd see her again, I suppose. But I knew her the moment I saw her, and it nearly did me in."

That was an understatement. Travers had had such conflicting emotions upon seeing Maggie that he wasn't sure how he really felt about her being here. All he knew was that her presence made him realize how very much he had missed her and how damned beautiful she had become.

"I guess she was surprised as well. What happened between the two of you, Travers? You've lived with a pain connected to her. I know you have. I could hear it in your voice when you spoke her name from your dream, and I hear it now."

He gave a slight nod, realizing that he needed to get this burden off of his chest. It was eating him alive, this memory, this slip of a girl who had haunted him for years. If anyone understood, it would be Laura.

"I guess I should start from the beginning. That way you'll understand the how and the why of it all. I met Maggie and her brother in Virginia years ago when they showed up at my clinic one fall day. I knew them to belong to a widow who lived down the road. The woman scraped together a meager living by sewing for the public. Her husband had died in less than favorable circumstances, so they were shunned for the most part by the people in the area. I noticed the children outside my clinic one day and acknowledged them. The next day, they made themselves at home on the porch of the place. I offered to pay the two of them if they would help keep the place tidy for me and keep wood for the stove. I couldn't help myself. I knew they needed help. I wasn't about to turn them away. After that, they seemed to become my shadows, especially Maggie. For two years she was my shadow, helping me in the clinic, sterilizing my utensils, making sure I had plenty of clean bandages. She even read my journals aloud to me while I updated patient files. Learned to make my coffee just the way I liked it. She used to tell anyone and everyone who would listen that when she grew up, she was going to marry me. I jokingly passed it off. She was a child after all. She didn't know her own mind."

He paused and ran his hand through his hair, taking his seat beside her again, though on the edge of the couch, his elbows on his knees, as he watched the swirl of the scotch in his glass. He had reached the critical point now and remembering was painful. He closed his eyes against the memory.

"Her mother became ill. When I reached her, she had apparently been ill for some time. How she managed to keep it from the children is beyond me. There was nothing I could do. She died the next day. Maggie was beside herself with grief, and she clung to me for comfort. Rance withdrew into himself. I tried to reach him but couldn't. Maggie, on the other hand, was convinced I would take them in. She was thirteen years old and growing up fast. I knew it wouldn't be proper for me to do that when she had living family. I sent for them, and it angered Maggie. She was convinced she was in love with me and that I loved her. I did love her, very much, enough to do the right thing for her and her brother. She panicked when her aunt and uncle showed up to take them away. She caught me off guard one day and kissed me, full on the lips, trying in her own childlike way to seduce me. I was shocked, to say the least. I put her away from me, and she collapsed into tears. She accused me of killing her mother, so I could send the two of them away.

"She said I should have been able to save her. There was nothing I could have done for their mother. I tried to reassure her of that. She raved then that I had raped her, that I was sending her away to hide my sins. Her aunt and uncle were livid. They almost had me arrested, but Maggie came clean with the truth. It could have ruined me. She knew that. She had a crush on me that she believed to be love, and I crushed her by sending her away. I had to. I'll never forget the look on her face as they rode away. Dejected and utterly lost.

"After they left, I questioned if I had done the right thing by sending for her family. They were strangers, to both of us, after all. I found out her uncle worked for a bank, and that he was well respected. So I took a chance and contacted him. After they left, I didn't hear from her again. I had no way of knowing if I had done the right thing or not and was too afraid to find out, afraid that I had made a horrible mistake. I got no letters, and the letters I sent were never returned. All this time, I've been haunted by a child . . . I never considered that one day she would grow up."

Laura had been listening with interest and understood the pain he must have felt over the issue. The children had become a part of his life in a way he had never expected, and he had hurt Maggie badly to do the right thing by her. He had been the gentleman. Now, however, she was back and full-grown.

"How are things between the two of you now?"

"She forgave me for everything, of course. She grew up and realized that I had only her best interests at heart. She chose not to find me, thinking it best to leave the past in the past. She outgrew her childish love for me and promised to marry another."

Laura sighed, studying her friend.

"Please tell me I'm not hearing what I think I'm hearing."

"Well, that's the clincher, now isn't it? After seven years she walks back into my life, and all I can think is, why the hell did I have to do the right thing?"

"You're in shock, Travers. It's only natural to think like that. She is gorgeous. Anybody would be blinded by her beauty."

"I'm not just anybody. I know her, Laura. She doesn't love

Bowers. I know she doesn't and I mean to make her change her mind where he's concerned."

"For her own protection, or for your own desires?"

"Both."

SIXTEEN

It was Hell, that's what it was. Jim Bowers had unleashed Hell on him. And in all probability, he had done it without knowing that his fiancé and the good doctor of the town had known one another for years. Travers chaffed at the idea of her marrying that man. He had seen little of her in the last several days. Rance was always there, escorting her, though he always looked as if he'd rather be elsewhere. Bowers had appeared in town, and Travers had seen them from a distance as they had spoken on the street to Sheriff Tate, Bowers attempting to appear the upstanding citizen. Tate let him.

Maggie had not attempted to seek Travers out again, and he figured that was for the best. If Bowers even thought that the two of them were friends. . . well, he didn't want to even think about what the man might do. Rance seemed to have a liking for the saloon, and Travers found himself going there, hoping to draw him into conversation. The first few times, the boy had been too drunk to even know Travers was there, so he had taken him back to the hotel and got him settled for the night. Maggie had only spoken through the door to him as it was late and improper to do otherwise.

Tonight, however, was a different story. Rance was there, but he had Tandy sitting on his lap. When the redhead saw Travers, she hopped up and gave the doctor a hug for greeting.

"Howdy, Doc. What can I get you to drink?"

"Whiskey's fine."

As she moved away, Rance followed her with his eyes.

"Nice lady, that one," he said aloud, not really to anyone in particular.

"Yes, she is," Travers agreed. He watched the kid, thinking he looked unwell. He looked gray as if he wasn't getting enough air.

"You feeling alright, Rance? You're looking kind of peaked."

"I'm just fine, Doc. Nothing' wrong with me that a little liquor can't fix."

He wouldn't look at Travers, and that bothered him. Something was wrong. He tried again to draw him into conversation.

"So, your sister and Jim Bowers. What do you think about him? Is he good to her?"

That got his attention. He turned and faced Travers with a puzzled look on his face.

"Now, why is that any concern of yours what I think? You never gave a damn before."

There was no love lost there, Travers thought gravely. Apparently, the boy harbored ill feelings about something.

"You know that you and Maggie both have always been important to me. How could you have ever believed otherwise?"

"You certainly showed that from all those letters you wrote," he said, unable to keep the sneer from his voice.

So, he thought he had been abandoned as well. Time to set that matter straight.

"I *did* write, Rance. Your aunt burned the letters. She admitted it to Maggie just recently."

"I don't believe you. You never gave a damn about anything but your precious reputation. You certainly never cared about two pitiful little orphans who might ruin everything for you."

"You're wrong, Rance. I did care. I still do. That's why I'm concerned about your sister getting involved with this Bowers fellow. I think you have no love for him either." Travers was getting angry, his voice gruff and low.

"Well, you're right. I don't particularly care for the man. I think he's a toad. He doesn't fool me. He can put on all the airs he wants, but I know he's trash."

Rance took a gulp of whiskey and grimaced loudly, his lips drawn back over his teeth. He turned to watch Tandy return with Travers' drink. She placed it before him and returned to her position on Rance's lap, her hand cupping his cheek.

"What's the matter, sweetie? You seem a little blue?"

"Just missing' you, darlin'. How about me and you disappear for a bit?"

The redhead smiled and rose, pulling Maggie's brother after her. The two didn't bother to bid Travers goodbye. He lifted his glass to them anyway, thinking the kid may not be half bad after all if he hated Bowers. Time would tell, he thought. With that in mind, he quit the saloon and went next door to Flora's. She was in the parlor downstairs, holding court with a few gentlemen who were waiting for companionship above stairs. When she saw him, she rose to meet him as he came in. Caught by surprise, surely, but she brightened and sashayed towards him like a true courtesan. He smiled in greeting.

"Hello, Flora. How've you been? Haven't seen much of you lately," he said as he took her hand and raised it to his lips. She smelled like flowers. Always did. He had noticed it the first time they had met and knew he could probably find her in the dark if need be, though he wasn't counting on needing to.

"Why, Dr. Gage, I am fit as a fiddle. I do say, this is an honor. You so rarely come into our humble abode anymore."

He laughed. "Humble abode? Darlin', this place is hardly humble." Indeed it wasn't. Flora took great care in her decorating the place to look like a mansion inside. It was not overly done, but the furnishings were fine as any he'd ever seen in the finest houses in Virginia.

"Shah," she sputtered, her eyes twinkling. "Where have you been keeping yourself, Trav? It has been a while. I hear tell that there's a new lady in town with the looks to rival even me. Tell me you haven't succumbed to her beauty over mine!" She sounded indignantly offended, and Travers threw back his head and laughed. Flora was so pretentiously vain that he knew she was teasing him. He decided to give as good as he got.

"Alas, I'm afraid to admit, I have been struck by her beauty as if by lightning. Her smile alone can render me speechless."

Flora pouted prettily, her voice smoky with pretended hurt, and her hand fluttered delicately to her bosom.

"It is as I feared. I've lost you for good. I shall have to rid this town of that hussy once and for all. Else I won't stand a snowball's chance in hell with you."

"Flora, Flora, Flora. You do have a knack for setting your cap for the unattainable. I warned you before that I'd break your heart."

She huffed loudly. "Well, you can't blame a girl for trying. After all, you are the cream of the crop around here. And a girl does get lonely."

Travers gave a laugh at that. Flora could have her pick of any man around, but she still teased Travers that he was the one she wanted. He knew better. She only pretended to want him because it amused her to see him get flustered by her advances. But he had turned it around on her, playing along with her instead. She had come to accept this banter as their own private joke and loved him for it.

Flora had heard the tales about Margaret Pritchard. And she was lovely, just as they said. The fact that she had already encountered the woman and been rebuffed by her, Flora decided to keep to herself. And the good doctor was said to already be an acquaintance of hers. Hmm . . . How interesting.

"I hear you know Miss Pritchard from Virginia. Is that so?"

"Um—hmm."

"Well? Is that all I get? I'm curious, come on. Throw a dog a bone. I've not heard any juicy gossip in so long I'm starved for it. Liven' my night!" she quibbled theatrically.

"There's nothing really to tell. I knew her when she was just a child. I haven't seen her in seven years or so. It was quite a surprise seeing her again."

"I'll bet, with her looking like *that*!"

Travers nodded. "She is a real beauty, no denying it."

"And engaged to Jim Bowers," she said, her lip between her teeth. "That must rub you something raw, huh?'

"Rawer than a bullwhip full of cockleburs." He informed her in no uncertain terms.

"Well, the wedding's not until June, right? You've got a little time to persuade her otherwise. Maybe I could help with that." Her raised brow gave him pause, but no. He wouldn't use Flora that way.

"No, but thanks. I'll handle it in my own way."

"Suit yourself. It could be fun, though. For me, anyway, if not for you."

Travers rose and lightly poked her nose with his forefinger before adding teasingly, "There you go again, thinking only of yourself. Whatever am I going to do with you?"

"I'm still waiting to find out," she sighed, her green eyes soft and full of humor, her southern drawl even more pronounced.

"Well, dream on, angel. I've got to go. But do me a favor? Rance is with Tandy tonight. Kind of worried about him. He's got a lot of anger and no love for his future brother in law. Keep your eyes and ears open for me when he's around if you will."

"It might cost ya'," she warned playfully.

"Well, put it on my tab. We'll settle up later. Somehow." His eyes danced with humor at her jab.

"Careful. I might just make you pay up, mister."

Travers went to the door and stepped out, but turned as he left to toss back at her, "Honey, you've got to catch me first."

Her laughter followed him out the door.

SEVENTEEN

He ran into the two of them at the post office of all places. They were coming out of the place when he practically ran them over. Travers backed up immediately lest he bump right into Maggie. He tipped his hat and bid her good morning without a glance at Bowers who hovered over her like a mother hen.

"'Morning, Maggie. How are you? Didn't mean to run you over like that. Guess I'd better watch where I'm going." He had actually been engrossed in the new medical journal he'd just gotten from Pete at the general store.

Maggie smoothed her skirt and looked from Travers to Jim, noting the ugly way her fiancé was looking at the doctor. She hurried to stem the outburst she saw coming.

"Oh, Dr. Gage, it's perfectly alright. No harm done."

Jim wasn't going to let it go. He looked as if he would have an apoplectic fit when Travers called her Maggie. She cringed inside.

"No harm done? No harm done? The man practically ran you over, and there's no *harm* done? He should learn to watch where he's going. Someday he'll run over the wrong person, and they won't be as obliging. And my fiancé's name is Margaret, Dr. Gage. Margaret Pritchard. I'll thank you for remembering that. I don't recall introducing the two of you. Your use of such a vulgar pet name implies something I don't think I like, Gage. You will address her properly from now on, is that clear?"

Travers' eyes had hardened at the brutal tone of Bowers' words. He could see Maggie cringing beside them, her hand going to Jim's arm, attempting to placate him. So, she was finally getting a view of the man's atrocious temper. About time.

"Jim, darling, Dr. Gage and I knew one another before you and I ever met. He's an old friend."

Bowers glared at her, his chest puffing out belligerently.

"And you're just now telling me this?"

"Well, I didn't know that the two of you knew one another. After all, you never mentioned him to me before."

Jim's eyes flew to Travers', noting the interest he was having in their conversation. He grabbed Maggie roughly by the arm and informed Travers,

"You watch yourself around my fiancé, Gage." With that, he practically dragged her away with him. Travers could only watch as Maggie struggled to keep step with him. The man was a cad.

He had no affection to bestow on anyone and Maggie had to see that for herself. She would learn. Slowly but surely, she would learn.

———◆———

Jim Bowers was beside himself with rage. He had looked the fool in front of Gage and Margaret today. They had both acted as if they shared some secret joke with the joke being on him. He itched to put the man in his place. Travers Gage didn't know who he was messing with. But he would know. He surely would. Jim Bowers would not be made a fool of by any man. Nor any woman for that matter. Margaret would have to learn her place if she was to become his wife. He would show her soon enough. And he had just the thing.

"That man has a lot of nerve. He thinks he runs this town. Him and his high falutin' friends. You are to stay clear of him, you understand me?"

Maggie stopped in her tracks, jerking her arm free of the bruising hold Jim had on her, now that they were out of sight of Travers. She rubbed her arm, her brows drawn together in a frown.

"I'll have you know, that Travers and I go way back. He is my friend, and while you are my fiancé, you are not my jailor. I will speak to whomever I please. If you think that I am going to be manhandled and dictated to, you have another think coming! I love you, Jim, but I won't be treated like some piece of property or hired help. This marriage will be one of mutual understanding, love and respect, or there won't be a marriage! Do I make myself clear?"

The heat that crept up Jim Bowers' neck could have fried an egg, so hot it scalded his blood. He glared down at his wife to be, thinking how utterly naive the girl was. She actually thought that she was laying down the law about how things were going to be between the two of them. Well, wouldn't she be in for a surprise! He reined in his temper and simmered down. They had a few months before she utterly belonged to him. He could afford to play along. For a while. Forcing a smile of chagrin to his face, he said, "I'm sorry, Margaret. It's just that I can't stand the thought of any other man touching you except me. I know I shouldn't be jealous, but what can I say? You are so beautiful, and every man who looks at you wants you." He pulled her gently into his arms. She came into them stiffly, but as he rubbed his hand against the back of her neck ever so softly, she weakened and smiled.

"You know you have nothing to worry about, Jim. I accepted your proposal of marriage. I can't wait to be your wife." She said the last softly, seductively, hoping to receive a kiss, however chaste it may be since they were still in public. Jim merely grinned back and put her away from him, causing her to frown. He always pushed her away when she wanted more.

"In a couple of months you will be Mrs. James Bowers, and you'll live like a queen on the prairie. I can't wait for that day as well, my love." His smile held a secret satisfaction that only he could know. Margaret would rue the day that she had challenged him. And she would learn exactly what it meant to be his wife.

<hr>

Travers had thought about the situation with Maggie and spoke with Laura at length about it. Laura was reluctant to talk much about it, knowing that he was going to do whatever he wanted as far as that woman was concerned. She hurt for him, knowing this could not end well for the two of them. She knew Maggie to be very pleasant, but she was blind where Jim Bowers was concerned. She tried to stay out of it, but Travers insisted that they have them over for dinner one night. She knew if she refused that he would be angry, so she caved and sent a written invitation to the girl and her brother at the hotel. Within minutes, the invitation was accepted much to Laura's surprise.

Travers was waiting impatiently on the porch for them, pacing and smoking a cheroot, something he rarely did. The man never touched the stuff unless he had something weighing on his mind. Laura guessed that there was more than enough to keep him occupied these days. Maggie seemed to be a constant in his thoughts, though he spoke little about the situation now. After the first few weeks after her arrival, he had ceased discussing the girl with her, apparently knowing it was doing neither one of them any good. The purpose of this dinner was to be neighborly. Or so he said.

They showed up right on time, and he met them outside, taking Maggie's arm and escorting her inside. Rance followed along quietly, sullenly, his hat in his hand. As they entered the room, Laura was struck by how much the two of them looked as if they belonged together, and she began to have second thoughts about Travers pursuing the girl. They seemed to be totally unaware that each was enamored with the other. How odd.

Maggie's dress was amber silk and modest to a fault, the row of buttons reaching her throat. The small ruff of lace there accented her ebony hair which she had twisted at her nape and entwined with a golden ribbon. She was really stunning. Even Flora could see that. Laura had invited her as well as the Moss's, and they were all already inside.

Rance looked every inch the gentleman in his vest and frock

coat, but Laura noted the look of illness about him. She made a mental note to speak to Travers about him. Rance barely acknowledged the other guests, but Maggie made an effort to shake hands with every one of them, smiling graciously in return. Flora's brow shot up when she was introduced, and the girl acknowledged her as if they were meeting for the first time. Perhaps she didn't recall the little scene in the store with her fiancé, or maybe she was trying to make up for her rudeness from before. Throughout the evening, Maggie was civil to them all, more so to Laura and to Travers. She made every effort to draw Laura into conversation as if she somehow felt that she must win Laura's approval since she was Travers' friend. Travers made sure that Rance was brought into the conversation as well, though he gave clipped remarks and cast sullen looks at Clayton and Sarah often as if their presence were a sacrilege.

Laura found herself warming to Maggie despite herself. The girl seemed to be looking for a friend, as she had no one out here except her fiancé. Travers was a given, but she needed female companionship out here and perhaps thought Laura was the obvious choice. If Travers trusted her, then why shouldn't she? Laura found that the two of them had much in common, both of them losing their parents at an early age. Maggie loved to quilt, something that Laura had always loved but found little time for. It was Maggie's idea that they should form a quilting circle, and promptly invited Flora and Sarah to be part of it.

"Oh, it would be great fun! It would give us a chance to know one another, and since I'll be living in the area, I really would like to get that chance."

She sounded so earnest, but Laura had concerns.

"Well, Maggie, you'll be living a good piece out of town. Do you really think you'll be able to find the time to come to town that often?"

"Of course! Jim has the ranch to keep him busy much of the day. I have to do something to occupy my time besides keep house. Besides, I'll be providing a much-needed amenity for the winter. I hear the weather can be quite bitter out here."

"Honey, it gets so cold out here that men have been known to spoon themselves." Flora hooted. The others laughed, knowing that was pretty close to the truth. A man never knew what to expect out of the weather and sometimes got caught without protection. Dead men had been found practically folded double, the cold being too much for them to handle.

They spoke frankly about the harshness of the land, the fact that there had been Indian raids along the Colorado border. Just the previous year, General Winfield Scott Hancock had taken command at nearby Fort Larned. The famed Yellow Hair, as the Indians called him, George Armstrong Custer was one of his field officers. The army had tried to route the Cheyenne and their allies in the territory, to no avail. The Indians were always just a step ahead of them. They raided in the area, but so far had left Gold City and the immediate area alone. Custer had made a foray into the town for supplies just before Maggie's arrival. Thankfully, his troops were gone within the hour.

Maggie had not known much about the area, but she was learning fast. There was danger on every hand, and Maggie knew a tad of fear now that she knew she would be going to the ranch, a woman alone. Jim would have thought of everything, she knew. He was such a considerate person. Her protection had always been paramount to him. That thought comforted her.

Flora chose at that point to regale her with the tales of Travers' gunfights, and Maggie's blood turned cold. She could not bear to think of her friend facing such paramount danger or doing something so stupid as to face a killer intent on gunning him down in the street. She watched Travers as the stories unfolded and noted the drawn look on his face. So, he hadn't wanted her to know about that. He was a changed man. She knew so little about what he had done with himself the last seven years, though she had heard tales that he had fought in the war. Tales that were surely just that: tales. But she would not think on those just now. She hungered for tidbits of his past and got so few.

Travers finally noted the late hour and hinted at it, suggesting to the others that maybe they could try dinner again another time. He succeeded in politely getting rid of his guests, though everyone knew the real reason he was calling it a night. He did not like being the star attraction any time, let alone after-dinner conversation. They all gave in graciously and headed home. He walked Maggie and Rance back to their hotel.

At the entrance, he turned to Maggie.

"Don't believe everything you hear, Maggie. Flora has a way of making things seem more than they are."

"Oh, I don't know, Travers. I strongly suspect she didn't have to embellish a thing. You forget I know you."

"Well," he said, watching Rance go on inside without saying goodnight, "I've never been one to back down from anything."

"That's what I know."

"Ummm. Are the two of you coming to the church picnic next Sunday? It is open to the town."

She hedged a little. "We weren't sure. I mean, no one had mentioned it to us, and since Jim isn't a member, we weren't sure if we were invited."

"Consider yourself invited. Laura and I will make sure you're not left unchaperoned if Rance doesn't want to come along."

"I'll think about it."

"It's been thought about. You're coming to the picnic." He was leaving her no choice. The darkness and the nearness of her were doing him in. She was feeling it as well.

"Alright." Her voice was soft, and her eyes devoured him. He noticed and she lowered her eyes self-consciously. Before he could speak, she murmured a hushed "Goodnight," and hurried to the hotel, leaving Travers to stare after her. With a shake of his head, he turned and headed home.

EIGHTEEN

The town couldn't have picked a better day for a picnic. The sun set high in a cloudless blue sky, and a gentle breeze cooled the otherwise scorching air. It was May now and hot already with the gentle humming of insects' background music for the affair. Children played tag near the creek and the women set about laying out the food on the cloth covered tables someone had erected between two massive sweet gum trees. The men entertained themselves with conversation and an occasional smoke while they waited for permission to chow down on the spread being laid. 'Dinner on the ground' was what the elders called it, and that is exactly what it was. Blankets and quilts lay scattered everywhere, coloring the grass with various hues of patchwork.

The reverend stepped forward and blessed the food, then loudly told everyone to dive in. The men needed no further urging and were the first to help their plates before wandering off to settle in on a quilt with their families close behind.

Rance and Maggie had come to the service that morning with Travers and Laura, though they had been waiting for Maggie's fiancé to show up. Throughout the morning service, her eyes had gone to the door, hoping it would open and Jim would walk through. It never did, and he had yet to put in an appearance. The brother and sister had graciously accepted the invitation to stay for lunch and Travers was having a hard time keeping his eyes off of Maggie. She was wearing a pink and ivory cotton sateen dress, the sleeves stopping just below the elbow to billow out trumpet-like with a ruff of ivory lace. The fitted bodice accentuated her tiny waist and Travers knew she was small enough to span with his hands. She was like a porcelain doll he had seen once in the general store, her complexion translucent, her eyes shining like polished sapphires. She was exquisite, and he never would have guessed the child he remembered from long ago turning into such a head-turner.

Travers had a problem and didn't quite know how to fix it. With one simple word, his name, he had lost his heart to her. That angered and puzzled him in a way. He had never been a rash person. He was always careful about all aspects of his life, and he didn't understand why she had affected him so. He had tried to tell himself it was because of Bowers, that he would have tried to dissuade any decent woman from becoming involved with the likes of him. But Travers knew it went deeper than that. He had loved her at first sight. What really galled him though was the fact that she pretended to feel only friendship for him. He knew better. She looked at him with eyes that revealed much. It was one aspect of Maggie that had not changed. She had never been good at hiding her feelings. Her eyes tended to give her away.

Maggie caught Travers staring at her. Their eyes locked and Maggie was the one to turn away.

"Laura, I wonder if maybe you could stand up for me at the wedding," she asked shyly.

Laura's eyes rounded and darted to Travers who busied himself with scarfing down the remainder of his pound cake lest the words stuck there on the tip of his tongue come tumbling out.

"Well, Maggie, don't you think you should have a close friend do that?"

Maggie looked a bit uncomfortable.

"I know that's the way it should be, but all my friends are back home, and you've been so kind to me since I arrived, I was hoping you'd do the honors."

Laura folded her napkin slowly, studying it, a frown on her face. Then she smiled and nodded.

"I'd be happy to stand up for you, Maggie."

Maggie smiled, and Travers thought he'd go blind. He had to get away from her before he said or did something. Rising from the blanket, he said,

"Rance, I'm gonna see what Clayton's up to down by the creek. Care to join me?"

Rance pushed his spectacles up his nose and looked down at the creek where a crowd of men and kids were gathering.

"I think I will," he said and rose to leave with Travers.

Laura and Maggie watched them go, and Laura saw the longing in Maggie's face.

"Why can't you admit your feelings to him?"

Maggie jerked her attention back to Laura.

"I beg your pardon?"

Laura shook her head. Gathering Rance and Travers' plates, she said, "You're so blind you can't see the nose on the front of your face, child, even though everyone else can. You are in for such a rude awakening I'm afraid." She offered the girl across from her a sad smile then rose and took the plates to be washed.

Sarah Moss and Clara Johnson were already scrubbing, and Laura rolled up her sleeves to help. Sarah had been watching the girl and Travers. Travers was in over his head where she was concerned. That girl may have feelings for the doctor, but she had been raised in the south, and in the South, women were honor bound in marriage commitments. If she had agreed to a betrothal to that Bowers character, then she would not go back on her word. The stiffness in the girl's spine told Sarah all she needed to know. And she hurt for her friend because that girl would break his heart.

Clara Walker had been thinking the same thing.

"That girl needs a good shaking," she muttered as Laura began to dry the dishes.

"Well, it won't come from me," Laura said. "I've already put in my two cents. Besides, she asked me to stand up for her at the wedding."

The dishes rattled as they fell in the washtub as the two women gasped and looked at Laura disbelievingly.

"Surely you said no," Sarah said.

"No. I said I would, and I'm going to do it. She doesn't have anyone out here except Rance, and he's a lot of help," she rolled her eyes at the women who nodded knowingly.

Down at the creek, Clayton was showing some of the boys how to hand grab a fish with rousing participation from everyone watching from the banks.

"Show'em how it's done, Clay!" Sheriff Tate yelled from between cupped hands, laughing as the child nearest the blacksmith promptly fell on his rear, splashing Clayton full in the face. The big man came up gasping, his paw grasping the hefty ten— year—old up by the back of his suspenders. The boy floundered a bit before finding sure ground and promptly headed for the safety of the bank.

"Aww, Will, Giving up so soon?"

"Whatsa' matter boy? Little bit 'a water ain't gonna hurt nobody."

The teasing from the bank was all in fun, and Travers noted that Rance had taken out his notebook and was writing furiously, pausing to watch the action in the water, then sketching it in his book. The doctor shifted his weight to his other leg so he could get a better look over Rance's shoulder.

He was surprised. The young man had talent. The sketches were very good, the detail accurate to a fault. He had even captured the look on ol' Clayton's face when the Moser boy had nearly drowned him. A thought occurred to him.

"Say, you ever done any portraits?"

Rance never looked up. "A few."

"You ought to advertise. Photographers are rare out here. Some folks might like a portrait of themselves or their families. I know I would."

Rance shrugged a shoulder, his eyes on the scene before him, but Travers could tell he had sparked his interest.

"Why don't you do a portrait or two to show. When people

see the quality of your work, they'll be lining up at your door."

Rance looked up then.

"And you? Would you be interested?"

"Well, sure."

Maggie's brother seemed to think that over.

"All right. I'll get with you about a time and date then."

"Great," Travers said and walked a little closer to the creek where Clayton and the other youngsters had begun to make their way from the water. The big black man looked exhausted and exasperated. He plunked down on the grass near Travers, his chest heaving. Travers squatted down beside him.

"What's wrong, hoss? You gonna let a few sprouts get the better of you?" He chuckled as he plucked a piece of grass and stuck it between his teeth.

"Sprouts? Them *sprouts* could take down a bull," Clayton finished with a snort. He was fighting a smile. It had been a long time since he had played with kids. Ever since Samuel's death, he had avoided them. He had needed space to grieve. Losing a child was hard, but today, these chil'ins had made him remember the fun they could be. Ever since Sarah had taken to tending those babes for Celia and Babs, he had longed for the sounds of his own little one again. How he missed that boy.

"Been a long time since I played with kids," he told Travers quietly, his eyes going to the few who remained nearby, splash-ing one another in the creek, the men having broken ranks now and moseyed back to help their women load the wagons for the trip home.

"He was a good kid, I hear. With you for his pa, how could he be anything else?" Travers grinned.

Clayton cocked his head to the side, his brows arched as he remembered.

"He was a good boy. But his maw taught him those man-ners. She was strict and firm with him. He hardly ever had to be whupped, which was good, cause I hated like rip to whup 'im," he said with a grunt.

"I hate I never got the chance to meet him."

"Well, just goes to show you life can be shorter for some than others. I don't grieve for 'im no more. I just miss that boy something awful. There was so much I wanted us to do—to-gether. Now . . ." he shook his head sadly.

Travers studied his friend for several long seconds, noting his pain.

"You're sure Sarah can't have more children?"

Clayton twirled a blade of grass twixt his fingers, watching his wife.

"It's been so long, Trav, even if she were able I wouldn't ask her to. We gettin' on up in years. Life's hard n'nuff out here. She's happy tendin' them babes for the girls. 'Sides, that midwife said Sarah had such a hard time with Samuel, it'd likely be hard to get pregnant again. She bled out, and we like to have lost 'em both."

Travers thought on that a while. He wouldn't pry into matters that didn't concern him, but he felt for his friends. They had lost their only child, and that just didn't seem fair to him. He let the matter go.

Clayton stood up and stretched, his arms raised heavenward, blocking the sun from Travers.

"Whew! I think it's about time to go lay before the Lord!"

Travers laughed. He could about go for a nap as well. The two of them walked over to where Laura and Sarah were conversing animatedly. They hushed when they saw the men. Travers eyed then, thinking they were certainly acting peculiar, but he said nothing. Clayton just shook his head, thinking 'women' and let it go as well.

They gathered their things, loaded their baskets and set off towards home. Rance and Maggie had moved off to stand beside the creek and were deep in conversation. Agitated conversation. Everyone else had left, and that meant Rance and Maggie would be left out here alone. Travers handed Laura's basket to Clayton, who grinned at the hopeless fool before him but said nothing.

Travers watched them go for a few minutes before easing up to the brother and sister. They didn't even notice him; their exchange had become so heated.

"I'm well aware of your feelings for him, Rance. All you have done since you've met him is be rude!"

"*I'm* rude?!" He was supposed to escort you to the picnic, Maggie! Where the hell is this fiancé of yours? Hmm?"

If Maggie hadn't already been red in the face from arguing, she would have blushed furiously.

"I don't know," she muttered softly. Then her chin rose. "I'm sure something came up at the ranch. He's a busy man, you know. He has responsibilities. Unlike someone else I know!" she hissed at her brother.

Rance stepped forward, his finger pointing in agitated frustration at the ground.

"Responsibilities or not, no man leaves his fiancé hanging as much as you have been. I can't believe you would tie yourself to a man who shows you so little respect. I can see now what Travers was talking about. If you had a lick of sense in that head of yours, you'd be throwing yourself at him instead!"

Maggie gaped at her brother, furious that he would make

such a comment. Her sharp intake of breath and rounded eyes alerted Travers to the fact that she was suddenly aware they were no longer alone.

"How long have you been standing there?!"

Travers smiled, enjoying the indignant look on her face and the smug one on Rance's.

"Long enough," he said as he came closer. Turning to Rance, he said quietly,

"Why don't you run along? I want to have a word with your sister."

Rance crammed his hat down on his head and grumped, "Gladly!' before hurrying off.

Maggie turned to follow, calling, "Rance, you come back here!"

Travers grabbed her and held her fast.

She turned on him.

"Unhand me, now! You—Ohhhh!"

"You and I are going to talk."

Her eyes shot sparks at him, and her lips thinned, a sure sign that she was truly angry.

"Why, you —"

"Calm down. I don't bite. Often." He added, teasingly, hoping to wipe that searing look off her face. "Walk with me."

She stared at him for so long he thought she would refuse, but finally, she turned and began to walk along the bank of the creek, not waiting to see if he followed. Travers stepped after her, and they walked for a while, neither speaking, each lost in their own thoughts. She was breathing easier now, her color back to normal. Travers was loath to speak, just enjoying being in her presence. The sun was sitting low in the sky, leaving a golden glow over everything it kissed, including Maggie.

"I didn't mean to eavesdrop back there," he said finally, his hand motioning back to where he had come upon her and Rance arguing.

"You should have made your presence known immediately. A gentleman would have."

Ouch, he thought. She was sure good at throwing about barbs. No matter.

"I don't recall claiming to be a gentleman." His teeth flashed as he looked down at her.

"Apparently not, otherwise you wouldn't have sent my brother back to the hotel leaving me alone with you without a proper escort." She smiled smugly up at him.

Her words hit him, and he realized she had laid her own trap. He stepped closer.

"Afraid to be alone with me, Maggie?" His voice was soft,

with a hint of tease, but intensely sensual and touched her with all the force of a passionate kiss.

"I'm—I'm not afraid." She couldn't meet his eyes. He had always said she revealed too much of herself that way. Fortunately, he let the moment pass.

They walked past the church and graveyard, past the lumber mill, following the creek enjoying the sound of the rushing water and the occasional drone of bees. It was Travers who broke the silence.

"You shouldn't fault your brother for looking out for you. That's what brothers do."

She sighed. "I know. I just wish he would lay off of Jim. As far as my brother's concerned, he can't do anything right."

"Well, you have to admit, he does leave you hanging an awful lot."

"I know. But he is busy with the ranch and all. I understand that he has to sacrifice a few things, and so do I."

"Has he taken you to see the house yet?"

"I've seen it from a distance. He wants it to be a surprise for our wedding night."

"And, how was it?"

"It's huge!" she gushed. "I never dreamed I'd live in anything so grand!"

Travers had to admit, she acted happy, thrilled to be marrying this crook. Maybe she did love him. But he wasn't above still trying to talk her out of it.

"Don't you think it's going to get awful lonely out there?"

"I've thought about it, but no. Town is close enough that I can visit as often as I want. There are dozens of men about."

"And women?"

That gave her pause. She couldn't recall seeing a single woman out there nor had Jim mentioned there being any on the ranch.

Travers noted her frown and asked, "No women on a ranch that large? Isn't that a little odd?"

"I don't know. I've never been on a ranch before. Perhaps that's the way it's supposed to be."

"Maggie, all ranches have women, for cleaning, cooking, and gardening."

"Well, perhaps I'll remedy that problem when I come to it," she offered.

He would let that subject drop for the moment. There were other things he wanted to know.

"Have you ever wondered what your life would be like had you stayed in Virginia? I mean, if your mother hadn't died?"

He sat down on a fallen log nearby, his foot raised atop it as well, his arm propped on his knee as he toyed with a new spring flower that had somehow pushed its way through the gravelly bank of the creek.

"Sometimes," she admitted. "I'm sure life would have been much different for all of us." A wistful look crossed her face.

"Maybe. But the war would have changed everything. Did change everything." His eyes became clouded, the memories as strong as ever.

"Tell me about it. Where were you? Did you enlist?" She moved to sit next to him on the log, her attention fully on him, hungry to find out more about his past.

"I did enlist. With the Union Army." She stared out at the creek that continued to flow by them, the music of it unheard now as she registered that last remark.

"I guess I should have suspected as much. Knowing you the way I do. I imagine the neighbors weren't too happy with you."

"To say the least," he said, grimacing.

"Mmm. I imagine you saw a great deal of horror out there."

He nodded slowly. "Horror doesn't begin to describe it. I was kept to the back of the lines for the most part. As you can imagine, doctors were much in demand on both sides."

I'm sure," she agreed, her eyes studying him, seeing the haunted look in his eyes.

"Sherman was right when he coined the phrase 'war is hell.' There's nothing like watching the man in front of you get his head blown off."

At his words, Maggie blanched. She had seen the men at the depot waiting to catch the next train home. Some of them had arms missing, some legs. A few were missing both.

She could only imagine the carnage Travers had been subjected to.

"But you survived. You're whole. That's something to be thankful for," she said softly.

He gave her a long hard look before staring off into space again.

"No man is whole after coming through something like that. He may still have his limbs intact, but a part of him will always be missing."

She thought about that for a minute.

"I guess not," she agreed.

She rose from the log and went to the creek where she found a few smooth stones. One by one she skipped them expertly across the water. She had changed so much he thought, yet so little. She was clearly all woman now, yet she still had that childish spark to her. He had taught her to skip stones years ago. He had taken her and her brother fishing down at the lake behind his family home. They had spent a pleasant Sunday afternoon there, the two children catching a string full of fish, which they proudly took home to their mother who had been tickled pink by the gift. Travers had volunteered to clean the catfish and was promptly invited to stay for supper. At the dinner table, he was amazed at how well the two children behaved. They had scrubbed their faces and hands until they were pink and had quietly led them in saying grace. Now, ten years later, she still carried a hint of the child she had once been.

An old itch started in on him, and he reached to scratch it. He should have known better. He had never been able to reach it that way, so he looked around for a stick. As luck would have it, there were none in the vicinity. He cursed under his breath.

Maggie noticed his agitation and walked back over.

"What's wrong?"

"I've got this damned itch, and I can't reach it," he growled.

"Here, I'll scratch it for you," she offered.

Travers hesitated, thinking her hands on him might not be a good idea. The itch on his back decided the matter for him.

He gave her a look of thanks as she moved behind him, her hands resting lightly on his shoulders. She began to scratch where he indicated though her scratching felt more like a feather brushing his skin.

"You've got to scratch harder than that," he deadpanned.

She dug in this time, almost eliciting a yowl from him, but he gritted his teeth and endured it, the itch slowly beginning to fade.

Maggie had felt the scar beneath her fingertips and was dying to know about it. It felt like a bullet wound, she thought, probably a souvenir from the war.

"You were shot?" she asked softly.

He stiffened noticeably, drawing slightly away from her hands, which had ceased to scratch but still moved lightly over his shoulders.

"Yes."

"Was it bad?" Her voice was close to his ear, her breath easing along the curve of his jaw and down his neck.

"Bad enough." He sounded hoarse suddenly and attempted to clear his throat.

"May I see it?"

"I don't think that's a good idea." No way was it a good idea. He needed to get up and leave.

Right now.

He didn't move.

"I'm not squeamish, you know."

"I'm well aware of that," he retorted. Any kid that could skin and gut squirrels like she could was definitely not squeamish. "It's just that there's nothing to see."

She heaved a big sigh.

"Maybe I just want to see for myself that it healed properly."

"Maggie—"

"Travers, for a wound to itch like that something didn't heal right. Now let me see it!"

He sighed, deciding it couldn't hurt. She would pester him to death if he didn't. He unfastened the first few buttons of his shirt and slid it back to expose the scar on his back. The cool touch of her hands on his flesh nearly sent him running, but he stayed right where he was.

Maggie frowned.

"This is an exit wound. A very torn up exit wound, I might add. Who on earth patched you up?"

"Does it really matter?" he growled.

"Turn around. I want to see the other one."

"Maggie—"

"Turn around!"

He didn't know why he did it, but he did. She was standing between his spread legs, her hands moving over the scar just under his clavicle. Each tried not to notice the intimacy of their position.

"This side doesn't look as bad as the other. What happened?"

He sighed. He would have to tell her or she would pester him to death about it. He knew her too well.

"I went to the aid of a fallen general. Some rebs were about to capture him. I got to him first."

"And you were wounded in the process?"

"Yes."

She stared at the scar, her thoughts a jumble. She cared for this man so much.

Always had. Her vow to marry Jim had been made in good faith. Yet, she found herself wanting Travers to know that she cared for him as well. Not as the child who still harbored a crush on the man she had come to adore, but as a woman. She couldn't throw herself at him as before, for she was a lady now and ladies did not do such things. Did they?

"I heard the rumors, Travers. About a doctor saving a union general from capture and the men he killed. No one ever said anything about the doctor being shot."

"Yeah, well, rumors never give you the full story, do they? That's why they're called rumors. They're hearsay, not fact."

She bit her lip on the retort she had ready for him.

"Was it bad? The wound I mean."

He looked away from the concern he saw in her eyes.

"I worked on the general for two hours. After I finally closed him up, I saw five more patients before someone informed me that I was bleeding profusely. By that time, I had lost so much blood I passed out. I woke up two days later patched up. The doctor who did it was a drunken sadist that I had previously refused to share a medical tent with. He let the wound get infected. General Sharpe, the man whose life I saved, got his personal physician on my case. He saved my life."

Her hands were on his cheek now, lightly tracing the outline of his face. He had almost died, and she had not known.

"I prayed for you every day. I didn't know where you were, or which side you were fighting for, but I prayed just the same."

He reached and pulled her hand away from his face, holding it in his, noting the slim length of her fingers and the buffed smoothness of her nails.

"You were never far from my thoughts as well."

He raised his eyes to hers and was transfixed. It was like looking into the purest blue waters and seeing one's soul.

"You thought of me, then?" she breathed.

"At the oddest of times," he admitted.

She smiled softly at him, ducking her head a little.

"Do you remember how I used to proclaim that one day I would be your wife?"

He smiled as well, remembering vividly.

"It was a childhood fantasy of mine, Travers. You were my dream, my ideal. You were handsome, had a good home and I knew you could provide for a wife. I wanted that for myself. A good home where I wouldn't ever have to worry about where my next meal came from because I knew my husband would be capable of taking care of me. I thought that meant being *your* wife. Then suddenly, you were gone."

She sat beside him then, so close their legs brushed and he breathed in the strange vanilla scent of her.

"I missed you terribly, for so long. I was still of the foolish notion that one day, you would knock on my door and sweep me off my feet. But it never happened, and I realized that it was just a fantasy. Though I did wonder what I would do if you really did show up. But you never did. Then Jim came courting, and I realized that happiness was right before my eyes. I didn't fall in love with him overnight. I took my time. There was still you to consider, after all. There were days when all I did was think about you. But Jim was gentle and kind, and he gave me time to know my own heart."

She paused and sighed deeply, sadly.

"I never thought I'd see you again, Travers."

He had listened intently to what she was trying to tell him; an explanation of her actions from so long ago and her hopes and dreams that had been dashed. She did truly care for him, though she was betrothed to another. She really did feel the attraction that he had been fighting from the moment he saw her. His hand crept to her lips, his fingers whispering over them, feeling the petal softness of her mouth. They trembled at his touch and her eyes darkened, her breathing shallow and erratic.

"Maggie . . ." he breathed and lowered his head, his eyes locked with hers. He nipped at her lower lip lightly with his, sucking it gently before running the tip of his tongue around the outer edge of her upper lip, causing her to gasp sharply at the utterly sensual nature of it. She was in his arms suddenly, and she was not sure how it happened though she certainly didn't care. She was lying half across his lap, her arms finding their way under his shirt to caress his back.

He was lost in her. Totally, completely lost. He breathed in the unique scent that he had come to associate with her alone. Her hair smelled of sun-ripened fruit, orange in particular, and her skin of vanilla.

It was an unusual combination to be sure, but it drove him insane with want. He felt he could devour her, his need was so great. It shook him to the core that she should have such an effect on him and he eased back, breaking the intimate contact of their lips to study her face mere inches from his.

She was breathing heavily, her eyes closed, still in the throes of passion. She licked her lips, then pulled her lower lip between her teeth to hold there in consternation, her eyes flying open to find Travers staring down at her flushed face.

He eased his hand along her rib cage, the heat of it burning through the cotton of her dress. Up past her breast, careful to skim along the side, which evoked a gasp at even the merest touch, his hand slid to cup the back of her head, his thumb toying with the lobe of her ear. She shuddered in his arms, her eyes closing the breath of a second before opening to drink in the desire displayed in his.

He dipped his head ever so slowly, their eyes locked, his tongue teasing the corner of her mouth before tracing the ridge of her upper lip. Another shudder. Her tongue darted out to duel with his before he claimed her mouth fully, the intensity of the kiss mind shattering.

Maggie closed her eyes against a world that had begun to spin wildly around her, feeling only the need to be consumed by this man. The heat in her belly was driving her mad, and she pressed closer to him. Somehow, they were suddenly upon the ground, and his knee was between her thighs, her skirts now in disarray, his hand searching, seeking. . .

Jim had never made her feel like this.

Her eyes flew open. The thought of her fiancé had the effect of ice water being thrown in her face. Her hands flew to Travers' shoulders, pushing frantically.

Travers knew the instant she left him, her body freezing on him. He pulled back seeing the panic in her eyes.

"Get up!"

He didn't budge.

"Get up! Get off me!" she hissed frantically, pushing at the unyielding wall of his chest.

He moved then, sitting up, pulling her with him. He passed a hand over his face, then rubbed the back of his neck in frustration. Maggie was scrambling to get her skirts in order, her motions jerking, angry.

"I'm sorry, Maggie, I forgot myself apparently."

She cast petulant eyes his way and struggled to stand. Travers rose and helped Maggie to her feet. Each seemed unsteady on their feet, and their eyes met briefly with the realization. Maggie's face flushed hotly, and she turned away. Travers took her by the arms forcing her to face him. She had nothing to be ashamed of in his eyes.

"Maggie, are you all right?"

She ached to lean into his arms, to let the deep concern in the timbre of his voice soothe her, yet she dared not. She swallowed the lump in her throat.

"I'm—fine."

He wasn't convinced.

"You don't look fine. You look like you're about to pass out on me."

"I'm fine. Really. Just a little . . . dazed," she said softly. Her lashes fluttered low over her cheeks reminding him of those gorgeous ostrich feather fans again. She looked lost, unsure of herself for the first time and Travers stepped up to take advantage of that weakness. If there ever was a time to reach Maggie it was now.

"This changes things, Maggie. You can't deny what just happened."

Her eyes raised to his, clouded with uncertainty.

"This changes nothing!" she insisted, her jaw set.

"Yes, it does. You've allowed another man to touch you. A man, *not* your fiancé."

"A fact which you will never divulge, Travers Gage," she ground out from between clenched teeth. Her eyes were stormy now. "To anyone. Is that clear?"

Travers grabbed her by the shoulders, the urge to shake her violently, uncontrollable.

"Maggie, you cannot deny that we almost made love! If you truly loved that man, you would not have responded the way you did!" he said incredulously.

"All right! I can't—won't deny what just happened. But it was wrong. *I* was wrong. For a brief instant, I let my childhood fantasy consume me. But it was a mistake, and it will never happen again." She ground the words out, her finger jabbing at the air demonstratively, trying to drive that fact home.

Travers stepped back and snorted.

"You can't be serious!"

"Oh, but I am. The wedding is still on, and I would appreciate it if you would refrain from these attempts at convincing me otherwise. If anything, you're only making a fool of yourself."

Travers took another step back, feeling as if he had been slapped. Hard.

"Is that a fact?"

Maggie turned away from the look of hurt on his face. They stood there in silence for a few moments, Maggie gnawing at her lip, Travers watching her, thinking, wondering how she could be so blind. Finally, he asked her softly,

"If I'm the fool, Maggie, what does that make you?"

Maggie raised her head defiantly, her eyes hard as obsidian. He shook his head, then held out his arm.

"Come on. I'll see you back to the hotel."

She ignored the arm and stepped ahead of him stiffly. He shrugged and followed. Neither spoke on the way back, but their silence was noted by the few folks they passed on the street back in town, their expressions raising a few eyebrows. He left her at the door to the hotel and turning on his heel, stalked away.

He had no idea that she raced up the stairs, slammed the door to her room only to go to the window where she watched him storm off from behind the lace curtains. When he was out of sight, she turned from the window, unfastened her dress with a frustrated yank and collapsed into a heap on the bed. It was a long time before she got control of herself, her desire for him a tangible thing. It was only then that she allowed the tears to come.

Travers grabbed the bottle of scotch from the library on his way up to his room, taking the stairs two at a time. He didn't see Laura step from the kitchen to watch, drying her hands on her apron as she did so. Turning back to finish with supper, she felt a heaviness in her chest for her friend. There was trouble ahead for him. Thirty minutes later, she mounted the steps and knocked quietly at his door.

"Go away."

She could barely hear him. Trying the knob, it turned easily, and she eased the door open. He was sitting on the bed, his boots tossed carelessly to the side, his long legs stretched before him, the bottle in one hand, a half-empty glass in the other. His brow was furrowed deeply, focused on the contents of the glass.

Laura sighed and walked over to sit on the bed beside him. He didn't look up.

"Am I playing the fool, Laura?"

"Oh, I don't know. I think the two of you are doing a pretty good job at denying what's really in your hearts. She's honor bound to fulfill her commitments. Following her heart just doesn't enter into the equation."

"And what about me? What am I denying where Maggie is concerned? Haven't I made it clear that I want her for myself? Why can't she see that marrying that man is going to destroy her? She deserves better than him."

"But at what expense, Travers? Sure, you want her, but why? To thwart Bowers? Do you even really know why? Does she?"

"What are you talking about, Laura?"

"Oh come on, Trav. You've been haunted by this girl for seven years. Obviously, there was a deep affection for her even then. Perhaps you've been denying it to yourself. She kissed you, remember when she begged you to let her stay. Perhaps you knew even then how violently she had a grip on your heart."

"She was a child, Laura."

"She was thirteen years old. Lots of girls from the South married at that age."

"I never thought of her in *that* way, Laura. She was a child whom I adored, the same as her brother for that matter."

"Perhaps. And perhaps it's not the fact that you sent her away all those years ago that have plagued you so much as the memory of that kiss and what it showed you. The fact that you could feel something more for Maggie than the love for a child."

Travers didn't want to think about that. To do so would drive him mad. A child. . . Maggie had been a child. He felt ill. Had it really been as Laura was suggesting? Had he sensed it even then? He had known the two of them had always had a special bond. In a look . . . in a touch. They had seemed connected in a special way. Perhaps that is why he refused to allow her and her brother to stay with him. He had staunchly denied any feelings for her other than that of a guardian. He had known he was doing the right thing by the two of them. Then why had it hurt so?

Laura eased from the room, seeing his thoughts were in chaos. He had a lot to think about. If he truly loved her, he would find the answer within himself about how to deal with this. Maggie, Laura was convinced, had replaced Travers with Jim in the hopes that he would be to her what Travers had failed at—the love of her life. She had worshiped him, and he had turned her away. The hurt was still there, though. Laura saw it every time she saw Maggie look at Travers. She covered it well, however, for Travers was still blind to it. Whatever came, she hoped it worked out for the best.

Jim Bowers was fit to be tied. His new man Curtis Hokes was proving to have been a mistake. The man was inept. Bowers had given the man explicit instruction about disposing of his victim's body. He hadn't. Instead, he had left the man hanging for all to see. Proud of his handiwork, he had untied him, trying to leave the impression that the poor soul had committed suicide. Bowers had given him orders to leave town after taking care of the matter, thinking his orders would be followed to the letter. When the body had been found hanging, Bowers could have crocheted barbed wire with his teeth, he was so angry. Now, here Hokes was, finally venturing back to the ranch weeks later, belligerent even in the face of a furious Jim Bowers. He gave a lame excuse about putting the fear of God into the folks of Gold City. Jim felt like a firecracker had been lit under his skin. He nearly choked the man to death before Bailey pulled him off the desperately gasping man, his face purple and eyes bulged. He didn't want the town folk sniffing at his heels any more than they already were. He meant to keep his nose as clean as possible and with Hokes around, that would be impossible. With a look and a nod at Bowers, the foreman hoisted the new hire and took him outside where he lashed his hands and feet together and tossed him over his horse. The terrified man fought and strained but was weak from his struggle with Bowers. The look on Bailey's face told him his time was short and he struggled in earnest to get loose. It was useless.

Bowers watched the two men ride off. Sam Bailey was proving to be a real hand at this sort of thing. He had picked right when he had chosen him as his foreman. The man had a vicious streak that wouldn't wait, and he was fine with the fact that Bowers wanted no blood on his own hands. He relished it actually. That left more for Bailey to mete out.

He recalled the first time that he had introduced the foreman to Margaret and had noted the rapacious look of lust on the man's face. The man had made no effort to disguise it, and Margaret had excused herself quickly, removing herself from the man's presence. He had terrified her. Jim didn't know if that was a bad thing. He knew he could control Sam Bailey. The man liked his job too much. But now, her terror of the man could come in mighty handy. She had proven to be a little on the fiery side, and he would not stand for his wife being uppity. She would not be allowed to speak her mind so quickly as she was want to do presently. The doctor may see that as a form of defiance on her part and as her husband, Jim would not have it.

She was spending far too much time with the doctor and his circle of friends. That would have to be stopped. He would have to make the time to put in more appearances for her sake. He was sure the tongues were wagging as it was already. His absences had not gone unnoticed. Dr. Gage had certainly made himself available for her. That rankled. The man took too much upon himself where Margaret was concerned. Margaret had asked him once why he had never mentioned the fact that Travers was the doctor here. It had never really occurred to him that it was important. He had not known of their association, and if he had, well, he would have done something about it before now. Now, he would have to suck it up and pretend things were just fine between the two of them.

His reasons for hating the doctor had nothing to do with Margaret, though that did add fuel to the fire. Travers Gage would find out soon enough why he was targeted for death by the wealthy landowner. Until then, Bowers would lay low and let the fervor over this latest murder die down.

In the week that followed, two people came to town that Travers thought would change the dreadful way things were looking. Maggie's Aunt Netta and a land officer, Lloyd Ates. Netta Howard he hoped was going to be a staunch ally for he soon learned that she had little love for Bowers as well. Ates was going to come in handy for keeping Bowers in line.

They arrived on the same stage, and Maggie and Rance were there to greet their aunt, though Travers thought he noted a coldness between the two women. The elder woman's visage softened as she greeted Rance and Travers guessed that there was some bit of emotion behind that cool facade. They settled her in a room at the hotel and took lunch in the restaurant. The three of them spoke little, and to all who were curious enough to stare, they seemed an odd trio to be considered family.

Travers made the woman's acquaintance later in the week when the three of them happened to stop by where Travers was watching Clayton, and some of the locals build the new theater in town. Just past the hotel, they were going up with it fast. Rance had stopped to question Travers about the place, for already there were signs posted about the first show coming to town.

"You think it'll be ready in time, Dr. Gage?"

"Sure. With time to spare, the way Clayton's been pushing this crew."

"Well, this is certainly a change, seeing Negras in charge."

Travers turned a frown on the boy, the urge to hit him upside his head alarming. The boy had a lot to learn.

"Careful, kid. Clayton's not one to take offense, but I do. That man is my friend, and if you can't show him the respect deemed a man, you'd best be moving' along."

"Hey, no offense meant," he stammered, looking at Travers over the top of his glasses.

"Well, now. I still haven't gotten that portrait done. You still interested?" the doctor wanted to know.

"Anytime you're ready."

"Soon," he promised, before turning to look at Maggie and her aunt whose attention was on the building going up.

The woman was of a height taller than her niece, by several inches. Her hair had already greyed and was tucked up under her hat in a bun. She was not an unattractive lady, quite the opposite in fact, and that led Travers to wonder if that could have been a reason for the woman's coolness towards Maggie. It happened frequently, when an older relative found a child an up and coming beauty, they tended to push them away lest they are forced to compete for attention. Surely that was not the case here. The woman had quite a few years on her, to what purpose would she be forced to compete?

She still had a youthful figure, despite her advancing age and the smile she turned on Travers revealed the beauty she had once been.

He stepped forward to introduce himself.

"Travers Gage," he said with a tip of his hat.

"Ah. The doctor from Virginia. I remember now. How do you do?"

Travers had only a slight recollection of her from when she and her husband had come to get the children after their mother had died. The woman had not stuck out so in his mind, as the uncle was the one he had dealt with closely. He couldn't even recall his face now, for all he could picture from that time was the agony on Maggie's face as they rode away.

"I'm fine, thank you. I hope you had a safe journey?"

"As good as any," she admitted. "I was sure we'd be attacked by Indians. I hear they are getting riled up out here."

"Yes, we have been lucky so far," he admitted. "General Hancock has been keeping them on the move, though. I expect we'll hear from them soon enough."

"I hope I'm gone from here when they do decide to pay a visit."

"So do I, ma'am. Are you here for the wedding?"

Maggie's eyes flew to his, and he noted the anger embedded there. Apparently, Aunt Netta was not a fan of her fiancé.

The woman made no bones about it. With a grandiose sigh and a roll of her eyes, she said, "I suppose I must attend. I do hope she comes to her senses before then. She won't listen to me, however."

"I take it you have no love for the man, either?"

"Quite the contrary. He's a rake and a rapscallion. I wish she'd never set eyes on him."

Maggie stepped up her mouth agape.

"Aunt Netta! This is hardly a conversation to be having with someone off the streets!"

"Darling, I hardly think Dr. Gage is 'just anyone.' He is an old friend from home, is he not?"

The woman looked, for her part, as if she were inquiring about the time of day. She tried to appear so innocent, but Travers knew she was pitching the ball to him, hoping he would run with it. The look in her eyes was pleading. He felt he better lay it out for her the way of things.

"I'm sorry ma'am. I've already had this conversation with her, and it did absolutely no good. She's bound and determined to marry that man, and I don't think God himself could stop that wedding."

"Well, she already knows my opinion on the matter. I promised I would stay and see this through, as much as I hate to. I fear she's in for it."

"She's heard that one, too. Time will tell."

Maggie spun on her heel and flounced off, her petticoat flashing unladylike. Aunt Netta leaned closer to the doctor, her voice lowered conspiratorially,

"I think betwixt the two of us, we can get her to change her mind."

"I'm afraid your niece is more stubborn than ever, Mrs. Howard. She has refused to budge on this. I think she really believes that she loves him."

"Surely there is something we can say or do?"

Travers turned to escort her back to the hotel, offering her his arm which she took without hesitation. They crossed the street, and he offered a final word on the matter.

"Ma'am, I have tried everything but offer to marry her myself. I think she would brain me if I stooped that low. I fear we're just going to have to let it go."

"Perhaps you should see where your proposal takes you. She loved you as a child. Surely there is still something there for you. Dr. Gage, I fear for her. I fear that marriage and that man do not mix. I'm begging you, talk to her again. She'll listen to you. She just has to."

He sighed in aggravation, knowing that the woman was asking the impossible of him. Maggie had shut him out of her life. Their friendship had been stretched to the limit ever since he had asked her to reconsider. He didn't want to take another chance alienating her further. Not knowing what else to say, he let the matter drop.

NINETEEN

It was a hot night, steamy and uncomfortable. Travers had removed his necktie to allow for a little ventilation. He had thought about calling it an early night and going on up to bed. Something inside him wouldn't let him. He had been down here in the smoking room nursing a drink, thinking of her for the last hour or so. She was making a foolish mistake. He had tried to reason with her, tried to make her see things as he saw them. He had hoped that if anyone could get through to her, it would be him. He was wrong.

She was going to go through with this marriage to Jim Bowers. And she would suffer dearly for it. Bowers was a dangerous man. Travers knew it; everyone knew it. The mysterious disappearances of men around the area had Bowers' fingerprints all over them. He had a small army of reprobates that would kill for nothing. But Jim Bowers was a rich man, and one could be sure, he paid his men well for their services to keep his name out of it. But people talked. People from the town suspected he was the one responsible. Sooner or later, the truth would out.

Travers strode out to the porch and leaned a shoulder against a post, observing the nightlife down the street. It was relatively quiet here on this end of town. Down the street, however, loud, raucous laughter, breaking glass, and the banging of the piano could be heard. He shook his head.

He had never understood why some folks felt the need to blow off steam that way. It was vulgar, disgusting and disruptive to the town, but the townsfolk tolerated it because it was good money: for the local carpenter who was paid to repair the damage to the saloon, the general store who replaced broken glasses and mirrors, and for Travers as well. He did a lot of patching up the morning after.

Travers gave a smirk and shook his head. At least there didn't seem to be too much brawling going on down the street tonight. Unusual, since the hands from Bowers' ranch were in town. They had a way of lighting the place up when they were around. He thought that he'd have a lot of time on his hands in the morning when he heard the boards creak nearby. It was Ras come for his nightly chat.

"Evenin', Doc."

"Evenin', Sheriff," Travers acknowledged without even turning his head.

"Seems purty tame tonight, don' it?"

"Yeah, pretty quiet. I was just wondering if it was the calm before the storm,"

Travers remarked, raising his snifter to take another sip of the brandy he'd been nursing.

"Yep, know what'cha mean. Still early yet." The sheriff spat a stream of tobacco juice a few feet in front of him.

"Um hmm." He and Travers stood there in companionable silence for a few minutes, listening to the sounds of the night, each lost in a thought process of their own. Tate thought he should have run Bowers out of town long ago. Now he seemed to have free reign here, and he was not a likin' it. He itched to put the idea to Travers to call him out, but he wouldn't. Travers was waiting for the man to slip up, and show his hand. Travers had a way about him that Tate liked and respected, and if Travers said to wait him out, that's what they were going to do.

He started to broach the subject of Bowers and his bride to Travers but thought better of it. The doc seemed to have a lot on his mind tonight, so he decided to amble on.

"Well, I guess I'd better finish my rounds. See ya' in the mornin'." Tate ambled off the porch and crossed the street. Travers watched him go, checking doors and windows as he went. He was a good man. A little old for the job, but he handled everything pretty well. He had called on Travers more than once to break up brawls in the saloon and to stop a drunken cowboy intent on shooting up the town. If Tate had a deputy, he guessed he was it, although Tate had never officially given him a badge.

He worried for Tate. The man was getting on up in years and in a town growing like this one, with rowdier crowds of folks pouring in, a sheriff's days were numbered. Erasmus would be no match for even the klutziest of killers should he be faced with one. The only real trouble in town, Travers had taken care of personally. But with Jim Bowers living close by, the bad element was always a presence.

He leaned his head back to drink in the beauty of the night sky. The stars danced overhead, and some looked close enough to touch. They looked like diamonds upon black velvet, and his thoughts turned to Maggie once again. Soon now, she would be wearing diamonds, though they would not be from him. They would be from a man he loathed, and the one she was convinced she loved. Somehow, he must find a way to convince her she was wrong.

Accepting the fact that he loved her was hard. He barely knew the woman, though he had known her well as a child. He had thought long and hard about what Laura had said about his feelings for her and decided there had to be some truth to it. It was the only logical explanation to why she had haunted him for so long. The Maggie he knew was a child, but she had always looked upon him with complete trust and a faith that had staggered him. In her eyes, he could do no wrong. Until the day he had sent her away. The look on her face had crushed his soul, for it was like he had torn a limb from his own body. It was that look, that child he had carried in his memory all these years. He had given no thought to the fact that one day she would grow up.

That day in town when he had heard his name spoken and turned to find her standing there, he had felt as though he had been struck by lightning. He had known her instantly and been at a loss for words. She had left him speechless with her beauty. For an instant, he had dared hope that she was there to make good on her silly childhood promise that she would one day be Mrs. Travers Gage. So much for that.

His eyes took on a hard look, and he tried to reign in his thoughts. It did no good to think about what would never be. He would never be able to shower her with diamonds or pearls like Bowers. But he found himself wanting at least a chance to make her happy.

He shook himself. His mood was sour now, and he felt the need to dunk himself in a cool tub of water. The heat he was feeling now had nothing to do with the sultry night air. He drained his glass and, not bothering to glance down the street again, went inside and proceeded to finish off the bottle of brandy in his room.

⸻ ⸱ ⸻

The knock at his door and the morning call to breakfast woke him. He lay in bed with his eyes closed, dreading the light. He was not one to imbibe often, and today he was paying for it. He was a social drinker and knew his limitations, but last night . . . well, last night he had needed something to dull his racing thoughts.

He knew he was late, but right now he couldn't seem to move. His head throbbed as if he'd been hit with a sledgehammer and he vaguely recalled that this was one of the reasons he limited his drinking. Hangovers were hell.

He eased one eye open. The room was dimly lit, the sun apparently behind a cloud, for his window always caught the morning sun straight on. God . . . He eased himself into a sitting position, massaging his aching head for a minute or so, then rose and bathed himself quickly. He rinsed his mouth several times to get rid of the sour taste and brushed his teeth. The act of bending over the wash basin gave him pause, for he began to see pinwheels of bright colors that he knew weren't on his walls anywhere. He had to sit down to dress, and he chose the black button front pants with a white shirt and grey satin vest. He rolled the cuffs up on his shirt to his elbows and ran a comb through his hair. He figured he looked presentable enough, not bothering to look at himself in the mirror. He didn't want to see the effects of last night. He found the door with just a hint of a stagger and closed his eyes, leaning his head against it for several seconds, breathed a prayer to help him get through the day. With that, he quit the room, following the scent of freshly brewed coffee.

Joseph and the O'Neal brothers were already seated in the dining room, their breakfast half eaten. He took a seat at the other end of the table, raising brows from the other men. He should have known better, for they only raised their voices to be heard from their end of the table.

"Top o' the mornin' to ya, Doc," Jack said, lifting his glass of juice to him. Travers offered a token toast himself with his coffee cup before taking a sip of the rich hot brew. He closed his eyes against the renewed pounding in his head, hoping the three men would let him alone just this once. Thankfully, they seemed to have business to tend to themselves and hurried through the rest of their breakfast. As the last of them was leaving, Flora bounced through the door. Seeing, Travers, she made a beeline straight for him.

"Good mornin', handsome!" she smiled sweetly. "What can I getcha this glorious morning?"

Travers grunted, thinking it was anything but. Curiosity got the better of him. Laura was always here at breakfast.

"What brings you about so early? Where is Laura?"

"She and her new *friend* are going to the dressmaker for fittings for their dresses for the wedding."

"Oh."

"Come on. Is that all you can say? What happened to you sweeping that girl off her feet? Don't tell me she was immune to your charms!"

"Something like that," he said and took a sip of the coffee.

"Oh, Trav. I'm sorry. I really am."

"Don't be. She's not married yet. Besides, there are two more weeks to work on her. Although, I'm about ready to resort to kidnapping. Maybe then, I'll be able to get a decent night's sleep."

She raised an eyebrow and propped a hand on her hip.

"Rough night, huh?"

"The worst," he admitted.

"You know, I'm real good at massaging aching heads," she

purred, leaning in closer, intimately, brushing against him.

Travers chuckled despite himself.

"I'll just have toast if you don't mind. Anything—heavier—might not sit so well with me."

"Suit yourself. Two pieces of toast coming up." She turned and headed for the kitchen.

"Heavy on the butter," he called after her.

In a few minutes, she was back with two nicely warmed, butter slathered pieces of bread. She made herself at home while he ate, and informed him that he had a package waiting for him at the general store. She had popped in there earlier, and Pete had told her to tell Travers it had arrived. He let her chat on, his thoughts on the day before him. The coffee was good and strong and was easing his aching head. He would stop in at Pete's and pick up his package first and then head over to the barber's to check on the man's infected thumb. He had treated him last week and was certain it would be better by now. If not, well, Travers would have to think on that. Pulling his watch from his pocket, he saw he was running behind. With the last gulp of coffee, he rose and bid Flora good day before heading out.

Sure enough, Pete was waiting for him to arrive.

"Mornin', Pete," he greeted the proprietor with a curt nod.

"Mornin' there, Doc." Pete was doing figures at the counter but put them away when he saw Travers.

"How's the missus this morning?" Travers was referring to the woman's foot. He had treated her for a sprain the day before.

"Oh, much better, Doc. She's taking it easy like you said. Grumbling and complaining, says she needs to be about her chores but taking it easy just the same."

"Good, good," Travers said and pointed to the box on the counter. "This mine?"

"Yes, sir. Came in on the early coach 'bout an hour ago."

They talked for a few more minutes before Travers headed to his clinic. He was a few steps away when he saw Laura and Maggie come from the dressmaker's. He paused, considered approaching them then thought better of it. He tucked his head and moved on, not knowing that the two women had spotted him and froze.

The look on Maggie's face was pitiful. She stared after Travers with such longing that Laura had to look away lest she open her mouth and let fly with her opinion. The girl was hopeless when it came to affairs of the heart. She swallowed her tongue and pulled Maggie's attention away from the man down the street.

"Why don't we have a cup of tea at my place? I'm sure you could use a bit of something to calm your nerves. You seem to be all a' jitter with the wedding fast approaching."

Maggie cast a thankful look at the blonde woman, knowing she was reading her right.

"I'd love a cup of tea, Laura. Thank you for the offer. It's very kind of you."

"Kind? I'm just doing what all bridesmaids do, aren't I? Keeping you from losing your mind?" She laughed lightly, hoping to raise the girl's spirits.

"You are right on the money there. This wedding is more stressful than I had anticipated. I had no idea that it would be this way."

"Well, the outside stress doesn't help, I'm sure."

Maggie sighed. "No, it doesn't. And you've really been a friend throughout all this when you didn't have to be. I know you think that Travers is right and I'm making a mistake, but you've been really kind about it."

"Well, I don't like being told what to do either. Never have. If you truly believe you love this guy, who am I to say otherwise?"

Maggie cast a grateful look at her. "You are a true gem, Laura. No wonder Travers thinks so highly of you."

Laura laughed. "Travers *tolerates* me. He is always telling me how I'd make some man a good wife, so I figure he's about had enough of me. I told him I have no intention of getting saddled with a husband. I don't want that burden."

"Burden?" They had reached the boardinghouse and Laura opened the door for Maggie to precede her inside. They went into the parlor where Flora had left a steaming hot pot of tea for them. Laura poured them each a cup of the stuff and seated herself across from Maggie, who thanked her for the tea. The girl took a sip then, turned the conversation back to what they had been talking about before.

"You said you didn't want a husband because he would be a burden?"

Laura nodded. "Men are such children. They have to be the man of the house, provide for the wife and think that the wife's place is only in the home doing the cooking, the cleaning, etc. etc. I find that totally offensive. Look at me. I'm beholden to no one. I make my own living, though I do clean and cook and run a boardinghouse. But I've chopped wood, shot my own dinner. I don't need a man for that. Sure, I wouldn't mind not having to work so hard all the time, but I wouldn't change that for my freedom any day. I like what I do."

"You certainly seem happy. I've never thought of it that way. I've always wanted a husband, though, someone to spend the rest of my life with, someone to love me the way I love them. It just seems the way of nature. Even some animals mate for life."

"Well, this animal would be kin to the praying mantis, I'm afraid. Sooner or later, I'd be biting my man's head off," Laura laughed.

"Ugh," Maggie said, but couldn't help laughing herself. "That is not a pleasant thought, Laura. Not pleasant at all."

"No, it isn't. But the temptation would be too great if I were married. No man controls me, and they never will."

"I applaud you, madam. You are truly one in a million. I'm afraid that us fainter of heart must submit ourselves to be cared for. I, for one, actually like the attention Jim bestows upon me." She fingered the string of pearls about her neck that Jim had given her a few nights ago.

"I'm sure you do. Hell, if I had a man who gave me baubles like that, I might reconsider my stance on marriage."

They laughed nervously, each knowing they were treading dangerous territory in talking about Jim Bowers. Laura eased the tension by passing Maggie a plate of cookies. She took one and thanked her, nibbling at the buttery softness of it.

"Wow! These are delicious. Maybe I could get the recipe? Jim has such a sweet tooth, and I know he'd love these."

"Sure. I'll get it for you before you go." She took a sip of her coffee before turning the topic to Maggie's aunt. "Has your Aunt Netta been on your case again?"

Maggie opened her mouth to reply but never got to as there was knock at the door. Laura excused herself to see who it was and returned with the object of their conversation in tow. Aunt Netta swept into the room, her satin petticoats swishing, her carriage erect, her face a mask. Maggie had been in the process of sipping her tea, and one look at her aunt's face had her sitting the cup back on its saucer. She obviously had something on her mind.

"Aunt Netta? What a pleasant surprise," she said, hoping she sounded more pleasant than she felt. This was not going to go well.

Netta Howard looked from Maggie to Laura. "I'd like a moment with my niece if you don't mind, Ms. Murphy?"

Laura knew the two of them were not close and she looked to Maggie for confirmation before she made to leave the room. At the door, she paused and looking back, informed them, "I'll be right across the hall if you should need me, Maggie." With that, she closed the door to give them some privacy.

Maggie silently thanked Laura for her show of support, both of them knowing that her aunt was here to once again try to talk her out of this marriage. She indicated a chair which, her aunt sank onto gracefully, her features looking as if they could have been carved from granite for all the emotion she showed. She fidgeted, and Maggie knew this not going to be pleasant.

Maggie cleared her throat and offered her aunt a cup of tea, which thankfully the woman turned down. The woman took a lace handkerchief from her reticule and folded it nervously, then finally found the courage to speak.

"Margaret, I know you, and I have never been extremely close, but I'm sure you know I have always tried to do right by you, regardless of how I felt about you."

That raised Maggie's eyebrow, for in truth the woman had always seemed to prefer Rance to her. She nodded, encouraging her aunt to go on.

"I know you think that I could have been more motherly, and you're probably right. But I suppose I just didn't know how. I regret that. Honestly, I do. And what I have to say to you now may seem harsh and cruel, but I would not be doing my job as your guardian if I did not. Please reconsider this marriage. That man is a user, and I see only hurt for you, dear. He is cruel. I see it in his eyes. Your uncle was not the best judge of character, I'm afraid, and I believe his association with that man contributed to his death."

Maggie raised rounded eyes to meet those of her aunt's. "Aunt Netta, you should be ashamed of yourself. Uncle Charles died of a heart attack. We know that."

"Yes, child, and he had been in perfect health before meeting your Mr. Bowers. I know he didn't kill him straight out, but Charles knew something about that man's background and refused to share it with me. He knew something, Margaret, something that scared him. He feared for you as well. He told me so many times."

"Aunt Netta, if he was so worried about me why did he never say anything?" Maggie was not liking the turn this conversation was taking. Now even her aunt was speaking of Jim as if he had some dark, evil side to him. She knew better.

"Your uncle thought you would meet someone else and you would forget about Jim. He prayed for it."

"Well, I didn't, so if you'll excuse me, I think this conversation has gone on long enough."

She rose and went to the door which she opened hoping her aunt would get the message. Netta Howard sat there staring at her niece.

"Margaret, please don't throw your life away on this man. He does not love you. I know this. Come home with me. I'll help you find a suitable husband. One who will love you and be gentle."

"I think you should leave now." She indicated the door and thankfully this time the woman took the hint. She paused at the door, however, and turned back to Maggie.

"If you should need me, you know where to find me."

With that, she walked out. Maggie stood there for a minute, trying to get control of her slowly rising temper. Thankfully, Laura appeared, having heard the door close behind the woman. She stepped into the hall gingerly, noting the expression on the girl's face. She gently took her by the arm and led her back to her seat by the window and handed her a cup of tea. The girl took a gulp, nearly choking on the brew. She was upset. Angry, heartsick. No one seemed to be happy for her. Laura could sympathize, but she had to know. Taking the seat opposite her once again, she waded in.

"Maggie, I'd like to ask you something. I'll understand if you tell me to mind my own business, but truly, I'm trying to be your friend here. Why are you so determined to go through with this marriage when everyone but you is against it?"

"Laura, I love him. I know that is so hard for you and everyone else to understand. None of you know Jim the way I know him. He's kind, he's gentle, he's funny, he's romantic. He treats me like a queen. I truly don't know why none of you have ever seen that side of him, but I have, and he loves me. I know about the disappearances. Travers made sure I knew about them. But there has been no proof that Jim had anything to do with that. The last I heard, a man was innocent in this country until proven guilty. He has never been anything but the perfect gentleman to me, and I refuse to believe him capable of such things. That is why I am going to marry him." She sounded tired, Laura thought, tired of defending herself to everyone. Laura knew her mind was made up and she would not try to change it for her. But she needed to know that if she needed a friend she would be there for her.

"Maggie, I always heard that bought knowledge was the most precious of all. I hope you are truly happy with him. If you should ever need me, I'll be here for you."

Maggie gave Laura's hand a squeeze. "Thanks so much, Laura. That means a lot."

"Well, let's get you married, girl!" Laura struck up a jovial tune of 'Here Comes the Bride,' humming it which sent Maggie into giggles. It broke the spell of gloom that had clouded the morning, and the two of them spent the rest of the day planning the wedding dinner at the hotel. Laura would protect the girl as much as possible, but the time would come when she could not. God help her when that time came.

TWENTY

Sitting and staring at that ominous cloud was getting her nowhere. She should be getting ready for her wedding. There were things to do, last minute details to see to. Yet, she sat there frowning at that solitary black cloud in an otherwise sunny sky. The gentle breeze coming through the window ruffled the lace at the neck of her nightgown and lifted her hair away from her face. Her frown deepened as she recalled the events of last night. Travers had shown up at her door, and Aunt Netta had let him in, hoping for the same thing that he did. To change Maggie's mind.

The moment they were alone she had turned on him.

"Please tell me that you've come to wish me well. If not, then please leave." Her arms were folded defensively across her chest, her heart seeming to thump painfully. She wanted his blessing so bad. Why, why couldn't he seem to give it?

Travers strode over to her, his hands fisted helplessly at his side. He searched her face, looking for that spark that had flickered between them and flamed the day of the picnic. She was hiding it carefully. She refused to meet his eyes, knowing he would see her pain. She backed away from him.

"Maggie, I'm begging you, don't do this."

Maggie had groaned aloud, grinding her teeth even.

"Travers," she said, rubbing the bridge of her nose, eyes closed in exasperation. We have gone over this, what, a thousand times now? I gave my word to Jim, and I have every intention of keeping it. Give it up. There is nothing you can say or do to change my mind." Her eyes pleaded with his now, hoping he would accept it and leave. He didn't.

"His life is a lie, Maggie," he said, grasping her roughly by the arms and giving her a shake. "And so is yours if you have convinced yourself that what you feel for this man is love. Have you so quickly forgotten what it was like between the two of us? Should I refresh your memory?"

"No!" she had gasped and struggled free of his grip. He had continued.

"You certainly didn't kiss like a woman in love with another man. Quite frankly, I would have guessed, had I known you any better, that all your affection was directed to me."

The heat had crept up her neck and suffused her cheeks all the way to her hairline. He was telling the truth. She had acted disgracefully. To herself and to Jim. She would never admit it to Travers, though.

"Travers, I don't want to lose our friendship over this. I thought you understood that I only reacted to you before out of, well, curiosity. I had adored you for years. Surely you won't hold that against me. I thank you for trying to look out for me. But this has to stop. You've no right."

"No right? No right?" he asked quietly as he moved closer, his eyes boring into hers. "I know you, Maggie. You're infatuated with him. That's not love. What you felt when we kissed, that's love. And you know it."

She had raised panicked eyes to his. He was reaching her.

"Maggie," he said, raising his hand to brush his knuckles across her cheek, his finger tracing her lower lip. "Marry me instead." There. It was said. The words lay there like a gauntlet, his eyes daring her to accept the challenge. His heart was in his eyes, and she wanted to believe him so badly.

Maggie's throat had closed instantly at his words. Her eyes darkened at the vague memory that very notion had once been her dream. She could even recall the moment it had first taken root in her mind. She was watching him treat this little old lady, noting the gentleness of his touch and the intensity of his professionalism. He honestly cared about his patients, and she had known he could be her way out of the poverty she and her family had endured. She had craved marriage to Travers the way a squirrel craves a nut, thinking it was her only means of survival. Then she had met Jim. He had shown her that other good, decent men existed outside of Travers Gage.

The feel of his thumb on her lip was unnerving, and she trembled from head to toe. If only he would stop touching her! Before she could pull away, he pulled her into a kiss that curled her toes. She was tingling all over and her eyes closed, her breathing choppy and strained. She touched him with fingertips that seemed to have lost their feeling, and she heard him groan aloud at her touch. She could not, would not do this again. What must he think of her? What would Jim think of her behavior? Dear God. . .

"Stop!" She tore away from him, panting to catch her breath. Travers backed away, his hand going through his hair, distractedly. He seemed shaken as well.

Several minutes passed before she could wrap her tongue around a thought and verbalize and when she did, Travers knew he had lost her.

"That was clever, Travers. You almost had me convinced. But I know you would do or say anything to get me to stop this wedding. I'm sorry to disappoint you."

He had looked at her with such pain that she had almost caved. Almost.

"It's a mistake, Maggie. One you'll regret for the rest of your life." She had not replied, and he had left. She had watched him go, noted how he never looked back and knew they had lost something precious.

Yes, that cloud bothered her. She tried to push the doubts away. *Nothing* was going to ruin this day. Not some dark cloud on an otherwise sunny sky, not Travers, not even her aunt, who had somehow managed to 'forget' to wake her this morning. Tearing herself away from the window, she turned her thoughts to what was going to be the happiest day of her life.

Laura and Aunt Netta were sipping tea in the restaurant downstairs when Maggie finally joined them. She had chosen a soft blue day dress to wear and would change into her wedding gown before lunch. Her hair was piled fashionably atop her head, her cheeks flushed with color and a smile on her lips. It was Laura who noted the circles under her eyes.

"Rough night?"

"Oh, it's just nerves, I suppose. I think I was so excited I couldn't sleep."

Laura and Aunt Netta exchanged looks but let the subject drop. Something had kept Maggie up, all right, but each doubted it was the thought of marrying Jim Bowers. Both suspected it was her conscience and how she had refused Travers at every turn. Laura kept her mouth shut and cut her eyes to Netta Howard, implying she should do the same and the woman took her cue. They would help Maggie become Mrs. Jim Bowers. As much as it pained them to. Getting married was the easy part. It was the undoing of it that was difficult. They each felt Maggie was sure to learn.

TWENTY-ONE

They had kept the wedding small, with only Laura, Aunt Netta, and Rance as Maggie's witnesses and Sam Bailey, the ranch foreman and two drovers as Jim's witnesses. Maggie had been extremely nervous, the butterflies in her stomach clamoring to get out. One look at Jim had settled her down. He had dressed in his finest suit for the occasion, a black pinstripe worsted with a crisp white shirt complete with boiled collar and blue neck kerchief. He was the picture of calm, self-assured and had beamed at her as she walked down the aisle to meet him. He had taken her hand in his, and his warmth had enveloped her, causing all doubts and fears to dissipate. She had barely heard the preacher as he had spoken and had to be prompted to speak her vows. Jim had calmly repeated his vows and when the ceremony concluded, planted a chaste kiss on her lips. Too chaste. Then he had abruptly turned and paid the preacher who excused himself after congratulating the couple.

They had all dined at the restaurant afterward, Maggie having arranged for a special meal of pheasant and rice with vegetables. Dessert was a surprise wedding cake that Laura had Clara Johnson create. It looked and tasted divine, of buttercream icing and spice inside. The meal, however wonderful, was strained, the conversation forced and hesitant.

None of Maggie's witnesses seemed to enjoy her new husband's company, and it showed. There was no lingering over the meal. Laura excused herself first, giving Maggie a hug and wishing her well with her new life. Aunt Netta and Rance had followed shortly after, but not before assuring Maggie they would be out to check on her in a few days.

That had been two months ago.

She had seen neither her aunt nor her brother since. That was probably a good thing, she thought. Jim would not allow her to leave the ranch. He had been into town a few times merely to put in an appearance and make sure everyone knew they were the perfectly happy newlyweds. Why he just kept his little bride worn out with his devotion to her! Well, there was one thing for certain. Jim was happy all right. Jim was the only one happy.

Their wedding night had been an utter disaster. Maggie had waited for Jim in their bedroom wearing a long white lacy confection that was both revealing and demure. He had come to her, taking her roughly in his arms, his mouth tearing across her flesh impatiently. At first, Maggie had thought it was just his need for her was so great that he was beside himself with passion. In the past, she had timidly offered herself to him, wanting to know the touch of him as her lover. He always had gently refused her offers, kissing her gently on her forehead as if she were a child. As his assault on her began, she had thrown herself into the moment, aching to be his wife in every way. His roughness was desire, she thought. What a fool she had been. The passion soon became anger and Maggie began to become seriously frightened. Something had not been right from the start, and up to the moment of truth, she could never have guessed. Jim had strained and bucked and pumped, but there was no penetration which Maggie had steeled herself for.

Realizing his predicament, she had shyly tried to touch him, to arouse him and Jim had slapped her hands away. Jim had finally pulled away in frustration, leaning over her watching her silently for several minutes before he hit her. Hard. The slap sounded like a pistol shot in the silent room and was followed by Maggie's astonished gasp as she held her hand to her stinging cheek. She had lashed out at him then, striking at his chest trying to get him off of her, terrified.

It was not the wedding night she had expected at all. She had dreamed of love that would take her breath away. Well, that had happened, but not in the sense she had hoped. Fear had made her mouth dry, her breath coming in small shallow gasps as she fought her husband off of her. Jim had finally scrambled from the bed, threw on his clothes and left.

He was gone three days. The cook, Slim was his name and rightly so for he was thin as a rail, had seen to it that she ate well and had water for bathing. He didn't talk much, and when he did, he was abrupt and to the point. 'Eat," he had said that first morning when he had brought her a breakfast tray of eggs, ham, and biscuits. She had gingerly picked at the food, then found herself devouring the tasty fare. The old man had proven to be a splendid cook, and she cleared her plate whenever mealtime rolled around. Slim never said a word about it, just grunted when he collected the dishes. Once, she thought she saw a flicker of a smile cross his face.

Jim had left her alone until last night. Dear God, last night. Maggie felt herself get queasy at the memory. He had come to her again, intent on fulfilling his husbandly duty by her. He had taken more time with her, arousing her until she was quivering with need. His kisses had held true passion, and he had allowed her more access to his body, his flesh heating at her touch. Still, he had not been able to perform. Maggie had lain there stunned. She had asked him softly what was wrong if there was something she could do. He had risen and paced the room angrily, saying he didn't know. He had apologized and left her to spend the night alone. Again.

They avoided one another, newlyweds yet to experience the marriage bed. They were civil to one another, and that was about it. She deplored the fact that Jim went into town and would not let her. But she knew his purpose behind that. He was making sure that Travers got the message that she was being serviced. It galled her, but he had that right. She let him have that small victory, but that was all he had.

Travers. She had thought of him often since her wedding night. Dreamed about him, in fact. Dreamed that it was him, she went to bed with at night instead of her pillow which soaked up her tears of regret. He had known. He had known and tried to tell her. She had been such a fool.

Travers had spent Maggie's wedding night getting good and drunk. He had wandered down to the saloon, having drained his last bottle of whiskey, in search of more liquor. Flora was there. He had approached her to talk, but she had taken one look at him and tried to walk away. He had stopped her, and before he knew what was happening, he was leading her back to her place. Hell. Who needed Maggie when he could have the most beautiful woman in town?

Flora had dragged her feet, giving him every chance to bolt and run. He didn't waver. Not until Sheriff Tate intervened and Flora sighed in relief. She wanted Travers, but not when he was drowning his love for another woman. She treasured their friendship too much to take advantage of him that way.

The next day, she went to check on him and found him 'indisposed.' So, the man had trouble holding his liquor. She smiled, barged into his room and doused him with water from the pitcher on his washstand. He struggled to his feet, dripping wet and furious, his eyes burning into her. Flora should have been scared. She wasn't. She was angry. Angry to see how a woman could bring this man so low.

"I have a few things to say to you, Dr. Gage, and you are going to listen to every word."

She poked him in the chest with her finger, and he folded neatly back onto the bed. Some of the fight went out of him, whether it was from her matter of fact statement or his hangover, Flora didn't care.

"You are looked upon by this town as a man of integrity, Travers Gage. You *are* human, we realize that. But what you have to understand is that, even though you are hurting, you must face facts. You must go on with your life, even though it doesn't seem worth living because you have a responsibility to these people. They need you, depend on you. I need you. Not in the way you wanted last night, but the same way everyone else in this town needs you. I need to know that there is still someone I can look to who can give me hope, that there are still good men out here in this cursed frontier who have refused to let their morals go for the sake of money or greed. Someone to protect us from people like Jim Bowers and his kind. Someone who can stand out in a crowd and pull people together in a crisis the way you always have. Now you get off your ass and stop wallowing in your hurt. It only makes the pain worse."

He listened to her, his mouth drooped open at her sermonizing before ducking his head. She was right, he knew. Trust Flora to do the honest thing. She was ever after him to get him in bed, but at crunch time, she had gladly begged off. That was friendship, he thought.

She sat beside him on the bed, her hand covering his as it rested on his knee.

"I know all about rejection, Travers. I could write you a book on it. But sinking into this mire will give Jim Bowers a victory you don't want him to have. He must never know how much you truly care for Maggie. If he ever found out, he could make your life, and hers, a living hell. Consider that before you sink any further into that hole you're digging."

That jolted him to attention if anything else hadn't. Flora was reading the writing on the wall. There was more at stake here than his wounded heart. Maggie. If Jim ever found out, he could manipulate the situation to his advantage. . .

He grabbed Flora into a hug so fierce she squealed, but he held on for a moment longer. Then, surprising the redhead further, planted a kiss on her full lips, sour though it was.

"Flora, you're a gem. I don't know how to thank you."

She sat there, bemused, her lips tingling from the contact. Giving a small chuckle, she said, "I think you just did!"

He mussed her hair and shooed her out of his room before bathing hurriedly and heading to his clinic. He had a responsibility to this town, and he meant to fulfill it.

TWENTY-TWO

The land officer that Travers had hoped would keep Bowers in line proved to be useless. After two or three visits to his office, Travers surmised that the man was pretty much in it for the money and whoever lined his pockets got what they wanted. The man made an effort to seem otherwise, but Travers read him well. Sure enough, Travers had seen Bowers pay the man a visit. He didn't linger long enough to actually lay down the law to the newcomer. But Travers guessed he pretty much informed the man who was in charge. After that, Bowers kept his distance, a sign that puzzled the doctor to no end. He was slick as glass, he was.

His little forays into town after his and Maggie's wedding riled Travers, but he refused to let Jim Bowers see him hot under the collar. The man always made a point to speak to the good doctor when before he had carefully ignored him. Travers was no fool. His subtle hints about marital bliss were usually countered with Travers' jibes about Maggie'.

The man hated that use of her given name, and he snarled every time Travers called her that. It tickled him to turn the table on the man, it surely did, for Travers was so frustrated he could hardly stand himself. The agony of knowing that Maggie and Bowers were intimate turned his stomach. He buried himself in his work after their marriage and to finding proof to bury that bastard. It mattered not that Maggie might get hurt in the process. Her feelings didn't count when it came to putting away a murderer.

He lay awake at night and wondered what she was thinking, what she was doing. If the two of them were at that very moment in the throes of passion. The memory of their time by the creek rose before him nightly, and he tossed and turned fitfully trying to escape the lingering emotions. He was on the border of insanity, and he had to do something to relieve the pounding in his blood. As he lay there in bed at night, he pretended that Bowers was stepping into a noose and that he was the one who pulled it tight around his neck. One day soon, he thought. It *would* happen.

* * *

Maggie was sitting in the parlor mending a lace shawl that had once belonged to her mother when her husband walked in.

He seemed to be in quite the mood and struck up a conversation with her, a curiosity in itself since they never seemed to talk anymore.

"How are you, my dear? Hope all is well. You are looking fit."

"I'm fine, Jim. And you?"

"The same. I'm sorry we've been at such odds lately, but I mean to remedy that. How would you like to come into town with me? I've business there and at Fort Dodge that will take several days, and I fear to leave you all alone out here. The Indians are on the prowl again, it seems. George Custer informed me of such just this morning. They were passing through on their way to Fort Wallace. The men will be busy with the cattle, and the cook will be needed out there as well, I'm afraid. Besides, I'm sure a few days in town would lift your spirits. You could shop, visit with friends, your aunt, and brother."

Maggie stared at him, the shawl forgotten in her lap. He was actually pleasant, and for a moment she caught a fleeting glimpse of the man she had fallen in love with. He was charming and dressed impeccably in his fawn-colored jacket and brown pin-stripe pants. He could have walked off the pages of the Sears catalog. She sighed inside herself, knowing that pictures were deceiving and considered his act of 'thoughtfulness.' At least he was showing a bit of protectiveness towards her. That had to account for something.

"Town sounds wonderful."

"Very well. We'll leave within the hour. Pack your trunk. A week's worth of clothes should suffice."

A week! Maggie could hardly contain herself. She could barely keep the smile that lurked at the corner of her mouth from spilling over her lips. She was beginning to think she would never get back to civilization.

"I'll be ready."

Jim gave a curt nod before going back outside to give orders and ready the carriage.

Maggie was upstairs before the door closed behind him.

TWENTY-THREE

Travers was in his clinic and didn't see the drifter ride into town. He was poring over his medical journals to reacquaint himself with experimental treatments. Out here medicine was scarce, and he could always use an alternative method for treating patients. He was busy making notes when he heard the loud bellow of his name being called. He calmly finished the sentence he was writing, lay down his pencil, and leaning his elbows on the desk, steepled his fingers. Another gun in town. This was just getting to be ridiculous. He could hear the excited voices of the people on the boardwalk lining the street. They wanted to see Dr. Gage at work at his other profession, the town trash remover.

He sat there, hoping the nut would give up and leave. For fifteen minutes he sat there, hoping his blatant disregard for the man on the street would see the man slink away. He didn't. Travers walked over to the wall and took down his 12-gauge shotgun. It was loaded with squirrel shot, but the man outside wouldn't know that. Maybe just the sight of it would deter the man down the street.

Stepping outside into the sunshine, he squinted into the light thinking again how aptly named the town was with the sun glowing at just the right angle on it. A gentle breeze stirred his hair and eased into his nostrils, causing them to flair. The storefronts were crowded with folks come to watch another man taken down. They knew the doc's reputation. The man out in the street was in for a rude awakening. He was young and full of juice but spoiling for an early death to be sure. Everyone quieted down when they saw Travers step from the porch, his eyes mere slits, his face a mask of almost indifference. There was no anger or fear there, just calm self-assurance that bordered on impatience.

Travers stopped about fifteen yards from the man and took a good look at him.

He was a kid. Seventeen, maybe eighteen years old. Damn. They were getting younger and younger. He raised his gun so that the barrel rested casually back on his shoulder.

The kid down the street fidgeted, eyeing the man he had come to kill, his firm countenance and the shotgun that he carried with authority. Throwing out his chest he bolstered himself. The man was an easy mark, he told himself. He was bad enough to take this man down and anyone else he chose to call out.

Travers spoke finally.

"This is your only invitation to leave town."

The kid laughed nervously and shifted his gun belt.

"I'm leaving, all right. As soon as I plug you and put you six feet under."

Travers let loose a huge, exaggerated sigh and shook his head.

"I don't make a habit of killing children," he stated flatly, looking the kid in the eye, his own eyes cold, hard.

That did it.

The kid reached for his gun only to hear the bellow of gunfire that wasn't his. He felt shattering pain in his leg and looked down. It was a bloody pulp. He collapsed into the street, writhing in pain, blood pouring from what was left of his knee.

Travers strode over to him casually, knelt down and pulled the pistol from the boy's belt. He looked at the wound, then back at the boy who was now whimpering like a girl.

"Well, best get you to the clinic."

The boy grabbed Travers' arm to hold him there when he would have risen.

"Why?" he asked, and Travers answered, "I told you. I don't make a habit of killing children."

Some of the men who had witnessed the affair came out and carried the fallen boy into the doc's clinic and placed him on the examining table. Travers thanked them then ushered them out when they showed no signs of leaving. He wanted to be alone. He washed up and disinfected his tools and began cutting away the kid's pants leg. The leg was a mess, but at least the boy wasn't dead. He would probably walk again but with the aid of a cane. Travers sobered at the thought. He gave the boy a quick drink of laudanum to help with the pain.

"What's your name, son?" he asked as he began to clean the wound.

"Deke. Deke Lowe."

"Well, Deke Lowe, what on earth possessed you to pull a stunt like you just did?"

"Heard my cousins talkin' bout you. They said yore fast. I told 'em I was faster."

Travers grunted harshly.

"Trying to prove you're a man, Deke Lowe?"

The kid caught his breath against the pain in his leg.

"Something like that."

Travers picked up a pair of tweezers and started picking out pellets. Not taking his eyes off the leg, he said, "Being a fast gun is not what makes one a man, Mr. Lowe. It's knowing when to use it and how to use it — properly," he emphasized. "Guns are not always the right choice in a fight."

"What's that supposed to mean?" the kid grumbled back.

"It means guns don't make the man. Any man who hides behind a gun is not worth the leather in his gun belt."

The kid let out a sneer.

"That's a matter of opinion. My cousins *Frank* and *Jesse* might have something to say about that."

Travers paused. He pinned the kid with his fierce eyes.

"Frank and Jesse—James?"

The kid chuckled, thinking he had put a little fear into the doc now.

"Yeah. Heard of 'em, have ya?"

Travers went back to work on the leg, a little more aggressively, causing the boy to squirm and clench his teeth.

"I *know* them. You tell Frank that Travers Gage says hello."

"Humph," the boy snorted and closed his eyes before he finally had to know.

"Really, why didn't you kill me?"

Travers weighed his answer before giving it, wondering if this boy would understand his point.

"I've seen a lot of men come through this town, a lot of them gunning for me. Few of them left here alive. I'm no gunfighter, but I don't tolerate people bent on murder. My life is just as precious as the next. A lot of men lose sight of that fact, so much so that they become like rabid animals, killing for sport, rather than survival. You've got a lot of life left to live, kid. Be careful that your cousins don't help you lose sight of that fact. They've had it rough, and I don't blame them for the life they chose. But sooner or later, they're gonna lose sight of everything but survival. They'll be hunted down like animals. And when that happens, they'll be taken out. Hard."

Deke seemed to be letting that soak in. He asked after several minutes, "You said you know them?"

"Yes."

"How?"

Travers hesitated, not sure he should divulge that bit of information, but something about this kid drew the truth out of him. It was a part of his past that he did not regret.

"Frank studied under me for a few months. He was preparing to go to medical school, but he needed some help with his entrance exam. His stepfather had written me and asked if he could send him to me. Frank had expressed an interest, and he felt he would make a good doctor. Things weren't good at home though. Trouble had started before he ever left for Virginia. Border wars and all that. His family was caught right in the middle of it. After four months, he decided he best go home. That was a month before the war broke out."

Deke didn't believe him. Frank had never mentioned the name Travers Gage or the fact that he was ever interested in being a doctor.

"You're joshin' me. It must have been another Frank James. I would have known something like that."

"Really?" Travers asked. "Frank's a very private person. You really think he'd admit to something like that? A man doesn't care to admit their dreams have been dashed, son. But he would have made a fine surgeon. Steadiest hands I've ever seen. Crack shot, too. A little slow on the draw for my constitution, but his accuracy with a rifle is downright scary."

Deke's eyes rounded but he said nothing. The doctor *did* know his cousin! Frank could be awful slow in a fight, but he'd knock a gnat off a fly at a hundred yards. He was what folks called a deadeye. He never missed. And he had a methodical way of studying people like he was seeing them inside. Sometimes, he would look at Deke that way and the boy would shudder. Frank was always too quiet and studious for Deke's taste. Deke tended to be loud and brash, trying to get Frank to act like he and Jesse. Jesse could throw down when he wanted to, and could go on a tear that rivaled anything Deke put out. And that rubbed Frank raw quite often. He liked to keep a very low profile, and Jesse didn't, and more times than not refused to. Jesse loved attention, as did Deke, but they always kept Deke's involvement in anything illegal on the down low. He was always masked and more times than not relegated to only holding the horses. He had never entered a bank, nor stepped foot on a train, and that rankled his hide. Deke knew he was good. He just had to prove it to them. And so that was what had brought him here.

They had been sitting around a campfire in the distant vicinity when the doctor's name had come up. Jesse had mentioned to Frank that he heard there was a doctor in the area who was damn fast with a gun. They had exchanged looks, but Deke had not caught the unspoken message passed between the brothers. He had seen it as an opportunity and had pounced on it.

The absurdity of it hit Deke. Why had Frank never mentioned that he had studied medicine to him? Then he figured the truth of it. Deke liked to talk. He had a hard time knowing when to keep his mouth shut. The fact that Frank had medical knowledge might be a bone of contention with the local law. The James' tended to take care of themselves. He had seen Frank tend the wounded many times after their gang got shot up, but it had never clicked. Until now. It had to be true. There was no denying it.

"Well, I'll be. Frank studyin' doctorin'."

The laudanum seemed to finally kick in and eased the boy into a slumber. Travers continued to work on his leg, saving what tissue he could. He snipped and sewed, picked out bone fragments, and finally closed the wound. He sat back and looked at his handiwork before bandaging it up. He sat there for a long time looking at the damaged leg, knowing he could have chosen not to fire at all. He had saved the boy's life. He hadn't wanted to hurt him, but he knew if he hadn't fired, the boy would have killed him.

Life was strange, and it never ceased to amaze Travers how fragile it was. He began to bandage the wound and wondered if Maggie had heard about the episode yet. It wasn't like he expected her to come running, but it would have been nice to know that she cared about him the least little bit. He rarely saw her anymore. She came to town sporadically, and when she did, she did her best to avoid him. He had tried to seek her out once, and she had refused to see him. He had let it go. After all, she was a married woman now. That thought set a churning in his gut and his jaw clenched hard as he cut that thought process off at the bud. No use even going down that road again. What was done was done.

He tied off the bandage and rising, went to the basin where he washed his hands, scrubbing the blood from them. He studied them for several moments. At least it wasn't the boy's lifeblood that stained them. They were already covered in enough of that. So much so, that he thought that he would never get them clean.

Walking back to his office, he went back to work on the notes he had been making when the kid had called him out. He spent the rest of the day doing so, his patient sleeping soundly as a babe.

•———•———•

Maggie had been in town and had heard the challenge from the street. She was up in her room at the hotel and had rushed to the window, careful to remain hidden behind the lace curtains. Travers had taken his time coming out, though she had prayed that he wouldn't appear at all. He had managed to keep from killing that boy. She had gone weak from relief, and her knees had suggested she find a chair fast. She had been terrified for him, but Travers had taken control of the situation quickly, effectively.

She was in Hell. She knew it. Travers had been right, and she had been proud.

Travers had always been right. About everything. But pride

wouldn't let her go to him in her hour of need. If he ever knew . . . Maggie shuddered at the thought.

Travers must never know.

———◆———

The next day, Travers examined his patient who was now fully awake and full of chatter. He spoke non-stop about exploits he was supposed to have gone on with Frank and Jesse and how he was going to join up with them as soon as he was able. Travers told him that could be a while. Deke sulled up and proceeded to down a half a bottle of whiskey against the pain. He would be out for a while, Travers decided, so he gathered his medical satchel and headed out, leaving the boy to sleep it off. He made a few calls on locals who had been feeling a bit under the weather and checked on the newborn and his mother from the previous week. All were doing well, and Travers was pleased to know that he had helped in even the minutest fashion. Life in this town was good, even if it did have its drawbacks. He had never regretted his choice to stay here until Maggie showed up. Life. .It had a twisted sense of humor.

TWENTY-FOUR

Months passed quickly, even for a small town such as this. The kid he had shot, Deke Lowe, had stayed for two weeks healing up then had disappeared. No note of thanks or to say where he was going. He had, however, left two dollars on the front desk. Travers hoped that he had gotten through to the kid. If he did rejoin his cousins, he would be dead soon for sure. That was a certainty.

Other things were happening now that Travers had observed from a distance but given little thought to. He should have. The sight of Loyd Ates riding out of town had not triggered the mental red flag that it should have. Travers was usually too tied up to follow the man when he left town on his occasional excursions, and Sheriff Tate had only managed to track him once without success. It was obvious the man was meeting someone out on the prairie, but there was no way of knowing who for certain or why.

━━━◆━━━

Clayton and Sarah had designated Thursday nights as game night at their house. Cards, charades, anything they were in the mood for. They had invited Travers, Laura, Flora and the Tate's. Sarah and Laura had baked cakes and cookies and had coffee on brewing to get them through the night. This one looked to be a long one. The men were deep in conversation about the missing men, and the women were exchanging recipes. The games had yet to be played. The conversation shifted to the fact they were looking for a new schoolteacher. Flora was thrilled. She had been volunteering at the school but had no proper training to teach. She had been so happy there, her heart already taken with some little towhead girl. She would come and sit on her lap while she read stories to them. Flora had taken to baking them cookies. The little girl had been hesitant to warm up to Flora, but as Flora continued to read to them, she had migrated from the back of the room to her lap. She was a tiny thing, and Flora had to wonder if she was even old enough to be in school since the darling refused to talk. She would simply smile at any attempts to get her to talk.

It was Laura that brought the lateness of the hour to everyone's attention.

"If we don't get busy, we won't get out of here by midnight.

159

I thought we were here to play cards."

Ras piped up. "We was waiting on you womenfolk to get through with your jawin'. I'm ready for a slice of cake. I didn't et much supper. I'm hongry."

"You not waitin' on us women, you old coot. We a'waitin' on you men. Ya'll gossip worse than women any day." Louella couldn't help herself.

"So says the woman who could be a reporter for the society pages. You know more about what goes on in these parts than the nearest newspaper's gossip column." Clay and Travers couldn't help but laugh at that one. It was true. If a person wanted to know what was going on with someone in and around town, all they had to do was look up Louella.

"Well, somebody has to do it," she insisted, "Seein' as how they ain't no newspaper for miles and miles."

"Woman, get them cards and serve that cake a 'fore I die of hunger. Us workin' men need our sustenance."

"Workin' man? Just what do you do every day, Ras, besides sit on yore rump at the office? You really hurt yourself."

Travers cringed comically, as did Clayton.

Ras saw and leapt into the fray.

"If I want to sit on my rump, I will, woman. I'm an old man. I can't be gallivanting' all over the country like these young whippersnappers here," he told her, indicating the doctor and blacksmith. "And since you know so all-fired much, why don't you lurk about and find out what ole' Bowers is up to? We get you on the case, we'd be done with this matter and him out of our hair."

"Aww, you just too lazy to do it yourself. You men kill me. But you mark my word. It'll be a woman that brings him down. Be it Margaret or whoever, he'll get what's coming to him. There ain't no telling what'll come out when it does. Man's a snake."

Travers piped up. "Well, we aren't going to get to the bottom of it tonight, so let's get to some poker, why don't we? And a piece of that cake sounds mighty fine about now." He smiled brilliantly at Laura who had just brought Ras a piece and plunked it with little fanfare before him. She rolled her eyes and went to fetch him a piece as well. Men. What on earth would they do without them, she thought, hiding a grin of her own.

Travers knew that there was nothing to be done but wait out Bowers. He would know when the time came to bring him down. In the meantime he could be patient, watching, waiting.

TWENTY-FIVE

Flora was about to step into the general store when she stopped in her tracks, the breath she had been about to take stuck somewhere in her throat. A man had just stepped down from the stagecoach two doors down and was busily swatting the dust from his hat and coat. Sandy blonde hair and broad of shoulder, he took her breath away. He turned towards her momentarily and their eyes locked, her green ones large and round, his blue, with a slight crinkle at the edge as he looked her up and down appreciatively. The cast of his lips was sensuous without trying to be, and the very thought of his lips on hers made Flora break out into an unladylike sweat. Flustered, she lowered her eyes and darted into the store where she casually maintained a presence near the window so she could observe him unnoticed. She gasped. Her eyes were not deceiving her, he was coming this way! She whirled around, intending to dart between the fabric aisles, and sent a basin and pitcher display crashing to the floor.

Pete came rushing over.

"Ms. Flora! Are you alright?" he asked, concerned, noting her agitated state.

Flora was gritting her teeth and flexing her hands. Dropping to her knees, she began to pick up the larger shards of the broken items, her hands shaking. Pete knelt beside her, taking the pieces from her.

"Now, no need to fret. I'll take care of this."

"I'm sorry, Pete. I don't know what's gotten into me. I'm not usually so clumsy."

He patted her arm and helped her back up

"You look like you could use a good stiff drink. Tell you what. I got a pot of coffee in the back. I'll pour you a cup and add a bit of bourbon to it. It'll ease those jitters."

She offered a weak smile.

"No, I'll be fine. But I think I will go home now. You be sure to put that—whatever—on my bill," she said, gesturing at the mess with her hand.

Pete just waved it away.

"No, ma'am. It was purely an accident. Besides, I owe you," he added, wagging a finger at her.

She flashed a smile at him, knowing he was referring to the time she'd had to nurse him back to health when the town had influenza. His wife had been ill herself to the point of death.

Flora had taken charge and had even crawled into bed with the man when the chills wracked his body. Pete's wife had been mortified to learn that her husband had shared a bed with the madam, but she promptly forgot all that when she realized the woman had saved her husband's life.

"Tell Genevieve I said 'hello,'" she called back to him as she hurried out the door.

"I will," he said and went to get the broom and dustpan to sweep the remaining fragments up.

The stranger had come in, unnoticed, as the two had carried on over the mess the woman had made. He had slipped down the aisle near them and watched the scene unfold, his eyes missing nothing about the woman who had caught his eye earlier.

She was beautiful, with deep green eyes and rich red hair, not the brassy color but a luxurious mane that he knew would feel like silk to the touch. Her complexion was as smooth as ivory, and when she had smiled at the storekeeper, the hair had risen on his neck as if she had breathed on it. He watched her hesitate at the door as she looked both ways before hurrying outside.

As she stepped from the store, he eased to the window to watch her make her way towards the other end of town. As she went, she was stopped and greeted by several men and a few of the women. Each time, she looked over her shoulder as if to see if she was being followed. She wasn't. At least not by him. He was still watching her when Pete came back from discarding the broken pitcher.

"Can I help you, sir?" he asked as he joined the stranger at the window.

The stranger turned, startled to have been caught so unaware. He actually blushed. He gestured out the window.

"Just enjoying the view." He cleared his throat and followed Pete back to the counter.

"I believe you have a package for me. Name's Daniel Mc-Cullough."

The storekeeper's eyes lit up.

"Ah! The new schoolteacher. I do indeed have something for you." The man turned to the shelves behind the counter and examined a few before withdrawing a large crate. Depositing it on the counter, he gave the man his total. As Daniel counted out the money, he asked about the woman who had just left, his voice impersonal.

Pete's attention was perked immediately. So that's what had interested the fellow so.

"That was Ms. Flora McDonough. A beauty inside and out," he informed this Daniel fellow. He was a brawny fellow for a schoolteacher, Pete thought as he looked the man up and down.

"She's very—striking," Daniel agreed.

"She is that and more. A kinder heart you'll not find in this town. Why every man for miles around here has gone a'callin' over to her place. 'Course the only man she would even consider having' is the doc, but he's got eyes for another, supposedly. She runs the Velvet Rose down by the saloon. Big two story house. You can't miss it."

Pete didn't know it, but his words had a lightning effect on Daniel.

A whore. He should have figured. No decent woman looked the way she did with those cat eyes of hers and lips that begged to be kissed. She was a woman who obviously enjoyed men's company, and from the smile, she had bestowed on Pete, he had sampled her wares as well.

"Well, good day to you, sir," the schoolteacher said, tipping his hat. With the crate under his arm, he quit the store and headed to the sheriff's office. The old man gave him the key to the house that would be his, and he soon found it and found a thick coating of dust covering everything in sight. It billowed upward like smoke as he deposited the crate on the table. Anxious to see its contents, he carefully opened it lest he stir up another cloud of dust. Everything he had requested was there. Books, maps, slates, chalk. There was even a copy of 'A Tale of Two Cities' by Charles Dickens, his favorite author.

He spent the afternoon cleaning, and the sheriff popped in to invite him to supper but didn't linger long as the dust was still as thick in the air as fleas on a dog. Daniel had kindly refused the invitation, and the sheriff told him the hotel served good food and stayed open late. Once he had the dirt and grime under control, he went and picked up his trunk at the stage office. He splashed himself with water and changed clothes, finding his appetite. He decided that hotel food might look pretty good about now and headed in that direction.

He was about a block and a half away when he saw her, the redhead, speaking to a man on the street. She was laughing at something the man had said and then suddenly, she threw herself into his arms, kissing him full on the mouth. She withdrew a little and seemed to whisper intimately in his ear, her eyes beseeching him, her mouth mere inches from her lover's. Again she kissed him, and he kissed her back this time, before disentangling himself from her arms. He sent her away with a thwack to her behind, and she giggled loudly, sticking her tongue out at him over her shoulder. She darted into the two-story house they were standing in front of just across from the hotel. As she disappeared, the man turned to face Daniel, giving him his first glimpse of the man's face. Shock and recognition rooted him to the spot. It couldn't be!

❖

Travers had been taken quite aback at Flora's actions. She had never been so bold in her teasing in public before, but when she had whispered to him 'Please Travers, play along. I'll explain later,' he had followed her lead and returned the kiss. The minx was up to something. There was an urgency in her kiss and the way that she clung to him that led him to believe that this little act was for the benefit of a man. Shaking his head, he had about run smack into the person striding towards him. Travers pulled up short to apologize and, his smile spread from ear to ear.

"My God, Daniel, is it really you? How long has it been?"

Daniel grinned and extended his hand, which Travers pumped furiously, pulling the man into a backslapping hug. "How are you, Trav? Been a long time."

Travers laughed. "Too damned long. What brings you to town?"

"I'm the new schoolteacher."

"No kidding?"

"Nope."

"Well, I'll be. I knew they were looking for someone but didn't know they had actually hired one. This is great news. We need some new blood around here. And looks like we got ourselves some genuine blue-blood to boot." He laughed, referring to Daniel's family background. Oxford-educated, his grandfather, had founded one of the first newspapers in Chicago. Daniel had attended Oxford as well, and he and Travers had met at the start of the war. Travers had been assigned briefly to the same regiment as Daniel before transferring to the 7th West Virginia Volunteer Infantry under Lt. Col. Jonathan Lockwood. The two men had struck up an instant friendship.

"Uh, Travers, since when is lip color fashionable on a man?" the blond man teased.

Travers wiped at his mouth, finding a trace of Flora's lip rouge on his fingertips.

"That little minx! I tell you, if I didn't know better, I'd think—"

Travers hesitated, seeing the intense interest in Daniel's eyes. He grinned suddenly, thinking it was all very clear now. He chuckled to himself. Flora must really have it bad for this man to go to such extremes as making a public spectacle of herself for him.

"Well, Flora is a handful, if you know what I mean," he kidded, his brows raised knowingly.

"Really? I take it the two of you are—friends?"

164

"Why, Flora and I share everything! But a temper! Heaven help you when her temper gets riled. It's that Irish in her, I guess." Travers scratched at his jaw, thinking that these two were certainly suited to one another. Yes, sir. This was going to be fun.

"Irish, you say?" The schoolteacher's interest was rich.

"Yeah. That red hair and those green eyes make for a lively change of pace around here. Say, why don't you come have dinner with us this evening? I was just on my way to the clinic, but it can wait. Come on. I'll introduce you."

Daniel seemed to hesitate.

"I wouldn't want to intrude."

Travers hastened to assure him, "Oh, no! Besides, Flora will be thrilled! Any friend of mine is a friend of Flora's!" Thrilled his ass, Travers was thinking. She'd likely skewer him on her dinner fork before the night was over. He was going to enjoy this!

The two men walked back to the boarding house where Travers explained to Daniel that he lived there, along with a few other tenants and that Laura Murphy owned the place.

"Laura's one of the best cooks around. You'll enjoy the meal, I promise you that," he said as they entered the dining room.

Laura was laughing about something Flora had just said, and Flora looked mortified. When the two men walked in, Flora froze, her hand shaking around the bowl of peas she had been in the process of putting on the table. Travers walked over and rescued the peas before they could be scattered across the floor. Once they were safely deposited on the table, he gathered Flora close, his head near hers, nuzzling her neck.

"Darling," he fairly purred, "I have someone I want you to meet. He's a good friend of mine. We met during the war. His name is Daniel McCullough. He's just arrived in town and guess what? He's the new schoolteacher!"

Travers saw the look of horror that crossed Flora's face and held her in place when she would have run from the room. He smiled down into her panicked eyes and through clenched teeth, muttered, "Smile, darling. I thought I'd make this easy for you."

Flora returned the smile but the look she shot Travers could have felled an army. Travers was shaking with mirth now and Laura, who had witnessed the scene with curious eyes now understood. This was Flora's heartthrob. And as luck would have it, Flora's use of Travers had backfired. She had caught herself in her own web. Travers obviously knew the man very well. One look at Flora and Laura decided she'd better step forward now.

"Daniel, is it? We'd be delighted to have you join us for dinner."

The blond man nodded at her, barely casting a glance her

way, his eyes hungrily taking in the sight of Flora and Travers. He did manage a "Thank you, ma'am."

Laura cleared her throat.

"Flora, why don't you get another place setting?"

Flora disappeared in a flash and Laura popped Travers on the arm with the back of her hand. Daniel didn't notice. He was watching the doorway where Flora had disappeared.

"Stop teasing her! She'll leave if you keep this up."

Travers chuckled. "No, she won't. She'll suck it up and endure it, even if she has to put on another face to do it. But stay she will, and I won't have to force her."

Flora came back at that moment with another place setting and promptly sat down. The others followed suit, and after Travers said grace, all began helping their plates.

"So, you're the new school teacher?" Laura asked politely, hoping to break the silence that had fallen over every one of them once everyone had helped their plates.

"Yes, ma'am. I just arrived today."

"Well, I hope you found the house to your liking. I'm afraid no one had a chance to get over there to clean it for you. We weren't sure when to expect you."

"That's purely alright, ma'am. Wasn't sure myself. And the house is fine, thank you. So is this meal. You are a mighty fine cook."

Laura beamed under the praise, her eyes going to Flora, who sat stiffly in her chair, pretending to eat by rearranging her food on her plate.

"Well, I had help. Flora prepared the dessert. It's her specialty. Marbled Fudge cake. It is absolutely divine!"

The schoolteacher's eyes went to the redhead again, noting how quiet she had become. He wished she'd make conversation for he wanted to hear her voice again. She had the most southern accent he'd ever heard, but on her, it sounded like heaven. He watched the byplay between her and Travers and noted something didn't seem quite right. What, he couldn't quite put his finger on. Travers was especially attentive towards her, but she looked like she would just as soon go through the floor. She mumbled her responses and poked at her food, darting nervous glances the schoolteacher's way. The meal passed much too quickly, and the ladies soon disappeared into the kitchen to clean up. Travers led Daniel into the parlor and poured each of them a drink. They settled into the chairs before the fireplace and Travers took out a cigar and lit it, offering his friend one. Daniel rarely smoked but thought this might be the one occasion he might. He needed a slight calming of his nerves.

"So, you'll be staying a while I guess. The new schoolteacher.

I figured you'd be off on some exotic adventure writing. You never struck me as the teacher type," the doctor said, smiling at his friend.

"Well, I did a bit of traveling. The writing never took off, though. Always had too much to do."

"You mean too many women to entertain, don't you?"

"Well, there was that as well," the blonde man admitted, laughing. "India is such an incredible place, you're afraid you'll miss something if you take your eyes off the scenery. The only real chance to write is at night, and that can be dangerous if your mind isn't on your surroundings."

Travers sat forward in his chair, his hand on his knee. "You went to India? When?"

"The year after the war. Had to get away, find a little beauty left in the world."

"It must be something to behold, with all that wildlife in its natural habitat. Did you hunt any while you were there?"

"No. Couldn't bring myself to shoot at anything. Though lucky for me I had several guides who were more than willing to. We had to kill a few big cats who thought to have us for dinner."

That brought a chuckle from the doctor. "I bet they were fascinating up close."

"Most beautiful creatures you'll ever see. Bengal Tigers. You know, the ones with the black stripes. Massive animals. One of the guides made me a necklace of the claws. I'll have to show it to you sometime."

Travers sat back and looked at his friend. The man seemed older, wiser, much the way Travers felt. The two of them had seen way too much in their lifetime. No wonder the man couldn't bring himself to fire a gun even to save his own life.

"I'd like to see it," he said, remarking on the necklace.

Daniel nodded, and they fell into silence, each savoring their cigar. Daniel finally rose and stretched, telling Travers he felt his bed calling him. He told him to give his regards to the women and to thank them again for supper, that it was delicious. Then he made his way back to the house he was to call home. Once there, he undressed and crawled into bed, the events of the day catching up to him. He went to sleep with flashing green eyes and rich, red hair dancing through his thoughts.

TWENTY-SIX

Travers was on his way to lunch at the hotel the next day when Porter, the telegraph operator stepped out the door and flagged him down. He crossed the street and stepped into the office. Porter had another customer, but he quickly concluded his business with her. He turned to Travers after the woman departed.

"You've got a telegram from a General L. Sharpe. Says it's urgent." He handed the envelope he had tucked it into to Travers who tore it open and scanned the message quickly.

Doc. T. Gage Stop. Am in Nicholsville KS Stop. Need You ASAP Stop.

Gen. L. Sharpe Stop.

He folded the paper and put it in his vest pocket and spoke to Porter. "Send this message back for me: Gen. L. Sharpe Stop. Will leave immediately Stop. Arrive tonight Stop. Doc. T. Gage Stop."

Porter finished writing the message down and settled the bill with Travers.

"Hope everything's all right," he called as Travers left the office and hurried to his clinic. Then he turned and began to tap out the message to Nicholsville.

Travers grabbed a few extra supplies and tucked then securely in his medical valise. Whatever had caused the general to call for him must be urgent. He looked quickly through his medicines and grabbed a few different varieties just to be safe. There was no telling what he would find when he got here. He locked up the clinic and went next door to ask the tailor to keep an eye on the place for a few days. The man said he would be glad to and wished him a safe journey.

Back in his room, he changed into sturdier travel attire and let Laura know he might be gone for a few days. She tried to give him some food to take along, but he told her he would eat when he got to Nicholsville.

He made an impressive figure as he stepped out onto the porch, pausing to place a black Stetson on his head to shield his eyes from the blazing sun. He was wearing a suit of lightweight worsted, black and tailored to fit. His vest was pearl gray satin and had a black pinstripe. His snowy white shirt was open at the neck, his tie tucked inside his valise. The long riding jacket was also black and fit him superbly. He didn't notice the many females who stopped to stare at his fine form unabashedly as he strode to the stable where he kept Cirrus. At the stable he had the boy call his horse, and he saddled him while the boy fed his horse an apple, a favorite treat of his. In no time he was on his way to Nicholsville.

He rode into Nicholsville around six o'clock and headed straight for the hotel. Dismounting, he tied Cirrus securely to the post before the hotel and unhooked his satchel from the saddle horn. With a swat of his hat against his pants leg, some of the dust disappeared, and he replaced his hat. In the hotel, he found the clerk asleep behind his desk. Travers cleared his throat, and the man only grunted in his sleep. Having little patience, Travers turned the register that sat atop the counter and scanned it for Sharpe. There, in room number 11. He turned the register back around. The clerk never cracked an eyelid. Travers went up the stairs and down the hall to the right, following the numbers. He noted that the hotel had seen a few improvements since his last visit. New paint and wallpaper. Big-time improvements for such a small town. He stopped before the appointed room and gave a brief, solid knock. A rustling could be heard within, and in a second the door was opened just a crack. Travers could barely see the slight figure on the other side.

"Yeah?" The voice was indiscernible and cautious.

"I'm looking for General Sharpe."

"You Dr. Travers Gage?" The voice rose slightly in pitch.

"Yes. He sent for me."

The door opened, and the figure reached out and pulled him quickly into the dimly lit room. He could make out the form of the general lying upon the bed, his jacket opened all the way down. He appeared to be sleeping, and as Travers stepped closer to the bed, he could hear a tell-tale rattle in the man's chest. He tore his gaze away from the sick man and addressed the room's other occupant.

"And you are. .?"

"Sal. Sal Sharpe." A small, slender hand was extended. Travers shook it and held it, refusing to let go when it would have been pulled away.

"Short for Sally?"

Startled green eyes rose to meet his. The oversized clothing she wore might hide the curves he knew she must possess, but curly chestnut hair peeked out from underneath the oversized hat, and Travers noticed that although the hand was slight, there was a steel-like quality to it. This girl had seen hard times, was accustomed to working.

He grinned down at her and finally released the hand. He tipped his hat to her, saying, "Nice to meet you, Miss Sharpe."

Sally Sharpe pinkened furiously and turned her back to Travers, walking to stand on the other side of the bed. Reaching over, she touched her father lightly on the shoulder, giving him a slight shake. Lawrence Sharpe woke to a fit of coughing and Travers could see the blood mingled with the spittle on the handkerchief he used to cover his mouth. He knew a heaviness in his chest for he knew without even examining him it was consumption. But he would examine him thoroughly to be sure and to estimate properly.

When the general was finally able to speak, he addressed Travers.

"Doc, it's been a while."

"Yes, sir," Travers agreed, his hands folded in front of him.

"The local doctor was dead drunk when we rode in. The clerk downstairs told us you were nearby. Hope we didn't upset your schedule."

"No, sir. I'm glad you sent for me. I wouldn't have it any other way." He sat his valise down on the nightstand and removed his riding jacket carefully, taking care to lay it across a chair next to the door, lest the dust that still clung to it from the ride over send the general into another coughing fit. His hat he removed as well, placing it in the chair along with his coat. Running his fingers through his hair, he turned back to find Sally observing him closely. She blushed again and turned her face to focus on some unseen object on the far wall, her chin raised pertly. Travers smiled to himself, thinking he would have to become better acquainted with Miss Sharpe. First, he would see to her father.

"Okay, General, let's get you into a sitting position," he said and moved to aid the sick man. Lawrence Sharpe was weak and didn't refuse help from Travers or Sally as they maneuvered him around on the bed. Sally propped pillows behind him, and he leaned back, winded from the slightest bit of exertion. Travers took out his stethoscope and hung it around his neck, checking his pulse first. He found it faint and erratic. Then he listened to the man's chest, front and back. Taking his time, he checked everything carefully. Sally and the General sat quietly, waiting for Travers to finish his examination. He took about fifteen minutes to complete it then stepped back. His face held the truth that Lawrence Sharpe had known.

"How long?" the older man asked.

Travers shook his head. "Three weeks, three months, maybe, but it's highly unlikely. You're very advanced. When were you diagnosed?"

General Sharpe grunted. "About a year after the war."

Surprised, Travers pulled up a chair next to the bed and sat down.

"Well, sir, it's a miracle you've lived this long."

The general nodded, knowing he was living on borrowed time. He hated it for Sally, hated the idea of leaving her alone in the world. He reached for her hand and grasped it weakly. Travers' gaze slid to the slight figure across from him. Tears glistened in her eyes as they drank in the sight of her father. She seemed to be trying to memorize his face.

"I know, dear. I know. We've been ignoring this for so long as if we thought it would go away. But, it's time to pay the piper now. You've got to be brave for me, girl. You're a general's daughter, remember."

Tears poured down her face then, and she said brokenly, "I will, Papa. I will."

The general pulled her into his arms and held her close, his own eyes misty. Travers slipped silently from the room, giving them a few moments of privacy. Grief was such a personal thing, and he often had to walk away from it. He found himself downstairs and calmly greeted the clerk who was now awake. The clerk's eyes widened upon seeing Travers coming down the stairs.

"Well, good day sir. I didn't know you were here."

"That's because you were asleep on the job when I arrived."

The clerk had the grace to flush.

"Boy, don't you know that anybody could have stumbled in here and robbed the place?"

The clerk's Adam's apple bobbed up and down. "Yes, sir. I'll remember that sir," he stammered. Travers made small talk for a few moments more then moseyed back upstairs. He gave a slight rap on the door and was bid to enter. He did so to find the general sitting on the side of the bed with Sally helping him button his jacket.

"Now hold on there. Where do you think you're going?"

The general looked up at Travers, a smile on his face.

"Supper. I hear the restaurant next door has decent food."

"But, sir—" Travers began to protest.

The general's hand went up.

"Now look here, son. I'm dying. I think we all know that. But I refuse to do so lying down. Until I'm forced to, anyway. Besides, I can't think of anything better than to spend the evening with an old friend toasting old times and catching up, can you?"

Travers sighed, knowing Lawrence Sharpe was doing this as much for himself as for his daughter. He would not debate the issue with him further.

"All right. We'll go to supper."

Pleased, the general took his daughter's hand and told her,
"Why don't you go change for supper, dear?"
Sally hesitated.
"I'm fine, Papa."
"Young lady, I want to see you in a proper dress for a change.
Why don't you put on that lovely green flowered one we bought
in St. Louis? And maybe style your hair a little less severe. I long
to see it once again without you cramming it up under that ten-
gallon hat."

She turned blood red, her chin jutting out just a bit, hating to
have been put in such a spot. Travers watched her awkward exit
from the room, thinking she looked quite angry and wondered
why. Her father just requested that she look more like his daughter than his son. Where was the harm in that? Besides, he found
he couldn't wait to see the true Sally Sharpe.

The general rose gingerly from the bed and eased himself
into the chair that Travers had pulled up earlier. Sensing his intent, Travers knelt and helped him pull on his knee-high boots.
He sensed the man was irritated that he needed help with such a
mundane thing, but he didn't voice his displeasure. That simple
act had winded him. Travers noted the weary expression on his
face as he took a seat on the side of the vacated bed.

"General, are you sure you're up to this? We can have supper
brought in."

"No. I want to do this while I still can. It may be the last time
I'm able to spend quality time with my daughter and my dear
friend. I'll be bedridden soon enough. Then you can pamper me
all you want."

Travers nodded, understanding, for the general had a very
valid point. And he longed to be a part of his friend's last days,
for he didn't really feel that the man had three weeks left. What
Travers heard in the man's chest had spoken more of days, and
Travers was sad for his friend and his daughter.

His thoughts turned to Sally Sharpe. Much like himself, when
her father died, she would be very much alone in the world for
she was the last of their family as well. Her mother had died
before the war, and she had stayed with friends, grudgingly so.
When her father had returned from the conflict, she had latched
onto him with a tenacity that rivaled a Pit Bull, according to the
general. He had written Travers once while he was still serving
out his time in the army.

His thoughts were interrupted by the man coughing.
"What on earth are you doing in Kansas, General?"
The man gave a flourish of his hand.
"Oh, it was Sally's idea. My health had gotten worse, and
she thought that the drier air out here might help. For a while,

it seemed to. We've been traveling for some time, now. Sightseeing, you know. Sally wanted to come out West. Wanted to see it before it became too civilized. She's tough as nails, that one. She's had to be. I've been unable to provide and protect like I should, but she stepped right up and handled everything. She can shoot better than I, believe it or not!"

Travers chuckled at that, knowing that must be a source of pride for the aging man. He admired strength in any woman. There was something about Sally that appealed to him. He wasn't sure exactly what it was. She wasn't unattractive. He could tell that much right off. When the door to her room opened, and she stepped through it, he had his answer. Where Maggie was ebony velvet and fine ivory, Sally was peaches and cream. Her cheeks were rosy with self-consciousness, but Travers thought she couldn't have looked lovelier. He rose and gave her a slight bow, causing her to color even more so.

"Ma'am, you are simply radiant. You should dress so more often. It's a shame to hide such beauty under those other clothes."

Lawrence Sharpe grunted, noting the look of interest in the doctor's eyes.

"Another idea of hers. Although I must admit, it's come in handy on occasion, her propensity to dress like a man. Lots of riffraff about."

"You've not had trouble have you?"

"Nothing that 'Sal' here didn't handle rather effectively."

The pretty young lady rolled her eyes at that, but Travers sensed her pride in her father's praise. The general struggled out of the chair with a bit of assistance from the doctor, and the threesome made their way downstairs and out into the street to the restaurant next door. Few people were about, and they seated themselves in a quiet nook away from the door but close enough that it didn't tax the sick man too much. When the waiter had taken their order and disappeared into the kitchen, General Sharpe turned to Travers.

"So, how is it we come to find *you* in Kansas, son? Last I saw you, you couldn't wait to get home."

"Nothing like a trip home to see what one really has, sir. I guess I figured I needed a change of scenery."

"You wouldn't be running, would you?"

"Perhaps," Travers admitted with a grin.

"From the war or the reputation?"

"Maybe a little of both."

Sharpe nodded soberly. "I'm sure your neighbors didn't welcome you back with open arms."

"No, sir," was the grim reply.

"You know, Travers, I've learned a lot in my many years. One thing is certain. At some point in time, every man is forced to stand alone. When that time comes, it either makes us or breaks us. You seem to have weathered the storm just fine. It was a piece of luck us finding you. I told Sally just the other day how much I would love to see you. If only to thank you once again for saving my life."

Travers nodded. Life is strange, he thought. He turned to Sally, who had sat silently observing the two of them. She was pretty, he thought. Even though he couldn't help but compare her to Maggie, he decided he had a liking for peaches and cream.

"Sally, you're very quiet. We didn't mean to exclude you from the conversation. Your father says that you have a keen interest in the West. Anything, in particular, caught your eye out here?"

Sally fingered her napkin, blushing now that their attention was on her.

"Oh, there've been so many things. The buffalo are magnificent. I can't imagine what it must be like living out here all the time. They say the Indians are on the warpath, but Father and I haven't seen any at all. A blessing, probably."

"Well, it's true. But there are ways of dealing fairly with the Indians. Some know when you're honest with them. Others just don't care. They'd just as soon scalp you as look at you."

Sally sat forward in her chair, noticeably. "Have you run into any Indians out here, Doctor?"

"A few. They steer clear of the larger towns. I ran across a few outside of Dodge a few months back. They steered clear of me, and I steered clear of them."

"What tribes are in this area? Are they as fierce as everyone says?"

"Some are. Some just have a reputation for slaughter because that's what the government wants everyone to think. It gives them an excuse to exterminate at will."

Lawrence Sharpe interjected.

"Surely things haven't gotten as bad as that."

"They're worse. Custer is one of the worst. He's a braggart and an instigator. I don't like him nor do I trust him. The Indians despise him."

"What has General Scott been doing out here? Sitting on his behind?"

"Practically. I hear Phil Sheridan is on his way out here. If he is, Lord help us."

"You think things will get worse? Surely not. The Indians will have to see there's no use in fighting anymore."

Travers looked at the general, thinking how little he knew of what was happening out here. The man had no idea. The army was slaughtering innocent tribes along with those who were waging war. It wasn't right.

"Sir, anyone out here with half a brain knows what is truly going on. The government has no immediate plan to civilize these people. They have every intention of exterminating them. The Indians stand in the way of what the government wants, and that is more land, and gold if what the miners are saying can be believed. These people welcomed us in the beginning. They quickly saw that we weren't simply passing through or going away. We're encroaching on their land, killing off their food supply. Wouldn't you fight if you saw your way of life being destroyed? I thought the war would have opened your eyes to that. The South was lacking in industry, sir, not heart. That is why they lost the war. The same will happen here, friend. These people will fight to the bitter end. They don't fight the way we do, and that has been why they have succeeded thus far. They are adept at hit and run tactics, guerrilla warfare if you will. They have been able to disappear into the wilderness because we don't know this land the way they do. But the time is coming for them, I'm afraid. Soon."

General Sharpe grunted and raised his eyebrows at Travers.

"You sound as if you're on their side."

"I have no ax to grind with them. They've left me alone even though they've come across me traveling alone on more than one occasion. I admire them. I think that what our government is doing to them is a terrible waste. We could learn so much from them, yet we refuse to listen. Higher ups are of a mind to make this nation stretch from coast to coast. Neither one man nor one tribe of Indians is going to stop them. I think it's a shame what the government justifies in the name of 'progress.'"

That brought a sigh from the general, and he eased back in his chair, studying the man who had saved his life. The doctor was a man of integrity. He fought if he had to and he picked his battles carefully. He noted that Sally was studying him as well, a frown marring her brow. She was letting what he had said sink in deep. The waiter brought their food then and the moment passed, and they moved on to other things. Sally laughed at her father's attempt at jokes. He had never been good at them, but she humored him, and so did Travers. The evening passed pleasantly, and Travers hated to see it end. He walked them back to their hotel room and gave the general something to ease his coughing spells should he have another attack. Bidding them goodbye was hard. Sally had opened up a bit more over supper, and he wanted to get to know her better, but he also had to get back to town. He informed them he would be back before the week was out and took his leave.

TWENTY-SEVEN

Travers had settled into a routine of trying to get back to normal as if his life had not been turned upside down by the appearance of Maggie and her marriage to his enemy Jim Bowers. They had still not found proof to link the man to any of the deaths and disappearances of the men from the town. Time was ticking along at a snail's pace. They were all seated in the parlor at the boarding house one night, Laura, Travers, Flora and Daniel nursing drinks and shooting the breeze when Travers finally got wind of how the newlyweds must be fairing. Flora was the one who volunteered the information.

"Poor girl. She was so convinced she was in love with him. I'll bet she wishes she had her nickel back. Celia says he is one more hoot."

Laura cut her eyes to Travers who seemed to appear uninterested in the conversation. He wore a slight frown and his finger traced the rim of his half-full bourbon glass. But he was interested all right. Keeping her tone casual, she asked,

"What do you mean, Flora? They seem to be very happy."

Flora gave an undignified snort. "Well, let's just say, she's not suffering from the marriage bed. From the lack of it, maybe."

Daniel chuckled. "You mean he won't sleep with her?"

"Not won't. Can't"

That really got Travers' attention. Nervous chuckles burst from everyone in the room, even him. Laura was the one to finally come out and ask.

"So what's the matter with him that he can't perform his husbandly task?" Her question was laced with laughter. Flora got control of herself long enough to answer.

"Back at the start of the war, seems he enlisted to fight under Forrest. Apparently, he was rough on his horse. The horse didn't take kindly to mistreatment, threw him and proceeded to bite him. In the privates no less. Hard. I hear the men thought they were under attack from all the yellin' and screamin' going on and rushed into battle. Instead, they found Bowers screaming and bleeding like a stuck pig. Rumor has it that horse was actually grinning." Flora was doing some grinning herself, her expression reminding Travers of a Cheshire cat.

Yes, he would have loved to have seen that, Travers thought to himself. He listened to the others carry on about the incident and their own speculations about what had really happened.

Flora said that Celia was exhausted after his visits. He apparently could only function if the woman showed fear. Maggie had apparently not done so for him to seek out another woman's bed. He was concerned for her. If she and Bowers had not shared a bed, then she must be miserable. Maggie was a passionate creature. He knew. She had tried to tamp down her desire for him the few times they managed to be intimate. He knew she didn't love that man. She had been blinded by his flattery, his wealth, and his charm. Somehow he had failed to make her see her husband as everyone else did. Now, maybe living under the same roof with him would be an eye-opener. Maggie had endured enough unhappiness in her life. She deserved someone to love her and care for her. He had tried to become that man for her. She wanted no part of him.

Travers stifled the sigh that threatened to rise from his chest. He would not think about Maggie anymore tonight. Turning to Daniel, he asked him how the school was coming along.

"It's doing surprisingly well. We have several new students from the nearby farms now that I've split the day up. It allows for some of the older children to come and they can still do their chores."

"I thought it was an excellent idea. Enrollment is up, and the children love Daniel. He makes it fun to learn, not a chore," Flora chimed in, her eyes beaming.

"So you've actually been to the school to watch him in action?" Laura chirped, amused.

"Well," Flora admitted, blushing furiously, "I dropped by a batch of my famous oatmeal raisin cookies. I thought the children might enjoy them." She went on to tell Laura about her trips to the school and how she had sat and listened to him teach right along with the children.

Daniel sat back and listened to Flora go on about the school and the work he was doing there, watching her eyes dance as she described how he got all the children involved and included her in some of the activities. He enjoyed Flora's company so much. She was vivacious, surprisingly intelligent and loved children. Her wit and sharp tongue could slice a man to ribbons though. He had been on the receiving end before and knew how her tongue worked. She was a curiosity. For some reason, she had singled him out to tease, and on more than one occasion he had caught her watching him as he went about his business in town. Realizing she had been caught, she had actually blushed, profusely so, an amusing and surprising thing for the town madam.

Her trips to the school were legitimate, he knew, for she really appeared to love the tykes. Little Hannah Mason was her favorite. She had lavished the child with so much affection that some of the other children were starting to get jealous. Hell, *he* was starting to get jealous. She had actually stayed and participated in class much to the children's amusement. He had worried about how the parents would react to having her at the school so often, but so far no one had anything negative to say to him about it. Flora had always dressed with decorum and modesty when she came to the school, so he felt that as long as she behaved herself, she was free to come and go as she pleased.

In the meantime, he was going to tread lightly where she was concerned. He didn't quite know where things stood with her and Travers and he had not pressed the issue. However, Travers seemed to be of the mind that she was free to do whatever she pleased. Daniel wasn't looking for a wife. He was a confirmed bachelor who had little time for one woman. He liked them all. But he could sure use a friend. As long as she didn't complicate his life too much.

Flora was halfway participating in the conversation now, having noted Daniel's quiet perusal of her. She fought the blush she felt rising and avoided his eyes which seemed to penetrate, searching for something in her. Looking for an excuse to evade him, she noted the late hour and rose to leave. Laura tried to protest, but Flora insisted that she really must be getting home. Travers made an attempt to offer to walk her home, but she refused his offer. Daniel watched the play between the two of them. He shot Travers a look, and Travers returned it with one as if to say 'She's a big girl. She can take care of herself'. That riled Daniel for some reason. They walked Flora to the door and Travers didn't even kiss her goodnight. Daniel spoke up then and said he should be going as well, his eyes on Flora who quickly stepped outside, avoiding his stare. Travers and Laura looked knowingly at one another. There was a romance budding here.

They closed the door on the unlikely pair, Laura chuckling to herself and Travers shaking his head. The schoolteacher and the town madam. Boy, they were going to catch some grief!

On the porch, Daniel and Flora just stood there awkwardly, looking everywhere but at each other, the tension thicker than molasses on a winter morning. Finally, Flora broke the silence.

"Well, I had a lovely time tonight. Laura and Travers are such good friends."

Daniel grunted, still chaffed that Travers had not taken it upon himself to walk Flora home. They were supposed to be a couple. Even madams deserved to be walked home in the dark of night. He looked down the street to her end of town.

"Since you're lacking an escort, I'll see that you get home safely." He moved to take her arm, the abruptness of it catching her off guard. The contact startled her, and her eyes flew to his. Daniel's face was drawn into a scowl. That riled Flora to no end and she lashed out in self-defense.

"I'm perfectly capable of seeing myself home, thank you!" Her chin went up a notch, anger clipping her words. She wished he would stop frowning so as if the thought of touching her were sinful. She jerked her arm out of his grasp and before he could blink she was off the porch and sashaying down the street. Daniel hesitated but a second before he bounded off the porch and caught up with her in a few strides.

"You will let me do the gentlemanly thing here and see you safely home," he grated through clenched teeth.

Looking straight ahead, she gave an eloquent shrug of her shoulder, saying "Suit yourself."

It was a fairly quiet night, few cowboys were in town, and most of the girls appeared to be at the saloon. The only light appeared to be in Celia's room. Still, Flora went to the back entrance, leery of being seen with the schoolteacher at her front door. She fumbled for her key in her reticule, muttering to herself before she finally produced it. Jamming it into the lock, she found it wouldn't turn. She glared at it in frustration, the urge to stamp her foot rising dangerously to the surface. Daniel, seeing her frustration, stepped forward.

"Allow me."

Taking the key, he jiggled it for a moment before it moved. This time, the lock slid open easily. Flustered, Flora was glad he couldn't see the effect he was having on her. She wanted so badly for him to grab her and kiss her. It had been a long time since she had reacted this way with a man. Travers had never affected her this way, though she was physically attracted to him. She loved Travers but realized what she felt was nothing compared to what this man made her feel. He was driving her to madness. She gave him a muted 'Thank You' before opening the door to go inside. Daniel caught her hand on the knob, his body mere inches from hers, causing her breathing to stop.

"Have dinner with me tomorrow night."

She turned her head ever so slightly to find his lips a breath away. She tore her eyes from them to find him watching her, his eyes unreadable in the dark. Her mouth had gone too dry for words, so she gave a slight nod of acceptance. He seemed to deflate with relief, she thought. Hmmm. Maybe she was affecting him more than she thought. Daniel stepped back and let her close the door, thinking she looked somewhat bemused in the dim light coming from inside. When the door closed on her, he turned and headed home. Tomorrow night he would find out what was on her mind.

* * *

The next day, Travers was headed out of the post office when he literally bumped into Maggie. She began to stumble and reacting quickly, he grabbed her around the waist to steady her. Her bonnet slid back over her head revealing her carefully coiled tresses, the scent of it coursing through him, forcing intimate awareness that he could little stand at the moment. The second he touched her he had felt her tense up, and her eyes remained chest level. For some reason, she would not look at him.

"Maggie? Everything alright?"

Flustered, she stepped back before informing him, "I'm fine. You really should watch where you're going. You seem to make a habit of bumping into people."

Travers let an easy grin spread across his face. "Well, as long as I have a lovely lady such as yourself to catch each time, I'll continue to make a habit of it," he drawled sensuously.

Heat suffused her cheeks, and she turned to flounce off, stopping short to adjust her bonnet.

"Maggie, how's the honeymoon?" It really wasn't meant to be a goad, but he couldn't resist. She froze, her back to him and she went straight as a board.

"It's wonderful. Thank you for asking," she muttered as she hurried away, her gown swaying with the swiftness of her step. Her body language told a different story from the one he had just received. Things were not wonderful between the newlyweds and anyone with a good eye could see that. He must find the time to get her alone and talk to her once more. Divorce was an ugly word, and he didn't like to think of himself promoting it, but Maggie had grounds for it. He meant to show her what life could be like for the two of them. She had not believed him when he told her that he loved her. This time, he would make sure that she knew it was fact. He watched until she entered the dress shop and then made his way to his clinic.

* * *

Laura was laughing at her. Laughing! She had come to offer her support when Flora had told her about her date with Daniel. Upon seeing the state Flora was in, Laura had convulsed with laughter. The madam had emptied out her trunk, her closet, her chest of drawers, all the contents piled onto the bed. She had nothing to wear! She was standing there in her bathrobe, her bottom lip clenched tightly between her teeth. This was not good! And Laura, her best friend in the world was laughing at her!

"Will you shut up, already! I have to get dressed! Help me!"

Laura snapped to attention, her smile magnanimous. "Flora, you're in love."

Flora whirled around. "What! I am not—"

"Yes, you are! From the moment you laid eyes on him, you've had stars in your eyes. This is rich. Even you must see the humor in it. The madam and the schoolteacher. What an unlikely pair!"

Flora was getting more flustered by the minute. "I fail to see the humor in this! I have a date, my first date in years I might add, and you are proclaiming that I'm in love! Hogwash! I'm simply, irresistibly attracted to the man is all. And I have no idea what to wear! Nothing fits, nothing works!" She threw her hands up in agitated frustration, "That's it. I'll just have to cancel. He'll understand. I'll just cancel, and that is that."

Laura moved to stand next to her friend. "You will *not* cancel. You deserve this night. You have so many wonderful dresses, something will work. We'll make it work. It's just nerves, Flora. Calm down. Here, how about this one?" She held up the royal blue and gold dress that was her favorite. "This one looks divine on you."

"I don't know. It seems a little much, don't you think? I'm not going as my alter ego, you know. I simply want to be me tonight."

"Ahhh. But you still want to look your best, don't you? Perhaps downplay your fire a bit, something a little more practical. Why don't you wear this? It's crisp, demure and I think if you wore your hair down, it would be just the thing." Laura was examining a sleek, black suit and white blouse. Flora came closer to examine it, thinking Laura might have something there.

"I like it. Will you help me with my hair? I think I'll put a bit up and let the rest fall free. Laura, I don't want to blow this night. It's the first real date I've had in years. And Daniel, well, I don't want to lead him on if there's nothing there, you know?"

Flora was hopeless. She was head over heels and from the looks of things, Laura figured there was mutual feeling on Daniel's part. Flora was a born flirt, no two ways about it. She knew what men wanted, but for too long, she had never stopped to consider what *she* wanted. Laura figured that it was high time her friend deserved a bit of happiness for herself. She was just so happy for her.

"Sure, I'll stay, honey. I'll even wait up for you if need be, in case you want to talk afterward."

"Thanks, Laura." They got Flora dressed and fixed her hair, and as they were putting on the finishing touches of a bit of perfume, Tandy came knocking.

"He's waiting downstairs. My, don't you look — different."

Flora frowned. "Good or bad — different?"

Tandy smiled. "I'd say *very good* — different. You're gonna blow him away, Flora."

Flora's smile could have been seen for miles. "Thanks, sweetie. That's the idea."

She hugged Laura and Tandy and hurried downstairs.

He was waiting by the front door. He looked uncomfortable in a three-piece suit of black worsted, and he kept tugging at his collar as if the tie was too tight. He looked up and saw her on the stairs, and she could see him take a deep breath. He looked so nervous, she almost ran back upstairs. Then he smiled at her, and her heart did little flips flops in her chest, and she smiled softly back at him. She somehow made it down the stairs, and he met her at the landing.

"Flora. You look very nice."

Very nice. That was not quite what she had hoped for, but she kept the smile on her face. This was going to be a long dinner, she thought. He offered his arm, and they strolled across the street to the hotel.

At the hotel restaurant, they were seated and brought drinks. Flora asked for coffee, and Daniel asked for red wine. Each seemed as nervous as the other.

Daniel couldn't seem to take his eyes off of the redhead. She seemed different tonight. Almost as if she had cloaked herself in a different persona. She smiled shyly, her eyes darting at him before darting nervously about the room. What was she so nervous about? She had literally peeled one of her fingernails off.

"What say we try the veal? I hear it's delicious." Daniel folded his menu and studied her as she pondered the menu, a knot between her eyes. She folded the thing and agreed that the veal sounded fine to her.

"This is nice, having a free night. We've been so busy at the house lately that I've had little time to myself." It was Flora's attempt at small talk. Unfortunately, the topic was not a good one. Daniel's brow furrowed. He attempted to change the subject.

"I take it you enjoy the lessons at school. Am I to understand that you didn't receive much in the way of an education?" Another flub. He had not meant it to sound as if he thought her to be dumb, but after saying it could have kicked himself. Because that was how it had to have sounded to her. Her furrowed brow indicated that she must be thinking that very thing. The date was not going well.

"No, I didn't. I was always good at numbers, though. Had to be. Had to know when I was getting cheated. I had a knack with figures." Flora decided to volunteer that information, hoping that the conversation would steer another direction.

"You seem to love kids."

Flora smiled. "I do. You?"

"I'm a schoolteacher, aren't I? Ever thought of having any of your own?"

"Maybe," she sighed. It had been something of an elusive dream for her. She had always wanted children. Her lifestyle could have, should have provided her with plenty, but Flora couldn't bring herself to conceive that way. The job was stressful enough without a child to look after. So she had waited for the right man to come along. A man like Daniel.

He saw the wistfulness in her eyes. "Why didn't you?"

"What?"

"Why didn't you have any kids of your own?"

"It just never seemed the right time, I guess." He was delving into an area that was a little touchy to her. She knew what he was thinking. He thought that she had him nailed to father her children In a sense he was right. She was wildly attracted to Daniel. She would love to have his children, but she wanted a relationship, an understanding built on love, trust. He was looking at this from a totally different perspective, she knew.

Daniel was getting uncomfortable. He was getting the vibe that she felt she had found the man to settle down with. He shifted in his seat, his necktie seeming to choke him.

"And you? No little ones in your future? Or past?"

"No. I tend to travel a lot. Not conducive to family life."

Silence fell then lingered. And lingered.

Flora prayed their food would hurry and arrive. It did. Ten minutes later.

She startled Daniel then with a most unusual thing. She asked him to give thanks for their meal. The schoolteacher looked as if he had been slugged.

"What's wrong?"

Daniel shifted under her gaze. "Well, I just find it a little surprising that the town madam would like to offer thanks to God for her dinner."

Flora looked miffed. "I do fear God, Daniel. I also go to church. I know that it is only through His divine intervention that I wound up in Gold City. Do you honestly think me so jaded that I cannot give God thanks for my dinner? Is that how you really see me? As a heathen who cares for no one but herself?" Her eyes were clouded, demanding an answer.

Daniel squirmed. She had nailed him. "I really don't know, Flora. You just surprise me at times, is all. I don't really know you that well. I just figured that a woman of your—reputation—"

"Reputation? And what reputation is that? That I'm a whore? Of course, I am. I own the biggest cathouse around. I *must* be a whore. Here I thought I was pulling the wool over your eyes."

She smiled at him then, sadly. Diving into the food that had once looked so appetizing before but now had the consistency of ash, she avoided conversation with him again. The meal passed in uncomfortable silence, Daniel not realizing how he had cut her with his assumption about her. She had hoped to tell him about her life now. He didn't appear interested. He didn't speak again until their waiter had taken the plates away.

"I'll see you home."

"Oh, there's no need. I'm just going across to Laura's."

"I can still see you to Laura's."

"Don't bother." She rose, and he did the gentlemanly thing and rose as well. She brushed past him and darted out the door ending the worst date of her life. Irritated and out of sorts, she opted to go home instead of to Laura's as she had told Daniel. In her suite back at the house she realized with chagrin that for the first time in a really long time she had failed to give thanks for her dinner.

◆———◆———◆

Maggie Bowers was not having a good night either. Jim had come home drunk. He had been to Dodge on business and had finished off a fifth of whiskey with Sam Bailey on the ride home. The two had barely been able to sit their horses when they had ridden in hours before. Bailey had slithered off his horse and pulled Jim from his, shuffling him through the front door, knocking the coat tree over in the process, waking Maggie who had been asleep on the couch. They were unconcerned that it was after midnight and might wake her or anyone else for that matter. She remained on the couch, attempting to remain as inconspicuous as possible to the two men. Bailey dumped Jim in a nearby chair and turned to leave, stopping short when he saw her cowering there. His lips turned up in a greasy smile, and his eyes darted to his boss before starting towards her, his intent not to be borne. Maggie flew off the couch and up the stairs, hearing the cumbersome tread of Bailey just feet behind her. Thankfully, he had to pass his employer, who threw his leg out, blocking the path of the foreman. The man went headfirst into an expensive Chinese vase that Bowers had bought in Georgia, sending it crashing to the floor into several pieces.

"I think you best be gettin' out of here, Sam. The wife and I have business tonight."

Sam gathered himself sullenly off the floor and made for the door. His boss wasn't so drunk he couldn't give orders. He cursed under his breath as he lumbered outside. The woman was getting under his skin, and he wanted a taste. But his time would come. He could be patient.

Jim sat up, rubbing his throbbing, whirling head. He managed to get to his feet and made his way upstairs where he found his wife had locked herself in her room. Shaking the doorknob, he called out to her, "Open up, Margaret. Your husband is home."

Maggie sat in the middle of her bed, her fear turning to relief upon hearing her husband's voice on the other side of the door.

"Go to bed, Jim. It's late, and you're drunk."

"Open the door, Margaret. I need to speak with you. Now."

Maggie climbed off the bed and went to stand by the door. "Jim, I'm tired. I waited up for you, and it's after midnight. We can talk in the morning."

"We will talk now, Mrs. Bowers!" He stepped away from the door and raising his foot gave the panel a mighty kick for one so soused. The doorframe splintered and the door flew open, hitting Maggie in the shoulder even as she dodged the panel as it flew inward. She staggered back, her hand grasping the injured area.

"What on earth! Have you lost your mind?"

"Just found it, actually. I believe it's high time that you understood that you belong to me, wife."

Maggie frowned, not liking the tone of his voice. A frisson of fear ran the length of her.

"Of course I belong to you, Jim. I married you, didn't I?"

"Oh, you married me alright. But you don't respect me, do you? What, no answer? Come here, wife."

Maggie backed away even as he advanced. "Jim, you're drunk. Don't do something you're going to regret."

"I have no intentions of regretting a thing, darlin'. Now come here."

"I won't."

"What did you say?" His eyes pinned her.

"I—I won't."

He moved like lightning, grabbing her by the hair and held her within a hair's breadth from him.

"Don't you ever tell me no, darlin'. Ever. When I say jump, you ask 'how high?' You got that?"

"Jim, you are hurting me." She struggled against the punishing hold he had on her, his fingers digging into her cheeks now.

"I am the head of this household. Do you deny that? You refer all decisions, all business transactions through me. You will submit to me as your husband, Margaret. And that means whatever, whenever and where ever I so desire."

Maggie almost laughed, would have if he didn't have such a painful grip on her.

"Yes, Jim."

Apparently, he wasn't so drunk as to miss the disdain in her voice.

He released her only to send his fist into her stomach. She stumbled back, the wind knocked out of her, doubled over in pain, but she didn't hit the floor. That in itself seemed to anger him. Before she got over the punch to the gut, he backhanded her across the face, sending her reeling. Her lip was cut and bleeding. Maggie closed her eyes against the pain, wondering how far he would take matters this time. He had never done more than threaten her before, but this was over the top. She prayed he would wind this up quickly. She knelt there on the floor on her knees, her head bowed in submission. It helped. Jim took it that he had gotten the message through to her and walked away. He didn't see the slight figure that lurked in the shadows of the hallway as he stormed to his rooms down the hall. When the door closed behind him, the figure separated itself from the darkness of the shadows.

She was lifted into arms that had a bit of age but still had steel in them and carried to her bed. She didn't even bother to open her eyes, her senses telling her it was Slim even as he went to try to repair the door so she could have some privacy. In a few minutes, he was back, this time with a wet cloth that he applied to her swelling face and lip. She winced at the touch.

"Easy, now. Don't have much to help the swelling but got some laudanum to help you rest. You need it, Ms. Margaret," he told her when she would have argued with him. She hated the taste of the stuff. But she feared he was right. She would have pain tonight. Her stomach already felt as if an elephant had stepped in it. Her face, well, she might have fared better falling down the stairs. But Slim was there to help. He cared, even if no one else did. She let him give her a big dose of the white liquid and found that he was right. Within minutes she was out like a light.

TWENTY-EIGHT

The night of the dance turned out to be quite pleasant. A gentle breeze stirred the branches of the shade trees and lent a little relief from the sweltering heat. It had showered earlier in the day, and that had helped to cool things a bit as well. Travers was standing near the gate wondering why on earth he had allowed Laura to talk him into coming here. Couples were already on the dance floor, their laughter contagious as they twirled past him. The vision of Daniel and Flora sweeping past him caught his attention. Flora was gazing up at the schoolteacher, her heart in her eyes. Daniel was doing his best to appear bored, though how he could was beyond Travers. Flora looked quite lovely in a fawn colored skirt with a matching peplum blouse, cinched tightly with a wide, colorful silk sash. Travers shook his head. The man needed a good kick in the rump. Poor Flora was all but throwing herself at the man and Daniel was playing hard to get. He was going to have to have a heart to heart with his friend it seemed. It was wrong of him to do Flora this way. She deserved better.

Clayton was talking to him again.

"I'm sorry, what was that you say?"

Clayton grinned, nodding at Daniel and Flora.

"He's a jughead. Dancing with the purtiest woman out there and looking the way he do."

"Yeah, he's giving her a hard time. I'm going to have a talk with him about it. Soon."

Clayton snorted and chuckled.

"Well, while yore at it, thump that ridiculous look off'n his face and tell him I told you to."

Travers chuckled as well. Daniel wasn't an easy man to talk to these days, let alone thump, but he humored Clayton with a clap on his back and excused himself to wander over to where Laura was sitting alone.

"What's this? No line of beaus clamoring for a dance?"

Laura smiled. "I sent them all packing. They've got nothing I want."

"Oh come now, surely one of them has caught your eye."

Laura just crossed her arms and shook her head. "Not a one."

Travers pulled up a crate and sat down beside his friend.

"Well, you'd make a good wife for any man here. You're a

damn fine cook and keep a clean house, that's for sure."

"What makes you think I need a husband, Travers Gage?"

He paused a moment, sensing a bit of temper in that question. Her eyebrow was arched expectantly, anticipating his response.

"Well . .er, every woman desires a good man they can depend on. Someone they can grow old with."

Laura sat ramrod straight. "So why should I be any different?" She flung her hand around agitatedly. "Well, let me tell you a thing or two, Dr. Gage. There are very few men that I respect in this world, you being one of 'em. I don't need a man to validate me. I'm a woman alone who enjoys being in charge of her own life. I make my own money, am independent and have good friends to boot. Now you tell me, why do I need a man?"

Travers had watched her throughout her tirade. She was animated and honest. He thought he would throw her a tidbit to gnaw on.

"To keep you warm at night?"

She produced a smug little smile. "That's what flannel gowns are for."

He burst out laughing then, and she did too, despite herself. There was an ease between them, like family, and each of them realized it and knew it for what it was. Travers reached and took her hand in his, patting it.

"You're a gem, Laura, and right as always. You know what you want for yourself which is more than most folks do. But I got a feeling, someday, some man is going to come along and change your point of view."

Laura smiled and snorted very unladylike. "Horse pucky."

The dance was in full swing, and the entire town and the folks from the surrounding area had turned out in droves. Maggie and Jim Bowers had arrived late with the hired help in tow. Maggie seemed to be even more remote this evening, Travers thought. He had not had the chance to speak to her yet but made a mental note not to let the evening pass without doing so.

He was watching Clayton, and Sarah cut a jig when he was grabbed from behind. He pulled the perpetrator around, knowing exactly who it was before seeing the unbound russet tresses. The music had just ended, and this time the musicians struck up a hauntingly beautiful waltz. Flora began to pull him towards the dance floor. He began to protest mightily. Flora stopped, took one look at his features and hissed under her breath, "Travers Gage, you are going to dance with me even if I have to throw a fit to get you to do it."

The way she had her hands planted on her hips and the look in her eyes told him she would do just that. He suppressed a groan, knowing he would never hear the end of it now. Taking her hand, he led her into the midst of the other couples, and with a deep swirl they spun away causing Flora to laugh gaily up into Travers' eyes. It had been a long time since he had waltzed and Flora was a very adept partner. They seemed to float across the floor, and people began to take notice. Travers could feel the stares and turned his gaze upon his friend.

"Everyone is staring at us."

"Good," she smiled back.

"It's a little unnerving."

Flora moved closer, their bodies touching and she stretched to whisper in his ear. "Are *they* looking?"

"They?"

"The only two people you and I need be concerned about."

He knew instantly what she was about. He raised his eyes to scour the crowd. A grin spread across his face, and he leaned closer, his arms tightening around her. If she wasn't sly . . .

"Most definitely."

Flora returned his smile.

"Oh, that's just wonderful," she sighed.

Travers threw his head back and laughed. To everyone else, it seemed he was truly enamored with the lovely madam. Inside he was dying. Daniel was finally getting a taste of his own medicine, and from the look on his face, it was a bitter pill to swallow. Maggie, on the other hand, was standing there watching them with the appearance of stone. He got the impression she was staring through them, not at them. She was standing alone, a glass of punch held in her hand untouched. Her husband was engaged in conversation with a few of the men from town, but he was keeping a close eye on his wife that was for sure. Maggie didn't look well, and that bothered Travers. He kept the smile plastered on his face for Flora's benefit but made a mental note to seek Maggie out later in the evening.

The moment the waltz ended, both Flora and Travers were swarmed by would be partners. Travers, however, made his excuse and headed for the punch table only to find his path blocked by Daniel.

"So, you and Flora seemed to be having a good time." Daniel's face was turned down into a scowl.

"Why, yes. Flora and I always have a good time when we're together. She just seems to have that effect on people."

Daniel's face darkened if that were possible since his face already looked like a thundercloud. "I hear she's been trying to get you into her bed for quite a while now. I guess she finally succeeded."

Travers looked at the man he had long called a friend. Shaking his head, he put his thoughts into words.

"You know, to be an educated man, you've got to be one of the dumbest when it comes to women."

Daniel stiffened and stepped forward belligerently.

"Just what the hell are you saying?"

Travers sighed and turned to walk away, leaving Daniel to ponder his parting remark.

"You figure it out."

The spread the ladies had prepared for the night was to die for. Travers had already sampled a variety of the dishes and was on his way to filling his second plate of the night when Clayton and Sarah joined him at the buffet as well. The two of them had put on quite a spectacle on the dance floor performing a lively square dance. Poor Clayton had the appearance of a chicken when he danced, and the crowd had roared and clapped, cheering them on. Those two had certainly worked up an appetite from the looks of the food going onto their plates.

Travers suppressed a chuckle. "Now, slow down there, Hoss. This spread wasn't meant to serve us two-legged creatures *and* our livestock. I don't recall that horse of yours liking fried chicken and apple pie." Sarah guffawed at that and tried to cover her plate, shielding the towering mound of food from Travers, who peered smiling over her shoulder.

"Ain't no horse gonna see any of this here food. This is how a *man* eats, Doc."

The big black man thrust out his chest and grinned.

Travers gestured at the man's plate. "You eat all of that, you gonna be as *big* as that horse of yours."

Sarah came to his defense. "Well, that's alright by me. I happen to like my men big. Ummm, um, ummm!"

"Why, Sarah!" Travers blushed at the look in Sarah's eyes, and she covered her face with her hand, giggling like a schoolgirl, startling even herself with that last remark.

Clayton just shook his head and smiled. "You stepped right into that one, hoss."

They found a table with a few seats left nearby and joined their neighbors. Travers got halfway through his food and wondered what on earth he was going to do with what he realized he couldn't eat. He listened to the chatter going on around him, responding when necessary. His mind had begun to wonder, though. Across the way, he had gotten another look at Maggie. She didn't appear to have spoken a word all night. He decided it was time to saunter over and pay his respects. He asked Sarah to cover his food for him. He had decided to take it home with him. He hated to waste what he couldn't eat at the moment. He excused himself from the table and wandered over to where

Maggie stood so still. She was thin. Her profile was almost gaunt.

"Maggie?"

She practically jumped at the sound of his voice. She had not heard him approach, and his nearness made her uneasy.

"Hello, Travers." Her voice seemed a mere whisper.

"Lovely night, isn't it?"

She nodded.

"Yes, it turned out to be a lovely night after all." She had feared the heat would make things unbearable, but it had cooled a bit after the shower they received earlier in the afternoon. They stood in silence for a while, each watching the dancers, their thoughts digging up the past.

"How are you, Maggie? I haven't seen much of you lately." His voice was low, inquisitive without prying.

Keeping her eyes on the dancing mass before her, she shrugged. "You know how it is. One just gets busy with everyday life."

"Mmmm. And your new husband. How's he treating you?"

There was a rigidness to her now. She was on guard. "Like a queen." She turned to face him then, and there was a look of resignation on her face. She looked tired. Her eyes didn't have that gleam that he always remembered. Something was wrong.

"Are you ill, Maggie? You don't seem yourself tonight."

Maggie sighed, turning partially away again. "Travers, go away."

A voice broke in from behind.

"Yes, Dr. Gage. Do go away. I believe you have harassed my wife long enough this night." There was an edge to Bowers' voice as he moved to take his wife roughly by the arm. Maggie winced visibly, and Travers took a step forward to intervene but caught himself. Let the bastard do what he would in public. The town would have a fit if they knew he was mistreating his wife. He hoped he wasn't the only one who saw the exchange. He wasn't. The sheriff and Mrs. Tate had also noted the rough handling. The sheriff stepped a little closer and commented,

"I'd watch how I handled my wife, mister. We treat our women with respect around here. Including the 'working women' in this town. You're pert near close to stepping over the line. The least of punishments for such a crime in these parts is tar and feathers. I think, in this case, however, we could do a lot of assuming' and dole out the maximum. I get the feelin' you're extremely fond of necktie parties. Perhaps we'll throw *you* one."

The sheriff was deadpan and right on target, his boldness burning Bowers' blood. His face turned almost purple, his hand nearly cutting off the circulation in Maggie's arm. She remained dead still, however, not wanting to draw any more attention to herself. The night would not be a pleasant one.

Travers noted how pale Maggie had become.

"Maggie, perhaps you'd better come to the clinic tomorrow. If you're ill—"

Bowers thrust himself between the two, shielding Maggie from Travers' perceptive gaze.

"My *wife* is none of your concern, Doctor. You had best learn to keep your nose out of matters that don't concern you." His voice was low, measured for control.

"*Maggie*," Travers goaded, "does concern me. She's my friend. I only meant to inquire as to her health. If she is physically ill, she needs medical attention. A husband should know that, and with you being a man of *wealth*, I would think you shouldn't hesitate to see that she received the best of care."

Bowers was in his face now. "You bastard! You stay away from my wife! I'm warning you. You step out of line just once with her, and you'll be sorry the two of us ever met."

"You're the one stepping out of line here, Bowers. I find out you're responsible for her ill health, in any way, and you and I are going to settle up. You newlyweds have a lovely evening." With that parting remark, Travers sauntered away.

Later in the evening, Travers got another chance to speak to Daniel about Flora. He corralled him away from all the simpering young ladies vying for his attention. They were reluctant to let him leave, and Travers looked back at the six or eight ladies who continued to hover nearby.

"Looks like you've got yourself a small entourage there, hoss. You planning on building a harem?"

Daniel sighed, grinning magnanimously, patting himself on the chest. "Well, you know how it is. I can't seem to beat them off with a stick."

"Well," Travers murmured thoughtfully. "That's unfortunate for them because as of tonight, you are off the market." He smiled and gave his friend a hearty slap on the back, his eyes panning the crowd nonchalantly.

Daniel looked at his friend as if he had just lost his mind. "I beg your pardon?" His brows were drawn, and his mouth pursed sourly.

"From this moment on, you will dance with no other woman save Flora. And you will talk to her and treat her with respect. Then you will escort her home where you will give her a chaste kiss goodnight but not before making a date for a picnic next week. Then you will play the gentleman and leave."

Travers' little matter of fact speech had Daniel's eyes practically popping out of his head. Before the doctor even finished, Daniel was sputtering, shifting from one foot to the other, crossing his arms, waiting for the good doctor to finish. When he did, Daniel let fly, his arms akimbo.

"I'll have you know that I am not off the market! And anything that goes on between Flora and me is none of your business. Actually, it should be since the two of you are supposedly involved. She's been throwing herself at me. Apparently, you've not been keeping the home fires burning, Trav. She's looking for a husband, that's what she's doing, and figured you weren't going to make a move anytime soon. Well, I'm not husband material. I enjoy her company, but she can be a little too—much—if you know what I mean. She stares at me with those mesmerizing green cat eyes of hers, and it's rather unnerving. She's always baking cookies for the kids and bringing them to school. She loves those kids, I know, but she's well, she's always there, and sometimes she makes me so angry that I just want to wring her lovely little neck. One minute she's hot, the next she's cold and ignores me, and then I really want to wring that porcelain neck of hers." Daniel's hands made the motion of surrounding a neck and squeezing. Travers just let him ramble on. This was getting interesting.

"She's so damn beautiful, God help her, that sometimes, I don't think she even knows it. She can walk down the street and every man in town, married or not, goes out of his way to tip his hat to her, open doors for her, speak to her, which I'm sure sets the other women on fire. And she acknowledges them all, even though she doesn't really flirt with them, she just, well, everyone knows what she is!"

Daniel paused to catch his breath, but before he could continue, he realized that Travers had gone stiff and was looking beyond him. They were no longer alone. Turning slowly, he found Laura and Flora had come up behind him and had heard the last of their conversation. Flora seemed frozen for a moment, her eyes huge in her face. Then her eyelids lowered, and a sensuous smile plastered itself to her face, and she looked Daniel in the eye.

"Why, indeed they do, Mr. McCullough." She walked closer to him, her hips swaying, her accent as southern as pecan pie. "Every man in this town knows that I own the only whorehouse for miles, and my girls, well, they do know how to treat a man. After all, they learned from the best." Her voice had lowered seductively, her lids hovering so low her lashes fanned her cheeks. She was a breath away from him, but for all her sugary words, Daniel knew it was a facade. She hovered close only seconds longer, then without looking at him, turned and walked away.

He watched her go, her spine stiff for about fifty paces, her head held high, then she seemed to wilt like a lily in the summer heat. She kept going, never looking back.

Travers and Laura had watched in silence, knowing instantly when she had transformed back into Starr. She was only Starr inside her place, Flora about town and to her friends. And to Travers and Laura, it was very apparent that Flora felt that Daniel would never accept her as anything other than the town madam. He considered her a whore. Thus, from that moment on, that was the only persona he would ever see from her. Laura looked at Travers who nodded for her to go after their friend. She hurried away, her dress thrown up before her, throwing Daniel a glare as she went. Daniel looked at Travers, noting the naked anger he saw in his friend's eyes.

"Wha—"

He never got to finish, Travers' fist sending him staggering back, his lip pouring blood.

"On second thought, stay away from her. You don't deserve her." Travers clenched and unclenched his fists in anger before stomping away. The party was beginning to break up now, and few people had witnessed what had transpired between the two men. Travers didn't care. Daniel had deserved it. Even if Daniel had spoken the truth about Flora, a gentleman never spoke about a woman so carelessly. Travers had learned long ago, never to judge people until he had walked in their shoes for a while. Appearances were often deceiving. Flora was a sure fit into that category. She may have served her time on her back, but she was a lady as far as this town was concerned. That was the reason the men went out of their way to tip their hats to her. And the women were not jealous of her. They were angry at themselves for lacking the courage and strength that she exhibited in adversity. Damn, but the temptation was strong to seek Daniel out and punch him again.

He changed his direction, having been headed to Flora's, heading to his office instead. Somehow, he didn't think Flora would welcome the company of any man right now. He poured himself a whiskey from the bottle he kept for medicinal purposes, held the glass for a moment, just looking at it, thinking maybe, —oh what the hell, and downed it in a gulp. He was in a foul mood. The episode with Flora and Daniel had been the icing on the cake of a sorry evening. It had not started out that way, but then the scene with Maggie and Bowers had certainly been enough to dampen anyone's jovial mood. And now this. Daniel would not forget easily, he knew. The man was thick as mud when it came to women. Travers was sorry to have it come to this.

• — • — •

Laura caught Flora as she was headed upstairs to her suite. "Flora?"

The redhead stopped on the fourth step and turned slowly. Her eyes were rivers of tears, and her lower lip trembled ever so slightly. She was a woman who prided herself on her self-control, but for once she felt shattered. Laura mounted the stairs, joining her friend there, placing her arms around her shoulders and led her up to her quarters. Once inside, she pushed her into her favorite overstuffed chair and set about making some tea. Within minutes they were sharing a pot of tea. Laura produced a clean handkerchief as Flora was weeping silently.

"He'll never accept me, Laura. He's got in his head that I'm not good enough for him. Maybe, maybe it's true."

Laura snorted. "Horse shit! That man is the biggest jackass I've ever met! Don't ever let me hear you say that you're not good enough for any man. I know better and so do you."

"I guess I knew it was too good to be true, that he would actually be interested in me. We have nothing in common. He's educated; I'm not. Street smarts is what I've got. It's the only way to survive out here when you have nothing." Flora gazed down into the dark liquid in her china teacup, her thoughts as dark as the drink.

"Flora, I think that his reaction was fear. I think he really cares about you, else he wouldn't seek you out so often. He's afraid of his feelings for you. It's normal in men. They're such babies when it comes to relationships."

"I don't know, Laura. He seems pretty determined to steer clear of anything deeper than friendship. Maybe it's me, trying to rush things. Am I? Trying to rush a relationship with him? Am I so obvious that it appears I'm chasing him?"

Laura smiled behind her teacup. "Flora, all anyone has to do is look at you when you look at him. You are in love. Apparently for the first time in your life. The fifty thousand dollar question is, does Daniel love you? I've learned that sometimes in life, one has to be careful and not show their hand too early in the game. I think maybe you jumped the gun on this one. You need a new tactic. The trick is to let him think you're over your 'infatuation' of him. He'll get curious, and start wondering if he's lost his charm. He'll seek out other women for the express purpose of building his self-esteem back up, but soon that won't work. It won't salve his ego. You have a lot of power here, Flora. He took an immediate shine to you when he got to town. That should mean something. The spark is there. Eventually, he'll discover that all those women can't fill the void that has developed in his heart. He'll get to wondering what happened, why you don't still seek out his company. And he will make his move, then. When he thinks you've lost interest. But you have to learn to play hard to get. That's what men want. They want to do the chasing."

Flora began to smile. Perhaps she had been going about this the wrong way. It was time to change her tactics. She and Laura plotted deep into the night.

———◆———

Back at the hotel, Bowers had seen Maggie to her room. Taking the key from her, he unlocked the door and ushered her roughly inside. She jerked away from the bruising hold he had on her arm, rubbing the now tender spot, knowing that in the morning it would be black and blue. She kept her back stiff, her eyes averted from him, hoping that if she ignored him long enough, he would go away. Not this night.

"How long has the Doc been sniffing at your heels?"

Maggie rolled her eyes, an exaggerated sigh escaping her tense body. She just closed her eyes and shook her head.

"You're imagining things, Jim."

"I don't think so," he said, slapping his riding gloves against his leg, coming closer. "I've heard the way he calls you 'Maggie,' slaughtering your given name. His voice goes soft as butter when he addresses you." He studied her intently for a moment, her rigid form with her profile to him.

"Exactly how well did you know this 'childhood friend'? Did you sit on his lap and 'play doctor'?"

Maggie gasped, her eyes going wide as she swung around to face him.

"How dare you imply that he would take advantage of a child!"

Bowers moved closer, his eyes boring into hers, already damning her without the truth.

"Did you squirm for him, Margaret? Did you whimper on his lap or did you take it like a woman?"

"I was thirteen years old, you bastard! He never touched me in any inappropriate manner," she grated between clenched teeth, looking him straight in the eye.

"Thirteen . . . umm . . . most girls get married around that age where I come from."

Maggie allowed a sneer to curl her upper lip.

"Yes, I can see why. If you're the only breed of man coming from the hills of Arkansas these days, it's understandable why you take child brides. After all, children are so gullible, so easily manipulated, so easily cowed. They tend to see the good in everyone. Even those who would break their spirit."

"All the better to train properly in the ways of pleasing their husbands." He smirked.

"You are a sick man. I'm no child. And I'm not afraid of you. Not anymore. There's nothing you could do to me now that would frighten me. I know that you're guilty as sin of getting rid of those men whose land you ended up with. You picked the wrong town to do your dirty work in. Your greed is going to be your downfall, *husband*." She sneered the moniker at him. "This town will find out the truth. And I won't have to help one little bit. Before you go spreading lies about Dr. Gage, you better remember, *you* are the one who stands to lose big here."

In a flash, he was before her, his fingers digging deep into her arms as he jerked her to him, her eyes level with his, her toes barely touching the floor. She flinched from the pain in her arms and the fury in his eyes, feeling it scorch through her.

"Careful, wife. One more word out of you and the good doctor could disappear as well. And we wouldn't want that now, would we?"

His voice was soft, almost caressing. He smiled, and she began to shudder. An eyebrow raised.

"I see I've made my point." He lowered his lips to hers and kissed her savagely, drawing blood. Then he threw her to the bed where she landed half on it, half on the floor, her skirts tangled about her.

"Sleep well, love. Perhaps you'll dream of me," he taunted as he quit the room.

She was to the door before it was shut good, turning the lock against him, her breathing uneven and labored. She stood there a moment, then dashed to the balcony door and waited. Sure enough, he exited the building and headed for the Velvet Rose. To Celia. Somehow, she knew the woman was in for it tonight. Better her than me, she thought. Better her than me. And yet a thought began to take form. The more she thought about it, the better she liked it. And tomorrow she would present that plan and set it in motion. But Travers must not know. She had endangered him tonight by riling Jim. She should have just kept her mouth shut, but she had not, unable to allow Jim to speak so vilely of Travers. She knew Travers was a man well able to take care of himself. But now, she was afraid. Jim was a man who thrived on not playing on a level playing field. Travers had tried to warn her. Dear God, she had been so blind. But now she knew, and that could cripple her with fear if she let it. Maggie was not a religious person, but that night she prayed. She was going to need all the help she could get in bringing the devil himself to heel.

TWENTY-NINE

In a month's time, the general was dead. He and Sally had stayed on in Nicholsville at the hotel and Travers had ridden out often to evaluate his patient and make things as easy on him as possible. The laudanum had helped, but the coughing spells had worsened, resulting in many sleepless nights for them. Travers and Sally had comforted each other as best they knew how as her father lay dying before their eyes. In the end, he had gone peacefully in his sleep. Travers had been grateful for that. Often he had seen people in this condition go out in terrible fashion, coughing up huge quantities of blood before drowning in it. Sally had been spared, a kindness from God no doubt. She had wept uncontrollably that night, and Travers had held her a long time. She was now alone in the world, in the same boat, he had once been in.

He felt her pain, for he had highly regarded this man as a soldier and as a friend. He had left her alone to grieve privately for a while, allowing her to say her goodbyes to her father alone. The tears finally stopped, and she took control of the matter at hand. There was the matter of a military funeral to prepare and telegrams to send. Travers had offered to handle such matters, but she had been adamant that he leave it all to her. Besides, it was what her father would have expected of her. Travers had to admit, she was handling this better than he had expected she would. Once her tears dried over the initial loss, she was through crying. She did not even weep at the funeral. She held herself with dignity, her eyes focused on some object unseen by anyone but her.

It was a nice funeral, small but in full reverence to such a prominent man as General Lawrence Sharpe. Soldiers from nearby Fort Larned had come and seen to it that he was sent off in style. The flag that they presented Sally was the one that Travers had thrown across her father years before on that day on the battlefield. Somehow it just seemed fitting that his coffin be draped with that emblem. The general had given it to Travers as a memento of courage under fire. Travers felt that Lawrence would want Sally to have it now.

They buried him on a hill in the town cemetery, under a vast Sycamore overlooking the open plains. Sally said he had commented that it might be a nice spot for that eternal sleep, a spot where one's soul could look out and see forever. Travers had commissioned a marker for him.

Gen. Lawrence A. Sharpe
1st Division, Company A
Maine
Respected Soldier, Citizen, Father, Friend

Sally had been pleased with it, smiling her thanks to him, unable to voice her thoughts over the lump in her throat. She had given Travers a crushing hug, and he had wrapped his arms around her, holding her for a long time. He had remained at her side throughout the funeral and burial, her shadow lest she should falter. She didn't. Not once. Travers admired her even more. She was indeed her father's daughter. After the funeral, he escorted her back to their room, and he saw that she was packed for travel. Concern knitted his brow.

"Sally?"

She pretended to ignore him at first, checking drawers and chests to make sure nothing was being left behind. Travers just stood quietly watching her, waiting for her to answer. She moved then to her father's valise, opened it and took a letter and wrapped package from its depths. She looked at them a long time before she spoke.

"These are for you. Father asked me to give these to you after his death. He said you were like the son he never had." She placed them on the bed, closed the valise, and finally turned to face him.

"I'm leaving. I've bought a small farm north of here. It's a nice place, plenty of land. I'll be able to support myself."

"Sally—"

She held up her hand to stop him.

"Travers, this is the best thing for me right now. I appreciate everything you have done for us. Words cannot express. I need some time to find my footing. And I'll be fine. I promise."

Travers offered a noticeable sigh. There was no point in arguing.

"So, will I get invited to dinner?" he asked, hopeful. That brought a slight smile.

"We'll see."

He walked over and stood before her, close. She didn't move, but she didn't look up either. He used the knuckle of his forefinger to lift her chin so he could see her face, look her in the eye. They stared at one another, forever it seemed, then he moved his hand to cup her cheek, sliding his hand beneath her ear and into her hair.

She wanted him to kiss her. Had wanted it from the moment she had opened the door to him that day he had walked into her life. She closed her eyes against the sweetness of his caress and

199

moaned softly, wishing, waiting.

The moan did it. Travers pulled her close, noting how soft, supple and wonderful she felt in his arms. Her arms crept about his back and held him close. The kiss, when it came was beyond anything she had ever imagined, like an ebb and flow of the heat of the sun and a cool ocean breeze. It seemed to go on and on, and Travers finally pulled away. Sally laid her forehead upon his chest, savoring the tingling still threading through her lips and body. Travers held her tightly to him, his hand caressing her back, his head resting atop hers.

"You'd better make that invitation soon."

Sally chuckled aloud and looked at him then. "Soon," she agreed and kissed him briefly on the lips before pulling away.

Travers helped her load the wagon she had waiting outside and made her promise to send word that she had arrived at the farm safely and had settled in. She paid the bill at the desk and in short order was on her way. Travers watched her go, hating to see her leave. She had become important to him, but he knew she needed this time to herself. She was a strong-willed woman who chose to be alone. She needed to be self-reliant. He considered following her but thought better of it. She might not take too kindly to that. He had best be getting back home. The town may have need of him.

———•———

In his room back at the boarding house, Travers pulled off his coat and cravat, loosening his collar as he did so. He was rolling up his sleeves when he remembered the letter and package Sally had said the general had left for him. He sat at his desk and opened the letter first.

> *To my good friend Travers Gage,*
> *Who could have guessed that a Virginian and a dyed in the wool Yankee General could have become such good friends! You are a man of noble character Travers, and the fact that you fought for your beliefs against severe opposition proves that. That fateful day on the battlefield was an act of God and no other. I have often thought of that day, and it never ceases to amaze me still. You appeared to me like an avenging angel, intent upon exterminating your fellow man for the sake of the life of a stranger. It wasn't just a matter of restoring a country. Few men, very few men that I know of would have pulled such a stunt as you did. My life has never been the same. I have learned that life is too precious to waste and have tried to encourage my daughter to live with conviction and character as well, even though in present times it may not be the popular thing to do. She is a strong woman, and I am very proud of her. She has been*

my rock throughout my illness, and we are exceedingly grateful for your help and support.

I fear she will take my death hard and it is my hope that you will continue to be there for her in my absence. She is young and eager to make her own way in this world, and I fear she may leap too soon into the fire. I ask that you be her advisor and voice of reason when need be, although getting her cooperation may prove to be a challenge. She respects you, as do I, and I know with you in her life, she cannot go wrong.

Thank you, my friend, for all you have done for me these past few weeks. You have made a sick man's passing much easier, and your company alone has been medicine for my spirit. I have taken the liberty to leave a few of my personal items in your care. One is my personal journals which I think you might find interesting and the other are some things that I happened across when my unit marched through Virginia. On closer inspection, I found that they indeed belonged to you! I hope you will be pleased with their return.

May God keep His hand on you son. Never fail to follow your convictions. I could not have loved a son more.

Yours affectionately,

Gen. Law. A Sharpe

Travers sat there, letting the man's words flow through him. The pain he felt was that of losing *his* father, and that was blinding. He had never had any really good friends, preferring to keep to himself and bury himself in his work. Frank James and Thomas Allen had been the closest to him until the general. The man's loss hurt like hell. He rose and went to the bed where the package lay. He untied the string and unwrapped the box. Inside there were four journals belonging to the general, and underneath was a treasure he had never thought to see again. A folding portfolio, charred about the edges but still whole, opened to reveal portraits of his mother and father. How on earth they had survived the fire, he would never know. And underneath was a framed 8x10 oil painting of his home. He sank to the bed and stared at the painting of the place he remembered so well, yet often couldn't remember details about. Some days the picture he carried of it in his mind was so clear, yet there were times when he couldn't even recall how many rooms the house had. It had been his parents' pride and joy and Travers had seen to it that it was kept spotless after their passing. Thankfully they had not lived to see it reduced to a pile of ash. Travers sat in his room for a long time that night, staring even as darkness fell, remembering.

THIRTY

A month passed before Travers got that invitation. When it came, it came in person. Sally caused quite a stir when she rode into town dressed in pants and tied her horse up in front of the doctor's clinic. As she dismounted, she could feel every eye in the town upon her, it seemed. She was an oddity out here. A woman in pants was not something that was seen in these parts. She tried not to let it get to her. They were just curious, after all. She straightened her back and headed for the door. Before she could take two steps, the door opened, and Travers stepped out onto the sidewalk. His grin was spread from ear to ear.

"Well, it's about time. I thought I was going to have to go calling myself to get that dinner invitation."

Sally grinned sheepishly.

"I've been busy. The place was a total mess, and I wasn't about to have visitors until I got it into some kind of order."

Travers laughed. "Point well taken. How about some lunch? I'm just about to head to get a bite to eat back at Laura's. Join me?"

"Sure." This wasn't so bad, Sally thought. She had been extremely nervous about riding in here. Not knowing what to expect from Travers, thinking maybe she had read the situation wrong. Perhaps she had read more into their kiss than he had. His warmth told her otherwise. He offered her his arm, and they walked to the boarding house, knowing that the eyes of the town were upon them every step of the way. Travers shrugged it off. He could feel the tension in Sally as they were inspected thoroughly by the people of the town. He chuckled to himself.

"Don't worry. They're really not busybodies. Just curious. They don't often see me with a companion is all. They're really good folk. Save a few."

Sally laughed, the tension flowing out of her. It helped to know that the doctor was not a womanizer. Her father had spoken so highly of him before his death. The time that she had spent with him when he had come to check on her father had given her a good idea of the sort of man he was. He was charming, in a quirky sort of way. And he appealed to her. They were both reserved individuals, yet careful to make their own way in the world. Both of them had no brothers or sisters. They were both alone in a vastly changing world. She felt solid when she was with him. And that was a welcome thing.

At the boarding house, Laura was just putting some sandwiches on the table when they walked in. Her brow arched at the sight of Sally.

"Well, hello there. I'm Laura Murphy, and Travers didn't tell me we were having guests for lunch, else I'd of put on the dog!"

Travers waved that last comment away and eased Sally closer for introductions.

"Laura, this is Sally Sharpe. She just rode into town a few minutes ago. Had no idea she was coming, or I would have given you warning. Sally, this is my good friend Laura. She owns the place, and she's an excellent cook, be it soup and sandwiches or Thanksgiving turkey. One never leaves Laura's table hungry, I can promise you that."

Laura came forward and shook the girl's hand.

"Why, you are the general's daughter. Sweetie, I have heard so much about you and your father, and I'm so sorry for your loss. Travers spoke so highly of him. I'm sorry I never got the chance to meet him."

Sally was a bit taken back by the warmth she found in the woman.

"Why, thank you. He was a great man. One who is sorely missed. Travers was a real blessing. When my father found out he was nearby, he sent for him immediately. I don't know what we'd have done without his help. He made my father's passing so much more bearable."

"Honey, Travers is hard to beat in a crisis. But you'll never hear him admit to that. No, the doc isn't one to wallow in praise."

Travers grunted at that last comment and sat down, already helping his plate. Taking a sip of his coffee that Laura brought him at that moment, he told Sally, who was still standing nervously nearby, "Grab a seat. We don't stand on ceremony around here at lunchtime. Dinner is another matter, but lunch is pretty much caught on the go."

The girl took a seat across from him and began filling her plate as well. She was soon deep in conversation with Laura and they pretty much excluded Travers from their conversation. They were swapping recipes and ideas for gardening when he finished and indicated he was about to head back to the clinic. Sally looked at him guiltily before rising to walk with him to the door.

"I didn't mean to ignore you through lunch. It's just, Laura is so nice, and I've not had any female companionship in so long."

Travers shushed her quickly, his finger gently pressed to her lips. "You don't fret one bit about that. Stay as long as you like. I know Laura would like the company. But you did forget one thing."

Sally's brow furrowed. "What's that?"

"You still failed to actually *invite* me to that dinner you promised me."

Sally laughed. "Consider yourself invited for Saturday evening at 5 o'clock. How about that?"

"Much better. But perhaps you could ask a little sweeter? Perhaps with a 'pretty please'?"

Sally leaned in and whispered in his ear ever so softly, "Pretty please?"

Goose pimples shot down Travers' neck. "That did the trick. Five o'clock sharp Saturday it is. I will be there with bells on, Miss Sharpe."

Sally laughed at Travers before giving him a soft peck on the cheek. Travers left her then, heading back to the clinic, and Sally went back inside where she spent the remainder of the afternoon with Laura.

✦━━━◆━━━✦

Someone had seen that exchange on the front porch. From her vantage point high above the street, Maggie had seen, and her heart had fallen to her knees. Watching him go about his life from afar was killing her. Travers had every right to see any woman he wanted. He didn't belong to *her*. She had no ties to him except a childhood friendship. And a love that she could not forget.

✦━━━◆━━━✦

Sally had just placed the pie in the oven when she heard the sound of hoof beats coming lazily into the yard. Smiling, she doffed her apron and patted her hair nervously. Even through the door, she could hear him speaking softly to his horse, giving him a gentle pat before knocking on the door. She hadn't meant to rush, but she opened it on the second knock, his hand still paused to strike upon the wood. His mouth stretched into a wide smile at the sight of her, noting happily that she had dressed for the occasion. Her hair was pulled back into a braided bun, a few tendrils escaping here and there to curl gently about her face. She wore a white cotton blouse that she left open at the neck and a blue gingham skirt that accentuated her slim waist. She looked truly fetching, Travers thought as he doffed his hat.

Sally had noticed the way his eyes had traveled the length of her and felt a blush rising to her cheeks. She turned away, moving to the table.

"Won't you come in? Everything's ready except dessert, but there's no rush for that. It will be done by the time we're ready for it."

Travers stepped inside the quaint little cabin, noting how efficient she had made her home. His eyes traveled back to her, noting the anxious look in her eyes.

"It's very nice, Sally. You've done wonders with the place," he told her as he shut the door behind him.

Her face brightened instantly under the praise. She had been nervous about what he would think about the place since she bought it and she could tell that Travers truly meant every word.

"Thank you. It's been a rough few weeks, but everything's coming along nicely."

Just then, Travers got a whiff of a mouth-watering aroma.

"Well, if the food is as good as it smells, I'll think I have died and gone to heaven."

She giggled happily.

"Hungry?"

"Starved." The grin he gave her said he was hungry for more than food and heat suffused her cheeks again.

She came forward to take his hat and found he wouldn't release it. They stood there for several seconds, each with a firm grip on the hat, their eyes meeting, a silent understanding passing between them. It was Travers who broke the silence.

"You look mighty fetching today, Sally Sharpe."

The husky timbre of his voice rocked her back on her heels, literally. Her eyes lowered, and she jerked the hat free, turning to place it on a peg near the door.

"Thank you, Dr. Gage. I thought it was time that I proved I do know how to dress like a proper lady." Her voice chided him gently, forcing Travers to recall the times he had teased her about her usual mode of dress consisting of men's shirts and britches. Not that Travers minded seeing her backside molded into those pants, but he had seen so little of her in women's clothing. Twice to be exact. The night they had first met, and he had stayed to take dinner with her and her father and at her father's funeral. He chuckled at her jibe and moved to take a seat at the table where she had indicated, noting the care with which it was laid.

"You *are* a lady, Sally. Clothes can't change that fact."

She came to the table with serving spoons, placing them in the bowls of food she had just placed before him. "Well, it's hard to do men's work in skirts and petticoats. Saves on the repairs, too. You men don't know how lucky you are to have such freedom of movement."

"I guess not. Then again, I've no hankering to see how the other half lives by strapping on a corset and skirts either."

Sally couldn't help herself, laughing at that picture. "I hope not."

She sat down then, and Travers offered grace. They passed the evening eating and talking, just enjoying each other's company. He helped her wash the dishes and put them away, and they moved out onto the porch where a gentle breeze stirred the air. She had two straight chairs that she kept outside for just this purpose. She had made them herself and proudly told Travers so.

"Why, Sally Sharpe, you are handy. You aren't looking for a wife by any chance?"

Sally laughed. "Lord, no!" She knew that Travers was teasing her, letting her know that he thought she could take care of herself just as good as any man. She was not looking to get tied down to any man for a while, and she hoped that Travers' interest did not lean in that direction. She liked the companionship that he offered, and he made her feel like no man ever had. But tying the knot was not high on her list of things to do. Her father, God rest his soul, had required much care during his lengthy illness. She had had little time for herself. But he had always told her, whenever the subject of marriage came up, that she must always marry for love.

"Life is too short to settle for less than you deserve. Fight for it if need be, Sally. Love is the grandest thing if it is true. It can be hell if it isn't."

She had always remembered those words. And she had determined within herself that she would not settle for less than that.

"You seem a long way away. Care to share?" Travers was smiling.

"Oh, I was just thinking about something my father used to tell me. He told me to live my life the way I saw fit, and everyone else could be damned!"

That brought a light chuckle from him. "He's right, you know. We're living in a new world, Sally. The war, it changed a lot of things. People are coming around to a new way of thinking. Life is hard enough. Living a life, not of our own making can be hell."

Sally nodded. She was never one to beat around the bush. "What do you want from me, Travers?"

He studied on that a moment before giving her the truth.

"I want to spend time with you. Get to know you. If it leads to something more, then, perhaps we could pursue it. I'm not looking for marriage. I don't think you are either. But I'm lonely. There was someone once who is now beyond my reach. I had strong feelings for her. I won't lie about that. But I'm tired of thinking about what might have been. I like you. I think you like me. Perhaps, together we can keep the demons at bay."

Sally let that sink in. "I appreciate your honesty. I do like you, Travers. You've been a constant on my mind. But I'm not ready to settle down, either. This young lady of yours was a fool, I think." She smiled at him.

She rose and took him by the hand, leading him into the house. Travers followed her, knowing she meant to get right down to business. Turning at the bed, she pulled back the covers, slowly, deliberately. Then she turned and faced him, pulled the pins slowly from her hair. Travers watched her, his breathing accelerating. Yes, he could definitely forget about whatsher-name for a while. She moved closer, her hands brushing his chest, slipping the buttons free on his shirt. He helped and found he couldn't get rid of his clothes fast enough. She forced him to slow down. They tumbled onto the bed half dressed, their passion rising like a hot August wind across the plains. She strained against him, and he found her, taking what she offered so unabashedly. He lost himself in the woman he had come to care for, this fiercely independent spirit so like himself. She refused to let him keep the upper hand. They made love all afternoon, finding comfort in each other's arms.

For once, Travers didn't feel the need to rush back to town. It was the wee hours of the morning when he managed to make it home.

THIRTY-ONE

It was late at night, and Travers was still at his clinic working on an article he was preparing concerning a special case he had come across in a patient. He was trying to get it finished so he could mail it tomorrow to be published in the next medical journal. The only light in the place was an oil lamp that he had drawn near. There were no street lamps on this side of the street, and the shadows were long and deep here. He was so engrossed in his writing that he didn't hear the knock at the door. He did hear the noise of the door clicking shut.

"Hello?" he called and got no answer.

Uneasy, he dimmed the lamp, and pulling his gun from the holster he kept hanging on the back of his chair, eased to the door that led into the waiting area. A tall figure stood there in the dark.

"Who's there?"

The figure stepped closer, cautiously, still in deep shadow.

"Hello, Trav." A step closer and Travers's eyes widened in surprise.

"Frank! Damn it all to hell! That's a good way to get yourself shot!"

The man grinned, and Travers could see that even in the darkness he looked gray.

"Well," the man responded, "it wouldn't be the first time tonight. Think you could help an old friend out?"

Travers went and secured the door, pulling the shade down as he went. He kept the gun handy and motioned for Frank to follow him into the exam room, carrying the lamp and setting it on a table nearby, turned it up to get a good look at the man. Sure enough, the man had been shot in the right shoulder. Blood streamed down his arm and covered the front of his shirt.

"Looks like you got something of a mess here. Let's take a look." Travers helped him remove his shirt. The bullet was deeply embedded. He told Frank to lie back on the table as he made quick work of washing his hands and gathering his already disinfected tools, turned to eye the man.

"By God, Frank. It's been a long time. I never expected to see you bleeding all over my clinic."

Frank James looked at his old friend and grinned.

"Yeah, well, get busy, will ya'? This thing is killing me."

He took a deep drag from the bottle of whiskey Travers

handed him.

"Ready?"

Frank nodded and braced himself.

It was deep. It took Travers ten minutes to dislodge it from near the shoulder blade. By the time he was through, Frank was white as a sheet and close to being drunk.

"Yewh! For a minute there I thought you had lost your touch," he said smiling weakly at Travers.

Travers tossed the bullet and tweezers into a basin and poured whiskey into the free-flowing wound, eliciting a sharp hiss from his patient.

"You're damn lucky to be alive, Frank. You've lost a lot of blood, my friend." Travers pressed clean linen to the wound, applying pressure.

Frank sighed. "Yeah, well, I'm sure I'll lose a lot more before I leave this sorry world."

Travers looked at the man, thinking he had aged, especially around the eyes.

"Another bank?"

Frank shook his head. "Stage."

"When are you going to give this up? Don't you understand you're not infallible? Some people 'd give anything to be known as the killer of Frank or Jesse James. One of these days, your luck may run out."

A frown crossed Frank's face.

"I didn't come here for a lecture from you."

"And I don't mean to lecture, Frank. It's just, I care about what happens to you and Jesse, whether you believe that or not. There are some folks about who still believe that you're in the right. But they're few and far between."

"Nobody stood up for us before, Trav. Nobody. What makes you think that if we gave up our guns that we wouldn't be strung up without the benefit of a trial now? The feds never gave us a second's consideration when they opened fire on my family, shooting up my mother, killing Archie and almost killing our Paw, hanging him over and over again. All *that* in front of Jesse after beating the tar out of him. He was just a kid. No, I'm covered in blood, Trav. Blood that won't wash off with a simple 'I'm sorry.' I think it's a little late for that. Don't you?"

Travers hung his head, shaking it, knowing inside that his friend was right.

"How is Jesse?" he asked as he checked the bleeding, finding it slowed. He helped Frank sit up and bandaged the wound tightly, knowing his friend was in for a hard night's ride.

"Well, he's faring better than me, that's for sure. The kid's faster than greased lightning with a gun and could find his way out of a mud storm. Sometimes I'd swear that boy is Apache. He can find places to hide that I'd never have imagined.

Travers gave a low chuckle "A true outlaw's outlaw, huh?"

Frank nodded. "Yeah."

Travers stepped back and looked at his handiwork. Satisfied with the binding, he picked up the ruined bloody shirt and tossed it into the heater. Going to the closet in his office, he produced a plain blue cotton shirt and helped Frank slip it on.

"I had a visitor a while back. Kid by the name of Deke Lowe," Travers told him as Frank buttoned the shirt, concealing the bandage.

Frank's eyes rose to meet Travers'.

"Yeah. I could have kicked that boy's butt after he told me the stunt he pulled."

"So you have seen him."

"Oh yeah. He's back in Missouri. Jesse and I sent him home. Kid ain't got a lick of sense."

Travers pulled up a stool and sat, crossing his arms over his chest.

"You're his hero, Frank. He was hoping to make a name for himself the way you and Jesse have."

"He's a kid."

"He's 19 years old. Older than some war vets are even now."

Frank was shaking his head.

"He had no business out here. He shouldn't even be carrying a gun."

"Well, now, out here, I'm afraid that's just a fact of life."

A deep sigh escaped Frank as he stared into the flame of the lamp.

"Yes, sir. That is a fact."

Frank changed the subject then, asking about Travers. They talked about what he had been doing since they had last seen each other, the war, Maggie. Travers told him that she had come to Gold City and married, though he was careful to keep the conversation light and impersonal. Frank, intuitive as he was, picked up on the undercurrent when Travers mentioned Maggie. He would have liked to deepen that conversation, but he knew time was of the essence. They had already talked for too long, and Frank rose and put his hat on his head, saying he must be going. Jesse was waiting for him just outside of town.

Travers rose as well and grabbing his hat and coat said, "I'll ride out with you. That way, if anybody sees you, well. . ."

Frank hesitated, not wanting to place his friend in that situation.

"Alright," he said finally. Frank slung his holster over his shoulder, his right arm snug in a sling.

Travers strapped on his gun, and we went to get his horse, careful to stay in shadow. In moments they were on their way. Frank led the way, and they rode in silence for about a mile when Frank pulled up.

"He's just ahead. You go on back now. No need to deliver me like some parcel."

"If it's alright, I'd like to at least say hello."

"Suit yourself," Frank said giving a shrug. They rode for several more minutes until they drew up under a cottonwood tree. A mounted figure separated itself from the base of the tree.

"Evenin' Doc." His voice was even, measured.

"Jesse. It's good to see you." Travers offered his hand, noting the hesitance with which it was shaken. It was a gunman's hand, not much different from his own, smooth, yet hard.

"You got to be taking better care of your brother, son. Seems he's getting a mite slow. Old age must be setting in."

"Slow, my ass," Frank grumbled.

Jesse chuckled then, and the tension seemed to ease. Travers loosened a small satchel he had tied to his pommel and held it out to Jesse.

"Here. Take this. I put together some things you might need: laudanum, bandages and such. Next time I might not be around when you need help."

Jesse eased his horse forward and taking the small satchel from the doc, strapped it to his horse. "Much obliged."

"Frank, you were lucky this time, coming into town the way you did. I can't guarantee your safety again. It's full of some real hard cases. Some of them would gun you down for a dime."

The tension was back.

"I won't be back Travers. I won't put you in that situation again."

Travers just looked at him.

"It's not me I'm worried about. I don't hanker to see my good friend dead from a bullet on the streets of my town, nor swinging from the gallows before a bloodthirsty mob." His voice was harsh.

Frank swallowed the lump in his throat. It had been a long time since anyone other than his brother had expressed concern for him. It felt strange, but he knew that Travers meant every word he said. They were friends. The war had not changed that, and their paths, though different, had fortunately crossed once again. He shifted in his saddle and extended his hand.

"Thanks, Trav. For everything. And I won't be back. If I should need you, I'll send word to you and use the name Wallace. Remember that weasel from Virginia?"

Lew Wallace was a neighbor of Travers' who was small in

stature and had the facial expression of a weasel. His eyes darted inquisitively and furtively about, his body language on edge like that of the creature as well, always nervous, jittery. He was a chronic hypochondriac and Frank had met him shortly after his arrival in Virginia.

Travers smiled.

"Yeah. He was a true pain in the ass. Wonder what happened to him."

Jesse grunted. "Injuns kilt him. He was headed west after the war. Got no further than Texas."

Travers had not heard about Wallace. He wondered how Jesse would know of him being killed by Indians but he knew this was not the time to broach the subject.

It was time to part. Neither seemed willing to move. Finally, Jesse set them in motion. "Frank, we got a long ways to go."

Travers eased his horse closer to Frank, and they shook hands once again, for what Travers feared might be the last time.

"Frank, take care of yourself out there."

"I will. My thanks. Again."

Travers shrugged it off. "That's what friends are for."

Frank clicked to his horse and eased away. Jesse sidled up to Travers.

"Thanks, Doc," he said, being the first to extend his hand this time. Travers grasped it firmly.

"You keep your head down out there, Jesse. And watch out for Frank. He's getting too old for this mess." The last was loud enough for Frank to hear.

"You bet." Jesse swooped his crumpled hat from his head and kicked his horse lightly, and it jumped away to follow Frank, leaving Travers there under the tree. He stayed there for a while, making sure no one from the town followed before heading back.

◆———◆———◆

The next morning, Sheriff Tate joined him as he walked into his office.

"Someone tells me you've been moonlighting as of late."

"I don't know what you mean, Ras." He knew exactly what he meant but pretended otherwise. He took a medical journal from the shelf and pretended to busy himself.

"A couple of fellers say they seen Frank James stroll into town and park it here as purty as you please last night."

Travers stopped what he was doing, looking Sheriff Tate in the eye.

"Is that a fact?"

"Yep."

"Well, I think some fellows need eye exams. If they were so convinced they saw Frank James here, why didn't they pay me a visit last night?"

Tate shrugged. "Figure they was leery of Jesse lurking about."

Travers let an understanding look cross his face and gave an "Ah." That surely explained it.

Tate shifted his stance. "So. Was he here?"

Travers gave the Sheriff a disgruntled look.

"Now, Tate. You know that I have to protect the privacy of my patients. If I had a visitor last night, the fact that he came at dark must surely imply that he wished to remain anonymous. Therefore, I am not at liberty to divulge privileged information."

"You mean yore not gonna tell me, don't you." It wasn't a question.

"That is absolutely correct."

Tate sighed. "Doc, you know I don't get into yore business much at all, but if that was Frank James here last night, it is my duty to ask you that he not present himself here again. I'd hate to think this town had anything to do with sendin' him up for all his crimes. Hell, if I were given his situation, I'd probably do the same thing. But that's neither here nor there. He's done wrong in the eyes of the law, and as a sworn lawman, I cain't look the other way. Now, thar it is. You take it an' run with it." With that, the man quit his office. Travers shut the volume before him and leaned back in his chair, studying the sheriff's parting words.

THIRTY-TWO

He ran into Rance in the general store a few days later. The young man was getting more paints, it appeared. It occurred to him that he had never gotten that portrait done that he had mentioned to Rance at the church picnic before Maggie had gotten married. He wanted a portrait of Maggie but wasn't certain if that was a good idea or even how to go about asking for one. Travers knew he should kick himself before he even opened his mouth but he didn't.

"Howdy, Rance. How's the painting coming along?"

The man pushed the spectacles up his nose and gave Travers a look that he didn't expect.

"I have orders running out my ears. I can't get finished with one before someone else is requesting one. I'm looking into opening my own studio."

"Well, that's—amazing." Travers didn't know what to say. He was a bit surprised that business was that good out here, but apparently, he had been right. A traveling photographer was hard to come by.

"Thanks for the idea, Dr. Gage. I assume I'll be getting to you before too long as well?"

"Just say the word, Rance. I'll be there with bells on."

They parted then, and Travers watched him go. It was as if a new light had come into the man's eyes. He had found his niche here, and that gave him a newfound confidence Travers could see written on every line in his face. Rance's talent had been spread by word of mouth, and that was the best advertisement in the world. Travers began to think more heavily concerning that portrait.

✦

Maggie seemed a dream to Travers. He rarely saw her these days, and that could be a good thing. He tried to stay busy and keep himself occupied with work, but Jim Bowers was a shadow that loomed persistently. No more deaths had occurred, but that meant nothing. The man had to be brought to justice. There was no statute of limitations on murder. But they had to have bodies to prove murder. That little bit of evidence seemed determined to elude the sheriff and the doctor. Thinking about Bowers led to thinking about Maggie, and that was hard on the nerves. Travers did his best to focus on the issue at hand. Finding proof.

He had no idea that the fates were conspiring against him, forcing Maggie into his circle yet again. Sheriff Tate and Louella were planning a huge dinner party and had invited several couples from the town and neighboring ranches—Bowers and Maggie included. When Erasmus had informed him of the party, he had grimaced mightily until he realized that Ras was up to something.

"The way I got it figured is to keep our friends close and our enemies closer. Louella's been after me to have some folks over. I figure it's the perfect settin'. Pretend to make nice with Mr. Moneybags. If we include him, he may get the notion that we've let go the idea that we consider him a suspect in the disappearances. Besides, Louella likes that wife of his purty well."

Travers didn't know about the idea that Bowers would fall for the wining and dining but he supposed it was worth a shot. But *he* didn't want to show up without a date. He had to show Maggie that he had moved on as well.

"Alright if I bring someone, Ras?"

"Sure. Wouldn't be that little curly headed gal I've seen about town from time to time would it?" He gave a knowing grin.

"Her name is Sally, and she and I are—seeing one another. For the time being."

Tate gave a little nod of understanding. He knew that Travers didn't dally much with the women, knew that his heart lay with the one woman he couldn't have. The truly unfortunate thing was that woman was Maggie Bowers. Dang woman. She was surely easy on the eye but hard on the heart, and she had broken the doc's clean in two. This little lady named Sally was welcomed to their table at any time if she could get the man's mind off of Margaret Bowers.

The evening was going well until Jim came unglued over a comment Maggie made. They were sitting in the parlor after a fine meal of roast duck and giblet gravy when Maggie commented that she loved duck and would very much like to learn to shoot so she could hunt duck or any other creature she so desired. It was a perfectly innocent statement, but Jim read the meaning totally aimed at him.

"I'm sorry to disabuse you the notion, but there is no way in hell that I or any other man is going to teach you to shoot. Your place is in our home, keeping it and yourself beautiful." The smile he had plastered on his face was not pleasant.

Maggie knew a moment of fear, realizing she had misspoken

somehow.

"I only meant—"

"I know what you meant, wife, and you can forget about it! After all, it is my job to see that food is kept on the table. Or are you now implying that you care not for the fare that has been afforded you thus far in our marriage?"

Maggie's head swiveled from side to side so quickly her curls met in front and back.

"Jim, that is not what I meant at all. It's just that you are gone so much—"

Before she could finish, he was on his feet, pulling her forcibly with him, uncaring that his fingers dug painfully into her arm. With a grim face, he nodded to Sheriff and Louella Tate, who by this time had risen as well.

"Enjoyed the meal, ma'am, Sheriff. We had best be gettin' back to our room. We've an early morning." With that, they were through the door and headed down the street.

Travers had risen and started to follow, but Daniel stopped him. Tate moved to stand at the door, staring at the departing couple, his hand scratching his chin.

"Now reckon what the hell that was all about?"

"I don't know, but if he so much as raises his hand to her, he's a dead man." The doctor spoke with such conviction that everyone in the room believed him. He moved to stand beside the sheriff and saw the couple disappear into the hotel, Maggie fairly jogging to keep up with her husband's long stride. Something was not right. Travers doubted the marriage had even been consummated as much as Bowers frequented Celia. Maggie must be enduring hell. And what on earth had gotten into Bowers to pull her out of there the way he had? She had not said anything untoward. Or had she? He could not think about that right now. He was at a party, with a date no less, and he should not forget that. Turning, he found her eyes on him, large and luminous, a stark realization written clearly in them.

Sally had watched the two of them all night, noting how carefully the two avoided each other, the over-polite way they spoke to one another, the way they stayed on opposite sides of the room. This was the woman Travers had loved and lost. She didn't know why that knowledge shook her so, but it did. She and Travers had always been honest with each other about having an open relationship, neither wanting to be tied down. Freedom to come and go as they pleased. Still . . .

"Sally, I must apologize."

She shook her head. "No apology is necessary, Travers," she told him, her voice low. "Don't ever apologize for trying to help a friend. Although," she added with a hint of a smile playing about her lips, "if I were in your shoes, I would have decked him!"

Travers' laughter helped to break the tense mood that had fallen over the party. An hour later, everyone finally began to find their way home. Travers walked Sally to her room at the boarding house that Laura had offered to let her use during her stay in town. There was a strain between them that had not been there before. Both knew it for what it was—Maggie had come between them. He wanted to say something, to explain, to mend this breach in their relationship that had happened so quickly.

She turned to him and rising on tiptoe, kissed him softly, her lips lingering, her hand cupping his jaw. He returned the kiss, but too late, both of them realizing his heart was not in it. She pulled away, reading the pain in his eyes. With a heavy heart, she wrapped her arms around him, pulling him close, knowing this might be the last time he would hold her. Travers knew the same feeling and held her close, breathing in the cleanness of her hair, the purity of her soul. Sally was real and open and never would allow anyone to be anything other with her. When she pulled away, he knew he had only been kidding himself where she was concerned. Maggie would always be there between them. Sally did not speak as she slipped quietly into her room. Travers stood looking at her door for several minutes before he turned and found his own room for the night.

THIRTY-THREE

Sally was washing clothes early in the day when she got a strange feeling that someone was watching her. She hovered over her work, her eyes darting in every direction, the hair on her arms and the back of her neck fairly on end now. She raked the horizon, scanning it for any living creature. On his previous visits, Travers had educated her concerning the Indians in the area—their appearance and what to expect if she ever encountered any. Something told her that today that education would be of the utmost importance. She scanned again, eyes searching, and then—there, just in back of the Beech tree. . . a figure sat a horse, watching her, unmoving. At this distance, it was hard to tell whether or not it was an Indian. Then he moved. Dear God! She had a Crow from the looks of him coming straight for her! He kept his horse at a slow, measured walk, wary himself it seemed. She froze, fear turning the saliva in her mouth to acid. Her legs felt like wood. She couldn't have moved right then if she had to. Had to. Had to move! Now! She watched him draw closer, watched him stop about fifteen feet away. They eyed one another for several long minutes, sizing each other up. Move, Sal, move!

The Indian looked weary, as did his horse, its head drooping. He had traveled a long way. Probably off scalping some innocent family of settlers, she stupidly told herself. Now is *not* the time to be flashing ideas like that in your head, Sal!! He looked around noting she seemed alone and looked at the clothing she had scattered about to dry and at the tub of dirty water. He licked his chapped lips at the mere sight of even that soapy water before looking back at her.

"You are new. Old man Parker died last winter."

He spoke English! She couldn't help but notice that his voice was rich in timbre, not what she had come to expect from these heathens, even as she realized that she could tell him to get off her land! She held her tongue, thinking that that might provoke him to violence.

"I bought the place from the land office months ago. This land belongs to me now."

She held his stare, not giving an inch. He nodded slowly. He continued to stare at her, leaving her feeling as though he had removed her clothing and was looking her over the way she imagined Southerners used to do slaves. It was uncomfortable. The horse drew her attention then, swaying slightly, his head drooping lower if that were possible. By sheer force, she made herself move, the weakness of the animal playing upon her heart. She walked to the extra bucket of water she had placed nearby for rinsing and brought it and a ladle to them. The warrior watched her keenly, his body straightening as she walked to them. The horse's ears pricked and his head rose at the scent of it, his foot stomping in anticipation. Sally walked boldly closer, noting the man's demeanor. He had tensed up.

Holding the bucket, she dipped the ladle into the fresh water and offered it to him. The Indian stared at her a moment longer before sliding awkwardly from the horse. Sally frowned, noticing his wince of pain that he desperately tried to hide. He stepped towards her, and she saw he limped. He came and took the ladle from her, careful not to touch her and before turning it up to his lips, smiled his thanks. He smiled at her. And her heart did funny little flip-flops. A heathen Indian had smiled at her and had more effect than Travers ever had. This was not good! Not good at all!

The horse nearly knocked her down. Desperate to get to the water she was holding, he nudged her shoulder forcefully, sending her staggering. She caught herself, laughing at the pitiful thing. The Indian stared at her wide-eyed as she handed him the bucket and grabbing the rope about the horse's neck, led him to the trough between the house and the stable. The animal nearly climbed into it. He drank and drank, and Sally rubbed him, taking her brush and rubbing him down, watching the powerful muscles ripple underneath its flesh. He was pure white, the color of the clouds above her. He was a magnificent animal. Almost as magnificent as his master, she couldn't help thinking. He was watching her as she worked, noting every movement she made. She could almost see his ears prick like those of his horse, so intensely was he listening to her speak softly to the animal.

Little Crow, for all his life, had never met anyone like her. She had seemed afraid of him at first, but now she acted as if he were family. She was a gentle soul. She had offered water immediately upon seeing the weariness of his horse. She was not unafraid, just cautious. He liked that. He had come here seeking water, and she had gladly given it. He would not push his luck with her. He would let his horse drink his fill, and they would push on. He still had a long way to go. He walked stiffly over to stand by her, watching her and his horse get along splendidly. A rare thing indeed. The animal usually disliked women. Had tried to bite one or two. This one seemed to have a calming effect on him. He told her so.

"He likes you. You calm him."

Sally looked up and smiled. "I think he's just so worn out and thirsty, he'd let the devil himself tend him."

"No. He's usually violent with women. You're the first he has not tried to bite."

Sally leaned over and seemed to whisper something into the creature's ear. The animal actually raised its head, looked at her for a second and shook his mane violently, sending a spray of slobber all over her. For a second, Sally stood there, her mouth open, her eyes wide with shock. Little Crow found the corners of his mouth turning up into yet another smile. He saw the look she shot him and finally burst into laughter. Within minutes, she joined him. When they finally could speak, he asked her, "What did you say to him to get such response?"

"I simply told him that I would not tolerate being bitten and if he wanted to water here ever again, he'd best mind his manners."

Little Crow laughed again. "He is a hard-headed one. But he has done well by his master. Always."

"You've come a long way. Are you from around here?" She observed.

"Two days' ride."

"Then you must be coming back from someplace far off." She was fishing, trying to find out more about him.

Little Crow knew what she was doing. He decided it best not to give her too much information about himself. Not just yet, anyway. He simply nodded in agreement with her observation. Sally realized that now was the time for introductions. She moved closer and extended her hand.

"Sally Sharpe."

The daughter of General Lawrence Sharpe. A friend to Doctor Travers Gage. She could be trusted. He didn't know the two men personally but knew their reputation. They were good men. Men of their word. She could be trusted. He had known it. His gut instinct never lied.

"Little Crow, of the Tonkawa nation," he said and shook her hand. He shouldn't have. Her hand was firm and soft, all at the same time. He dropped it like a coal of fire, noting her frown as he did so. He turned to go into the stable to get some oats for his horse, stopping short when he heard her sharp intake of breath. Turning his back to her had been a mistake. She was beside him in a second, and her hands were upon him, sending fire through his body like ribbon lightning. He swayed from the force of it as he staggered against the pain, his eyes closing against the light dancing before his eyes.

"You *are* hurt! I thought you might be. I saw that wince earlier! Why didn't you say anything?"

"And have you finish the job, white woman? I don't think so," he gritted between clenched teeth. She stomped her foot angrily at that comment and snapped, "I've a good mind to just let you ride out of here and die!"

"But you won't do that, will you?" He smiled even through the pain, unable to help himself.

Sally stood back and looked at him, her teeth playing with her lower lip.

"No. I won't. Now come into the house so I can fix you up. This may take some doing."

He grabbed her wrist and held her in place for a moment, searching her face. She stared back and then realized he must have been scanning her face for fear, placed her hand atop the one who held hers so solidly and said, "I'm not afraid of you. If you meant to harm me, you would have done so by now. Now, the question is, do you trust *me* to tend your wound? I'm afraid it may be infected. The pain of cleansing it may knock you unconscious. Do you trust me enough to let me work on you while you are oblivious to your surroundings?"

"I have little choice in the matter. You seem determined to help me."

"Oh, you have a choice all right. Let me try to help you, or you can go back out there on the plains and die slowly and painfully. I know which one *I'd* pick."

Little Crow found himself laughing under his breath again. The woman was matter of fact. It irritated him how she could elicit such response from him. He was not prone to smiles, let alone laughter. She made him feel—he wasn't sure. Laughter had not been a part of his world for a long time. Her kind had played a huge part in that fact. And yet, he found comfort in this woman. A white woman. The smile disappeared.

"I will let you tend to my wound. I feel the need for rest suddenly." He swayed again, and she gingerly thrust herself under his arm to help him inside the house. Little Crow could feel his lifeblood drain from him, making him weak as a newborn babe. She got him to the bed before he collapsed, fortunately onto it, face down, pulling her with him. He had passed out, weak from loss of blood or infection. She managed to squirm out from under his arm and careful so as not to disturb him, eased herself into a sitting position where she could view the wound.

It was bad. The clothing had been ripped away, and it appeared he had tried to tend himself to no avail. It was in such a precarious place on his back that he could not reach it. He wore a cotton weave shirt, much like the Apaches wore, with leggings and a breechcloth. His moccasins rose to his calves and had seen wear. The shirt would have to come off. Stepping away from the bed, she found her sewing box and rustled through it for scissors and needles. She found what she needed and went back outside to requisition hair from the man's horse. The animal looked at her balefully, but let her get the required items. She saw the animal had practically drunk the trough dry. He needed rest as well as his master. Leading him into the stable, she gave him the largest stall and filled his feed trough with oats and corn. He whinnied as she left, signaling that he approved of her treatment of him.

Back inside, she set about cutting away the shirt from the man Little Crow. It was a difficult task. Though ripped, it had become plastered to the wound by the dried blood and would have to be soaked off. She got a bottle of whiskey from the shelf and poured it liberally over the wound. He flinched in pain but didn't bat an eye. He was exhausted. He was a magnificent man, perfectly formed, tall, muscled in all the right places. He was nothing like she had ever seen before. A deep rich mahogany tone to his skin. He made the breath catch in her throat just looking at him. His smile had lit fires she never knew existed. Travers had made her nervous and flustered. Little Crow made her—hot. She flushed at the thought and set about trying to pry the cloth from the wound once again. It took ten minutes to free the material from what appeared to be a bullet wound several days old. A coldness settled on her. She struggled with his limp form, rolling him as best as she could, not finding what she desperately wanted to see. She had known it wouldn't be there. There was no exit wound.

She would have to dig it out. He would die if she didn't.

There was no time to reflect on the possibilities. Travers was too far to summon. Little Crow might only have minutes. She rolled her sleeves up and got to work. She found tools she thought might work and disinfected them with whiskey and set about probing his flesh with her hand before she struck the instrument into his flesh. Mercifully, he remained still.

Minutes passed, five, ten, a half hour. Then, suddenly it popped free, followed by a gush of blood and puss. She quickly pressed linen to it firmly, hoping to stop the flow. He could ill afford to lose more. She waited for a few minutes before dousing the wound with whiskey again and pressed again on it. He would have a tough recovery. Some of the flesh around the wound had begun to blacken. She had heard of doctors having to cut dead flesh from bad wounds, praying that they would heal. Sometimes they were successful. Sometimes. . .

After heating a pair of scissors in the fire, Sally began to cut, snipping and trimming, until the black was cut away, then she cauterized the wound. It hurt her almost as bad as she knew it hurt him. Just the thought of the hot poker entering his torn flesh made her queasy, but it couldn't be helped. An hour passed. She prayed that he remained unconscious, knowing the pain would send him thrashing about. Mercifully, God heard her prayers. He slept through the night, with Sally sitting beside him on the bed, her hand on his back so she could tell a change in his breathing should she begin to doze. Finally, exhaustion set in and she too fell into a deep sleep.

He awoke from the void of darkness into the pits of hell. He was consumed with heat. His throat and lungs felt parched as if he had been riding through a sandstorm. He shivered from a cold like nothing he had ever known. He couldn't decide which was worse, the heat or the cold. He heard the soft murmur of a gentle voice, and he saw her then. He had dreamed of her as he had hung suspended in the darkness. She seemed so familiar. He tried to talk, but she shushed him, putting a cup to his lips for him to drink. He did so and tasted what seemed to be the nectar of the gods. It swirled through his body, creating a comforting warmth that the hell had not created. His mind raced as he sought to pull himself out of the pit he found himself in.

"I'm not dead." His voice was a mere croak of sound.

"No, lucky for you I don't give up easily. At anything. That includes healing a wounded savage." The last was said with a soft smile, her eyes studying him intently. He realized she was teasing him.

"Ummm. .lucky for me. . ." his voice faded then into sleep once again, and this time he slept fitfully. The heat he had previously suffered so with gradually faded and he was surrounded by a comforting warmth he knew to be the white woman who had taken him into her house to tend. The sleep he fell into this time was a deep, healing sleep.

Sally studied the man lying in her bed. He had been dreadfully ill with fever for two days. Two days. She sighed, wondering now that the fever had passed and it was safe to leave him if she should go for Travers. She chewed that one over in her mind before deciding that she could forgo fetching the Doc. Somehow she wasn't ready to share the fact that Little Crow was here in her home, in her bed. Not that Travers would be angry, it was just, well, she wasn't ready to tell anyone about her new—friend.

She let him sleep the rest of the day and went about her chores.

⸺•⸺

Travers had just had lunch at the Tate's and was headed back to his office, his mind on the situation with Daniel. Almost two months had gone by, and Daniel still ignored him. It was just as well. Travers had been in a sour mood ever since the episodes with both Bowers and Daniel. He was not pleasant to be around. He was in mid-stride when he heard his name being called.

"Dr. Gage!"

Travers stopped, and it seemed the whole town did as well. People lined the boardwalk, their eyes taking in the figure standing in the street. He was a familiar face all right, and he was packing a gun, but he was packing a suitcase as well. The young man had apparently just gotten off the stage for he closed the door to it and began to stride towards Travers. Travers watched him come, wondering what the kid could possibly want with him now. The doctor noted that he walked with a pronounced limp now, but he strode with purpose as he made his way towards where Travers stood on the boardwalk.

The people lining the streets began to disperse, realizing there was nothing to see. The kid had been a mite slow the last time he confronted Dr. Gage. Besides, he didn't appear to be looking for a rematch.

Travers waited for the kid to stop in front of him before speaking.

"Well, Mr. Lowe, I'm assuming that that suitcase means you've come to stay awhile. Could it be our fair town grew on you a bit?"

Deke Lowe pushed his hat back on his head before extending his hand to Travers.

"Yes, sir. I'd like to talk to you about that."

Travers shook the young man's hand.

"It's good to see you, son," he said grinning.

The boy pinkened at the "son, ' but he grinned as Travers motioned for him to walk with him. Deke fell into step beside Travers, and motioning to the kid's seemingly stiff appendage, Travers asked him "How's the leg?"

Deke grunted.

"Well, it was sore as hell for the longest, but it's holding up all right. It helps to keep it moving."

Travers grinned, his teeth flashing.

"It itch much?"

"Like fire, man. I've never scratched so much in my life."

Travers chuckled. Ushering him into his clinic, he told him, "I would offer you some coffee, but I'm fresh out."

Deke waved the offer away. "Don't worry about it. I'll get something at the hotel later."

Travers studied the young man across from him. There was a difference about him, a calmer demeanor. "So what brings you to town?"

Deke doffed his hat and studied the braid around the crown

of it before answering.

"Well, Doc, I came to a conclusion, and I need your help. Frankly, I'm kind of expecting' it, seeing' as how you're the one who so kindly pointed out that I should find myself an occupation other than gunslinger."

Travers leaned back in his chair, his elbows resting on the arms, his fingers steepled before him. "What exactly did you have in mind?"

Deke leaned forward, his hands rolling his hat back and forth nervously between his knees.

"After I left here last summer, I went and found Frank and Jesse. Frank near walloped me for pulling that stunt with you. He sent me home with a fair amount of money. Said I needed to further my education, make something of myself. I tried to. But no one would give me a chance. I never finished school, and me being part of that family back home, well, that was like hanging a sign 'bout my neck saying 'jailbait.'"

Travers nodded, understanding. "How much education do you have?"

"Well, I got through the ninth grade before I dropped out. But I made good grades and I catch on real fast."

"It's going to take some work to catch you up. But it can be done. And you have to be willing to work hard and really want this for yourself." Travers pinned him with a severe stare, looking for any hint that the kid was anything but serious about this. He didn't find it. Deke swallowed the lump that had risen in his throat and squared his shoulders.

"I'm willing to do anything, sir." That was a first, Travers thought. He'd bet Deke had addressed few men that way and knew it must have been hard for him to do so now.

"All right then."

Travers knew the boy was being honest with him. He really did want to better himself, and it made Travers feel good to know that he had played a part in the change of heart. When they left his office an hour later, it was to see Pete at the general store for a job. Deke had told Travers that it had always been a dream of his to own his own business. Travers figured Pete would be glad to help. It would give Deke first-hand experience and an income while he furthered his education. But school would come first. Daniel would be their next stop.

As Travers had suspected, Pete jumped on the idea since he had trouble keeping good help. Pete and Deke got on well together, and Pete offered him more pay than Travers expected him to. Deke's eyes widened at the sum he mentioned, his eyes going to Travers in disbelief. The doctor said nothing as Deke stammered his thanks.

Outside, Travers told the one time gunslinger, "Deke, Pete's a good man. He knows your history, and he's going on a lot of faith here. Folks around here are more than willing to give a guy a chance if they see he really wants to change. You've been cut a break. Don't blow it."

They headed to the schoolhouse, Deke pondering the words of the doc. The man was going out on a limb for him, a man who had tried to kill him. It made no sense, yet it made perfect sense. He hoped the schoolteacher was as generous with his time. They entered the schoolhouse to find Daniel grading papers. He barely acknowledged them as they came inside the open door.

Travers strode up to the desk, noting the stiffness that had come over his friend's face.

"A moment of your time, Daniel."

"I've got nothing to say to you," Daniel said without looking up, his eyes scanning the papers before him.

"Well, that's too bad, cause I've got plenty to say to you, but right now we've got an audience. I've brought you a new student."

At that, Daniel looked up at Travers then over to Deke who stood there fidgeting nervously, his hat in his hand.

"Come here, son." Travers motioned for him to come forward. "I want you to meet Daniel McCullough. He's the schoolteacher here and was my best friend until recent events, but that's not why we're here." Turning to find Daniel glowering at him, he told him "Deke here needs his diploma. He wants to make something of himself, and we're gonna help him do just that."

Daniel looked from Travers to Deke and back again.

"And how much work are we talking about?"

"Two years," Travers interjected before Deke could say anything. He was skipping a year, but Travers had an idea that Deke Lowe was smarter than the average saddle tramp. "He's smart, and he catches on real fast." Travers grinned at that last bit of information, finding the humor in it. Daniel drummed his fingers on the desk, watching the kid fidget. It was going to be time-consuming, and—it was going to be time-consuming. He liked the sound of that. Staying busy would keep him from thinking about Flora. He frowned at just the thought of her.

Besides, this sounded like a challenge. Deke was a grown man, and he'd never taught anyone above school age before. And he figured there was a story here that he was missing, noting the by-play between these two. Travers was serious about getting the kid help, or he wouldn't be here. He had been avoiding him as of late. He wasn't the kind of man to find an excuse to seek him out. The challenge was met.

He rose from the desk and went to the bookcase where he removed two books. He handed them to Deke. "Read these from front to back over the next two days. Come back Monday at two o'clock, and we'll get started."

"You mean, I don't have to sit through class?" Deke couldn't imagine how this was going to work.

"No. Let's see where you are in your skills first. Then if you want, you can take regular school hours. I just thought you'd prefer more one on one, with you being considerably older than the other students."

"Whatever you think best, sir."

Daniel crossed his arms over his chest.

"Then I'll see you Monday at two o'clock."

THIRTY-FOUR

Daniel was enjoying his new pupil. Deke had an unwavering desire to learn, and that was unusual and refreshing to see in a young man such as he. Reading and science seemed to be his hardest subjects, math his easiest. Often when the boy was working the problems that Daniel had given him to do, he would strike up a conversation with the teacher, much to Daniel's consternation. Watching his pencil fly across the page had raised a knot between the older man's brows, for he was certain that the kid paid little to no attention to what he was doing. He had been quite stunned, however, upon examining the work. Every problem was answered correctly, the numbers perfectly legible, another unlikely characteristic the kid possessed, for Daniel knew that his handwriting was little more than hen scratch.

One evening, while grading a particularly difficult test, of which Deke received another perfect score, Daniel asked him where he had come by his math skills. Deke had grinned slyly before ducking his head.

"My cousin Frank taught me. Said it was important that a man know how to count. Especially money. In the business we were in, it was important that we all got an even share and nobody got cheated."

That piqued the teacher's interest.

"And exactly what business would that be?"

The boy seemed surprised, his eyebrows raised.

"Why, robbin' banks."

From the bland, doubting look on Daniel's face, it was obvious that he didn't know the truth about who his student really was.

"Doc didn't tell you, did he?" he asked quietly. "I thought he would have said something, you know. Warn you about who I was."

The eyebrow rose again.

"Warn me?"

"I rode with my cousins Frank and Jesse. James."

Daniel just grinned.

"Sure kid." He shook his head, slightly amused. The kid had a lively imagination. He was barely dry behind the ears and here he was trying to create himself a reputation with a few tall tales.

"He didn't tell you *anything* about me? How we met?"

"Nope. Just said you needed some educating. You heard

what I heard the day he brought you here."

Deke thumped his pencil upon his crossed knee.

"Hmmm. I thought the two of you were buddies. That you talked."

Daniel gave him a withering look.

"Guess not," Deke said, with a roll of his eyes.

Silence fell for several minutes as Daniel finished grading the paper. Deke was unsure whether or not he should tell the school teacher the truth and Daniel sat there, gnashing his teeth over the fact that this boy thought that Travers was his friend. Deke decide to take a chance.

"I came here to kill Travers."

Daniel's head whipped around.

"What!"

"That's how we met. I'd been riding with Frank and Jesse 'bout a year. Frank talked about him a lot. You know he tried to get Frank into medical school? But things turned sour, and he had to come home. Then the war happened. Rumors got around about the doc saving that Union general. I told Frank I could take him. I was convinced I could and came to town to prove it. Lucky for me, Dr. Gage slammed some sense into me. It took buckshot to do it, but it worked."

Daniel was sitting there, a stunned look on his face.

"Nawww. . ."

Deke sighed, then tugged his pants leg up above his knee. Daniel bent for a closer look at the mangled, pockmarked knee that seemed to be missing part of its kneecap.

"I was lucky. If he hadn't been a crack shot, I'd have lost my leg, and probably my life. But he patched me up good and sent me on my way. When I got back to Frank and Jesse, Frank nearly took a leather strap to me. Gave me a share of his money and sent me home to finish school. Told me to make something of myself. After tangling with the Doc, I figured robbin' banks wasn't such a bright idea anymore. That was my first real taste of lead and hopefully my last. I thought about it and decided to take Frank's advice. Only, back home, no one would help me cause everyone knew I was a James relation. Then it hit me. I figured if Doc Gage saw something in me worth savin', maybe he'd be willing to help. So, here I am. And that's that."

Daniel slumped back in his chair, his arms folded across his chest as he watched the kid pull his pants leg back down over the scarred knee.

"You're not lying, are you?" he asked incredulously.

"No."

"You're kin to Frank and Jesse James? You rode with them?" It came out more like a clarification than a question.

"Yeah, for nearly a year. Mostly I stood guard and watched the horses. But I rode with them, all right. After the Railroad took our land, Frank and Jesse weren't about to let sleeping dogs lie. Cole and his two brothers wouldn't take it lying down either."

"Cole Younger? You kin to him too?"

"Yeah. On my maw's side. Them Railroad men blew up Frank and Jesse's home with their maw and brother still inside. Little Archie died. That's when Frank and Jesse declared war on the railroad. Ol' Pinkerton and his men are some ruthless devils. They shot Cole's paw and almost got Cole, but Frank and Jesse yahooed the town. That Frank is one crack shot," Deke said, bobbing his head, smirking as he recalled the looks on those men's faces when Frank had severed the rope around Cole's neck with one shot.

Daniel sat up, his elbows propped on the desk before him, his arms crossed.

"Tell me about them."

The schoolteacher was fascinated. Frank and Jesse James were dang heroes out here. True, they had reason to wage war on authority. The law had never sided with them on the issue of their land because there was money to be made. Honest lawmen were a rare breed for sure, as their pay was barely enough to keep a cat alive, let alone a man. And the job was often a dangerous one, and that led many officers of the law to become as lawless as the men they were taught to protect the citizens from. And Deke here, well, he was a bonafide outlaw.

"Well, Frank's the quiet, smart type. He can sure shoot, but he takes too long to think on things sometimes. Now, Jesse, he's like lightning. Not afraid of anything or anybody. I've seen him walk into a hail of bullets, guns blazing, without batting an eye. Course, I imagine if he did blink, he'd be dead by now." The last was said with humor but had a sobering effect on the boy. He frowned down at his scuffed shoe, wiping at it with an agitated brush of his hand.

"They're not bad folk, really, just two brothers trying to survive, that's all."

They sat there in silence for a few minutes before Deke rose to his feet.

"Guess I better be gettin' on to work. Gotta earn my keep around here."

Daniel nodded, not saying a word.

Still, the young man hesitated.

"You—you're not gonna say anything to anybody, are you? I mean, about who I am—and them?" He played with the frayed rim of his hat.

Daniel studied the young man, seeing the uncertainty on his

face. The boy had taken a chance and come clean with his past. He was fearful that his second chance at life might be taken away, the fear that Daniel might turn him in plainly written on his face. Daniel knew immediately that he wouldn't do that. Everybody deserved a second chance. Especially a kid like Deke Lowe. Travers had seen something in him, and Daniel saw the potential he was showing, the promise of making something of himself beside a gun for hire. There was a hunger in him. Daniel would not be the one to turn him in.

"No, I'm not going to say a word about this to anyone. You've got a shot here of becoming somebody. I won't spoil that for you."

The relief on the kid's face was like watching the sun come out from behind a cloud. He tried to suppress a grin, but it leaped across his lips before he had control of it. Daniel grinned in return.

"Now go on. Get to work. And you have that book by Dickens read by Friday," he called after the hastily departing youth. The schoolteacher just shook his head, watching him as he went. Amazing. It was just like Travers to pull something like this on him. Pushing back from the desk, he rose and stretched before heading to find his so-called friend. He was still mad as hell at him, but the fact that he trusted him enough to turn Deke Lowe over to his capable hands eased the anger he still harbored towards the doctor.

He found him sitting on the porch of the boarding house. Daniel stopped in the street looking at the man. Travers was busy watching Maggie Bowers hurry into the motel just down the street. The man appeared to have it bad for the woman, and that was unfortunate with her being married. That thought brought him up short. If Travers was so in love with Margaret Bowers, why was he chasing after Flora? He felt the heat rising even as he stepped towards the doc, who became aware of Daniel's presence at about that instant.

"Evening, Daniel."

"Evening, Travers," Daniel grunted. Travers was taking note of his friend's flushed face and the knot resting between his eyes.

"That must be a mighty powerful headache you got going on to put such a knot between your eyes. Well, don't fret yourself too much. It'll pass soon enough. 'Course, if I had a head like that, I'm sure it'd ache for days."

Daniel just gave a bear-like grunt and plopped down into the rocking chair next to the doctor, causing the chair to creak uneasily.

"You have certainly pulled some good ones, Trav, but this

one takes the cake."

Travers sighed, not really wanting to know what he had done this time to irk his friend, but knew he was about to find out.

"What *are* you talking about, Daniel?"

"Deke Lowe. Why didn't you tell me who he was?"

Travers shrugged. "Would it really have made a difference?"

"Well, I might not have acted like an unbelieving buffoon when he told me you *shot* him!"

Travers chuckled at that.

"So he told you about that. Well, the boy does love to talk. Filled my ears full of what he was gonna do to me when he got well, bragging about all the banks they'd hit."

"I laughed at the kid! Til he showed me the leg. Nice piece of work, that. I bet you aren't so fond of that shotgun anymore."

The doctor sobered. "No, I'm not. But make no mistake. That boy aimed to kill me. I read it in his eyes. If I had doubted for one second otherwise, I'd never have pulled the trigger. He was fired up and full of juice. Young. Had never felt that nice burning sensation of hot lead. He learned fast that guns were meant to maim and kill and he wanted no part of it. Sending him home was the best thing that Frank could have done. Now, thanks to us, he stands a chance."

Daniel nodded. "Yep, he's bright, that one. Amazing talent with numbers. Says Frank taught him."

Travers reached into his pocket and pulled out a flask, offering it to Daniel, who took it.

"Frank has a brain like none I've ever seen. His stepfather was a doctor. I had met him some time back at a conference in Boston. When he married Frank and Jesse's ma, he contacted me, wanted me to tutor Frank. Said he showed interest in the profession. He needed a bit of fine-tuning. But he had such a thirst for knowledge, and he retained it like a reservoir. Loved Shakespeare. Used to quote it frequently."

"No kidding?"

"No kidding. Still, does it, I hear. Right in the middle of pulling bank jobs, no less. He has finesse, that's for sure. He would have made a damn fine surgeon. Steady hands, precision. He never got to take the entrance exam."

"What happened?"

"There were problems at home even then. The railroad meant to have their land, by any means. His stepfather almost died protecting those boys and Jesse couldn't hold off the wolves alone. I hated to see him go. I knew he wouldn't be back. It seemed such a waste of God-given talent."

"Sounds like the two of you were close."

"I became his mentor. But, he was more than that. I never

had a brother. I guess he helped to fill that void."

Daniel studied on that. "You ever meet Jesse?" Daniel was dying to know.

"Once," Travers admitted. "He had come up for a visit. Nice looking kid. Never would guess by looking at him that he's an outlaw. Meticulous manners, both of them. Their maw was very religious, so I hear."

Daniel was shaking his head. "Amazing. Simply amazing."

Travers took a sip from the flask Daniel had just given back to him.

"Yeah, well, theirs is a hard life I don't envy. Only a fool would."

Recapping the flask, he slipped it into his vest pocket. Giving his friend a long look, he couldn't resist asking, "So, you still mad at me?"

"I haven't decided yet. Just tell me one thing. Why are you so determined to chase Flora when it's so obvious that you're in love with another woman?"

Travers gave his friend a hard look before answering.

"You still haven't a clue, do you?"

"Clue about what?"

Travers was about exasperated with his longtime friend.

"I'm not 'chasing' Flora. I never have been. Flora is trying to make you jealous and using me as the pawn. I'd have to say that she's succeeded. Now, the question is, what are you going to do about it?"

Daniel frowned. He didn't like being played or made a fool of. "Why would she do that? Try to make me jealous? She knows I'm attracted to her. We have an—understanding."

"Daniel, Flora wants a relationship with you. A real relationship. She doesn't want to be your fall back girl, a mere afterthought when the others you are sniffing around are otherwise occupied. She wants a committed relationship. Why is it so hard for you to give it? She's one of the warmest people I know. Her heart is so big and so honest it's downright scary. Is it because she was a whore once? She gave that up years ago. She may not have led a pure and holy lifestyle, but hell, I know a lot of women of supposedly fine breeding who were little better than spawns of Satan. Flora is well respected in this town. Her past is just that, her past. All of us have a past. What's important is the future. What are you going to do ten years from now when she's married to someone else? You're going to live with a regret that you would never have had to face if you'd only taken the chance when it was first presented to you."

The pain and truth in Travers' words were tangible things. Daniel heard the regret in every word he spoke. He couldn't help but wonder if it had anything to do with Margaret Bowers. Had they known one another long ago? What made Travers speak as though from experience? He had seen the way the doctor's eyes followed her about town when he thought no one was watching. He had feelings for the woman, yet steered clear of her. Daniel didn't know much about Travers' past. The doctor was a man who kept things to himself, not letting his true feelings show. "You seem to speak from experience."

"I do. And it's a hell of a way to live life. Always wondering what might have been."

"Margaret Bowers?"

Travers turned to look at Daniel briefly before staring back down the street at nothing in particular, his thoughts dark as night.

"As I said before. Everyone has a past."

Daniel let the conversation drop then. Travers didn't seem to want to talk any more about it, and he knew the feeling. He had a lot to think about where he and Flora were concerned. About that time Laura came to the door.

"Well, hello, Daniel. I didn't know you were here. Why don't you stay and have dinner with us? I just came to fetch Travers to let him know it was time to eat."

Daniel and Travers stood, Travers, stretching as he did so.

"Well," Daniel said, scratching his belly, "I don't want to impose."

"No imposition," Travers said. "It's been too long since you came around."

"Well, all right. I'll stay," he told Laura with a smile. They followed her inside and sat down to pot roast, corn, green beans and rolls that were slick with butter. Watching Daniel consume the meal before him, Travers couldn't help but think how much easier the food went down now that his friend was back.

◆———◆———◆

It was a strained sort of friendship, but it was steadfast. Daniel proved that when he saw the riders come into town. They were dressed in haphazard, dear God, what appeared to be Confederate uniforms. Tattered, patched and dirty, they spelled trouble with a capital T. He was on his way to the schoolhouse when he spotted them. They seemed to slither into town, their eyes missing nothing, checking every detail, mentally ticking off everyone they saw on the street. Daniel knew their kind, and his stomach began to churn uneasily. Almost to Travers' office, he quickened his step, instinctively knowing they had come for the doc. Slipping inside, he was glad to see that Travers was just getting the morning started. No patients waited for him.

"We've got company."

Travers looked up to see his friend standing just inside the door to his office.

"Morning to you, too," Travers said as he completed washing and drying his hands.

"Trav, you've got visitors and it ain't no social call."

Visitors. Travers didn't like the sound of that word. His brow furrowed as he moved to pick up his gun, checking the cylinder, making sure it was fully loaded.

"How many?"

"Three that I know of. There could be more. Their kind travel in packs like wolves and these look rabid. They're hunting, my friend and my guess is they've come hunting you."

"Mmm. Three this time. Well, this should prove to be interesting."

"Trav. There's something else. They're wearing Confederate uniforms."

Travers' eyes met those of the schoolteacher, and he felt as if he had been punched in the gut.

His nightmare wasn't over. His past had caught up with him. They were here to avenge their fallen comrades. They had promised him this day would come. On the battlefield, the challenge had been issued even as other men had come to his aid and helped him drag the general to safety. They had made good on their word. He had known they would.

He didn't need this. The town didn't need this. It had been a while since he'd had to do this. Nagging fear began to rise up within him, but he fought it back, breathing deeply to settle himself to the task ahead. He strapped on his gun belt and hearing Daniel fumbling nearby, looked up to see him loading the shotgun he kept in his office.

"Just what do you think you're doing?"

Daniel didn't even bother to look up.

"I'm going out there with you."

"The hell you are!"

"Yes, hell I am!

"This isn't your fight," Travers grated to his friend.

"The hell you say! I'm not about to let my friend go out there and be slaughtered. Those men don't know the meaning of the words fair fight."

Daniel had never been witness to the other gun battles he had survived. War was one thing. Killing a man on the street was another. He was not ready for this.

"Daniel, you have no idea what you're doing. These men mean to kill. You will have to shoot to *kill*. Do you understand that, Daniel? This isn't war. In war, you shoot and move on, things happen so fast, you soon forget about the men you leave lying on the ground. You're not the one who has to bury them. Here, we're not at war fighting to preserve a country. You're fighting to survive, to live another day. This time, you get to get a real good look at your handiwork, up close and personal like. It isn't all guts and glory, Daniel. This, this gunplay, it carries a heavy weight with it. It makes men hard, harder than they ever dreamed they could be. And it exacts a high price, a painful price. Those men, if they're who I think they are, have been looking for me a long time. It's going to get real ugly. They're hungry, hungry for blood they promised a long time ago. Are you ready for that?"

Daniel recognized the haunted look for what it was and knew the weight his friend must carry having killed as he had been forced to do. But he knew that letting his friend go out there alone meant almost certain death. And his jaw clenched in determination. Travers noted his expression and sighed.

"Who are they, Travers?"

He let out a long sigh and moved to the window, easing the curtain back to get a look down the street. He saw them in the distance, getting off their horses before the saloon. They were certainly a shady looking bunch, but at this distance, he couldn't be sure.

"Well, if it's who I think it is, they were with the unit that tried to take General Sharpe. They promised revenge for their fallen comrades even as they received fire from some men coming to help me. It wouldn't have mattered so much had they not known I was from Virginia. But they knew. Word had gotten around that one of the blue bellies across from them was a Virginian. That just really pissed them off. No Virginian would be caught dead fighting for the North. They meant to rectify the situation. Show me what traitors get for turning against their home state. And one of them was my neighbor. He's the one who made that promise, and he means to keep it."

Daniel shuddered. Travers had not told him a lot about his time in the war. He had heard about the incident around the time it happened but had pushed it aside, thinking there was more fiction to it than fact. Perhaps he had been wrong to assume that. He had actually forgotten about it until now.

"Well, this time you won't be going out there alone."

Travers looked over his shoulder at his friend. Difference of opinion or no, Daniel was his friend, and he meant to stick by him.

"Let's get the party started, shall we?"

The two of them eased out onto the porch and scanned the street. Sheriff Tate was headed towards them carrying his shotgun as well. When he spotted them, a look of relief came across his face. They eased up and let him come to them, waiting to see what he had to say. The streets had begun to clear, people had taken note of the strangers riding into town. Clayton, also armed, was striding towards them as well. He and the sheriff reached them about the same time.

"Well, Doc looks like it's show time again. They's three of them durn drifters down at the saloon, questioning where they can find you. Got the look of Johnny Rebs about 'em. Confederate jackets and such. Real hard cases."

Clayton grunted. "Hard cases can be broken. What's the plan, Doc? We gonna take 'em at the saloon?"

Travers groaned. "Not you, too."

"You don't think I'm gonna sit back and let you face those men alone. If you do, then your head needs to be examined. I ain't about to lose you now. You mean too much to this town, to Sarah and me. I'll tear 'em apart bare-handed if I have to."

"I say four against three is purty good odds, Doc. A few years from now, I may not be able to stand by you this way. Better take the offer while it's on the table." Tate smiled at him, his eyes crinkled in a sad humor.

Travers looked about him at the three men he called friends. He could try locking them up in the jail but knew they would never forgive him and especially wouldn't if he got himself killed. These men were not going to take no for an answer.

"Alright. But I do the talking, and you follow my lead. The second one goes for his gun, you shoot, and you shoot to kill. Don't think about it. Just do it. They intend to win at any cost, and their idea of fair play is whoever pulls lead first. Remember that. They could have others scattered about the town. Keep your eyes open and watch your backs."

Nods all around. He looked them over and saw the determination in all of their faces. Satisfied that he could not talk them out of this, they turned as one and walked down the street.

They scattered out, Travers in the lead with Tate on his right and Daniel to his left. Clayton hung back to cover their backs, his eyes roving the street up which they had just come. Travers watched the street empty further and waited a few seconds before calling out.

"Luke Darnell!"

Silence. He had to wait only seconds before the man appeared at the swinging doors. His clothes carried a month's load of dirt and grime, his face unshaven and gray with illness and fatigue. A grin spread across the man's grizzled face, and he turned and yelled to the others in the saloon.

"It's him, boys! Drink a toast to the great state of Virginia and get your carcasses out here! We've a score to settle." He pushed out the door and stopped on the step to look down at Travers and the men who stood with him. His grin turned a sickening shade of evil when he spotted Clayton bringing up the rear.

"You really are a piece of work, Gage. I always knew you for a nigger lover but, this, having one protect your back, that's just downright sacrilege."

Travers just smiled, thinking that life had not been kind to Luke Darnell since the war. He looked diseased, and he knew from the cast of his eyes the man must have lost his mind a long time ago.

"That man is ten times the man you could ever hope to be. I figure you've been looking for me a while now. I've been expecting you. Figured you'd have found me before now, actually. Last time we met, the odds were heavily in your favor. They seemed to have turned. You remember what happened last time, Darnell? You watched your men fall one by one. You can walk away from this, and we can forget it ever happened. Or you can die just like they did."

Darnell wasn't biting. His face darkened. "You killed my men like dogs. You didn't even give them a chance."

"They didn't give me a chance. We were at war. People die in war. It happens. The war is over, Darnell. Let it go. Otherwise, men are going to die today. You right along with them."

Darnell's other two companions came out and spread out about the porch, flanking the man. They were just as unkempt as their leader, if not more so. One wore an eye patch, and his left hand had several fingers missing. The other looked like a walking skeleton, tall and gaunt to the point that his gun belt had to be slung over his shoulder instead of worn about his hips. All wore their hair long, and Travers suspected they were covered with lice. They sneered at Travers, the memory of what they had seen him do to their fellow brothers at Gettysburg boiling like hot oil in their bellies. They had waited a long time for this day.

Darnell's lip curled as he addressed Travers again. "Guess you got a shock when you went home and found it wa'nt there no more. Seems I weren't the only enemy you made when you fought for them blue bellies. Some of yore so-called friends were more'n eager to help torch that white mansion of yorn. Din't take hardly no persuasion at all."

Travers frowned, his eyes hard. His friends at Gold City had not been aware that he had lost his home because of his stand against his own state.

"Yes, it takes a real man to destroy a person's home when they aren't even around to defend it. That must have made you feel very much the defender of Southern pride. Tell me, was it a hollow victory Darnell, especially when you didn't find me in residence?"

"Naw. I crowed like a rooster for days. I just wish I'd a been there to see yore face when you saw that white mansion of yours reduced to a pile of ash."

"You didn't accomplish anything except prove yourself a coward. I know who helped you burn the place. The drunks who left Fellowship before the war proclaiming they were going to annihilate the North in one fell swoop. Their liquor ran out just after their courage did. Deserters and cowards. All of you."

Darnell had had enough of being called a coward. The man before him had always thought he was high and mighty. Uppity, as if he could shit and it wouldn't stink. Dr. Gage's heroics at Gettysburg had built a name for him, as a marked man. The day had come to collect on the promise he had been made a long time ago. Travers Gage was going to die today.

"You go to hell," he snarled and palmed his gun, aiming directly at the doctor's heart. The other two pulled lead at the same time, fanning further down the street, running for cover. Clayton, Daniel, and Sheriff Tate let loose with their guns as well, following Travers' lead as he poured forth lead, a bullet ripping through Darnell's chest, puncturing his lung, causing bloody foam to bubble forth as he fell to his knees, the wind literally gone from his body. The rebel tried to bring his gun up to bear on Travers, struggling to hold it steady with both hands. Travers waited until the man had his gun cocked and aimed before he opened fire on him again, this time finding his heart. The two goons with him had missed Travers with their first volley, one of them hitting Sheriff Tate in the foot, causing the air to turn blue with the language coming out of his mouth. They ran for cover, one behind their horses tied nearby, the other around the corner of the saloon. Travers stepped out of the line of fire, letting the others take care of the two outlaws. In a matter of minutes, Daniel and Clayton had dispensed of the remaining two with little effort. One was dead, the other bleeding from a grazed head and wounded shoulder. He lay prostrate in surrender on his stomach, his face in the dirt and hands on his head. He would live.

Travers turned back to Darnell, finding him lying face down half on the boardwalk and half off, his face in the dirt of the street. How fitting, he thought. A shame he hadn't been taken care of during the war. His kind rarely got their comeuppance by such, though. It usually had to be met out by those who stood for something higher.

Daniel and Clayton held the swearing sheriff between them,

their mouths turned up in grins as they listened to the man moan about the hole in his foot. Travers grinned, thinking that the old man would surely bend his wife's ear now, telling her tales of how he had been in a gun battle with Dr. Gage and outlaws. The man had few things to brag about, and Travers had a feeling this one would top them all. He was the law after all. Of course, he had stood with the doc. He could just hear him now. Chuckling, he led the trio back down the street, indicating to the growing crowd that they should get Limbaugh the undertaker and bring the wounded man to the clinic.

He tended the sheriff first.

"Well, Tate. I'd say that this is one lucky wound. Course, when Louella sees it, she'll swear you shot yourself drawing your gun." A hint of a smile creased his lips.

"That woman would argue with a fence post. But I got witnesses. You saw it all. One of them there dang outlaws did this." He shot a scathing look at the man being brought in to be tended. "How's that head, Johnny Reb? An inch over and I'd a kilt ya' dead."

The man cast a baleful look at the sheriff. He was thinking how much he wished he had killed the sheriff. His two compadres had succeeded in getting themselves killed, and he was left holding the bag. He would go to prison for attempted murder. He didn't like that thought one bit.

Daniel chimed in. "Afraid you'll be our guest for a while. Just awful that your buddies went and got themselves killed. Now you'll have to make new friends who don't make a habit of shooting at people. I figure Fort Hayes is just the place to find some more of your kind."

Travers just shook his head. "Don't go giving him any bright ideas. They're just liable to muster him into service, seeing as how the Indians are getting riled up again. They'll be looking for every able-bodied man they can find, and they won't be choosy about who they enlist. Ras can hold him in the jail here until the judge comes around next month."

That brought a string of protests from the outlaw and Clayton, and Daniel shoved him back in his seat when he would have bolted for the door. He continued to grumble under his breath, realizing he was going nowhere with these two guarding him. He needed to be patched up anyhow. His head was bleeding something fierce, and he was feeling lightheaded all of a sudden.

At that moment, Louella Tate charged through the door.

"What in the Sam hill do you think you are doing, old man? You ain't got the sense God gave a billy goat. I swear, you've gone and got yourself shot, I see! And in the foot no less! You hapless man. Couldn't you get your gun clear of your holster?"

The men looked at each other, and back at the little woman who was berating her husband. Tate's mouth was flapping, but nothing was coming out. Louella was flapping her gums at him, fussing over him like he was a child. He threw up his hands and snorted in frustration, not able to get a word in edgewise. Travers began to shake with mirth and Daniel, and Clayton soon joined him, their laughter soon drowning out Louella's fussing. Erasmus looked at the three men who were finding this situation so funny and threw his hands up.

"Aw, hell."

THIRTY-FIVE

Flora twirled in front of the mirror, complete disgust on her face at what she saw. Flora didn't know what had come over her. She desperately wanted this evening to be the evening their first date *should* have been. But nothing seemed to be right. The clothes weren't working for her. The hair—she exhaled in exasperation. Flouncing over to the bed, she threw herself down upon it.

Lying there fuming, she recalled what Laura had told her before. She was trying too hard. *'Be yourself.'* If only I could. Heck, she didn't even know what that meant anymore! For so long she had played a part, a role, the role of madam to this town and no matter how anyone saw her, that was always what she would be. Most of the townsfolk knew her and loved her regardless of what they knew her to be. But even most of those people who knew her believed she still serviced men. She had never disabused them of that notion because she had to play the part. Didn't she? Perhaps she should make it known the truth of her arrangement with the girls. She wanted so much for Daniel to see her as a woman, not some object to be used and cast aside.

With that thought in mind, she turned to the mirror and began to take the clothes off. She had some adjustments to make.

━━━━━◆━━━━━

He was early. Ten minutes early. He chalked it up to nerves. He hesitated before knocking, thinking he must be insane to subject Flora to this painful song and dance again. He had told himself after that last episode that he would rather chew glass than do it again. Now here they were, a week after his conversation with Travers doing the same darned thing. What was he thinking? Apparently, he wasn't. Was she thinking the same thing?

The door opened, and she was there. And was she there! He stood there for a moment, his mouth working, but no sound coming forth. She was more than stunning. She glowed with an inward beauty that the striped suit had little to do with. Her hair was piled atop her head in loose twists and curls, and she radiated sheer energy. And it touched him, leaving him breathless.

Flora had been stressing all afternoon, waiting for seven o'clock. She had been shocked when Daniel told her he thought they should give this thing between them another chance. She didn't know what had prompted the turn of events, but she was thankful that he had decided to see where it might lead. She had gone through several trial runs before settling on the ensemble she now wore. It was an emerald and cream striped walking jacket over a cream walking skirt. She looked like she had just stepped off the pages of a catalog. Classy, slim, svelte, and ever so much all woman. Her curves were covered, but accentuated, demure, yet enticing. Nothing blatantly sexual, but sensual in every possible way. There was a small ruffle at the high neck of her blouse and at the cuff of her sleeves, just peeking out from the sleeves of the jacket. Her makeup was minimal, yet just enough to accentuate her eyes, and his eyes kept going to the dewy moistness of her lips. She was perfection in every way this night, and they both knew it.

Flora had looked her fill as well while Daniel had perused her so thoroughly. He was dressed to the nines in his best suit. A dark russet material that looked so fine on him she wanted to cry. His hair was a bit mussed, but she had always preferred it that way. He looked utterly sensual, and she found herself standing inches away from him of a sudden.

"My, Red, you do clean up nice. I can't recall ever seeing you look quite so— " he struggled to find the right word.

Flora grinned. "—lovely? Divine? Beautiful?"

Daniel was doing a bit of grinning himself. "All of the above, though those were not the exact words I was looking for. No, I was thinking more along the lines of —heavenly."

Flora batted her eyes at that one.

"Well, I am no angel, that's for sure."

"Mmm. I'm curious to see if you have wings under that frock, 'course from where I'm standing, I'm just a step away from paradise."

There was a husky vibrato to his voice now, a different timber that had not been there before between them. The interest had finally turned to desire, and she didn't know whether or not to be thrilled or afraid.

Indecision made her bold.

"Perhaps I have horns and a tail instead."

"We'll see, Red. We will see. Soon." He leaned in and kissed her softly on the lips, leaving her filled with wonder.

It took her a moment to focus once they parted and she noticed the darkness of his eyes, the desire that he could no longer conceal. Yes, he wanted her. And after tonight, she had every intention that he know she wasn't to be taken lightly.

They went to the theater, newly opened in town. There was a variety show with traveling entertainment. Some were hilarious comic sketches, while others were, well, they were just sad. No talent whatsoever. There was a lady who ended the show who sang beautifully, some unfamiliar songs she had written herself. Lovely, haunting melodies that brought tears to Flora's eyes. She caught Daniel's eye to see if he had been affected by the music as well. He was staring intently at her. She blushed, even in the dark of the theater. His hand found its way to her face, and his finger wiped the moisture from her cheek. Her eyes were drawn to his again, and his hand went to the nape of her neck, caressing, playing with her hair. It shot goose pimples along her arms, causing her to shiver. Daniel felt it and drew her closer, his arm about her. They sat that way for the remainder of the program.

When it was over, instead of walking her home, he led her to his house, his fingers laced loosely with hers. Inside, he lit a lamp and asked her if she would like something to drink. She shook her head no, her eyes on his, waiting, hoping, questioning. Before she could blink, she was in his arms, and there was no doubt, no fear. She was overwhelmed by the feelings running through her. His mouth was wonderful, so demanding, so powerful, so soothing, all at the same time. She did not want to be soothed. She wanted to be loved, and she was ravenous with the desire to be ravished. But he held her away from him. It took some doing, as he was fighting himself as much as her.

"We can't do this right now. No!" He said as she made an effort to argue. He tweaked her nose, surprising her. "I have something for you." He led her to the bedroom where he opened the door. There was a table set up near the fireplace with covered dishes and, yes, that was champagne! And candles everywhere she looked. She turned to him.

"How—"

He shushed her.

"I really made an idiot of myself last time. And you are a special lady. You should be treated as such. Consider this a heartfelt apology."

Tears pricked her eyes. "You didn't have to do this."

"Oh, I think I did. And I had a little help from our friends, so thank them next time you see them."

She smiled brightly. "I will definitely do that."

He seated her and treated her to steak and stir-fried vegetables. And there were strawberries to go with the champagne. Flora was so tickled, she literally had to pinch herself to see that she was not dreaming. She had never in her life had champagne. She felt like a fairy princess. Especially when he asked her to dance with him afterward. There was no music, which she pointed out and he promptly showed her he could provide all the music they needed. He hummed one of the songs from earlier that evening, a lovely one that had especially moved Flora. She rested her head against his shoulder as he led her through the steps, her eyes closing in contentment.

An hour later, she was back on her doorstep. Frustrated but ecstatic. He had refused to make love to her. He had treated her like the perfect gentleman then kissed her goodnight. It was no light peck on the cheek. It had roiled her insides like nothing she had ever known. She was still tingling, still trying to get her bearings as she tripped lightly up the stairs to her apartment, a ridiculous smile on her face.

◆———◆———◆

Travers was taking the day off. He had it coming to him. He had been wrapped up at the clinic, and with the showdown with Darnell and his men, Travers was looking forward to some much-needed time alone. He decided he would surprise Sally. He had been to see her several times over the past few months, and they had spent many a pleasurable evening just enjoying each other's company. He had not expected to see much of her after the dinner party at the Tate's when she realized his lost love was Maggie but Sally had come to town one day on the premise of seeing Laura. She had pulled Travers to the side and told him that he was welcome at her place anytime. They had ended up in bed a few times, but Travers made sure that they kept it to a minimum. He knew that was putting Sally in a position she might have trouble with later on and he wanted there to be no regrets between them when and if they decided to part company. He got to her place just after lunch, and she smiled when she saw him ride into the yard. She was hanging clothes on the line to dry.

"Well, this is a pleasant surprise."

Travers smiled. "I was hoping you would say that. I am in need of a bit of relaxation."

"Rough week?"

"Rough month," he corrected. He dismounted and moved to help her put sheets out to dry. They worked for several minutes, making small talk and catching up. It had been a couple of months since Sally had been into town and Travers had not pressured her to come in. Sally would come when she wanted to. She was such a free spirit. She had done wonders with the farm. She was growing things Travers had no idea would grow out here. They went inside, and she poured them a cup of coffee she had left warming on the stove. They took their cups outside and sat on the porch sipping and shooting the breeze. Sally seemed to have something on her mind but she never said what it was and Travers didn't pressure her. He was simply enjoying her company and the solitude that the farm brought. It was so quiet out here. He could hear himself think. Back in town, even his own private musings had background noise. They had been visiting about an hour when he saw a figure coming towards them. He didn't like the looks of the man approaching. It appeared to be an Indian. He pointed out the figure drawing near.

"Expecting someone?"

"No. Not really." She seemed to hedge. There was something in her tone.

He cut his eyes towards her. "Well, either you are, or you aren't."

The Indian had drawn closer, his eyes boring into the man on the porch with Sally Sharpe.

Sally's eyes grew large, and she found she could not take her eyes off the man riding towards her. The Indian had locked eyes with her and seemed to be intent on ignoring Travers, making him suddenly seem like a fifth wheel. The Indian just sat his horse, as if willing Travers to disappear. Travers was watching this byplay with a bit of amusement. There was a story here that he was clearly in the dark about. He cleared his throat.

Sally jumped and tore her eyes from the brave, addressing Travers as she rose to her feet.

"Travers Gage, this is Little Crow of the Tonkawa Nation. He is a—friend. Little Crow, this is a good friend of mine, Dr. Travers Gage."

The man stepped forward and offered his hand in friendship to the Indian. Little Crow hesitated in taking it but a moment. Dr. Gage. The doctor from town. He had heard good things about this man. If Sally Sharpe were friends with him, he would be his friend as well.

"It is a pleasure to meet you, Little Crow. I've heard of you. I understand you're working as a delegate and liaison with the Crow nation. Under General Forsyth, isn't it? I've seen you in Dodge before, I believe."

Little Crow was impressed. The man knew who he was. He had not told Sally what he did, and from the look, she was giving him, she was quite put out to know that the doctor knew more about him than she did. He softened his face a bit.

"I am serving with the army as a liaison to the Crow. It has been difficult. There is much double talk."

Travers nodded. "I'm afraid that is true. I hope things are worked out soon, for everyone."

Little Crow nodded, looking again at Sally. Travers noted the look on his face and knew he was being dismissed. He drained his cup and handed it to Sally, who stood looking quite flustered. Travers laughed. He couldn't help himself. She seemed so embarrassed that Little Crow had caught the two of them together. Bless her, she seemed quite taken with the fellow.

Travers walked to his horse, and Sally followed him, her heart in her eyes. Regret for what Travers might be feeling but hope for what she saw with Little Crow.

Travers cupped her chin. "Sally, you've got company. Don't let this worry you one bit. If you've a mind to see where this leads, I say go for it."

She had been holding her breath. "Truly? You don't mind?"

"We aren't exclusive, Sally. I want you to be happy. The question is, are you okay with this?"

She nodded, her eyes sparkling. "I'm very okay with this."

Travers gave her a comforting grin. "Then don't let me keep you. From the look he's giving me, I'd say it's time I took my leave. I'd like to keep my hair."

She chuckled and hugged him before he mounted. "Thanks for understanding."

She watched him ride away before she turned to face Little Crow. He was watching her still. Devouring her with his eyes. It had been weeks since she had seen him. When he had been able enough to travel, he had left in the night while she slept. Beside him, in the bed. They had slept together, but that was all. He had been too weak to do more than walk for short spells at a time. She had tried to get him to stay, begged him to stay until he was fully recovered. He had slipped away in the cover of darkness without telling her goodbye or thank you, and that had miffed her to no end. She had hoped he would find his way back. Prayed he would. She had fought her attraction to him, knowing that it could backfire on her. She had tended him so carefully as he recovered from his wound, a wound that she realized now she should have had Travers examine before he left. Little Crow had stayed with her a week, allowing her to tend him. She had memorized the planes of his face and the texture of his hair, had been unable to keep her hands off him as he slept. He had caught her at it once and had grabbed her wrist, startling her. He had stared deeply into her eyes before he pulled her ever closer until she lay in the curve of his arm, her head lying against his shoulder. That had been the night he left. And now he was back.

Her mouth felt dry as cotton. He took a step towards her, and she found her voice.

"You left without saying goodbye." It was a softly voiced accusation.

He came nearer. "Because I was coming back. Surely you realized that."

She looked away, her eyes lowering uncertainty. "I wasn't certain."

Little Crow took her face in his hands, his eyes willing her to look at him. She did, her hope written clearly within them.

"You know that we are bound now. You surely saved my life. But we have unfinished business, you and I."

Her voice was a mere whisper. "Oh?"

Little Crow merely smiled and lowered his head to her by mere degrees, finally touching his lips to hers. His mouth opened fully, his tongue searching the depths of hers to tango with her tongue, causing a knot to form deep inside her. This man made her come alive. She ached to be crushed in his arms, and she threw her arms around him, grabbing at him, needing to get closer. She was rewarded with that crushing embrace she so craved. Before she knew what was going on, he had tossed her over his shoulder and carried her into the house, closing the door behind them. He followed her down on the bed, his hands and mouth as busy on her as hers were on him. After a long moment, he pulled back and looked deep into her eyes, the question there, hovering, unspoken, but there. Sally knew he could have just taken what he wanted and walked away, never to see her again, but that was not the kind of man he was. He was considerate, strong, and respectful. He did not take this intimacy between them lightly. He needed to know that she did not as well. It was in that long pause of baited breath that Sally lost her heart to him. She placed her hands ever so gently on either side of his face and pulled him down to her, her kiss telling him all he needed to know.

Three hours later, she lay there wondering how she had ever come to be so lucky, finding this man. God has surely put him in her path. She was cradled against his chest, his hand wound in her hair even as her hand played with a lock of his. He was built so solidly, his muscles rippling under his tanned flesh. She couldn't seem to keep her hands from him. He smiled at something and then turned solemn once again, looking deep in thought.

"What are you thinking?"

"Many things." He chose not to elaborate.

"You seem so serious. Is everything alright?"

He released a long sigh. "The negotiations are not going very well. The Crow do not want to cede any more land. They have refused to speak with the white generals any further."

"I'm sorry. I realize it must be very hard for you to be in this position."

He winced. "And I am sorry that I did not tell you that I worked for your government."

"Well, it's a relief to know that you aren't out scalping people." She smiled at him, hoping to lighten the mood.

"Did you know that the white man also engages in the taking

of scalps?"

That raised her eyebrows. "No, I didn't."

"Yes. They do. For centuries now." He didn't elaborate, and Sally figured that conversation could wait for a later date. It was just as well. If he did elaborate, he would have to tell her how he had learned that many tribes in the ancient world, in times of war, even before the time of the Christ these white man worshiped, had taken scalps as a status symbol of their bravery and power in battle. He would also have to tell her about his tribal history, how the Tonkawa had been known to kill and eat the flesh of their enemies. Somehow he did not think that would go over too well. Scalping, now that was a horse of a different color. When the time came to tell her more about himself and his tribe, he would tell her how they had fought the Comanche alongside the whites and been friendly with the Apache. But he would not tell her those things yet. For now, he was happy just being here with her.

"You lost your family because of the white man."

"My family, my tribe. We could no longer fight the terrible diseases your people brought to our country. My tribe was decimated. When we signed for peace, we signed our death warrant. I am the only male warrior left of my tribe. There are others out there, but my tribe dies with me."

"I am so sorry. I am ashamed of the color of my skin sometimes."

"Don't be. You have made me realize that not all white men are bent on evil."

"Just as every Indian is not bent on killing."

"Do you believe in the Great Spirit?"

"I do. I've never been very religious, but I believe that there is a Higher Power."

"I believe the Great Spirit put you in my path."

Sally sat up, looking hard at him. "I thought the very same thing not ten minutes ago."

It was a sign. Their hearts and heads were of like mind. A peace seemed to settle on him like he had not known since before his wife and tribe was decimated. A gentle breeze found its way through the little house.

"Then this was meant to be."

He pulled her back down into his arms where he proceeded to show her just how much they belonged together, how they fit in every way imaginable, leaving Sally without a doubt that they were indeed meant to be.

⬩————⬩————⬩

Little Crow was the one to bring it up at dinner that evening.

"This Dr. Gage. Was there something between the two of you?"

Sally tried not to let him see how the question she had been dreading affected her. She had just taken a sip of her coffee, and the black brew now refused to go down. Waiting for it to slip like hot mud down her throat, she pondered what to say. He knew. Otherwise, he wouldn't ask such a loaded question.

"We were—more than friends, yes. But that ended a while back. We will always be friends, Little Crow. Travers saved my father's life during the war, and when he died, Travers was there for us. He helped me through the loneliness, the loss, and I will forever be grateful to him for that. He's a good man, Little Crow. He cares about people, not just in medical terms, and that seems to be a rarity these days. He gives so much of himself and takes so little in return."

She paused, a frown marring her brow. She was thinking of Margaret Bowers and how Travers had lost more than his heart to her. He seemed to have lost his soul as well. Maggie seemed to be oblivious to that fact, but everyone who knew Travers well knew it to be so. The light in his eyes was different these days.

Little Crow was doing some frowning of his own. He had known Sally must have dallied with the doctor. And there seemed to be a continuing real friendship. He felt the need to make his intentions perfectly clear.

"It is good you have parted but remained friends. But that is all you will be from now on. From this point on, you are mine." The gleam in his eye left no doubt as to the fact that this was no temporary fling for him. The warmth that spread through Sally pushed a smile to her face. Reaching over, she placed her hand atop his where it rested loosely near his plate.

"Travers knows that you and I are together now. He is happy for us. There is absolutely no need for you to be jealous of him. We merely helped one another through some really difficult times in our lives. Give him a chance. He could be your friend as well."

Little Crow gave her hand a gentle squeeze. He had known a moment of jealousy when he had ridden in and saw them sitting together on the porch. But he had steeled himself to fight like a gentleman for his ray of sunshine. That was what he had come to view her as: his ray of sunshine. She was like a sunbeam to him, her warmth drawing him close, creating a longing to bask in her presence. She could leave him speechless at times, though he could not tell her that. She could not know how much power she had over him. To do so might mean the difference between life and death, not just of body, but of spirit.

THIRTY-SIX

She had seen him from a distance her first night back in town. Whether or not he saw her, well, there didn't seem much point in worrying about it. Not that she figured he'd come running to greet her. Far from it actually. Figured he'd run the other way if he did see her. She couldn't blame him if he did. She had been such a naive schoolgirl, just as he had said. But she had not listened to him. Laura had even let her do this thing, this marriage to Jim Bowers. A part of her now wished that they had tied her up and run with her. She wouldn't be in this mess now if they had. She had lots of time to think now since her husband preferred the company of the other woman in town. Thank God for small miracles, she thought. There was no way she would let him touch her in that manner. She had seen a side of Jim that had frightened her and hoped to never see again. She had finally seen the ruthlessness that everyone had warned her about. The night he had come home drunk and beaten her had left her cowed for a while. Weeks of the same harsh reality of violence had passed before she finally dared to stand up to him. Jim had been alarmed. She had seen it in his eyes. Suddenly, it seemed, he was not so sure of himself where she was concerned.

And that did not sit well with him. It rankled him. But he still loved rubbing Travers' nose in the fact that the two of them were still together and he frequented the town every chance he could. Maggie had let him have his fun for a while, now it was her turn. With a fire in her eye that had not been there for some time, she had packed her bags and called for Slim to bring the carriage around.

The old man knew from the moment he saw her what she had in mind, and he silently applauded her for it. She had guts, that one. Slim hated to see the little lady go, but he knew she deserved better than what she was getting from Bowers.

When he had brought the carriage around, she climbed in and snapped the reins, her eyes already scanning the horizon for Gold City. She had not even stopped to think about the possibility of Indians in the area but figured if Slim knew there was the chance that she might run into some, he would never have let her leave.

Within an hour's time, she was there. Curious eyes turned her way as she pulled to a stop in front of the stables. The young man who tended to the horses hurried forward to help her down, and she instructed him to have her trunk taken to the hotel. Taking her satchel, she headed in that very direction, her head held high. Thankfully, no one stopped her, and she stepped inside and released the breath she had been holding.

The clerk looked at her in surprise.

"Good day, ma'am. We weren't expecting you. Will your husband be joining you?"

He seemed to stumble over the words. Moving to the desk, she sat her satchel down and peeling off her gloves informed the man that she wanted the best suite of rooms available, preferably overlooking the street. She would be paying with cash, and the stay would be— indefinitely.

The clerk gawked at her. Maggie thought she was going to have to repeat herself, but he finally gathered his wits about him and clicking his heels together, yelled upstairs for a maid. Then, remembering himself, he cleared his throat and offered Maggie some coffee or tea while she waited for the maid to prepare her rooms. Maggie told him she would love a cup of tea and he showed her into a small parlor off to the right of the lobby. She silently commanded her legs to bend so she could sit down. She hadn't realized how taut her body seemed. It was like dry wood.

The news would travel fast. A good thing Jim was in Galveston for the week. Frankly, she didn't know if she was up to a showdown with him. The time would give her a chance to prepare for the confrontation she knew was coming.

◆———◆———◆

The evening Jim Bowers returned from Galveston, he came home to an empty house. Well, almost empty. The man called Slim that served as his cook was there making supper for the men in the kitchen out back of the house. His eyebrow lifted when he was questioned about Margaret's whereabouts.

"She left."

Jim slapped his hat against his leg. "Left? Care to explain that?"

Slim just shrugged. "All I know is she packed her bags and lit a shuck out of here Tuesday. Didn't say where she was headed. I didn't ask. That ain't none of my business. What happens between the two of you stays betwixt the two of you. I ain't gettin' in the middle of it."

Jim had stared hard at the man, knowing that he knew more than he was letting on. "You made no move to stop her?"

"No, sir. I figure she's free to go wherever she pleases."

"Well, I'm afraid you figured wrong. My wife belongs here. She should have been here waiting for my return."

"For what? So you could beat her again? I'm sure she was waiting anxiously for that." Slim spat sarcastically before he could stop himself. That brought Bowers up sharp.

"You have a problem with the way I treat my wife?"

He had said too much already, but he could stand by no longer without having his say.

"She don't deserve being treated the way you treat her. She ain't never done nothing to deserve it."

"How dare you—"

Slim came at him with a long two-pronged fork. "How dare *you*! You took a good woman and abused her. She would have made you a good wife. She loved you. Even, after all, she was told about you in town she still believed in you. You proved yourself, alright. Proved they were tellin' her the truth about ya' all along. And you broke her. Broke her spirit and her heart. So don't you go tellin' me *'how dare you.'*"

Jim could only glare at the tall, thin man in disbelief. He could care less what the man thought of him. And that the man had the very gall to confront him about the way he handled his wife was unspeakable, but that could be forgiven. The simple fact that he had allowed Margaret to leave him was a death sentence. He walked away before he could say more.

That night, Bailey paid Slim a visit. The man was bunking down when the foreman called him out of the bunkhouse. Mr. Bowers wanted to see him. As Slim stood to pull his trousers on over his long johns, Bailey thrust a long wicked looking knife low into his belly. Slim gasped against the pain and pushed away from him. Bailey thrust yet again, and Slim felt himself slipping away. Just before he lost consciousness, he felt himself being lifted and placed on a horse. Bailey rode for at least two hours northeast of the ranch. He knew that Mr. Bowers wouldn't want the man's body found on his property. He chose a washed out gully along the river in which to dump the body, watching as the cook slipped from sight down the wash. He hated to see him go. He had enjoyed his cooking.

◆———◆———◆

Jim's head ached, crushingly so. He tossed his hat into the corner, noting with irritation that it missed the coat rack. Let it stay there, he was whipped. It wasn't as if his wife was there to care that it was out of its proper place. Not that she would care anyway, for she had lit a shuck out of here faster than he could sneeze. Margaret had fooled him. She had seemed cowed for a while, the beatings he had given her seemingly kept her in line. For a while. Somewhere along the line, she had grown a backbone. He was certain that it had something to do with her friends in town, though word from his men was that she kept to herself, not seeking those friends out as he had supposed she would. She was known to frequent the hotel restaurant and sip tea for hours on end. After that, she disappeared to her room upstairs.

He longed to pistol whip Travers Gage. His rage at the man had reached new levels since his wife's thumbing her nose at him. It wasn't to be borne. Dr. Gage had much to pay for. He had what Jim Bowers so desperately wanted more than anything in this world. He had killed men for it, stolen to get it when he couldn't earn it and lied to get what he craved most: Respect.

So far it had eluded him in this town. He had come here with nothing and built an empire. His ranch was a spread to be envied. He was raking in money through his investments, thanks to Charles Pritchard. He remembered the day he had walked into the bank in Columbus, Georgia. The man behind the desk had looked at him as if he had slithered in from the street. He had grinned cordially at the banker, knowing something that the man looking so disdainfully at him had not. It was the day that had changed his life.

Jim Bowers was a man who had lived a hard, hard life. His father, Cecil Bowers, had farmed from the time he was big enough to sit a horse. He had raised Jim the same way. The Bowers clan was not rich, far from it. They eked out a meager living down in the hill country of Arkansas, but Cecil Bowers had a craving for the wide-open spaces and sprawling countryside dotted with cattle as far as the eyes could see. He played at being a rancher, even though the hill country of Arkansas was not his idea of the ideal place to raise cattle. They fell on hard times, and Jim's father introduced him to the world of avarice and vice. He pulled his six-year-old son aside one day and gave him orders to fetch their neighbor's milk cow under cover of darkness. Their own had stopped producing, and there was no money to buy another. Jim had been terrified, but he had seen the gleam in his father's eyes that day and had felt the thrill of coming home with the animal on a leash. His father had heaped praise upon him, telling him how proud he was of his big boy, though in private, lest word get out where the animal had come from.

What the world didn't know wouldn't hurt them. He had learned that keeping secrets came as naturally to him as breathing. And it was no wonder. His father had taught him well. Jim had grown to manhood under his tutelage, his ability to manipulate things to his advantage stood him as an equal to the man who had raised him. When Jim was sixteen, his father became ill. Putrid fever, they called it. He ranted and raved for days, his words making little sense. The third morning, he called Jim to his bedside. There was something very important he needed to know.

Jim was not his son. It had staggered Jim. He had sat there staring at his father, wondering why the man was determined to hurt him even as he lay on his deathbed. But the words continued to pour out. His real father had lost to Cecil Bowers in a poker game. Cecil had cleaned him out. He had nothing to pay with—except his youngest son. He was actually a twin, born only moments later than the firstborn. The man had already lost everything he owned. His wife had died in childbirth, and the man didn't know how he was going to raise two newborn sons. Unable to bear parting with the firstborn, he had offered the youngest to Cecil. Cecil had agreed to the exchange as all the children he had were a passel of girls. He had come to his hotel room that night under cover of darkness and presented the four-month-old boy to him. And so he had been raised in a household of girls by a spiteful stepma and taskmaster father.

Jim had sat there dumbfounded. He had managed to get the name of the man from his father before he died. And he had found that he had died a bitter, broken man, his brother having been raised by a foster family who adopted the boy and sent him on to school, and college. He had traced him to Columbus, Georgia to the local bank and had entered his life the same way he had exited it. This time, there were strings attached. He had a need for money and a thirst for travel. Charles Pritchard, he was certain, had shivered down to his gizzard when he realized that he was blood kin to the man standing before him. He would have done anything to keep him from revealing their blood association. It would have ruined him. And so he had dealt with him, making him his partner in crime, seeing that his 'investments' paid well for Bowers. It had worked well.

Upon his third or fourth trip to Columbus, he had met Margaret and knew that he had to have her. He had known that she would surely be the cure for his 'problem.' He had been bitterly disappointed. Their marriage had been a sham. Nothing had turned out as he had planned. She had not succeeded in making him whole again, and she was not the meek and pure one he expected her to be. She had run off and left him with mud on his face. It was not to be borne. She needed to be brought down a peg or two. And he had just the man to do it. But he would wait. There was a time and a place for everything. He would get back into her good graces and bring her home where she belonged. Right now she was too entrenched in the town. But soon. Very soon.

THIRTY-SEVEN

There was a stillness settling in, a coldness that could be felt to the marrow of his bones. He had known a few hard cases in his time but this one, well, he had a really bad feeling about him. He was a killer. Not like the other gunmen who had come after him. A cold, calculating man who enjoyed his line of work, this one. Travers knew this could be it for him. His gut told him so, though he hid his fear from Laura and his friend.

The black man was in another class from Bowers, for he had a hate in him that could not be assuaged. Travers had tried to rationalize the why of it but failed long ago. Some men were just born plain loco, and nothing could stop them from wreaking the havoc they desired, except for maybe a well-placed bullet. Now, Bowers, he was just plain mean and greedy. His evil had a logic to it, whereas the gunman waiting for him in the saloon down the street did not. Travers had seen it in his eyes when the man had leaned over his desk to inform him that he would be waiting down the street for him. He supposed some men just couldn't help themselves. They hated life but couldn't gather the courage to end it themselves, so they resorted to taking their hatred out on others.

Travers was tired. He wanted to simply disappear. This lifestyle was no good for a decent man. Losing Maggie to Bowers had robbed him of something. Sally had not filled that need. Losing her to Little Crow had not hurt him deeply, which told him something. Attraction and love had absolutely nothing to do with one another. Sally had become a treasured friend. Her budding relationship with Little Crow had shocked him, certainly, but he supposed it shouldn't have. He had always sensed that Sally was looking for something he couldn't give: all of himself.

He finished his work, his muscles tense and strained. Locking up the clinic, he headed to the boarding house to collect his gun. Upstairs he went to the pitcher and basin he kept nearby and splashed his face with the tepid water. He needed every sense alert. He also made careful work of donning his hat. The sun was beginning to set low in the west, and he would be facing that way when he stepped out to meet the killer known as Barney Hickson. As he checked his gun, he realized with a start that his hand was shaking. He flexed it and held it before him, studying it. It was still as if the quiver had been a fluke. Breathing deeply, he buckled his gun belt and with a firm tug of his hat, closed the door to his room behind him.

A slew of folks was waiting for him downstairs. Laura and Flora were there, each wringing their hands in nervous energy. Sheriff Tate and Daniel were holding the small crowd at bay at the bottom of the stairs. Daniel turned to him when he heard his tread upon the steps.

"I hope to hell you know what you're doing, Travers. That man isn't like the others. He's crazy. And you can bet he won't give you a fair shake when all is said and done."

Travers digested that, knowing the schoolteacher was right. He scanned the crowd and noted Clayton wasn't there. Odd.

"Any of you see Clayton?" Several folks looked around but admitted they hadn't seen the big black man.

Laura stepped forward. "Travers, don't go out there. He'll give up and leave."

Travers smiled ruefully at her. "You really think he will?" The look on her face told him she didn't believe that any more than he did.

"Step aside. I've business to attend to." They parted like a wave for him, following him closely as he went. Daniel kept stride with him, and Travers knew there was something he had to do.

"Daniel, if things go bad, you look after the girls, you hear me? They're going to need a steady man. And check in on Maggie from time to time, will you? I'm afraid for her. Something is not right in that household. She may need a hand before it's over."

Daniel, to his credit, did not break stride. He just looked at his friend and managed a nod.

"Will do. You just make sure that you come through this. I lost too many friends in the war, Doc. I don't intend to lose anymore. I wish you'd reconsider and let me help."

Travers shook his head. "No. Someone has to stick around here if I'm gone. I'm counting on you to do that."

Travers walked on then, leaving the schoolteacher behind and felt a sense of loss. He and Daniel had been through a living hell together in the war and knew how precious life could be. He was sorry that the two of them had not been better friends since his arrival. Flora had come between them. It wasn't her fault, really, for it was Daniel who couldn't see what was right in front of his face. He had treated her atrociously and lost a bond with Travers that had been very hard to breach. Each had tried in his own way to mend things, but being men, they were both proud and determined to stand their ground. Their truce had finally begun to take hold, and now Travers was off to face a man that Daniel was certain would kill his friend. He wasn't about to stand back and watch that happen. He slowed his steps, and as Travers moved on, he sprinted towards his house on the outskirts of town.

Down the street, Hickson had found himself a source of entertainment. Earlier, he had happened across Sarah sweeping her front porch and taken a fancy to her. She had not taken a fancy to him. Clayton had been in his shop when he heard a ruckus coming from the house. By the time he got to the front to see what was going on, the gunman had Sarah up in his arms, bearing her towards the saloon. Apparently, the man had knocked her senseless for her head lolled back and forth limply. Clayton saw red, and it had nothing to do with the crimson trickle that ran down the side of his wife's face. Hickson, seeing the big bear of a man bearing down on them, pulled his Bowie knife and pressed it against her side, stopping the huge blacksmith in his tracks. Satisfied that the man would be following at a more careful distance, he had taken her to the saloon and deposited her in a chair near the bar. Sarah moaned and held her head for a few moments before coming to herself. Upon seeing Hickson, she looked frantically around for her husband, and the relief flowed from her eyes as they landed on him near the door, though he gave a sharp jerk of his head to let her know she should stay put when she would have tried to come to him. Clayton was a patient man. Years of slavery had taught him that. This man would kill his wife at the drop of a hat if he tried to be a hero. Sarah was his life and if it meant playing the killer's game, then so be it.

The black gunman, having grown bored with waiting for Dr. Gage, was forcing Sarah to dance with him now, twirling with her about the place, the knife still pressed to her ribs. The customers in the saloon at the man's harsh command had stood back to watch him lead Sarah onto the makeshift dance floor, unsure what they should do. Sarah was remaining fairly calm and caught Clayton's eye several times, their eyes meeting in silent understanding that this would soon come to an end. The knife pressed against her side had nicked her several times, but she had clamped her teeth together and bore the pain in silence lest she alert her husband to the fact that she was bleeding. Right now, they could not afford for him to do anything rash.

They had just begun swaying to another lively tune when they heard Travers call to Hickson from out in the street. The black outlaw stopped and dragged Sarah with him over to the doors of the place. Travers stood just down the street, his feet planted firmly apart, his hat pulled low over his eyes. Sarah released a sigh of relief that did not go unnoticed by Hickson.

"You think that man out there gonna save you? You'd be wrong, sistah."

"Dr. Gage has come to take out the trash, you no good nigga'. You go out there and meet your maker." Sarah glared at the man who held her so cruelly, seeing no fear whatsoever in his eyes. It was like the man was dead inside. Travers would show him, though. He had to. With a yank, the man jerked her outside with him, and she began to struggle fiercely to free herself. Upon seeing her, Travers cursed silently under his breath.

"Let her go! Now!"

Hickson shook his head. "Nope. She's gonna watch me take you out and then her and me are disappearin'." He tossed her up on his horse tied to the hitching post nearby and lashed her hands to the pommel, ignoring her screeching, clawing and kicking. Clayton had followed them closely behind and was now getting worried. He had not bargained on this. Travers noted the man's fear and called to him.

"Clayton, she's not going anywhere. Trust me." His eyes remained on the man Hickson as he took up his position in front of the saloon. He had moved just in front of Sarah, keeping her in the line of Travers' fire.

Folks were everywhere, lining the street to see the action, concern for Sarah sweeping the crowd. They kept coming, and Travers knew a moment's hesitation, concern for Sarah and the others uppermost in his mind.

It happened fast. Before anyone could catch their breath, the black man fired and Travers was grappling for his gun, staggering, bleeding, but still on his feet. He had cleared leather but not gotten his shot off, his concern that he might hit Sarah making him hesitate. He steadied himself and as the black man aimed again, unloaded on him. Travers was hit yet again, and the man down the street crumpled over, dead from a bullet through his right eye. Travers stood there for what seemed like hours before he keeled over as well. The crowd stared in hushed shock before Sheriff Tate, Flora and Laura rushed to his side.

He was hit in the chest and the abdomen, bleeding profusely from each and had lost consciousness. Clayton, having released and made sure his wife was all right, rushed to his side as well. He scooped the smaller man up and bore him to his clinic, the entire town hot on his trail. Laura and Flora ran ahead to open the door and lay out the necessary tools. They met Daniel who was just now arriving, his gun in hand. He paled at the sight of Travers in the big man's arms.

"No. . .No. . ."

"He's not dead. Yet," Flora informed him. She shoved him out of the way as they entered the place and Clayton lay the man down carefully on the nearest bed.

He never moved.

THIRTY-EIGHT

The pain just would not go away. Funny little figures and colors danced on the backs of his eyelids, reminding him of a toy he'd had as a child. A kaleidoscope. His brain swayed dizzily with each cartwheel and turn the shapes and colors took. He could hear voices as if they were in a metal drum, close but muted and echoing. They were calling his name. He ignored them at first, concentrating all his energies on fighting the blinding heat spreading through his body. Fire. He fought it. The pain. The voices. Everything suddenly turned black and red. Fiery red. Pain. Like fire.

Ah, God, he had certainly died and gone to hell! The mere thought snapped his mind, and he began to thrash about. Hands grabbed for him, restricting him, binding him, and he surged forcefully against their restraint. He clawed at them, freeing one arm, which he began to swing wildly, connecting solidly with flesh and bone. He smiled in satisfaction. Lucifer and his mightiest demons were in for a surprise. He would not go willingly. He would not! He fought them, screaming at them, his increasingly heated flesh weakening, much to his despair. He fought until he could not, soon finding that even the merest of movements was like swimming in mud. He felt as if a wall had fallen on him suddenly, his breathing cut short. He did not want to stop, could not stop. He could not give up his soul without a fight. Logic told him he must rest. He would need all of his strength for another round with the demons. They only thought they had won this round. He was not through fighting. Not by a long shot.

◆━━━◆━━━◆

The three of them were exhausted. Laura was disheveled, her hair hanging in wet curls about her face, her dress soaked with an unladylike perspiration. Flora's hair had come down completely, hers hanging wetly about her face as well. She dabbed at a bit of moisture which had run down her face to the valley between her breasts with a handkerchief she found on a table nearby. Daniel raised his head slightly to look at the two women who had collapsed, one against the wall, the other in the chair beside their patient's bed. Flora was gingerly fingering her jaw, which was even now showing signs of bruising. She worked it several times, making sure it was still in working order.

"Ya'll all right?" he asked, noting the tears in their eyes.

Laura nodded, a little numb, fearing that things had just taken a turn for the worse for the man on the bed. Flora shook her head, tears brimming in her eyes. She opened her mouth to speak, but words would not come. She pressed her lips firmly together, her eyes squeezing shut, tears escaping down the side of her pale face. Daniel gingerly eased himself off the prone body of his friend who finally seemed to be resting. He knew without a doubt he would be black and blue all over in the morning. But he would heal. The man on the bed . . . that was a different story.

———◆———

At the Sharpe homestead, Sally and Little Crow were breaking a horse. Little Crow had found him running wild along the Colorado border. There was no lead on him, nothing to indicate he had lost a rider, so he had scouted the area to make sure. Satisfied that he was a rogue, he managed to rope him and lead him home. He was a beautiful thing. Fourteen hands of pure muscle, he was a chestnut-colored thoroughbred. And he seemed to like the brave until he tried to mount him. Then all hell broke loose. The horse went one direction, and Little Crow went another. He hit hard and stayed there a minute. Sally was watching and couldn't help but laugh. She could tell he wasn't seriously hurt, even from this distance, nothing but his pride.

"Hey! You want me to talk to him? It worked with Moon Walker." She was referring to his other horse, the one who liked to bite.

"No, thanks," he said with a wave of his hand, still flat on his back, taking in the blue above him.

"Suit yourself. But I bet I could get through to him. I have a way with his type. You know, the wild, wooly, fierce male chauvinists who really are just kids at heart. Riding the plains like they have no care in the world, but they always come back home to get their back scratched, and their heads petted. And their bellies fed. Can't forget who feeds them." She was trying her best to keep a straight face, her eyes dancing with laughter, her bottom lip firmly between her teeth.

He lay there just a moment longer, before sitting up.

"You need to be horsewhipped. I am no male chauvinist, and well you know it."

"Maybe, maybe not. But you do like to prove just how much a man you are, don't you? Like refusing to allow me to help with that stallion you got there."

He rose and made his way to where she stood just outside the corral fence.

"There is no way you are going anywhere near that animal. He is far too wild. Besides, he liked me well enough at first. But this one doesn't bite. He kicks, hard, and you have no business being near him."

"Fine. Since your concern is for my safety, I guess I will let it pass. For now." She gave him a sideways grin that insinuated much.

"In the meantime, why don't you show me again just how much a man you really are," she finished softly.

He cocked a brow at her. "Yeah?"

"Oh, yeah." She sighed, her voice dropping convincingly.

He was over the fence and had scooped her onto his shoulder before she could squeal in delight. And the afternoon was spent showing her just how tender-hearted he could be, especially where she was concerned.

Two hours later, he rose, dressing as he watched her stretch luxuriously like a cat. She was so beautiful, and he felt a certain pleasure that he had put that look of pure contentment on her face. She was happy with him. She had proved that time and again over the last month or so they had been together. He felt a chill race his back, and he stiffened against it. It unsettled him, and he wasn't quite sure what had caused it. He shook it off and turned to her.

"I'm going to ride into town and see if anyone is missing that horse. Talk to the sheriff there and see what he can tell me. He's a fine piece of horseflesh. I'd like to keep him, but I need to make sure he's free and clear."

He leaned over her and gave her a lingering kiss before heading out the door. Sally groaned and rose herself, got dressed and watched him ride away. She spent the rest of the day reading and baking. Tomorrow she could wash clothes.

* * *

Little Crow rode into a town in quiet chaos. The streets were relatively empty but for a few young children darting across in front of him heading to the General Store. The boardwalks were alive with what sounded like the drone of bees, muted conversation, concern, and uncertainty a palpable vibration. He rode for the sheriff's office and found Daniel and Tate deep in conversation. They turned as one when he walked through the door.

"What has happened?" He wasted no time mincing words of greeting.

Tate looked him over. "Who are you?"

"Little Crow. I scout for the army. Mostly for General Forsyth. I am also a friend of Dr. Gage. Is he here?"

The two men exchanged looks. The grizzled sheriff scratched his chin.

"You'd better sit down, son."

"I'll stand. What has happened?"

"Travers has been shot, that's what's happened," the younger of the two said coming forward, his arms crossed over his chest.

Tate moved forward to take over the story.

"A gunfighter came lookin' for him, young, black man. He took the blacksmith's wife hostage and planned on leavin' here with her. Travers intervened in time, but he was slower on the draw than normal. I'm sure it had a lot to do with Sarah's presence, scared she'd be hit, something like that, but he was hit. Twice."

"And this gunfighter, which way did he go? I can track him."

"No need," the sheriff said with a shake of his head, his hand raised to stop Little Crow when he would have moved towards the door. "He's dead. Travers may have been hit, and badly, but he knows how to follow through on his business. Drilled him through his right eye, he did."

The scout knew a moment of relief.

"Can I see him?"

"He's not regained consciousness. There's a bullet lodged, and we can't get it out."

That brought a frown. Little Crow knew it must be serious.

"There's no one to dig it out?"

"We've tried. Daniel here has done all he can do. It's lodged, and it's perilously close to his spinal cord. There's no one else around here with the skills to do this sort of operation."

Turning to leave, he remembered to tell Tate his reason for coming in the first place. Tate said he would put the word out about the horse.

"Where you stayin' so I can reach you?"

"At the Sharpe place, when I'm not on the trail."

Tate frowned. "You two—"

"Yes. Is that a problem?" Little Crow asked, noting the confusion on the sheriff's face.

"I thought –"

"Travers and Sally have been over for a while now. Now, if it's alright with you, I'd like to go see my friend." With that, he turned on his heel and exited, hearing the bemused sheriff mutter,

"Well, if that don't beat all."

⁕

Travers was bad. Very bad. He could tell from the moment he walked in. A woman sat by his side mopping his fevered brow with a cool, wet cloth. She stood when he entered.

"I'm sorry, but the doctor can't see you." She started towards him, but he held his hand up to stop her, moving closer to Travers' side.

"I'm a friend. Of the doctor and Sally Sharpe."

"Ah," the woman said as if that explained everything.

"I'm Laura Murphy, Travers' landlord, and his friend," she said with a gentle smile and as she returned to her place beside her patient and began to bathe his brow once again. "I'm Sally's friend as well, though I haven't seen her for a while now. You must be the reason why." She sent a sly smile his way.

"I am Little Crow. I've been scouting for the army. How long has he been like this?"

"A few hours now. Daniel and Ras are trying to decide what to do. The fever is getting worse."

He took Travers' fevered hand in his own and bowed his head, prayers going to the Great Spirit for his friend. Beneath the heat of his flesh, Little Crow felt a strong pulse, and a peace settled over him. This fever, this bullet, was not going to be the death of this man. The spirits told him so. Simply knowing that took the fear away.

He rose and assured Laura that everything would be fine with Travers. She smiled weakly, and agreed, but knew that unless they got that bullet out soon, his days were numbered.

THIRTY-NINE

Maggie was beside herself in the hours after the shooting. It had taken every inch of her willpower not to seek him out to see how he was faring. Within minutes, however, the truth was all over town that Travers was critically wounded and still had a bullet in him. The clerk had come to tell her himself, and he'd had to help her to a chair before she collapsed. Travers was not, could not be dying. They were all wrong. He was too strong a man to be laid low like this. If that man Barney Hickson weren't already dead, she'd have gone gunning for him herself.

Travers was not dying. He wasn't. Yet she stayed glued to her window watching the crowd still gathered outside his clinic awaiting word on his condition. Seeing the crowd, Maggie could only assume that it was entirely possible that he *was* in bad shape. She was dying to go to him. She dared not. Jim was out of town, but his men were around. She gnawed her lip until it bled and paced the floor, only to fly back to the window every few seconds. The worrying was eating at her, so she did what she could from this side of heaven. She prayed.

She climbed into bed well past midnight and was lying there wide awake, listening for every minute sound that might suggest a change in the condition of the man down the street when she heard a timid knock at her door. Jumping to her feet, she flew to it and opened it to find Daniel standing there. He looked haggard. His hair was standing up on end, and his clothes were rumpled and bloody. She couldn't seem to raise her eyes to his, they were transfixed on the stains covering the schoolteacher's white shirt. Travers' blood.

"Mrs. Bowers?" He had to say it twice before she tore her eyes away from the mess.

"Yes?" It was barely a whisper, but he heard.

"We need your help with Travers. He's sprung a fever from the bullet that's lodged in him, and we can't get it to break. Would you come?"

Maggie looked at the man who Travers called a friend and gaped. What could they possibly think she could do? She and Travers had gone their separate ways, and she had never had training in the medical field. The frantic look in Daniel's eyes told her that anything she could do would be appreciated. She left him at the door and went to fetch her cloak from the closet. Fastening it about her, she joined him, and they hurried down the dimly lit stairs and into the night. Everyone had gone from the clinic except Laura and Flora. Sheriff Tate stood guard outside and nodded to her, tipping his hat as they hurried inside. One look at Travers and her heart skipped frantically in her chest. He was so pale. His chest was wrapped in bandages that were already soaked through with fresh blood. For a second she couldn't move, just looked at him, her mouth dry with fear.

"It's bad, isn't it?" Her words were merely a whisper.

"Yes. One of the bullets is lodged near his spine, and we can't get it out. We're afraid it's gone into his spinal cord. I've tried to remove it, but can't get it to budge. I'm afraid to do more. He's so weak from loss of blood, and now he's running a fever and thrashing about. We had to subdue him earlier. He won't last long like this. We've pretty much run out of options and were hoping you could offer some. You grew up watching him, right? Maybe you remember something that he did before on someone else. If you can think of anything. Anything at all." The look on Daniel's face was despondent.

The doctor in the next town was out. He was a certified drunk, and Travers would rather die than be worked on by a drunk. Maggie wracked her brain but knew there was nothing she could do. Except—would Travers want her to? It was a stretch and would take time, time they might not have. She didn't know, but it would give him a fighting chance. She knew she had to try, had only seconds to make her decision, and she did.

Turning to Daniel, she said, "Go get Deke Lowe."

"What?"

"Don't ask questions, just do it."

Daniel just shook his head, but he disappeared out the door. Minutes later he was there with Deke in tow. She promptly pulled the young man aside and told him, "I want you to go find Frank."

"Mrs. Bowers—"

"Go find Frank. I know you know all of his hideouts around here. If you can find him, Travers just might have a chance."

The youngster looked from her to Travers' still body lying so pale upon the bed. The decision was already made. He would die trying to save this man's life if he had to. The man had given him another shot at making something of himself when he could have laid him in his grave. The man had integrity, and he meant to give him back his life if he could. He crammed his hat on his head and led the way outside where he, Maggie, and Daniel talked quietly with the sheriff for a few minutes. The old man gave a nod and walked away. In a few minutes, he was back with a horse, but he arrived at the back of the clinic out of sight of prying eyes. Deke climbed aboard and walked the horse away. Out of earshot of the town, he put the spurs to the horse and took off into the night.

Back inside, Daniel and Maggie herded the two women out of the clinic and to their homes. They did not want to go, but listening to reason, they finally gave in. This was going to be a touchy situation and the fewer people who knew about it, the better. Daniel and Maggie would take over the care of Travers for the night and the next day, hoping to give Deke time to find Frank and get back. Time was not on their side. It was quickly ticking away for Travers.

Daniel was exhausted. He dared not sleep, as Maggie would not be able to handle Travers alone if he began to thrash about again. He noted how her eyes seemed to devour the man on the bed, pain shadowing them. There was much water under the bridge where these two were concerned.

"Deke will find Frank. If he can't, he's a resourceful young man. He'll think of something."

"He'll find Frank. Frank is close by. He has a sixth sense about these things."

"Really?" Daniel's curiosity was aroused. She seemed so certain.

"He and Travers could have been brothers. They used to finish each other's sentences, knew what each other drank before being told. He knows, and he'll be here. He won't let us down."

"You know Frank James?"

"I was just twelve when he came to Fellowship to study under Travers. He wasn't there long, but he made a definite impression. Travers was in his element. His student challenged him, pushed him, made him study more on his own. He and Travers were really close. I envied them that."

Daniel watched the play of emotions run across her face. She was beginning to open up, reveal things about their past. Perhaps he could find out what had really happened between the two of them. Travers was never going to tell him, it seemed.

"What was your relationship with Travers, Mrs. Bowers? I seem to be in the dark concerning that. Everyone seems to know except me."

She rose and moved to the side of his bed, taking a cool, wet bath cloth and ran it over Travers' face, hoping to ease the fever he was running. He never felt it.

"Travers looked after my brother and me. Our mother could barely support us. He gave us money, helped keep us afloat. We could have starved, but he stepped in and refused to let that happen. Our neighbors never came around to check on us. We were poor white trash. Then Travers came into our lives, and it was never the same. When our mother died, he sent us to Georgia to relatives. We had a row about that. But it all worked out in the end."

"Just not happily ever after?"

Her eyes turned to raise briefly to meet the brown ones of Daniel.

"No. Unfortunately not."

<hr>

At three in the morning, Frank arrived, with Deke and Jesse in tow. Deke and Jesse took the horses back out of town out of sight lest someone come along and want to get nasty with the James clan in town. Maggie almost fainted with relief.

She hugged him the instant he walked in the back door.

"Oh, God! I prayed he'd find you!"

Frank James grinned down at the slight woman he remembered as a child.

"Ms. Margaret, good to see you. Deke didn't let his shirttail touch his back in getting back here. Travers is in a bad way, isn't he?"

The knot in Maggie's throat grew, and all she could do was nod in agreement. Frank would know what to do. He eased his coat and hat off, placing them on the peg by the door, his eyes already hard on the man lying on the bed. He knew they had precious little time left to save the doctor.

"I'll need these things washed and sanitized," he said, indicating the bloody utensils Daniel had discarded in frustration hours earlier. Maggie set about doing as he instructed, glad to have something to do to keep her mind busy. Daniel got his orders as well.

"I need you to bring in fresh water, plenty of it. Set some to boiling and save the rest for bathing. We've got to break that fever." He rolled his sleeves up and when Daniel had brought clean water in, poured a bit into the basin on the table and washed thoroughly with the lye soap Travers kept on hand. He scrubbed all the way past his elbows until he was fairly pink. Daniel stood back and watched the man work, wondering how on earth he had come to be here in this place in this time, watching an outlaw the likes of Frank James attempt to save his friend's life. It was beyond real.

Maggie poured the liquid sanitizing solution over the freshly washed utensils, her nose twitching at the familiar scent of the iodine mixture. It was funny, she thought, how scents from the past remained so vivid in one's memory. She never seemed to separate Travers from that smell, no matter how much she could recall the aftershave he wore, she still associated him with the iodine smell as well.

"Ms. Margaret, I'll need your help now. I'll need you to sponge and hand me things as needed. You remember all the scalpels and clamps?"

They had played surgery back then, she, Travers and Frank, where she was allowed to participate in learning the tools of the trade. They were prepping Frank for his entrance exam. Travers had never allowed her to be present during an actual surgery but had included her when it came time for teaching Frank the basics. Frank had not minded, had actually seemed to welcome her presence. They had spent many a long afternoon learning technique, listening intently to Travers as he explained the proper use of each utensil.

"I remember. I think." She prayed she did.

"It'll come back to you. We've got to go deep and quickly. You'll have to be ready to clamp when I say clamp. Are you up to this?"

Daniel stepped forward. "I'll help if she can't."

Frank looked from Daniel back to Maggie. "She'll do it. Her life depends on it."

Each of them knew he spoke the truth. Frank discerned a lot where Travers and Maggie were concerned. Her heart was in her eyes each time she looked towards the bed. She was unable to look but unable to tear her eyes away from the man lying so still and pale. As one they moved to the bed, and without being told which wound was the problem, Frank rolled Travers over and settled him on his stomach, carefully positioning him to keep his airflow unimpeded. Travers never moved, so deeply unconscious he was. Frank rubbed his hands together and held them above Travers for a moment as if anticipating where he should begin. He took a moment to fill his lungs deeply and took up his first scalpel, cutting with precision through Travers' flesh. Maggie mopped blood that poured forth, its color a putrid shade of dark red and yellow. He dissected Travers' back and began to bore gently ever deeper until he touched what he thought was metal. He tried to leave as little damage as possible in the dig into the doctor's back, his hole smaller than Maggie could have thought possible. There was no way a bullet was coming out of that hole. But pop free it did. Maggie jumped back, her mouth forming a little 'o' as she contemplated with a bit of shock the bullet protruding through the tiny opening on Travers' back, blood pouring freely from the wound, now, pushing the bullet free. Frank caught it with a pair of tweezers and tossed it into the small pan he had ready nearby. Maggie gathered herself, the suddenness of the bullet's release having surprised her so, and set about mopping the blood away as Frank dug into Travers' flesh, searching for the torn arteries, veins, and flesh that needed repair now that the offending object was dispelled. With one clamp and a few stitches, he had the flow of blood under control.

Just like that.

Maggie sagged into a chair, her knees weak with relief. Frank had made it seem so easy, but she knew it was simply that he knew where the problem lay before being told. That sixth sense of his. Amazing. Thanks to him, Travers stood a fighting chance. But he had lost so much blood, and his fever was still so high, she thought as she ran her hand over his damp brow. Frank was washing up, giving Daniel instructions.

"We need plenty of sheets. We're going to have to bathe him down with cool water. Even with the bullet out, his body is still so weak, he's going to have a hard time fighting the infection already set up in his system. But he's strong. And he's got us to help him, right?"

They looked at one another, the three of them a curious lot. A womanizing schoolteacher, a woman who had walked out on the richest man in the territory, and an outlaw with a hefty price on his head. Travers certainly had a motley crew of friends.

"Right." Maggie wasn't about to let Travers down. She could do this for him, fight for him because he no longer could, his strength gone, weakened by a bullet meant to kill him. Barney Hickson had not won this round yet. And he would not. Maggie meant to see that he didn't.

FORTY

Travers woke to find it dark in the room, a single lantern lit, casting a golden ring of light around the place. His eyes roved, searching for his bearings and he realized he was in bed in his clinic. He was sore. All over. He eased his body to find a more comfortable position on the bed and gasped at the searing pain that tore through him. His forehead dampened immediately with perspiration. He stilled instantly, his body arguing at the merest of movements. He was alone in the room. Someone apparently had been there. The fire was stoked in the heater, and he could smell fresh coffee which seemed to be brewing in the pot on top of the little heater stove. He sighed, gingerly, and lay back, closing his eyes against the burning pain that seemed to be awakening inside him. He prayed that someone would show up soon.

A quarter hour passed before they did. By that time, Travers was feeling the need to relieve himself something fierce. How long he had been ill, he did not know, but it must have been for some time for the need on him had become desperate. It was Daniel who opened the door and stepped through. Seeing Travers, awake froze him in his tracks.

"Thank God! I need to use the can."

The schoolteacher grinned as he hurried to his side and helped Travers sit up, taking extra care with him. He gave him a few minutes privacy then removed the jar and eased the doctor back down, noting the pale face beneath a fine sheen of sweat.

"All right, there, Trav? My goodness, you gave us a mighty scare. It's good to see you awake finally." Daniel's eyes crinkled, and he smiled at the man lying on the bed.

"What happened?"

"You don't recall?"

Travers gave a slight shake of his head, noting the pain slivering down his neck.

"No. Nothing."

Daniel eased into the chair beside the bed and clasped his hands together and rested them across his middle, reclining in the chair as he was wont to do.

"Barney Hickson is what happened. The black gunslinger."

"Who?" The name wasn't registering.

Daniel frowned. "Barney Hickson. He was a black gunsling-er. Came here to kill you. Nearly succeeded. Claimed he was a bosom brother with Dillinger, a man you killed a while back."

Travers lay there, absorbing that information. His memory was fuzzy, and he couldn't seem to recall anything. Daniel. What was Daniel doing here? The last time he had seen him had been during the war. Yet here the man was, in his clinic in Gold City just as if he had been here countless times before. He looked as if he had been wrung through a wringer, Travers would give him that. Apparently, the task of tending to Travers had fallen to him.

"So apparently he won." The black gunslinger could not be placed at all.

"He got you good. Twice. But you went down shooting, and he bought a first class ticket to Hell. We were afraid he'd taken you along for the ride. If it hadn't been for your friend Frank—"

"Frank?" Travers interrupted him.

"Yeah. It was Maggie who suggested it. Saved your life, he did. Not to worry though. Tate and Jesse kept close lookout lest anybody suspect anything."

"Maggie?" Travers felt sick suddenly, nausea rolling through him and his head began to pound. He hadn't thought about her for some time and here Daniel was speaking of her as if she were in the next room.

Daniel noted his parlor and frowned. Travers was acting mighty strange. He hadn't been able to recall the shooting, and now he seemed ill at the mere mention of Margaret Bowers.

"Travers, can I get you anything? Something for pain, something to eat? It's been ten days since the shooting. A bit of chicken broth maybe to help build your strength?"

Travers was having a hard time breathing. The pain was becoming intense.

"Laudanum. There's a bottle in my desk that I keep for my personal use. Hurry." He closed his eyes against the pain.

Daniel stepped into the office to fetch the bottle Travers had requested. In seconds he was back, his mouth still going.

"Clay and Sarah's sure gonna be happy to see you're awake. They've been beside themselves since the shooting. Course, they owe you. Hickson planned to ride out of here with Sarah. Clayton played it cool knowing you had everything under control. Scooped you up like a child and carried you here himself. I do believe that man would walk through fire for you." He gave the bottle to Travers who tipped it and pulled deeply from it, raising the schoolteacher's brow a bit. The doctor ran his hand across his mouth and recapped the bottle. He did not give it back to Daniel.

"Clayton carried me in here?"

Daniel nodded.

"And Sarah, she's alright?"

Daniel frowned. "Travers, you don't recall anything, do you?"

Travers sighed. His eyes still closed, he said, "No. I think I need to rest a while." He closed his eyes against the image of Maggie. Why would he mention her? His eyes flew open at the schoolteacher's next words.

"I'll get Maggie in here with something to eat. You could use it. Then you can rest."

"She's here?!" There was panic in the doctor's eyes.

"Well, she only went back to the hotel to change. She should be back any minute."

"For God's sake, don't let her back in here!"

"Travers, what is wrong with you?"

"Nothing. I just don't want—her to see me like this. I can't seem to recall a thing. About anything."

Daniel scratched his head. His friend certainly didn't act like he remembered a blooming thing. He sighed.

"Alright. I'll send Sarah in with a bite to eat. Sarah's been doing the cooking for us. Flora and Laura were tending you for a while until I relieved them. I don't think I've ever seen two women more emotional over a man before. Durn near had me squalin'."

Travers didn't respond, and Daniel left, his thoughts a' jumble. He intercepted Maggie just as she was leaving the hotel and informed him of Travers wish that she not return. The look on her face tore at him, but he could not go back on Travers' wishes. She turned on her heel and hurried back into the hotel lest he see her tears fall. He crossed the street to Sarah's place and gave Sarah and Laura the good news that the doctor was finally awake. After asking them to fix a bit of broth and to take it to their patient, he went in search of Flora.

He found her in her sitting room overlooking the small garden she and Laura had created out back of her place, and she appeared lost in thought. He considered not disturbing her but knew she would want to know the good news. He cleared his throat, and she jumped, her hand flying to her throat.

"I didn't mean to startle you. I thought you'd like to know, Doc is awake."

Joy flooded her face, and she launched herself at him, her arms about his neck clinging. He laughed at her exuberance and swung her about, knowing the joy she must be feeling. Inside, however, he felt he was dying. He had suspected all along. She was in love with Travers. Despite Travers' protestations to the contrary, he still believed that she was in love with the doctor. He would never figure into her life the way the doctor did. Even after the apology the other night, and the heated kiss that promised much, he still believed she longed for Travers. He'd had his chance with her, and he had thrown it away. He had been such a fool.

Flora pulled back and gazed up into Daniel's eyes noting the lost expression in them. She smiled at him, then surprised him by locking lips with his, and he stood there in shock before he crushed her to him and returned the kiss hundredfold. When he released her, they both gasped for breath. The question burned through Daniel, and he could stand it no more.

"I don't understand. I thought—" she put her finger to his lips, silencing him.

"I do love Travers. He's always been there for me. Losing him would be like losing a part of myself. The same way I'd feel if I lost Laura. But if I lost you, I'd die."

Her words hit him broadside, and it took a moment for him to digest their meaning. Her eyes glistened with unshed tears, but the smile on her face blinded him. Dear God. Could he possibly still have a chance with her?

"You mean—"

"I love you, Daniel. It's always been only you. Travers was just a way to make you jealous. He thought you needed your nose tweaked just a bit. There has never been anything but friendship between us. Ever."

Daniel smiled. "From the moment I saw you, I couldn't get you out of my mind."

"It was the same for me. The day you came to town and stepped off that stagecoach. One look and you took my breath away. Even if you have proven to be a blockhead who continues to believe I want another man." The last was said softly, seriously, accusingly.

Daniel had to grimace. "Guilty as charged, madam. I know I have a lot to make up for. How about dinner tomorrow night?"

"*Tomorrow* night?"

"Well, Red, it's like this. I'm dead on my feet. Afraid I wouldn't be very good company tonight. I'm running out of steam fast." His eyes were ringed from lack of sleep. Flora grinned.

"You're off the hook—for tonight. And you're right. You have a lot of making up to do, Mister." She polished that statement off with a kiss that scorched his lips and promised forever.

✦——✦——✦

Travers sighed with relief when Laura appeared, bearing a covered tray laden with a bowl of broth and tea. He had dreaded seeing Daniel again, though couldn't be sure why. His last memories of the man were during the war. What was he doing in Gold City? He had mentioned Maggie as if he knew her personally and spoke of Frank James as well. Travers had never told Daniel about either of them. It made no sense. The injury. Daniel had said that he had been unconscious for ten days. Laura could set things right. She would tell him what had happened.

Laura gave a sunny smile when she saw Travers was awake.

"It's about time! You sure know how to age a woman. I don't know what I'd have done without Daniel and Flora. You are a hand full when you're ill. Next time you decide to go getting yourself shot, I'm going on vacation!"

Travers offered up a slight grin, careful to move nothing more than his mouth and eyes. The simple act of moving the muscles in his face sent hot shivers down his neck and coursing through his spine.

"You are a welcome sight, I'll give you that."

"I'll bet you're starved. Daniel and Frank say you're to eat the minute you're awake. Seems we owe Mr. James a huge debt. He saved your life, you know."

"You met Frank James?"

"No," Laura admitted, with a negative shake of her head, "Daniel and Margaret were the only ones allowed to stay. Sheriff Tate felt it would be best that way. He and Deke kept watch out back at the schoolhouse. Flora and I were ushered out pronto. I have to admit, we were exhausted. We hit the sack back at my place and slept 'til noon the next day. We've all been taking shifts ever since, Clay and Sarah, Ras and Louella included. Margaret popped in when she could."

She fluffed the pillow up a bit and eased him up so she could feed him. She set the tray on the table beside his bed and took up the bowl of broth, spooning it. She sat beside him carefully and looked at him expectantly, indicating that he should open wide.

"Laura, what day is this?" Travers was so trying to be casual.

"Well, you've been out the tenth day. This is Tuesday, the twenty-first."

"No, I mean, what day, what year?"

That got her attention. She put the spoon back in the bowl.

"Travers, you know that it's April. We had that big cattle auction last month in town. And Daniel and the children had their spring pageant."

"Laura, the last thing I remember about Daniel is telling him goodbye during the war. What is the date?"

Laura could only stare in confusion at him.

"It's April 21, 1873."

1873. . .time had flown. He had come to Gold City in 1866. He remembered—the last thing he remembered was the train ride home from Boston. He had been to a medical conference there and had visited his friend Thomas Allen. That had been in spring of '68.

"Travers, what is wrong? What is the last thing you remember?"

"Coming home from Boston on the train. I had been to that medical conference."

"That can't be. That means you don't remember—" Laura clamped her mouth shut abruptly.

Travers was missing time.

Five years worth. Including Maggie Bowers' entrance to Gold City. This was in no way good. He would have to be told that she was here. Surely he already knew that. He didn't know the circumstances of why.

"Maggie?" Travers finished for her.

"You do know that she is here. You owe part of your recovery to her. It was her idea to fetch Frank. Fortunately, Deke Lowe found him quickly enough. You don't remember anything about her coming to Gold City?"

Travers frowned, thinking on it but finding his mind clean as a blank slate where Maggie was concerned. The memories of her as a child still haunted him. Didn't they?

"When did she arrive?"

"A few days before you got back from Boston. You ran into her the very evening you got back."

"Tell me about her. What does she look like?"

"Well, she's quite lovely. She has hair the color of pitch and the bluest eyes I've ever seen on a person. She's quite proper and petite, and the two of you have been at loggerheads ever since her arrival." There, she had said it. He needed to know.

"How so?"

Laura sighed, knowing this was not going to go over well. She set the bowl back on the tray, sensing that the broth might not get eaten this night.

"She's married, Travers. To none other than Jim Bowers."

Travers clenched his eyes shut against that image. Of all things he could have conjured up, that had not been it. Married to Bowers. Good, God! Had she gone insane?

"Please tell me that I'm dreaming, that all of this is just a really bad dream."

Laura shook her head. "I can't, Travers. It's the truth. Although, I will say that she finally grew a backbone and moved into town not long ago. They are still married. He comes to town to check on her, then abandons her for Celia." At Travers' raised brow, she shook her head, saying, "That's a story in itself. Maggie keeps to herself these days. Bowers escorts her to social functions, a chore that he has delighted in as of late. But for the most part, she stays upstairs in her hotel room."

"And she helped me?"

"Yes. She does still have feelings for you, Travers. I believe she loves you as you do her. But she had already committed to Jim before she arrived here. She couldn't be convinced otherwise. I believe she had true feelings for the man. She must have been devastated to learn how false he played her."

"We never got the proof against him that he was a killer?"

"No." She studied him closely, noting his frown as he swallowed that last bit of information.

"I suppose this means you'll have to go through a living hell once again where she's concerned. I don't know if you'll be able to stand it. I don't know if *I'll* be able to take it, watching you go through this yet again."

Travers sighed, knowing that what she said must definitely be true. Maggie had held such a tenacious place in his heart for all of those years, and her coming back into his life had to have been catastrophic. Enough to make him block her from his memory after being wounded so gravely. Perhaps it was for the best. His body and mind had shut the painful memories out to help itself heal. He had heard of amnesia cases before but had never seen one first hand. Now he was living it. It was an odd twist of fate. Maggie's memory had surely pulled him through the war, saving his sanity when he was surrounded by so much death. Now she was here, and he couldn't even recall her features. Each mental vision he brought to mind of Maggie was of her as a child. And yet, a nagging feeling tugged at his heart, a painful, painful feeling, as if a piece of him was missing. Laura had implied much with her last comment.

"You mean I took her being here hard?"

"Travers, she married a killer. You fought for her, and she chose him over you. You've— adjusted. You have your friends and your work. You're managing to go about your life as if you haven't lost a piece of yourself." She noted the dark frown. "Yes, Travers, I know how badly you wanted things to work out for the two of you. I tried to be that voice of reason for both of you. Hell, I was the maid of honor at her wedding! She wasn't just a person from your past, she became my friend, too. And I tried to talk sense into her. I did. But I also saw her point of view. She wasn't so jaded that she could see the evil that exudes from the man. But she learned. I say better late than never."

He was tired of talking about it. Maggie hurt to think about. She always had. He closed his eyes, hoping Laura was finished with her narrative on the matter. He didn't give her a chance to change the subject. He did it for her.

"And Frank? What was Daniel thinking, bringing him into

town?"

"I don't think he was thinking about anything except getting you help, Travers."

"Well, it was too dangerous. Frank and Jesse don't go into a town lest they are preparing to rob the bank."

Laura snorted. "Well, they didn't rob *our* bank! Frank James saved your lousy hide! I gathered that you two were friends. This memory loss you're experiencing must have sure enough addled your brain."

She gathered up her skirts and went to the door. "Since you're in such a glorious mood, I think you can feed yourself. I suggest you get to pumpin' that spoon. You're gonna need all the strength you can get when you face Maggie Bowers, I reckon."

With that parting shot, she flounced out of the clinic, her face flushed.

Outside, Laura had to get hold of herself. She knew she shouldn't have spoken so to Travers, but he was lashing out so. She knew it had to be frustrating for him to be in the predicament he was in, but his friends had given their all to see that he pulled through this crisis. It wasn't like Travers to be insensitive. Perhaps the injury was more severe than they had anticipated. She would speak to Daniel about it. Soon.

FORTY-ONE

Maggie had hoped that in the days that followed Travers would call for her. He didn't. Weeks passed, and still, she was unable to see him. He stayed in the clinic even after he was able to get around on his own. He was hiding from her, she was certain. Laura had told her that there was a complication with the injury, though nothing to be overly concerned about. She learned from Daniel that Travers was suffering from a bout of amnesia. He wanted to send for Frank again, but Travers had forbidden it. It was surreal to think that Travers didn't remember her. For so long, she had convinced herself that no matter what happened, she would always fit into Travers' thought process, even if they were enemies of the worst sort. Now, to think that he only recalled her as a child gave her pause.

She had re-entered his life so suddenly those years ago, never actually believing that she would ever see him again. Oh, she had prayed fervently for it to happen but had despaired of it actually ever coming true. The day she had seen him get off the stage after her arrival in Gold City had flipped her life upside down. Her heart had stopped, her tongue frozen to the top of her mouth as she had watched him bend the kinks from his body after being shut up in the stagecoach from an apparently long journey. He had seemed to step right out of her fantasies and life as she had known it had never been the same

No, fitting into Travers' thought process was the least of her worries at the moment. The most important thing was that he gets well. And her husband and the world could go to hell for all she cared. Just let Travers get well.

⸻ ◆ ⸻

The last several weeks Travers had managed to get his thoughts wrapped around the idea that Maggie was indeed here in Gold City. He had all but taken up residence in his clinic, trying to regain his strength and get his bearings. He felt all off-kilter, his mind all a' jumble and his body lacking the agility he once had. Travers hated illness, hated how it could tear a body down and destroy. Hated how it made him feel. He knew his temper had been on a short leash as of late with even his closest friends, and he knew he should apologize for his abruptness, but he was riding a tide of frustration that could not be borne. Travers hated helplessness in a man, and right now he was feeling

279

just that. There was no telling when he would get his memory back, and he had recalled nothing as of yet. That aggravation alone was enough to give him the disposition of a bear with a bad tooth.

He was peering out the window one afternoon when he saw a young man cross the street towards the General Store. He looked familiar, but Travers could not place him. At a distance, it was hard to see his features very good, but Travers felt he should know him but could not put a name to him. He waited for the man to exit hoping for a better look at him, thinking that he would jar his memory. He was to be disappointed. He drew a blank once again. Laura came that evening, and he asked her about the man he had seen. She frowned thinking, then nodded.

"You must be talking about Rance. Smallish, very slender with glasses? Real studious? Wavy hair? That's got to be him."

"He carried a large parcel from the General Store."

Laura nodded. "He's a very talented painter. He fancied himself a writer when he first came out here. But he's established himself as quite an artist since he's been here. Another thing he owes to you."

Travers frowned. "I don't follow."

"You noted how talented he was at the church picnic a few years back. Seems you convinced him to start painting portraits. He keeps quite busy, so I hear. Why you yourself told him you'd get one done. He's still waiting for that sitting, by the way." She continued to drone on about the goings on in the town, and Travers occasionally nodded when necessary though he was only half listening his thoughts silent chaos.

So, Rance was an artist. That was interesting. And it put a thought in his head . . .

⁕——⁕——⁕

Another day and it would be three months since he was laid low by the black gunslinger. Three months. After much consideration and desperation, Travers determined that the man had taken enough of his life. For the past few months, he had cloistered himself away from the town, mostly out of fear. He didn't want their pity. He didn't want their sympathetic, knowing looks. He wanted simply to get back to living. Only, doing so meant confronting Maggie, and he still had serious issues with that. He had hoped to settle his wildly scattered brain by harnessing the talents of her brother Rance. He had spoken to Daniel and got him to have Rance stop by one evening. The meeting had helped. Rance was not an overtly friendly person by nature, so his demeanor had kept things low key and undramatic. He tried to keep the true nature of his injury as secret as he could, simply putting the request to Rance for a specially commissioned paint-ing, one done in secret—of Maggie. Rance had simply frowned, thinking the prospect over and had finally agreed to the project. They agreed that Rance would come to the clinic to paint and keep Travers company as he did so. Travers had simply wanted to be part of the creation process. He didn't want to be shocked by the initial finished product. He wanted to see the image take form on canvas. He felt he could handle seeing Maggie a grown woman better this way.

And it had helped tremendously. Rance had appeared at two o'clock every afternoon and had set out his paints and performed magic on the canvas. A bit here and there, the outline of her on day one before Rance had to hurry to another sitting appoint-ment. It was frustrating, the waiting, but Travers knew this was the best way. When the day came that Rance presented him with the finished product, Travers could only stand back and stare. And stare. Even knowing, warned that the child had become a beautiful woman, he had been taken aback. And to think that he had come so close to having her as his own. Rance had outdone himself. He had captured the twinkle in her eye that Travers al-ways remembered from her as a child, that spark that she always had that set her apart from other children. But this was no child upon the canvas. The ebony hair that was so obviously silken to the touch was portrayed so vividly, and the porcelain of her skin reminded him of the creamy flowering magnolias from back home. Her eyes seemed to pierce him from the canvas, looking deeply into the soul of the person doing the viewing.

Travers barely remembered paying Rance for the portrait before he departed, on his way to another appointment, so en-grossed was he in the painting. And if Travers had fallen in love with Maggie Pritchard before, he suddenly realized that he could be accused of doing the same yet again. His heart twisted think-ing about her and the path that she had chosen. Jim Bowers was no man capable of true affection. If what Laura said was true, her marriage was a sham.

On more than one occasion he found himself drawn to the portrait, his hand reaching to trace the line of her features, imag-ining that the flesh he was caressing was alive, the ebony hair, slinking through his fingers. Only a skilled artisan could have created the piece before him. A man who knew his work knew his subject and held a love for the person in the portrait. Rance was good. Damn good. His work should be in a museum some-where, Travers thought, for he had brought Maggie to life on canvas with a vibrancy that shook Travers. Now that he knew what she looked like, he feared to face her.

FORTY-TWO

Travers succeeded in avoiding Maggie for a few weeks more. A soldier from Fort Wallace came in search of him and his services. They had been chasing the Sioux and Cheyenne back across into the mountains and foothills of Colorado and had sustained heavy casualties as well as having wounded prisoners. The doctor at the fort had sent for experienced help. Travers had hesitated briefly, thinking it might be too soon to jump head first into things, as he had not opened his clinic since the shooting. But it was time. He had hidden out for long enough, had healed as well as could be expected. He was as fit as he ever would be. He got a few things together and met the lieutenant out front where he had his horse saddled and waiting for him. On the way out of town, he stopped at Laura's and let her know the situation and told her to be sure to let Ras, Daniel, and Clayton know where he had gotten off to and that it would be some time before he made it back.

All the way to the fort, the lieutenant told about the 'stinking savages' and how they had routed them, forcing those taken prisoner to walk to the fort, the chiefs stripped of their headgear, feathers and such. It was meant to demoralize them, and Travers gritted his teeth, wondering how the officer gloating so across from him would hold up under the same circumstances. He would probably be begging for mercy. Travers set his goal then and there on treating the prisoners first. The doctor at the fort would probably have a fit, but he was not about to let them suffer at his hands. The soldiers could just be damned. Most of them had a death wish anyway if they thought that these people could be routed so easily.

He got a pleasant surprise when they reached the fort. Little Crow was there, and he came out to meet him when he saw him. Instinctively Travers knew him, although his memory had not completely come back. Seeing him, though, he was flooded with memories of the warrior and of Sally, the general's daughter. Laura had filled him on all of the people he had close contact with, and as time passed, memories came back. It was good to know that some of those memories were good ones of good friends. Travers dismounted and extended his hand in greeting. The brave took it somberly.

"I trust you are recovered from your wounds. I offered sacrifice to the Great Spirit in your honor."

Travers nodded. "I am much recovered. And thank you for your offerings. It was kind of you to think of me."

Little Crow shrugged. "One must do what one can for a friend. Sally sends her regards." He didn't mention the doctor's memory loss, though Laura had sent word to them shortly after the shooting that Travers may not recognize them if the occasion arose that he should run across them. It was good to be remembered.

Travers smiled, the creases about his eyes beginning to now show his age. A myriad of thoughts flashed across his consciousness. He couldn't help but think that while he had first thought this couple an unlikely pair that they were most definitely suited to one another.

"How is she? It's been a while since I saw her. I've been meaning to ride out and pay a visit, but I've only recently gotten my feet under me good."

"She is with child, I believe." The brave offered a smile of his own, one that stretched proudly across his handsome face. Travers could tell by the expression on his face that this was a most special occurrence. He clapped the man on the back and offered his congratulations, his heart happy for the two of them. He offered to ride out and examine Sally to confirm that she was indeed expecting and Little Crow gladly accepted the offer. He knew Sally would appreciate that he would let this man continue to be her doctor. Women had it hard enough out here, but pregnancy was a harsh reality on the plains. One might go for weeks without seeing another human being, and then they might not be of the friendly persuasion. They continued their chatter until the lieutenant cleared his throat loudly, grumpily, indicating that he was waiting to take him to the infirmary. Travers pointedly looked at the man before turning his back on him and resuming conversation with Little Crow, although he turned the conversation to the prisoners in the stockade. According to the scout, all of them had been taken to the stockade with no medical attention. Travers headed in their direction, his anger on a slow burn. Little Crow saw the reaction and knew a moment of pride. Travers Gage was not one to shirk duty or responsibility. He knew that in all cases, the critical of all men, soldiers or prisoners, were to be treated first. It had not been done in this case. He kept step with the doctor as they found the stockade.

A guard was on duty and seemed flustered when Travers demanded to be let in.

"But sir, Dr. Gibbs requires your assistance at the infirmary, not the stockade."

"It would seem that Dr. Gibbs has his hands full at the infirmary. I'll see to the wounded here. He can't be everywhere at once, corporal." Travers stared him down, his resolve solid as stone.

"I don't know, sir—" the young man was still hesitant. At that moment, a man appeared in the doorway of a building across the compound from them, his apron covered in blood, both fresh and dried. He waved briefly before striding over to them, his frown making known his consternation at being left waiting. They waited patiently for him to reach them. Travers could have groaned aloud when the man drew nearer. It was Creighton Gibbs, one of Morgan's lackeys from the war. Nearly as incompetent as his predecessor, he was one who thought highly of himself and his abilities but couldn't pour piss out of a boot without drenching himself with it. Travers' day was just getting better and better.

Gibbs pulled up and didn't offer his hand in greeting.

"Well, you took your time getting here, I see. And standing here talking to the riffraff instead of doing your job. I have men waiting to be seen to."

The man certainly had changed, and if anything, he was worse. Another Morgan, snide, whip-sharp tongue. No class. No respect for authority. *He* was the authority, or so he thought. Travers hardened his face against the man, the pot shot he had taken at Little Crow not about to go unaddressed.

"That man is my friend and a paid scout for the U.S. Army. Little Crow might allow himself to be spoken of in such a way but I won't. There is no excuse for ill manners. Next time your tongue makes such sorry conversation with him as the subject, I'll wrap it around your neck for you." The softness of his voice and the gentle grin belied the doctor's anger, and Gibbs took a step back, knowing he had pushed too far already. He puffed himself up like a fighting rooster and stammered plaintively, "I've got men waiting who need a surgeon."

"Are they critical?"

"Well, no—"

"Then they can wait until I have seen to the critical of the prisoners. Little Crow says there are several who need immediate attention."

Gibbs looked at the Tonkawa scout, the disdain in his eyes. Little Crow held his glare, thinking this man had much to learn about dealing with people. He read the hate and spite there, knew he had made an enemy this day without even crossing words with him himself. Travers had put the pompous little toad in his place and all because of him. No, the man would not be forgetting him or Travers. The man turned to Travers then.

"I'll be at the infirmary." With a quick spin, he darted back across the compound and back into the building from whence he had come.

Travers shook his head. "Let's see to the prisoners, shall we?"

They were distrustful of him, to be sure, but with Little Crow helping by translating, he managed to gain their trust and respect when they saw that he meant them no harm. Two were indeed critical, and Travers didn't know if one of them would make it or not. He had a lacerated liver, and he had done all he could, but the warrior had lost a lot of blood. He advised the war chief Dull Knife and the medicine man Little Wolf that they should offer up medicine and pray to the Great Spirit. They nodded their understanding and thanked him in their own tongue which Little Crow translated back to him. Little Crow began to question those being helped and found that they were actually a hunting party. They had been forced to leave their reservation because of the Pawnee and Paiute coming to steal their deer and buffalo. This was no war party. There was no war paint on their faces. They wore skins and hides to conceal their features but no paint. A grave injustice had been done here, Travers felt. He moved on to the others, encouraging Little Wolf to continue helping, as he had been doing upon Travers' and Little Crow's arrival, administering herbs and pastes to flesh wounds and treating them as they were accustomed. Travers examined all of the wounded to make sure they were in no danger of developing infections. He was pleased with what he found and told Little Wolf so. The medicine man said nothing, but his chest seemed to swell with pride that this white doctor had praised his work. Often, that was not the case. Medicine men were often seen as witch doctors and treated as freaks by the white man. But this one, he showed respect, and in doing so, he earned it in return. He watched the white man work as he went from warrior to warrior. He was patient, had a gentle touch that was sure and steady. He spoke directly to each man he treated, pausing to allow Little Crow to convey his words to his patient. He greeted each man with the same friendly chatter and never made any comment about them being prisoners.

Little Wolf was not the only one taking notice of the white doctor. Dull Knife was sizing him up as well. Travers knew this. He knew they were taking his measure and they had every right to. From all he had heard, these two were good men. They were not hot heads who jumped at the chance to fight. They could be reasoned with. They were distrustful and with good reason. They were looking for someone to trust, someone to speak for them to the white government. They had a people to protect, a way of life at stake. Of course, they would fight if push came to shove. Who wouldn't? Travers could well identify with that. But he knew they were done for. Before this fight for land and rights was over, most of the men in this stockade would be dead, their leaders included. It saddened him. Life was full of rotten apples. He turned to his work with more fervor, his mood even more sour than before. He treated them all before making his way to the infirmary.

———————

He was on his way home. He had been gone four days in all. Travers had taken one look at Gibbs' handiwork on the soldiers he had treated and gritted his teeth in frustration. How a man could be so incompetent was beyond him. Many of the wounded he had treated were so weak from loss of blood from wounds that could have so easily been stanched with the proper application of pressure, but apparently, Gibbs had no clue how to do even that, one of the simplest of things a doctor learned. Gibbs was no doctor. He couldn't even be credited with knowing how to apply dressings properly. He was a shame and disgrace to the uniform. After doing his duty to the men in blue, Travers sought out the commanding officer of the post.

Major George Forsyth was a veteran Indian fighter. He had been involved in several campaigns up to this point and felt he knew how to handle these insurgents. As if Indians weren't enough to deal with, here this Dr. Gage was telling him that the post's 'doctor' was no doctor at all.

"Dr. —Gage, is it? Well, I'm afraid he's all that the Army has to offer at the moment. No decent, God-fearing white man other than soldiers are eager to trek out here and set up shop. That is why we sent for you when we heard you were nearby. Custer came through here the day before we encountered the war party and said you were in the area. Said Hancock thinks mighty highly of you. If you're interested in taking over Gibbs' job, I could arrange—"

"No thanks. I'll be heading home now." He turned to go, then paused, turning back.

"Major, what will become of the prisoners?"

"They will be given a chance to surrender and go to the reservation. If they refuse, they will be sent to Fort Dodge and tried for murder."

"Murder! You can't be serious! They were merely out hunting, and you opened fire on them. Did you just expect them to lay down and die for you?"

"A pity they didn't. It would have saved time and ammunition if they had." The major's lip curled in distaste. He cared not one whit for these Redskins. They should all be exterminated in his opinion, but he didn't run the country. But Washington was a long way away from Kansas territory, and there were ways to deal with matters that Washington would never hear about.

Travers looked hard at the man before turning on his heel and stomping out. Little Crow was waiting for him. "Will you come to the stockade?"

Travers gave a nod and walked with him to where the hunting party was being held. There were eighteen of them, and all of them stood when he entered the stockade, even the one he had feared would die. His color was much better, and his eyes met Travers' with strength. He was being supported by Little Wolf, but he was on his feet. Dull Knife stepped forward and extended his hand in greeting. Travers took the warrior by his forearm.

"It is good to see everyone mending so well. I'm afraid it's time for me to go home. Is there anything else I can do for you before I go?" He knew there was, else he wouldn't be here.

Buffalo Hump spoke, haltingly, in English. "We hoped you would speak to the soldier chief for us. We have had no audience yet. Maybe you could speak for us."

Travers sighed. He had feared this was what they wanted.

"I have asked Major Forsyth what he planned to do with you. He says you will be given a choice to go back to the reservation or you will be sent to Fort Dodge and tried for murder."

Little Crow quickly translated for the others. There was a growing mumble, and Dull Knife's face became like a thundercloud.

"Murder? We fight because we must. They shoot first and take prisoners later. Why are we murderers?"

"I do not know, Dull Knife. But I have a feeling if you don't get out of here soon, the choice will be taken out of your hands."

The brave nodded. He had suspected as much. This man had spoken truth to him. It was why he had hoped for his help. When he looked at Dull Knife he saw not a savage, but a man. "We had feared such. We have the plan to escape but need help."

Travers looked at Little Crow who simply looked back at him, his eyes not giving away whether he had known they wanted his help for a jailbreak. This could not be good.

"What did you have in mind?"

Little Wolf pulled a leather pouch from inside his shirt. "Hops and Valerian root. Put in tea or coffee and make guard sleep."

Travers rubbed at his head, thinking. Okay, they needed help getting the herb into a drink and getting the guard to drink it. It could be done. Couldn't it?

"How much have you got?"

"Enough," the war chief told him confidently.

"Enough for two or more? It has to look good. And does it

smell?

"Like dirty feet."

Travers chuckled. "And you think anybody will drink something that smells like that?"

"Coffee mask smell, maybe. Have same effect. Make coffee weak. Strain roots after steep a bit. Make drink dark."

He scratched his chin. It could work. It could. They just had to have a plan.

Ten minutes later, he left the stockade with the pouch under his vest. He went to the infirmary and checked on the men left in there recuperating. Gibbs walked out when he entered. Good riddance, Travers thought. Only three men were remaining, and all had been placed on complete bed rest due to their injuries. One had a broken leg. The other two had been wounded several times by arrows. Most of them were not serious but had the potential to be if they didn't take good care of themselves and let their wounds heal. He checked them, changed the wounds and left. Gibbs was nowhere to be found.

Outside in the courtyard, he found the company getting ready to pull out. Forsyth and the soldier guarding the stockade were talking. A frown on Travers' face, he headed for them.

"Major, where are you headed? Surely you aren't going to leave when you have a stockade full of prisoners!"

Forsyth looked askance at him as he pulled on his gloves. "We've got orders to meet Colonel Reynolds at the Ladder River. They've tracked some more Cheyenne and Sioux near there."

Travers couldn't believe it. "And you're taking practically every man here to run them down? Why that's two hundred men!" He lowered his voice, giving the inflection that he didn't want to be heard by the prisoners who were watching all the activity from close by, turning his back to them as he spoke. "Major, you have eighteen men in that stockade. Seasoned warriors. Now, I've no quarrel with the red man, but I've no love for them either. Leaving a skeleton crew here tonight is not the brightest military strategy I've ever seen."

Forsyth snorted, rounding on the doctor. "And who made you an expert on military strategy, Dr. Gage? Those prisoners are going nowhere. The stockade is quite substantially built for holding hostiles. Besides, when we return, we will have more to put in there with them."

Travers bristled. "Well, if that's the case, Major, I think I'll stick around. I may be of further help around here, yet. I'm decent with a gun. If they try to make a break for it, we'll plant them where they lie." Major Forsyth smiled in dismissal at him, thinking perhaps Doctor Gage wasn't such a stickler, after all, his thoughts already on the journey ahead. He was ready to show those red devils that they didn't have a country anymore.

Travers nodded to Little Crow as the scout mounted up. Little Crow's left eye creased in what could have been a squint against the glare of the afternoon sun before he turned to make his way out of the fort. Travers watched them go. He watched them until they rode out of sight. He must continue to keep up the ruse. Worry that they all must stay alert lest the prisoners try and make a break for it. Scratching his head, he headed to the canteen and began brewing coffee.

Four hours and three cups of coffee later, the prisoners did just that. Travers had the guard outside the stockade and the one on the tower sleeping like babes. They left quietly, slipping from underneath the wall where they had dug a hole and covered it with a blanket to keep their escape route secret. They managed to round up their horses with little commotion and were on their way. Travers watched them slip away into the night, knowing that he had done the right thing. Those men would live to fight another day and one day may even kill him. But he doubted it. Dull Knife had trusted him, a white man. Few Indians trusted the white man. To an Indian, his word was his bond. The same held true for Travers. Perhaps they would meet again. Perhaps not. The world was not so small a place anymore.

◆———◆———◆

Forsyth did not take the news of the prisoners' escape well. He had cursed quite fluently and threw his gloves on the ground in frustration. They had come home empty-handed from their trek to the Ladder River. Gibbs had eyed Travers suspiciously but said nothing accusingly to Forsyth. Travers had been forced to use laudanum on Gibbs, as he had used all the herbs on the two guards. He had slipped it into his coffee, and the man went out like a light.

That had been two weeks ago.

Travers was feeling restless and the need to ride. He had come to accept what had happened between him and Maggie. There was nothing he could do. She had distanced herself even further from him after his rejection of her after he was wounded. He wanted to think about what to do where she was concerned. He couldn't do that in town. He had opened the clinic again and stayed busy. Everyone, it seemed, had a malady of some sort, though Travers was certain they came just out of curiosity to see that he was truly better. Travers was happy to be busy, but he couldn't keep his mind on his work as he had before he was shot. He needed space to clear his head.

Five miles out of town he reined in beneath the shade of a cottonwood. He knew he was being watched. He had felt the hair rise on the back of his neck about a mile back. He knew someone was out there and he waited, hoping they would come to him. He didn't have long to wait. Two men on horseback appeared downwind of him, slowly making their way towards him. He knew a moment's unease before he identified them as Dull Knife and Little Wolf, two of the Cheyenne he had helped escape from Fort Wallace. He dismounted and waited for them. They came slowly, their eyes scanning the area around them for any sign of danger. When they drew near, he smiled and raised his hand in greeting.

"Hello. It is good to see my friends are still thriving."

Dull Knife nodded. "And to you as well." Little Wolf raised his hand in greeting, and Travers acknowledged him also. "Little Wolf, how are the warriors who were wounded?"

"They are well. They send their regards."

"That is good. Tell them I hope they have long lives yet."

"I will."

Dull Knife pulled something from his shirt and nudging his horse forward, handed it to Travers. It was a medicine pouch, filled with herbs for healing. A warrior's medicine pouch was considered big medicine. He could not accept such a prize from this man.

"Dull Knife, I cannot accept this. This is yours."

The big man held up his hand when Travers tried to hand it back.

"No. It is a gift. For your kindness and bravery. We owe you our lives."

Travers protested. "But I really didn't do anything. You could have slipped out and been gone before those guards knew what hit them without the drugs."

The war chief nodded. "True, but you put your neck in the noose to help us. Our tribe is faltering. I fear what might have been if you had not been willing to help. Our women and children would have no one to stand for them, protect them. Now they do."

Travers knew to not accept the gift would be an insult. He held the beautifully decorated pouch before him. "Thank you. I will treasure it always."

The two men nodded their approval and eased away, leaving Travers standing where they had found him. He watched them go, thinking how very wrong about these people everyone was. The Cheyenne called themselves the 'Beautiful People", and they were right. They were striking in appearance, their complexions smooth, their posture regal. They were handsome individuals. He knew with the war being waged against them they would not be beautiful long. They would be ravaged by war, decimated, and destroyed as a nation. He hoped to never see it in his lifetime, but he knew it was coming far too quickly.

FORTY-THREE

There was no way he was going to let this happen. Yellow Bird was an instigator. He was angry, hot-headed and carried a huge chip on his shoulder because of the treatment of his people by the whites. For certain, he had reason to be angry, but his anger blinded him to the fact that his people were defeated. Even amongst warring tribes, the enemy knew and understood defeat. They accepted it and lived to fight another day. Not Yellow Bird. He seemed bent on dying today and destroying what was left of his tribe in the process. It puzzled Little Crow why the warrior even had a say at this council. He was no war leader. He was known as a thief in even his own tribe, though it had never been a proven fact. He was slick that one, and his slick tongue was fast grating on Little Crow's already stretched last nerve. With a face like thunder, he stood and pointed to the irritating brave.

"This one should not be here. He has no authority here. Leap Horn is war chief, is he not? To allow such talk from a small man like Yellow Bird is against all we ever held sacred. Only proven and tried warriors are allowed to speak at council. It should be such here."

Leap Horn nodded his agreement. "It is true, but his mother demanded his participation in the absence of his brother, Wind Chaser."

The absent warrior had been a highly respected man in his tribe and in line to be war chief. He had stood head and shoulders above his younger brother in every way, fair, honorable, and trustworthy. Wind Chaser had been killed the month before in an attack by the whites that had all but destroyed the Crow Village. Most of the warriors had gone hunting and were away at the time of the attack. Wind Chaser had chosen to stay behind, recovering from an infected wound from a previous skirmish with the white man. He had fought bravely and valiantly, his wound forgotten in defense of his village. He felled thirteen soldiers before he was brought down. Little Crow had witnessed the fight. He had led the soldiers straight to the village nestled along the Powder River, not knowing their true intent until they arrived. He had argued with Custer and been reprimanded, Little Crow had turned away, unable to stomach what he saw happening before his eyes. This life that he had known for so long, the only life he had known, was no longer. He felt lost in a world gone mad, knew only that he had to conform or die. Defeated people conformed or died. Little Crow was no coward. He had watched his people utterly decimated by these white men who came in scores across the plains in their wagons of wood and canvas. They encroached on the natives, taking, always taking, taking their sources of food and water, their very survival. They never gave in return. Scratch that. They gave disease, famine, and fire water that turned warriors into raving lunatics. It gave them bravado when they should have shown restraint. It turned brave warriors into simpering idiots. Oh, yes the white man enjoyed giving whiskey to his people. It furthered their cause.

Little Crow had fought the rising tide of whites in his country. Had breathed fire himself, once, believing that they could be stopped. Until he had journeyed to the great city of Washington years ago and seen the hundreds of thousands of them. He had known then that they could not be stopped. In an instant, he had seen his hope of a restored prairie dashed.

Yes, Little Crow could well understand hate. He had trod the same path as the warrior before him. Yellow Bird's hate had consumed him. His face was eaten alive with it. His eyes burned at Little Crow, who had dared to speak against him at the council. He stood as well, knowing that this man was respected and feared as a warrior while he was made to look as if he was nothing. He had always stood in the shadow of his older brother, had despised always being second best. He knew just as much as any warrior here. He would show them.

"I have a right to be here, while you, a *Tonkawa*" he spit the name as if it tasted vile on his tongue, "stand and speak as if you are the only one worthy of speaking at the council. You are not Crow. You have no tribe. You are a lone warrior who has no place to call home because you let the white man take from you all you held dear. We Crow will fight to the end if need be. We will never surrender to these whites! We will drive them from our lands for good!"

Little Crow kept his face a mask, refusing to let the indignant brave draw him into a battle of words. He would let the facts speak for themselves. He bent and retrieved a leather pouch from his saddlebags. Carefully, he opened it and removed small, flat pieces of images he had collected while he was in Washington. They were daguerreotypes, images taken with a device that captured people and places on a solid background. He spread them carefully on the ground before the elders, Leap Horn and Standing Elk reaching for them in consternation. They gazed over the images with a bit of shock and awe, unable to believe what they saw, the monstrous buildings, the people who littered the streets like ta-Tonka upon the prairie. He told them of the great white house where the leader of the white man lived and ruled, where laws were passed to get rid of the red man because they refused to surrender to the white man once they were defeated. He told of the homes made of wood and brick that towered over their lowly teepee, the large boats that traveled on the open water, the iron horse powered by trees and black fire that come from under the ground. He told them and showed them, hoping to make them realize that their way of life was at an end.

He could tell that he had made an impact with Leap Horn and Standing Elk. They passed the images back to Little Crow, and as they did so, Yellow Bird dashed them angrily from his hand, scattering them to the ground, one of them falling into the edge of the fire. It was of the cherry trees in full bloom. He had admired them so, their flowers so vibrant against the robin's egg sky. He had found an image of them in a store and had purchased it, wondering how odd that the Great Spirit had allowed something of such beauty to flourish among these whites who seemed bent on destroying everything in their path. He knew it was a sign, that even in change, there was hope. That is why he fought for peace. He knew there had to be a purpose for it all, the killing, the slaughter, the annihilation of a people who lived so close to the earth.

He calmly reached and pulled the image from the destructive flame and blew the fire out before it could consume the beauty it greedily held. He looked at the brave before him, thinking, how could he not see the truth before him?

"You are the last of the Crow to not conform. Why do you persist in warring against the inevitable? The white man has been your friend. You have been given good land to settle on. Many of your braves are scouts for the white man, same as me."

Yellow Bird sneered. "Yes, and they are outcasts. They have forsaken the old ways by putting on the garments of the whites. They talk out both sides of their mouth. All despise a double talker. When we wipe the whites from our home, they will go as well."

"How do you hope to win with so few warriors against so many soldiers? It is like sighing into a fierce wind and watching it steal your breath. You know the wind will take it, but still, you fight it until darkness falls upon you. Darkness has fallen. The rest of your tribe has seen the darkness and have built their campfires accordingly. They hunger for nothing, their bellies are full at night, their lodges warm with no fear of attack because they give no threat of rebellion."

Standing Elk gave a grunt. "I, too, wish to sleep warmly in my lodge with no fear. It is a hard bargain, to not fight for what is rightfully ours, this land that no man owns, the freedom to hunt for food without fear of being attacked by the whites. Our people have settled for the crumbs of the whites like dogs hunger for a bone. We cannot live on crumbs. Are we not people, too? Why are we less than the white man? The Crow do not live in lodges of mud and wood. We do not dress in clothing that keeps Mother Earth from speaking to us. They cannot hear her angry rumble of discontent. I think it is the whites who will learn that the time of defeat is at hand."

***

Council had not gone well today. Little Crow sighed, knowing that there would be a reckoning, a wakeup call to these white men who came through, taking everything in their path without asking first. He didn't know when, or how, but it would have to happen soon. And there was no way of knowing the outcome of such a thing. He could only pray that there be peace between these completely different races. Peace. He prayed for it, for he knew that all whites were not evil. His woman, Sally was not evil. She was kind and strong, her heart as big as the open waters at the end of the land he had seen in the white man's capital of Washington. And Travers Gage was not evil. In him, Little Crow had found a good friend. Although their worlds were so very different, Little Crow had felt a kinship with him. With his tribe being gone, Little Crow had found it difficult to make friends among the other tribes. Everyone saw him as a sell-out working for the white man. He wasn't working for the white man. He was working for himself. He was working for a better future for all involved, if only they could see it.

That evening, Sally noted the furrowed brow as he sat at the dinner table.

"Today did not go well, did it?"

He sighed heavily. "No. I'm thinking I should resign. The elders are listening to Yellow Bird as if he has suddenly become a war chief. I have tried everything I know to persuade them to take the land offered them by the government. I thought Standing Elk had decided to consider it, but no, he has cast his lot with the remaining warriors."

"You have done your job. Just because this band has decided to reject the treaty doesn't mean that you should give up. You are the voice of reason to and for these people. You speak their language with a knowledge and wisdom that they will come to respect and demand. You have lived that defeat. Somehow you will make them see." She placed her hand upon his, knowing the pain he must be feeling for his people.

The mention of defeat gave him pause. He had never really thought of himself as defeated. Certainly, his family, his tribe was decimated, but defeat? He had to shake the darkness that settled on his soul at that word. He smiled at Sally and ate his supper lost deep in thought.

Little Crow ran across Travers at the General Store in Dodge the next day. He found himself sharing with Travers about the failed council and about Yellow Bird's attempt to take control of the negotiations. Travers had listened and offered little advice but much consolation that Little Crow would know what to do, what to say to get through to the Crow holdouts. He hoped the doctor was right. Because right now, Little Crow was at a complete loss as to what to do to get them to listen to reason. Travers told him not to worry, that things would work themselves out. He also let Little Crow know he would be dropping in on him and Sally in the next few days. He still wanted to check on his friend with her pregnancy getting further along. They had a drink together in the saloon before going their separate ways. They did not notice the solitary figure sitting alone at a table in the darkest corner of the place. But he noticed them. Yes, indeed.

FORTY-FOUR

Travers laughed in spite of himself. Sally had Little Crow out in the garden weeding, of all things! He eased his horse up to the warrior and leaned his arms on his saddle horn, taking in the unique picture of a Tonkawa warrior doing a woman's work. The man looked up at the doctor with a look of chagrin on his face, noting the humor he saw there.

"You laugh, Gage. My woman needs help. She has no woman to help her. Only me. There is no shame in what I do."

Travers shook his head. "No, I suppose not. But I wouldn't want Yellow Bird to see you right now. He might take advantage of the situation and jump you for slighting him at the council."

Little Crow grunted disgustedly.

"Yellow Bird has never bested me. And he never will. Besides, he will not travel so far from his mother. She is a nag. She takes a flog to him if he stays away too long."

Travers watched him a few minutes longer before dismounting and offering a hand with the chores which the brave stubbornly refused. Sally was his woman, and he alone would provide for her. Thankfully, he had let Travers see her when she had realized she was expecting. He knew the value of a white doctor out here, at least. Sally had beamed when Travers had confirmed what she already knew. Travers had worried that maybe this was not such a good idea, but the look on Sally's face told him that she treasured this child already. Little Crow had been ecstatic. His first wife had not bore him any children before her death. He had gathered Sally up in his arms with a whoop and spun her around with his shouts of joy echoing across the countryside. Travers had silently taken his leave of them, knowing this was something to be shared in private. They never noticed when he left.

"Where is the mother to be?" he asked, looking towards the house.

Little Crow looked in that direction as well, a look of worry now crossing his face.

"Sleeping. She has not been well for days now. I make her rest."

"I'll take a look at her if that's all right?"

Little Crow nodded and rose, and the two of them walked to the house, slipping quietly inside. Sally lay on the bed with a blanket over her in the middle of July. Her face was flushed, and beads of perspiration dotted her forehead and matted her hair about her face. Travers did not like the looks of her. She seemed to be suffering from cholera.

"How long has she been like this?"

"Two days. The fever started this morning. It goes and comes. She was sleeping so I went outside to work in her garden. She has not been feeling well for a week now."

Travers frowned, the concern now eating at him. She was six months or so along with the child she carried, and this illness did not bode well for mother or child. He ran his hand across her brow, noting the warmth that was not a result of the summer heat.

Her lids fluttered weakly, taking several seconds to fixate on the man hovering above her. When she realized who was before her, she smiled.

"Travers, what a surprise. It's been so long." Her voice rasped in her throat, barely above a whisper.

"I had to come see how things were going out here. Looks like it's a good thing I did." He offered a smile of his own, hoping to put her at ease. "How long have you been feeling ill, Sally?"

"About a week."

A week. Hmm. That could be significant. "Any diarrhea or vomiting?"

She groaned, nodding her head. "Both. And it's so strange because I wasn't even nauseated. Now I can't seem to keep anything in me."

"And the fever. How often does it break?"

Little Crow stepped forward and sat beside her, taking her slight hand in his. He was worried, his face, usually so expressionless, was lined with a deep frown. Travers could well understand why. Sally was not well. Her breath rattled in her chest and was so shallow that she barely moved the mound of quilts that covered her weakened body.

"The fever started last evening. It has only broken twice but rises again too soon." Little Crow's voice was low, his eyes locked upon the woman whose hand he held. He knew she was slipping away. Travers nodded, understanding his concern. Little Crow had seen this before. In another time, another place.

Travers eased back the cover from Sally, and she gulped in a big gasp of air as if she were suddenly relieved of an oppressive burden. The simple act of uncovering her had caused such a chill to go down her body that she began to shake uncontrollably. Travers quickly covered her again, logic telling him to not make matters worse. He rose and went to where he had left his satchel on the table, opening it and rifling through it. He found a bottle of quinine and a measuring spoon, taking it back to her bedside.

He opened the bottle and poured a healthy amount into the spoon. He instructed Little Crow to help Sally sit up so she could take the medication. She was light as a feather in the brave's arms, he couldn't help but note. She managed to get the liquid down, and Travers pushed a cup of tea into Little Crow's hand.

"See that she drinks all of this. It will help her sleep, and hopefully, sweat off this fever."

The brave nodded, as he maneuvered to a better position behind Sally, propping her body back against his. She managed to sip a good portion of the brew that Little Crow had made earlier. Willow-bark tea. It was known to have a soothing effect and taking the quinine with it, well, she hoped to get some rest tonight. The last week had not been a good one. She slept but did not rest; she hacked and coughed, shivered and sweated. She prayed this medicine Travers had given her would kick in soon. She had not been there for Little Crow lately. He had been the one to cook and clean, something that a Tonkawa warrior did not do. That was women's work. But Little Crow had said not one word about the demeaning task of cooking their meals, working in their garden, or bathing her when she soaked through her bedclothes. He was right there beside her when she needed. Hovering like a mother hen.

It was hard for him to watch her unable to lift herself up to simply drink from a spoon. And her body against his was so hot and frail. It shook him. He knew a frisson of fear. He shut his eyes against the thought. It did not go away. He got Sally to finish the tea and helped her ease back into her pillows which were, of course, soaked through. The bed and Sally both smelled of dank, unwashed body, the fluids from her body drenching not only her nightgown but the covers and the pillows as well. Within minutes she had dozed off.

He turned to find Travers digging into his medical satchel. The doctor did not find what he was looking for. He looked up at Little Crow. "Do you have any sugar?"

"I think so. What is it, Travers?"

"I think she has cholera."

Little Crow was stunned. Of all the things he expected it had not been this. "Cholera?"

"Yes. We need to get as much fluid back into her body as possible. Sugar water will help, and the quinine will settle her stomach, hopefully. You say the fever has just started?"

"Last evening."

Travers ran his hand over his face, hoping they had caught the disease quickly enough.

"Then we might stand a chance of keeping her alive. But we need fluids poured back into her quickly. Sugar water will certainly help. And we need lots of water for bathing and soap. It's going to be a long night, friend. Let's get moving."

Hours later, they were exhausted. They had bathed Sally, gotten the water boiled for the sugar mixture and cooled it enough to get some in her when she woke up. She was sleeping more easily now, clean and the fever seemed to have abated. For now. She was so very weak, and Travers did not like the sunken eyes and wrinkled skin. She looked as if she had aged twenty years since he had last seen her. She was cramping, and her pulse was thready and irregular. None of these were good signs. She had been ill for some time, enough for the disease to get a firm hold on her. And Travers knew that without divine intervention, she could very well die.

Soon.

Little Crow needed no one to tell him what must be done. He had seen the hopelessness in the doctor's eyes, the fear. The man knew what he was about and he trusted him to tell him the truth, even though no words were spoken. After he washed thoroughly with lye soap, the warrior went outside and built a huge fire and danced and prayed to the Great Spirit the rest of the night.

◆————◆————◆

Travers was bone tired when he got back to Gold City. He had been at Sally's farm for ten days. Her color was better, and the fever had broken and stayed gone. She was still so very weak, though. He still feared for her and the child she carried. He warned both her and Little Crow that a setback could be costly, that she must keep herself well. Knowing that Sally needed all the care she could get at this crucial stage of recovery, for her and her child, Travers had stayed on to make sure she was on the mend. It had been good away from town. Sally and Little Crow had practically had to shoo him out the door, knowing he had obligations elsewhere, hesitant to monopolize his time, friends or no. Travers was truly in no hurry to get back to town. Maggie was in town, and he had no desire to see Maggie. Not yet, anyway. He had put off going back until he was certain Sally was on the mend. He was thinking to himself how fortuitous it had been that he had taken that ride out to see the two of them that day. Otherwise, things could have been on the opposite end of stellar for Sally.

His head ached, and his body creaked worse than a rusty hinge by the time he rode back into town. What he found back at the town was enough to send him running in the opposite

direction. Cholera.
     It had found its way into Gold City

FORTY-FIVE

It had been a long three days. Many from the town had survived their ordeal this far, but others were barely hanging on. There had been no deaths as of yet, but there would be. He was sure that the mayor's wife was done for. Once again they had a wagon train to thank for their run of disease. The load of folks from the Carolinas had rolled into town the day before he returned from Sally's. They had practically parked on his doorstep until his return. Some folks were just so ignorant of things, he thought. The wagon master had feigned ignorance that the disease running through the train was cholera, but Travers knew a liar when he saw one. The man didn't give a fig about anybody or anything, and his true colors showed on the second day of Travers' treating the sick members of the wagon train. The wagon master disappeared, leaving the train stranded without a guide to get them to Utah. The men who were still ablebodied were putting feelers out all over the town hoping to find someone who would take on the job of getting them to their destination. They were not having a lot of luck. No one wanted to be saddled with a bunch of disease-ridden folk hopscotching across the plains. Travers couldn't help but feel sorry for them, but he didn't want the job either.

He was washing up when Rance staggered in. The man looked like death, and Travers felt a lurch in his stomach. He was ill with cholera, just like all the others. One look told him that. His eyes were already horribly sunken in his head, his face flushed with an unnatural heat. Travers steered him to a corner away from the others and got him settled into bed immediately. Rance never said a word, just allowed Travers to direct and instruct and he followed his lead.

Less than an hour had passed when Tandy showed up. The little redhead parked her derriere in a chair beside Rance's bed and refused to leave his side. She had turned a deaf ear to the pleas from both Travers and Rance to leave, to get away from the deadly disease. She just smiled and pretended she hadn't heard a word they said. She administered the medications that Travers brought and saw to it that Rance downed the concoctions of sugar water and fluids to help battle the disease. She read from the Bible, the Song of Solomon, as Rance shivered and sweated.

•————•————•

The darkness pounded in on him, haunting, jeering, taunting. Sleep would not come this night, so he did not even attempt to seek it. There was no point. He could still hear the weeping, the moans, the denials that had been wrenched from Maggie as she had wept beside the bed of her brother who had lain so still, so, pale, so—dead. On her knees beside the bed, his cold, lifeless hand clasped in her own, she had wept silently, her body shaking with wrenching sobs.

It was not the way he had planned on renewing their acquaintance.

Laura had chanced upon Maggie the evening that Rance came in as she was headed home after helping out at the clinic. When Maggie learned how poorly her brother was doing, she had hastened to the clinic, ignoring her husband's orders to stay away from the place. Jim had paid her a visit just the day before, warning her of the spread of the terrible disease. Neighboring towns had been hit hard, burying entire families. Rance was the only family she had left out here in this God-forsaken place. Aunt Netta had at least had the good sense to go back to Georgia. No amount of persuasion on her part had gotten Maggie to hop the stage with her. More's the pity, Maggie thought, as she had clung to her brother's hand, speaking to him as he slipped away from her. Tandy had sat across from her, her head bent in grief, knowing he was crossing a bridge to the life beyond this one. Maggie didn't know much about the redhead, only that she was one of the girls who stayed busy at Flora's when all the decent folk's lights had long been extinguished. It wasn't in Maggie's heart to judge the girl, for she knew the pain written on her face was too real to be artifice. Whatever Rance had had with the young lady was real affection, be it love or friendship. It pleased Maggie to know that at least Rance had found a bit of happiness out here after he had fought the journey so hard. A journey of her making. . . It was her fault that he was lying before her, the life now gone from him. Life that was cut far too short because she couldn't be made to see reason, wouldn't change her mind. The cries that finally found their way out of Maggie were cries of despair for herself and for Rance. She held herself just as responsible as the sickness that took his life. Everything that Maggie held dear had somehow turned to ashes in the wind. She had thrown a life with Travers away. Her hopes and dreams of a fine marriage with Jim were deader than ten day dipped snuff. She wept for the loss of Rance's companionship, for the childhood that they had once shared so closely, the poverty, the ignorance, the spreading of wings to fly from a nest that had suddenly become so feathered. She wept for all the things she now realized Rance would never come to be, a father, an uncle . . . an artist the world would one day revere. Maggie knew her brother had found his calling out here in this 'desolate wasteland' that he was ever calling it. She had been astounded at the transformation she had witnessed in him, the confidence he had found in himself. The writing had never really taken off as he had hoped, but his paintings, how they showed such promise of a talent long hidden. And now the canvas would be forever blank. She had never approached him for a portrait or even a landscape. His own sister. And now she would never know the pride of owning any of his work. And that grieved her to no end. And so she wept for her brother and all the things that would never be as Tandy sat across from her and wept silently as well.

Travers had been unable to take it anymore. She had waltzed in and parked at Rance's bedside, not budging, her eyes on him alone. It was probably for the better. Travers hadn't known whether to speak or not, so he had let the matter alone. Flora had been at the clinic helping out, so she was there to comfort Maggie and Tandy as Travers stood helplessly by. He had watched for several minutes without saying a word before Maggie's sobs began to tear into him with such force that gave him no choice but to leave before he went insane. Even now he could hear them, hours later, in his room as he reclined upon his bed nursing a bourbon. His third. He closed his eyes against the sound in his head, and her image rose before him, but it was not the image of Maggie kneeling beside her brother. It was the image of Maggie long ago as she cried and begged, pleading with him not to send her away, that she loved him so.

FORTY-SIX

Life is a vicious cycle. We're born, we live for a while, some-times with a meager existence, sometimes with a wealth of love, money, and knowledge. And then we die. Death is no re-specter of persons. It does not discriminate, does not take just the weak in body, but plows forward as if our numbers are in God's giant raffle barrel which He pulls from, sometimes by the handfuls, sometimes one at a time. Gold City had barely gotten through the cholera outbreak when Indian attacks hit closer to home than ever before. A traveling Texas Ranger had stumbled upon the day-old bodies and burned out farms and had come to town for help. Two families living less than seven miles out of town were wiped out. Twelve people gone, their lives snuffed out in the blink of an eye. Seven of the dead were children. Travers had been sent for but to what purpose he never figured out. They were dead, all of them. All the animals, save the miss-ing horses, were dead as well. As he stood among the carnage that had once been bustling life, he could only shake his head in sorrow. He had never seen such degradation done to a human being before. To think that another human could inflict such atrocities on another. War was one thing, for in war it was man against man, and war came home even to the children in some cases, but not like this. Nothing like this. But the Indians were at war, he supposed. They had vowed to wipe the white man off the face of the earth. That meant making war against the white man and his seed.

Travers' first thought was of Yellow Bird, the renegade Crow that Little Crow was having such difficulty with. Travers knew it wasn't just Yellow Bird and his band that was making war. Countless others were raiding and killing and committing other atrocities even as he helped in the burial of the poor souls so recently slaughtered. He didn't know enough about him or his ways to point fingers or lay blame, but it just smelled of him somehow. He didn't believe this was perpetrated by the local tribes. For the most part, they had been peaceful towards the town and the surrounding farmers. The ensuing six months lent further credence to that suspicion. More farms were burned to the ground, the settlers killed, presumably by war parties, but to Travers and the men who traveled with him to the scenes of the slaughters, things looked staged. Travers had a nagging suspicion that though Indians might be involved, they were not the sole perpetrators. That thought sent a cold chill down him. But who? Renegades? Half-breeds? Either one was possible, he presumed, but he doubted it. Were Indians involved at all? Or were there just cold-blooded killers loose on the prairie using the situation with the Indians to cover their dastardly deeds? If they didn't find out soon what was going on, they might all be dead. The killings were getting closer and closer to town, the killers getting bolder. It was bad enough having to prove one man guilty of murder, but now he might have a whole passel of killers to get the jump on.

Damn . . .

That night as Clayton and Sarah lay in bed, their conversation turned to Travers. Sarah had noted how little time he now spent among his friends.

"I don't know, Clay. He seems so changed from the man we use to know. He flits from one place to another like he's avoiding. You don't think he blames me for what happened, do you?"

"Lord, no. Don't even think that, woman. Travers has a lot on his mind these days. He's avoiding Maggie for one thing. Rance's death nearly done him in. He feels he failed her. He was all she really had out here, and now he's gone. And Travers feels he's to blame. He won't ever admit that, but it's written all over his face. He's dealing with a lot from his past, too. Sometimes, a man just has to be alone to deal with the things in his life. Feels talking about it makes him weak. Don't mean he's any less a man. He's just a man. Ever since he came here, we've put a lot on his shoulders. We depend on him, heavily. And maybe that was wrong for us to get him to fight all our battles. But he's wise, and he knows when to listen instead of run off at the mouth like most folks. And we need to be there for him no matter what. And if he needs space, then we need to give it to him. Because he's our friend, Sarah. The best friend I'll ever have. And yours, too."

Sarah laid her head upon her husband's massive arm, knowing what he said was true. He had been the first person to actually befriend her here, remembering how the southern gentleman had brought her flowers that evening, his first night in town, and how he had manipulated the friendship between her and Clara Walker as well. Travers was the rock, the soul of this town. It had merely existed before he came here. And when he was gone, the town would flounder without him.

FORTY-SEVEN

Little Crow had been gone for two days. He had promised to be back in four. He had promised her. He never let her down. Never. He had made her promise him that she would wait until he got back to have their child, but she was having a difficult time keeping that promise. The pains had started in the night, nagging back pain that wouldn't ease no matter how hard she tried to find the softest section of the bed. Weakness had overtaken her. She had tried walking, but after a bit, her body, already so weakened by the bout with cholera, had just given out. She lay covered in sweat, her gown plastered to her pain-wracked body. She huffed and panted against the pain, knowing that she was utterly alone out here, giving birth to her child. She could not lose her head. If she and the babe were to survive, she had to concentrate. She had managed to boil water before her body gave out. Blankets and towels were already nearby, ready for use. She had been keeping them just so, suspecting her time was closer to hand than they realized. She clenched her jaw against a particularly excruciating pain that crossed her abdomen and ran up her back. It would not do to scream out here. Too many settlers had been slaughtered as of late. There was no telling who or what screams would bring running. She had gone over in her mind how some Indians gave birth, squatting and considered that. It looked so easy. She had tried but found that she couldn't hold herself up when the pains hit. Sally was not one to give up easily, but the pain was absolutely mind-numbing. She wrapped her hands around her belly and rubbed at the child that struggled to free itself from its haven of warmth, and insanely, she wondered why on earth it had chosen this moment in time to spring into the world. She laughed at the myriad of thoughts running through her head.

Her father had always said she had to do things the hard way. She could really use him right now. She missed him dreadfully. Her mother came to mind, and she knew a frisson of fear. Her mother had died before the war, just before Sally had turned twelve. Cancer had taken her away from them. It had not been a picnic, her mother wracked with pain almost constantly at the end. The cancer had spread to her bones, and finally her brain. Eliza Sharpe had been a mere shell of herself when she departed this earth. What hair she had left had hung in clumps, sparse now as she had pulled fistfuls of it out to direct the agony somewhere other than her body. It had nearly done Sally in, watching her mother suffer so. Her father had missed the roughest of it, being away so frequently as he was in the army. She remembered pouring pure opium down her mother only to watch it not work on the pain. She would have given anything, done anything for her mother not to have endured what she had. It had made a woman of Sally far too early.

She had loved her mother very much, and she was another loved one Sally could use very much at the moment. This birthing bit was not going as anticipated or as planned and she was in dire straits. She needed help, and she needed help now. Her contractions were so close she lost track counting how far apart they were. All she knew was she was well past the point of hopping a horse and scooting across the plains to town and Travers. She thought of him and sent him a mental message that she needed him. As time ticked by with no child and no Travers, Little Crow, or anyone else, for that matter, she began to pray.

✦——◆——✦

At the very moment that Sally was praying, Travers was tied up with a couple of soldiers passing through. Their company had been chasing Yellow Bird and his band for two days before engaging him across the Colorado River. The scrape had lasted for maybe a half hour before the band had broken for the mountains. The two soldiers had an interesting piece of information. Gibbs happened to be riding patrol with them when they came across the band unexpectedly, but Gibbs had acted quite strangely for a soldier who detested the prairie ruff. He had bungled shots and interfered with others who had been firing at the fleeing renegades. His horse had seen fit to ram the horse of the soldier that Travers was at that moment setting the bone for a broken arm, a result of being knocked to the ground by a careless and incompetent scruff who called himself a soldier and doctor. Gibbs had been unable to set the bone properly, causing grueling pain to the man. His buddy had knocked him on his butt, and once back in the territory, they had headed for Travers. Travers got the arm set, and the two troopers headed back to the hotel where they would be spending the night before heading out the next morning. He pondered on their conversation for a bit. He didn't know what significance the tale held the two men had, but he felt there was some in there somewhere, other than what Travers had known all along, that the man was worthless as could be. But that aside, he began to wonder if Gibbs and Bowers might have a connection. Why that question should even be asked stumped him as well, but it niggled at the back of his mind. He knew he was most likely jumping to conclusions trying to connect the two. It would certainly be killing two birds with one stone if they were. He shook that train of thought from his mind. There was nothing he could do about any of it tonight. His inner clock told him it was time to close up for the evening. He could almost hear Laura setting the table for supper.

Little Crow came home the third day, having cut his trip short a day. Unease about Sally had gripped him, and he had been unable to think of anything else. There was no sign of life in the yard. Strange. The yard animals all seemed to be gone. There was a strange horse tied up at the rail out front. It carried no saddle. The door to the cabin was open, flung wide. Little Crow leaped from his mount and, pulling his knife, ran for the cabin. The scene that met his eyes froze him in his tracks. Little Wolf, one of the Sioux prisoners Travers had helped escape from the fort, was there, praying over his woman, a sad chant that did not bode well. He lifted sage and prayed aloud, his voice mournful as he chanted to the Great Spirit to help the woman on the bed. Little Crow tore his eyes from the Sioux holy man and focused on Sally.

She was covered in bloody sheets, hair dank and matted about her face, her pallor ghostly white. She held their child wrapped in a swath of towel close to her chest. Eyes that should have been filled with joy and tears of gladness instead were vacant, glassy, unseeing, and the child appeared.

He could not bring himself to think it. Little Wolf stopped his chanting and pulled Little Crow to the side, his voice low so Sally could not hear.

"She is very weak, my brother, in heart, body, and in mind. I fear her spirit has left her as her child has."

Little Crow refused to believe this. "No! Sally!" He crossed to the bed, taking her by the arms and shaking her roughly, trying to get her to focus on him.

Little Wolf shook his head. "You will make it worse. She will come through on her own power soon enough. If you force it, she could be lost forever. She needs to know you are here and that is all. When she needs you, she will turn to you. Now she must fight the demons in her mind."

Little Crow backed from the bed, uncertain what to do.

"When did you find her?"

"Before dawn. The spirits told me to come. The child was already delivered. I could only pray." He shook his head regretfully. "I am sorry, brave one. He would have been a great warrior had he lived, just like his father."

Little Crow could not speak past the lump in his throat. He had feared the child would come early. That Sally was worried about this herself, he remembered. She had seemed so fragile of late. He had wanted to send for Travers, but each time he mentioned it, Sally had put him off. Now he knew that was a critical misstep. He thanked the old medicine man, and the man left. There was nothing else that could be done that had not been done. Except bury his child. Little Crow had barely looked at the child, so concerned for Sally that he saw nothing else. He knew getting the child from her arms would be a battle. He braced himself for it.

She never blinked. Her arms were frozen about her child as if made of iron. The expression on her face never changed. Her eyes stared into nothingness, the spirit was gone from them. He could not in all reasonability move her without the child to clean her and the bed. For several long hours, he debated what to do, agonizing, the reality of loss hitting him, forcing him outside where he rent the air with a cry of rage, agony, and loss. He danced to the Great Spirit to give him the strength to do what he knew he must do. Once he set himself on that path, he could not, would not veer from it.

When he had control of himself, he went back inside. Sally needed more than he could give her right now. And he knew who could give it to her.

◆━━━◆━━━◆

Travers was coming out of the clinic when he noticed the crowd gathering down the street. He paused to see what was holding their interest, his heart freezing when he saw. He waited for them to reach him, not trusting himself to move. Little Crow had Sally and their child wrapped in blankets before him on his horse, slowly walking the animal into town. When he reached Travers, the doctor could plainly read the distress on the warrior's face, and Sally was—absent was the word he could best find to describe her. No words were spoken as Travers took the woman from Little Crow's arms and carried her inside where he placed her on a bed away from prying eyes. The warrior followed him inside, closing the door on anyone who would have trespassed on such a private moment. When Travers got Sally situated, he asked Little Crow when it had happened. Little Crow explained how the child had come early, while he was away, and how Little Wolf had found her thus. He told Travers of his fears that this would happen while he was away and how she had refused to let him send for Travers. Travers shuddered, the agony that these two must be going through ripping him wide open. The child was something that had to be taken care of right away. Death was not a pretty sight two days old. How to get it loosed from Sally's arms was the tricky part. He could only think of laudanum, his mind was such mush, as he knew that Sally would fight them tooth and nail unless she was drugged. He put the bottle to her lips and told her drink, not even bothering with a spoon. He had to tell her the third time, but remarkably, she finally took a swig of it. In a matter of minutes, she faded into sleep. Ever so carefully, Travers eased the child free. He gave the child to his father then turned to examine Sally carefully, checking that other than her mind, she was well. For the first time, Little Crow got his first good look at their child. He was a fine boy. He took the boy to the back door and opened it and presented his son to the sky, giving him back to the God who had created him. He sang softly and held the child close, returning to sit at Sally's bedside, rocking, singing. His hand catching up that of Sally's as she slept.

Travers could only stand there and watch with a crushing sense of futility. He should have been there for Sally. She had counted on him. He knew that Little Crow traveled often. He had not counted on the child being early. He should have. He should have anticipated that, with her being so sick and all. Now, she was trapped in her own private hell, and there was no way of knowing if she would ever come out of it. He felt as if an elephant had stepped on him. He went to his office and pulled out his bottle of bourbon and contemplated getting soused. He could ill afford to do that. Sally might snap out of this at any moment, and she would need him. He could not afford to let her down again. He settled into the bunk he had squeezed into the corner and tried to sleep.

FORTY-EIGHT

There comes at times, great upheavals, and gentle settlings, and this seemed to be the case with Gold City. It gave that appearance, at least. The Indian attacks tapered off, the epidemics eased their assault, and summer turned into fall. A settling. A change of color in all aspects natural, personal, civil. Travers had run into Maggie a time or two on the street and on each occasion, she had turned away, practically dodging him to avoid conversation. There seemed to be a strain to Maggie these days. He had made a mental note of it, that he never saw her smile anymore. She had taken to her suite in the hotel and closed herself off from Laura and anyone who sought to draw her out. Bowers had become a regular visitor to the hotel, Maggie refusing to return to the ranch. The new groom had been forced to reshuffle his deck, now that the joke was on him. Whatever had happened between the two of them was widely speculated by the town. No one knew for certain what had brought Maggie back to Gold City and after months of her setting up house at the hotel, and Bowers' frequency of visits, everyone guessed it must have been a doozy.

Travers' memory came back in snippets, never really large enough to have complete clarity, but it was enough to piece together. He didn't like what was coming back. He had made an ass of himself where Maggie was concerned. He should have let things take their natural course and kept his nose out of her life. Duty had demanded he do otherwise. It was the damndest thing, duty. It was what had made him the gentleman in Virginia, what had led him to take her and Rance under his wing so long ago. Duty to see that no man starved if he could help it. Duty to protect those who could not protect themselves, to fill the shoes of the absent father, to bring light into a desperate situation. Duty to heal and preserve life as he had been trained to do. He had always done his duty, before, during, and after the war.

The urge to rip out his own tongue when he thought about Maggie was a common occurrence these days. But he learned to deal with it. She was no longer his concern. Apparently, she was no one except Jim's. Laura said she never saw her anymore. When Maggie had first come back to town, she had expressed interest in reforming their quilting circle. She, Laura, Sarah, Flora and Mrs. Johnson had met twice before Maggie sent her letter of regret to the next gathering they were to have. He had taken note one day as he stepped out onto the porch before heading off to the clinic, a slight movement at her window as if she had been there watching him from above before drawing the curtain back into place when she realized he sensed her there.

Flora had come to him one evening late, for a bottle of laudanum. She had given hers to Maggie she had said, a while back, around the time of Rance's death. Travers had asked her if she ever saw Maggie. Flora had given some vague answer that he could not even recall now. Apparently, Maggie had little contact with anyone these days. It was just as well. He wasn't fit company for anyone anymore.

Within days of Little Crow bringing Sally to the clinic, they had buried her. Her loss was not to be borne. She had never recovered her facilities after the birth of the child who had died. She had languished in a world of her own, her body continuing to go downhill fast. She had developed a fever that was common after childbirth and had died four days later.

Little Crow had been inconsolable.

Travers had walked away.

He had tried everything to get Sally to come around, to get the fever to break. She just had not the will, nor strength to fight. Little Crow had tried to pour his will into her, to make her fight for him if not for herself. She had given no sign that she ever heard him or even saw him. They buried her the day she died. Wrapped in the buffalo hide robe that Little Crow kept for the bitter winters, they placed her beside their son on the hill overlooking their little farm. That night, Little Crow rode away, once again alone in the world.

He would not be seen for months.

Travers did not work for months. He tried to rationalize the death of that precious woman and child in his mind. He could not. He should have known her time was close. That was his job. His skills, or lack of them, shook him to his core. No one who mattered to him seemed to survive his touch. He packed his bags and headed back east to Boston. He visited the hospitals there, sat in on some lectures by renowned surgeons. He observed some exploratory operations that he had heard were going on, amazing how the human body worked, yet understanding that life was so fragile and hung by a thread. He traveled extensively, avoiding people he knew well, looking for a place to settle his tormented soul. No place worked. Everywhere he went, he longed for Gold City. The memories of those gone haunted him. The memories of those still there waiting for him to return called to him. No one had tried to stop him when he had left. It was as if they understood his need to get away. They had seen the strain on him after Sally's death. Had known the pressure he had been under since Rance had died, his struggle to regain his memory. They had simply lined the streets as he had ridden out of town, praying, hoping he would one day come back.

————•————

Little Crow had taken to riding dispatch for the Army. He lived in a fog, more dead than alive now, his heart and soul eaten from his chest by the darkness that haunted him every day. He had dreamed of Sally almost nightly, her gentle smile telling him that she was all right. Though she said not a word, she communicated to him that she would come for him when it was his time. He tried to reach out to touch her only to have her fade into a mist. He knew from her smile that she was at peace. He wished he could find the same peace as her. He had thrown himself into the most dangerous of situations, hoping for a good death. It eluded him, month after month, after month. And as the days slipped into a new year, he grieved to see the rising of each sun.

————•————

Travers returned to Gold City, his manner more distant than ever. His friends offered their staunch support of him in their own ways, attempting to stay out of his way and give him the space he needed. Sally had been important to him, they knew. He threw himself into his work, traveling the countryside as well as working out of his clinic, calling on the nearby farmers and their families. The busier he stayed, the less he had to think about.

————•————

There was a feeling that Little Crow could not shake, a feeling that something was not quite right, a feeling as if he was not alone, perhaps in danger. It didn't stop him from continuing on, and he rode the rim of the canyon, forever looking, searching for the cause of his unease. He didn't know what to make of it. He had never felt this particular feeling before. It was as if bees were under his skin, fighting, trying to get out. The farther he rode, the worse it got. He topped a ridge and saw her. Sally. She simply stood there, not waving, not calling to him, just still as stone, though the wind ripped at her hair and dress until she dissolved like a fine mist. And then he knew. He hesitated but a moment before he nudged his horse to the edge of the cliff where she had appeared. His love was there waiting for him. He had longed for this, knew that his time was short for he had no desire to go on without her. And now she was giving him a sign.

He had known she would come, known she would not leave him to founder in his mourning forever. Her appearance had signaled that it was time. Sally had told him in a dream that she would come for him when it was his time. He had not expected it to be so soon but was now so glad of that fact. Life had been so hard without her. Her leaving had left him merely existing in a world that saw him as a misfit, a heathen that had no place here, his tribe decimated, no longer fitting in among the red skins or whites. It was time. He would not look back and long for a life that no longer held meaning for him. His friend Travers Gage had expressed much concern for him after Sally's death, seeing how his soul had looked into the distance searching for Sally and their child.

He considered the packet in his saddlebag that he was supposed to deliver to the fort this afternoon. He reached back and flipped the bag open, withdrawing the packet, looking hard at it. He didn't owe the white men at the fort one thing. They had given him nothing but grief for so long, calling him buck, red chief, and butchering his given name. He looked at the packet one last time before he tossed it aside, not bothering to see where it landed. His horse never stopped. At the edge he looked down, noting how deep the ravine was, almost sheer from a landslide where the river had carved itself a new path from floods earlier in the spring. The river was low now, and he eased ever closer. There was uneven ground immediately below, jagged rocks and debris from the current now exposed after months of little rain.

He heard something. Almost like a whistle. Then he was falling, his horse, Moon Rider, trying to find purchase on the ground that had suddenly turned to mush beneath its hooves. The rumbling grew louder, and dirt caved in on him even as he reached above him to grasp an exposed dead root of a long gone tree. It would not hold him long. Why he was even holding on to it was beyond him. He had seen Sally. It was his time, yet something told him to hold on just a bit longer. Within minutes he heard the pounding of hooves above him. Someone was there, and before he could worry if it was friend or foe, Travers' head appeared over the rim.

"What in the—You all right, man?"

"Don't I look alright?" Little Crow grinned up at Travers, the first he had seen in quite a while from his red-skinned friend.

"I'd say you've looked better. Hold on, and I'll have you back on solid ground in no time."

"No. You must take the packet to the fort that I dropped on up the ledge. I won't be coming back."

Travers gave a snort. "You'll be able to deliver it in person. Here, give me your hand." Even as he spoke, the root began to tear itself from the loosened dirt. Travers lunged forward, his hand grasping at that of Little Crow but found no secure grip. His grip was tenuous, and both knew it. Steel blue eyes met the black eyes below his as they hung there suspended for what seemed an eternity. Little Crow knew this man had done all he could to save him. He had been a friend to his woman, the sunshine goddess, and he knew the white doctor had loved her as he had. He had taken her death equally as hard as he had. This man had been his friend, too. He had never lied to him, as had many white men. The truth of their situation was in his eyes now. Little Crow longed to see his sunshine goddess again. She was waiting for him on the other side. He could sense her presence even now. So he told the white doctor what had to be said.

"Let me go."

Travers strained to keep his grip on the lithe brave.

"Not on your life," he gritted from between clenched teeth.

"It is my time. I have seen her. She waits for me. You must let me go."

Travers shook his head and began to tug even harder, trying to pull his friend up over the ravine that continued to crumple underneath them. The Indian seemed to dig in with his feet. He was not coming up. Frustrated, Travers stopped struggling, his eyes meeting the determined black ones once again.

"You cannot save me, my friend. Go away knowing that she awaits me. I long to go to her."

"I am so sorry, Little Crow. That I could not save Sally, and that I cannot save you. You have been a brave warrior, a credit to your people. I am proud to have called you my friend."

"My death is of my choosing. It is the way of our people. I go now. You are an honorable man, Gage. Let not my death be on your conscience."

They held for a moment longer, then with a yank, Little Crow pulled free. Travers watched him fall. He lost sight of him before he hit the rocks below. Travers hung his head, wishing there was something else he could have done. He had seen the loneliness in the man's eyes when he had spoken of Sally, knew he missed her terribly. Travers knew what that pain felt like. He had felt it many times. He would have chosen a more spectacular death for the man, though. He had deserved better than to fall off a cliff. He should have gone out fighting, as was his way of life, his people. Little Crow had simply lost heart, had given up, his people gone, then his woman and child.

He shimmied away from the precipice and pulled himself together before searching for the packet Little Crow had told him to deliver. Finding it, he opened it and looked at the contents. It contained several items of scouting instructions and a particularly interesting piece of news. A dishonorable discharge for Creighton Gibbs. Apparently, the man had not been up to snuff in more ways than one. His particular method of practicing medicine didn't hold a candle to the charges brought against him leading to the discharge. Fraud, dereliction of duty, and cowardice. It was more than enough to send the man packing. Someone in the Army had finally had enough of him.

Travers walked stiffly to his horse, the pain he had felt at losing Little Crow now intensified by the aches in his own body from the tumble he had taken just before finding the man dangling from the deteriorating cliff face. The horse whinnied and shifted nervously but steadied itself at the doctor's soothing voice. Travers rubbed the creature carefully, checking for injuries, smoothing it's now dusty coat. Thankfully the horse seemed to be only shaken. A miracle. Travers wouldn't have given a plug nickel for its survival when the two of them had plunged headfirst down the washout. It would have been a shame to lose the animal because of such a crazy mishap after it had survived four years of war.

He soothed the horse for a bit before leading him back to more solid ground. Something didn't sit right with Travers. Just before the ground had given way beneath them, he had heard a suspicious noise, much like that of dynamite being detonated. He decided to take a closer look at the area. There were indeed indications of explosives, the acrid smell of black powder still hanging in the air. Travers retraced his route to the cliff and found the telltale sign he had been looking for. Some tracks had been half brushed out of at least two horses. Whoever had tried to hide their tracks had been either very careless or in an all-fired hurry. He figured it was the latter. But it made no sense to him. Out here, if a man wanted someone dead badly enough, he sought him out personally to do the job. Unless that person was Jim Bowers, but Travers discounted that notion rather quickly. Bowers had no beef with the man at the bottom of the ravine. That he knew. Couldn't even say the two men had ever met. Little Crow was no gunfighter, but he was no novice when it came to fighting. True, he had many enemies, but this stank of vendetta and cowardice. The thought occurred to Travers that perhaps Little Crow wasn't the intended target at all. After all, he had come upon the brave just after the collapse of the ridge and had been caught in the melee as well, almost joining his friend at the bottom of the gorge. The tracks were a start, and Travers mounted his horse and headed in the same direction the tracks were leading off to. He was in no hurry. Justice had to be served for the senseless death of Little Crow. Whoever had done this to his friend would pay. He knew just where to start looking.

Sure enough, the tracks led back towards the fort. Travers was still a good three hours ride from the place when he jumped the two men up. It was Creighton Gibbs and some greaser he had never seen before. They were stretched out under a shade tree taking a break from the heat and dragging on their canteens when he rode straight up to them from behind. Apparently, they had not given much thought to the fact that they might be followed at all and were quite surprised when they turned around at the sound of Travers clearing his throat, to find that his gun was drawn and cocked as well, covering both of them quite sufficiently. Gibbs chuckled nervously, wiping his mouth with the back of his hand, his eyes on the doctor. The stranger with him looked ready to run.

"Don't suppose you gents have something you want to tell me, do you? Like where you were, oh, about two and a half hours ago?" His tone was anything but nonchalant, his body language telling them he was deadly serious.

Gibbs giggled like a girl, his eyes jumping to that of his buddy. Who did the man think he was questioning them? Nerve, and a lot of it the man had, seeing as how he was supposed to be dead. Something had gone wrong. The dynamite had not done its job. Travers Gage was supposed to be buried in a ton of debris down by the river. Instead, he was standing before them, grilling them on their whereabouts of the day.

"We was in Nicholsville gettin' us some grub. We been down to Dodge on business for the Army." Gibbs' eyes shifted again to his companion, trying to convey that he should keep his mouth shut and let him do the talking. "You got a problem with that, Gage?"

Travers shifted on his horse ever so slightly, his gun pointed straight towards Gibbs.

"I think I might, at that. See, I've been following your tracks for some time now, and you did not come from Nicholsville. You came from the direction of Gold City. Your tracks were lighter after you reached the river. Seems you unloaded something there. I bet I could tell you what it was. See dynamite has a mighty distinguishing smell. It hangs in the air for quite some time. Funny thing is, you didn't seem to want anyone to know you were in that area. Your tracks were scrubbed out, rather unprofessionally I might add. Now the burning question I'm dying to know is, why did you want Little Crow dead?"

Gibbs scratched his head on that one. He had not counted on the Injun being anywhere around when they had blasted the ledge. But he would take one as good as the other, he supposed. The prairie nigger had been uppity with him once too often without ever uttering a solitary word to Gibbs. No, he had wanted

Travers Gage at the bottom of that pile of debris. And here he was pinpointing their whereabouts with point-blank accuracy.

"I can't rightly say that I know what you're talking about, Gage. That Injun and me never got on, don't know that we ever even spoke. Why would I want him dead? Are you saying that he is?" He tried to make a good showing of feigning innocence.

"Well, I guess that answers my question. The dynamite wasn't meant for him at all, was it? It was meant for me." There it was, the accusation and clarification all in one tight little refrain. The man was good.

"Now Gage, you're awful quick to go assuming somethin' that just ain't got no merit. Why would we want you dead?"

"Oh, your friend there, I'm sure he's got no reason other than he's working for you. But now you, that's a different matter altogether. Perhaps it's because of what's inside the packet that Little Crow was carrying to your commanding officer. Seems he took to heart my appeal to have your credentials examined. He found more than enough to have you discharged—and like you, Gibbs, there is nothing honorable about it."

Gibbs bristled like a cur dog at that remark. "You high hatted piece of crap! I've had enough of your mouth. You thinkin' you're better'n me, talkin' like some city slicker who never saw a day's work in his life! You ain't about to outdo me. I'll show you yet!" Even as he reached for his gun, Travers kicked Cirrus into motion, knocking the man to the ground. The other man darted for his horse, and Travers shot him smack in the rump, watching him drop like a log, writhing and crying out in agony. Gibbs turned to crawl away and found his exit cut off by Travers and Cirrus. He got to his feet and pointed his gun at Travers once again only to have Cirrus ram him hard this time. As Gibbs spun around trying to break his fall, there was an explosion of gunfire, and he collapsed, unmoving, face down on the ground. Keeping the other man covered and letting him know it, Travers dismounted and rolled Gibbs over. He had fallen on his own gun, somehow causing it to go off. He was dead.

Travers secured his other captive and wrapped Gibbs up in his bedroll before tying him to his horse. Putting the other man on his horse, he headed to Fort Wallace. Let them do what they would with this one. He had avenged his friend's death, and that was all that mattered. Little Crow could rest in peace now, and Travers was sure that he was up here somewhere with Sally and their child. Little Crow said she had come for him. Travers wondered if he had seen her, heard her voice as she had beckoned. As he rode the plains towards Fort Wallace, the only voice he heard calling to him was the bottle in his desk drawer. He couldn't reach home fast enough.

FORTY-NINE

It was his rotten luck to run into Jim Bowers one afternoon as he was on his way to lunch back at the boarding house. Jim was headed to the hotel when he spied Travers and crossed the street to speak to him.

"Say, there, Dr. Gage. I was wondering if you happen to have any idea what could cause severe headaches. Margaret seems to suffer dreadfully from them, and nothing seems to help except laudanum."

Travers looked at the man before him with a touch of disdain. "Perhaps it's the company she's keeping."

Bowers, to his credit, had anticipated such a remark and offered one of his own.

"Or maybe it's the thought of what will never be. In any case, if the headaches continue, I fear I may have to take her to a specialist in New York or Boston. Perhaps there is a surgery that can relieve her of these 'symptoms.'"

"Surgery is the last resort for any malady. And I strongly suspect it is not even to be considered in her case. Headaches can be brought on by a food allergy, certain smells, even a woman's time of the month. Some women are just more prone to them. It is in their makeup, the genes. I'm afraid it is usually something they have to live with."

"Well, I find it distressing that my wife stays so indisposed. She hardly gets out of bed anymore. She's let her looks go, something that is so out of character for even her." He didn't mention the fact that he helped contribute to her indisposition. He had taken his fist to her several times as of late when she had pointed out to him just how much he stood to lose when everyone found out about his land deed scheme. After she shot her mouth off to him a time or two, he made certain that she realized just how fast Travers Gage could vanish from her life for good. His threats always seemed to have the desired effect.

"Perhaps a bit of laudanum from time to time would ease her suffering?" Bowers asked.

Travers nodded. "And a change of scenery might be the ticket. A lady loves to shop, you know. Spend her husband's money for him. One of the happening towns like Chicago or Boston might do wonders for her."

Bowers smiled, genuinely this time. "You know, you just might be on to something, at that. I think I'll arrange a getaway for the two of us. Much like a second honeymoon."

Travers kept the smirk from his lips that ached to respond caustically, "Don't you mean the honeymoon you never had?" Instead, he returned the smile and nodded good day to the man and headed in to eat his lunch that was probably getting cold.

Flora and Laura were having lunch together when Travers walked in and sat at his usual place at the table. The furrowed brow he wore was a given these days, a sure sign of the stress he was dealing with. They glanced at one another then back at Travers. Laura got up to pour him fresh coffee and patted his arm. "Smile, Trav. Break that frown that has become your face. Everybody who loves you is plumb afraid to speak, lest you snap their head off. Even Clay says he don't know how to talk to you anymore. And Clayton ain't never been one lacking for words. We're your friends, doc. Lean on us. You can't take on all the world's problems alone. You will break if you do, cause there is absolutely no bend to you."

He sipped his coffee and made a sandwich out of his chicken breast. His frown grew more severe if possible. He knew they meant well. They cared about him, just as he cared for them. But they had no idea the weight he carried, the guilt. He couldn't just pick himself up and walk on as if nothing had happened. He was responsible. He was so damned responsible that it gnawed on his gut at night as he lay in bed. He alone would shoulder the burden of his irresponsibility.

"You ladies have a nice day," he told them as he wrapped his sandwich up in a napkin and took his coffee with him out the door. He could not sit here and socialize. He had work to do.

Flora looked at Laura. "Kind of blunt, weren't ya? He's just now gotten to the point he will speak, and you go off on a tangent. Sarah and Clay have been trying to work up to getting him to come for supper soon. We all miss him, Lar, we just have to be patient. We don't know what he is going through. He feels responsible for so much, and he is so determined to get Bowers and has been unable to do it. How do you think you would feel if you were in his shoes?"

"Well, I don't know, Flora. Maybe I would talk about it with my friends, get a little support."

Flora laughed. "Since when do men need 'support'? Men don't need help with anything. At least to hear them tell it, they don't. No, leave Travers alone. He will come around soon enough." She finished her coffee and left as well, leaving a disgruntled Laura behind.

Humph, thought Laura. Flora didn't have to live with him.

She did, and that frown was beginning to get on her nerves. She felt like yanking him up and giving him a good shake sometimes, but knew she couldn't do that. No, Travers would have to deal with the events of the past few months himself. And she was going to just have to suffer right along with him.

FIFTY

He had been sitting there going over the conversation with Bowers in his mind. The man had gone out of his way to approach him. Unusual for him to do so. Maybe Maggie was really having problems that he should look into. "Not bloody likely," he muttered to himself, his teeth clenched so hard they hurt. Whatever had possessed him to think that Bowers was only looking out for Maggie's best interest? Hell, he should have known better. The man cared for no one but himself. Tossing the towel with which he had just finished wiping his hands on the back on the commode, he sat down at his desk and stared pensively into the flame that danced within the globe of the single lamp. He was a fool. Her marriage had not dampened the depth of his feelings for her. Sally, dear sweet Sally, had not even been able to take his mind off of the other woman. Even now, trying to recall Sally's face, it was Maggie's image that rose to mind. Raking a shaking hand through his already ruffled hair, he released a long sigh. Somehow, he knew in his gut, there would be no happy ending for the two of them. She was lost to him forever. That knowledge didn't stop the haunting memories of her spread out before him in the grass that day of the Sunday picnic. The feel of her skin beneath his hands as he had explored. God, he needed a drink. He was through mooning over a married woman, one who had chosen wealth over—he had thought to say love, but that was a little much. Affection would work. But affection seemed too trivial a word to describe his feelings for Maggie. She was, and he feared always would be, the only woman for him. That realization uncapped the bottle he had been pondering on his desk and brought it to his lips. He pulled on the liquid fire for a minute before setting it down again, corking it. Sitting here mooning over Maggie was not going to get his work finished. Reaching over to the stack of papers to his left, he took one down and got to business.

Evening fell and the night air came on hot and balmy, the sign of an approaching storm. The rising wind did little to ease the heat but stirred dust devil out in the streets. Travers still sat at his desk going over patients' records, making notations and filing them away as he went. He had three more to go as his mind had kept drifting. His mood was as black as the starless sky above the town tonight, and he was feeling the urge to hit the bottle once again. Sally kept rising before his eyes. Sweet, lovable Sally. She would have been twenty-six today. He missed her terribly. He had used her, used her sweetness, her passion, her friendship to take his mind off of Maggie, if only for a while. The weight of that guilt weighed heavy on him tonight. She had known that she was playing second fiddle to the other woman from the start and that had definitely changed the dynamics in their friendship. Now she was gone.

There was bitterness in him tonight, a harshness that he shouldn't be feeling. He considered going to the Velvet Rose when he finished but thought better of it. None of those women had what he wanted. Not even Flora. Not that she would allow it now, even after she had tried to nail him for years. Flora had Daniel. Or at least they played at having each other. Daniel still seemed quite afraid of committing to the redhead, and Travers had difficulty understanding why. Flora was everything a man could want in a woman. Notwithstanding her undeniable sensuality, she was beautiful, intelligent, and resourceful. She could cook, keep house. And she had a good head on her shoulders. She had set him straight time and again. She had a logic that few women possessed, and that was a good thing. She had begged off sharing his bed once even though he knew she would have otherwise been more than willing. But given the circumstances involved, she had done the right thing and turned him away.

Losing Maggie to Jim Bowers had done something to him. Sally had helped to clear his mind, if only for a short time, of the venom he had built up towards that man. He had given his word to General Sharpe that he would watch over her and he had to the best of his abilities. The two of them had shared something very special for a short time. He would probably have even married her if she had wanted, but Sally was a free spirit. She was not one who liked to take orders from anyone. When Little Crow had come into their life, she didn't stand a chance. He could tell, it had to have been love at first sight. For both of them. Over time, he had come to respect Little Crow and knew that he genuinely cared for Sally. He had been devastated as well at her death. His death had shaken Travers. The brave had lost his reason to live. He had been ready to take his own life he missed her so terribly. After the brave's death, for two days Travers had shut himself up in his room at the boarding house, drinking and refusing to come out. He felt like such a failure. He had become too needy. He had developed relationships he shouldn't have. He had let the people of this town into his heart. A mistake. He had known he shouldn't do it.

Laura, bless her, had made him see reason. No amount of beating himself up about their deaths would bring either of them back. Life handed out hard blows sometimes, and you either rolled with the punches or got knocked down. Travers already knew that. But his disposition had become so that even his closest friends stayed away, giving him space to grieve privately. He had begun missing meals, noticeably losing weight, and Sheriff Tate and Louella had finally insisted that he start taking lunch with them every day. Their company had been a big comfort to him. The sheriff was normally a man of few words, but he talked nonstop at the table during mealtime to cover the silence. Louella had clucked her tongue at him and told Travers he'd best start talking or she was going to have to shoot Ras to get him to shut up. That had brought a smile to Travers' face, and he had gradually eased into conversation with them. It had been a turning point.

But the bitterness still lingered, and he ached to place all the blame on Maggie. She was the reason for all of this. It was her fault, dammit that he was suffering so. He knew it was wrong, but it made him feel better blaming her for his pain.

He was so wrapped up in the thought that he didn't hear the click of the door shut and lock. He became aware of her just before she stepped into the room. Travers suppressed a huge shudder and refused to look up, to even acknowledge she was there. He pretended to busy himself with the files before him, a black frown on his face. He could smell her all the way from where she stood just inside the door. She smelled of wild flowers and vanilla, an unusual combination to say the least, but it suited her. From the corner of his eye, he could see her standing there just inside the door to his tiny office, the only light in the place the oil lamp on the desk. She was dressed in a long cape that covered her from head to toe. Soft kid slippers peeked from beneath the cape.

"Travers?" She spoke softly.

He still didn't look up. He continued to pretend his concentration was elsewhere. She continued to stand there. Several minutes passed before he finally looked right at her, asking pointedly, making no effort to hide his irritation,

"Is there something I can do for you?"

Maggie gnawed at her lip for a second before answering. "I need some laudanum. I have this really bad headache, and I seem to be all out."

Travers lay down his pencil, still looking at her, rose and went over to his medicine chest and found a small bottle of the liquid. Striding back to her, he placed it in her outstretched hand. He resumed his seat at the desk without another look her way and busied himself with the file in front of him once again. She remained, standing there silent as stone.

Dammit! What did she want? If she didn't get out of here

fast, she was going to regret it. He was fighting hard for control. She smelled incredible, and when he had handed her the laudanum, he could tell her hair was still damp from her bath. She had just come from her bath, and that thought alone was messing dangerously with his head. She shouldn't be here!

Maggie was in a quandary. This had seemed like a good idea at first thought, and she had acted impulsively, not completely thinking the idea through. And now he was sitting there ignoring her, damn him. Anger sparked in her eyes. She hadn't come here to be ignored. She was going to speak her piece whether he liked it or not.

"Travers, I haven't seen you in a while, and I was concerned."

Silence.

"Your friends say you're not yourself."

"I believe it's what they call 'mourning,'" he snapped at her sarcastically.

Maggie came further into the room, her back now up. "Travers, she's been gone a year now. I know she was your friend, we all do, but she's gone. This isolation you've brought upon yourself is not good for you."

"Get out." His eyes had closed tightly against her little speech.

"What? I will not. You're not the first person who's ever lost someone they love" Her hand flew to her mouth, her eyes large in her face like giant pools. She struggled to catch her breath, shaken by the very thought. Oh, God! He had been in love with that woman. Thus the reason for his withdrawal, his self-imposed isolation. Maggie had always denied the very idea. Because it had hurt, the thought of him with another woman. Now she knew she was only fooling herself.

"What's wrong, Maggie? Can't wrap your mind around the idea that I might care about someone else? Get out!"

Maggie just stood there frowning at him. His face a thundercloud, he shoved away from the desk and rose, coming towards her. She backed away instinctively, away from the intensity in his eyes.

"Yes, Maggie. I did love her. She was everything that you are not. And I loved her for that. She was a strong woman, without pretense or guile. She knew what she wanted and made no excuses for herself. And I loved her for it. But above all, she took my mind off of you. And I *loved* her for it." He had backed her against the wall behind his desk, stalking her all the while like a tiger, his eyes boring into hers.

"She's gone now, and while I loved her very much, I was not *in* love with her. She couldn't make my heart stop by simply walking into a room. It wasn't her that I dreamed about at night.

She never made me so angry that I could spit nails. And God help her, she didn't have your eyes." The last was said so softly, his voice full of anguish. His hand poised near her cheek, almost touching but he checked himself, knowing that would start a fire that could not be quenched by a mere touch. He was towering over her, his eyes angry, his body literally humming with frustration. The scent of him filled her nostrils, his words held her breathless.

"You have to the count of three to get out of here. If you don't, I can't be responsible for my actions. One . . . two . . ."

"Three," she whispered fervently, boldly, meeting his eyes. His gaze grew even darker, his silver eyes looking almost mad in the dimly lit room. For a split second, he didn't move. Then suddenly she was in his arms crushed against his chest so tightly she had to struggle for air. His mouth took possession of hers, ravaging it, taking away her will. It didn't matter. She was where she wanted to be. She had come here to comfort, hoping, praying for a sign that she still held a place in his heart. It was a selfish prayer, she knew, but right now she didn't care. He loved her. He had never stopped. She wrapped her arms around him and dug her fingers into his back pressing him closer if that were possible. It had been too long since she had been in his arms. The feeling was divine, and she wanted more, so much more. Tonight, she knew deep inside, she would not leave disappointed.

Travers was reeling. The moment she had whispered 'three,' he had known there was no going back for either of them. He wanted to hurt her the way she had hurt him, wanted her reeling from the emotion boiling up between them. He wanted to . . . he wanted to . . . take her then and there and by God, he would.

The moment he had taken her into his arms, he had known she was his, if only for this night. He devoured her mouth, his tongue raping, plundering, marking her as his as she clung desperately to him. He slid his hand to the back of her head holding her still to meet his assault. She whimpered softly, but Travers was beyond gentleness. He had endured long enough without her and tonight she would finally know what it meant to be possessed by him. After what seemed an eternity, he raised his head, still so close their noses brushed, his mouth scant inches from hers. Maggie licked her lips nervously, swallowing, trying to regain her breath. He watched her, wanting to see her reaction to his next words.

"You were warned, Maggie. I'm afraid you won't be going anywhere for a while."

She raised heavy-lidded eyes to meet his. "Oh, Travers," she breathed softly, her fingers tracing the tautly curved jaw before moving to feather across his bottom lip. He grabbed her hand

and turned it over, pressing an intimate kiss to the center of her palm sending hot shivers down her spine. His lips made their way up her arm to the curve of her neck, making her weak with too long suppressed desire. The cape disappeared and revealed a long white nightgown. The long billowing sleeves and neckline were gathered by a drawstring. Travers stepped back and just looked at her from head to toe for a moment, his eyes raking her hotly. When they touched upon her slippers peeking out from beneath her gown, he knelt and taking one foot in his hand, removed the shoe. His hand slid up the calf of her leg, pushing the gown with it. With every inch of skin revealed, Travers groaned low in his throat. She was naked underneath the gown. He bared her to the waist, his eyes hungry, and he shook with the need to touch. To taste. He did. He started with her navel, his tongue flicking into the cavity causing Maggie to gasp from the erotic pleasure of it. He teased her, tasted, moved lower and tasted there as well. Maggie was shivering, squirming, gasping for air, praying for him to stop, praying that he wouldn't.

He did. Travers rose to his feet, the light in his eyes rather frightening. His eyes locked with hers, he reached and untied the drawstring, pulling straight down on the neckline before easing it down, baring the creamy slopes of her shoulders and breasts. His eyes followed the gown as it crept lower and lower. It caught on her arms, but Maggie didn't care. Neither did Travers. He opened his mouth against the hollow of her throat, wreaking havoc on Maggie's nerves. His lips nibbled lower and lower until he found what he was looking for and clear lifted her from the floor. Maggie could only hold on, her head thrown back in rapture, her fingers raking through his hair. Travers was lost. He had known it from the moment she walked in. Somehow, he managed to open his trousers and, bracing her against the wall, her legs already about his hips, told her, "You're mine, Maggie. You were never meant to be his."

He entered her hard and fast and the pleasure of it was so exquisite Maggie almost screamed aloud. Travers covered her mouth with his and swallowed her moans and cries as she climaxed instantly. He could feel her convulsing around him, and he fought for control, the veins in his neck and temple in danger of popping. He was afraid to move, afraid it would all be over far too quickly if he did. He ended the kiss and leaned his forehead against hers, his eyes closed in ecstasy, his breathing hard labored.

"Dear God, Maggie. Maggie . . ."

Maggie was stunned. She had known it would be good between them. She had never imagined the emotions, the feelings involved. She felt bewitched, under a spell of his making and hoped it would never end. She rained kisses over his face, unable to stop herself. She loved this man. How could she have been so blind? Her breath caught and her eyes closed as he began to move once again within her. Maggie knew now that this was what Travers had tried to show her, tried to tell her about. She belonged in his arms and no others. Not even her own husband's. She clung to him as the world around her spun out of control, the very breath leaving her as she came totally, exquisitely, hopelessly—undone.

Travers could not get his fill of her. They made love on the floor, on the desk, in his chair, the cot, before ending up on the floor again. The hour grew late and the street lamps burned out one by one. Still, they lay in each other's arms. Neither wanted to move, for if they did, they knew that the night, their night, would come to an end. Maggie was still married and this night didn't change that fact. Finally, unable to stand it any longer, she rose and slipped her gown and cape back on. Travers watched her, knowing she was going back to her room on the second floor of the hotel, overlooking the street. He opened his mouth to speak, and she quickly covered his mouth with her fingers and then her mouth, kissing him softly once more.

"Don't speak. No 'if only's.' No matter what happens, we will always have this night." She kissed his forehead before slipping out the door and into the night.

Travers lay there, wondering how many steps lower into hell he had just descended. Surely that was worth seven or eight. He had just helped a woman commit adultery. Closing his eyes against the pain of her leaving, he came to the conclusion that his moral compass was definitely broken. He wondered when it had happened and could only nail it down to a why: a pair of blue eyes the color of sapphires. The floor soon grew cold, and he rose and made his way to a bed in the clinic where he would pass the remainder of a sleepless night.

———◆———

Maggie let herself into her room in the wee hours of the morning. She was tired and sore, but she felt alive for the first time in her life. She stripped her gown off and climbed into the bed naked and slept that way, remembering every touch, every kiss, every sigh, the feel of Travers' skin beneath her hands, the feel of the two of them coming together as one. She logged it into her memory, recalling every minute detail for she may never get the opportunity to share such passion again. It was well into mid-morning before she awoke.

FIFTY-ONE

Four days later, the town held its semi-annual dance. Once again, the committee in charge had outdone themselves. The food was a virtual smorgasbord of choice hams, turkeys, breads, fruits and desserts and the punch and liquor flowed abundantly. The square was lit up with lanterns strung across the street in rows and torches marked off the area set aside for the dance. The mid-June heat had the women wearing their shorter sleeves and lightweight gowns. A few twirls about the dance floor in this heat unprepared would have Travers working overtime if they weren't careful.

The square was already crowded when Travers arrived. He and Laura had just delivered her food to the buffet workers when he spotted her. Maggie was alone. Again. His first thought was to go to her. Common sense told him to stay away. He knew that the proper thing to do was keep his distance. He made small talk with the townsfolk and ran into Clayton. The man thankfully kept him entertained for a large portion of the evening. Laura had made her way to Maggie and spoken with her at length, and Travers noted how her face looked more relaxed as they engaged in conversation. Two hours had passed since the dance had begun and her husband still had not shown. She visited with others, Daniel and Flora, but eventually found her way to a seat a distance from the crowd.

Maggie was nervous about something. For an hour, she sat in her chair, a frown taking over her face, though she tried hard not to look so worried. Jim should have been here by now. Even though she and Jim were living separately, he still demanded that he escort her to public events. He had not arrived at the hotel when he said he would, and she had chosen to go ahead, knowing that would rile him. She sighed. He would not be pleased. The thought of what he might do began to eat at her. It had been a long time since he had beaten her. She didn't think he would try that again after what happened last time. But the not knowing set her lip between her teeth and she waited. And waited.

He had kept his distance from her all night, but the sight of her looking so purely angry, embarrassed and torn pulled at him. She was sitting across the dance floor from him, alone. Sheriff Tate had persuaded her to dance with him, much to Travers' surprise and Louella had thankfully plopped down in her vacated chair, fanning herself after engaging in such heavy foot stomping as her husband liked to call it.

Pete had danced with her, as well as Daniel who had succeeded in getting her to laugh. He could feel the impact of her smile all the way from across the room. That had been two dances ago. She had a look about her as if she could bolt and run at any minute. But Maggie didn't bolt and run. She held herself proudly, if uncertainly. She would not cow to her husband any longer on any terms.

Travers moved towards her, losing the battle against his better judgment. The night would be coming to an end soon. One dance. That's all he wanted. Just once he wanted to hold her in his arms. The need, the desire would not leave him, and soon he found himself before her.

She regarded him uncertainly, her eyes large, frightened. He stared at her, drinking her in, steel gray melding into blue.

"Dance with me," he said, brooking no resistance, his hand held out to her.

She knew she should refuse. Tried hard to think of an excuse to do so. She couldn't. From the moment she had seen him watching her from across the dance floor she had longed for this. She had been certain that he would keep his distance, feared he would. Prayed he wouldn't.

He was so handsome tonight he took her breath. His suit was crisp black, his shirt a snowy white. The vest he wore was red silk and his pocket watch contrasted nicely, the gold chain dangling luxuriously against the fine material. His jacket was superbly tailored, hanging almost to his knees. He had smoothed his hair back away from his face, but it fell free now, rakishly so over his right brow.

There was a fire burning in his eyes, one that she was familiar with, and it drew her like a moth.

There really was no question. She placed her hand in his, the warmth of his fingers shooting sensation up her arm. Funny things were happening inside of her, and she seemed to tingle all the way to her toes. He pulled her to her feet and led her to the center of the dance floor, his eyes locked with hers.

The music changed. Slow, melodic, hauntingly beautiful. Ah, a waltz. He pulled her into his arms, and the act itself was pure heaven. And pure hell. He must have been insane to think he could do this properly. Well, to hell, with proper. He had never professed to be proper. His hand went from resting lightly at her side to the small of her back, pressing her closer.

Her eyes darkened, and he could feel the air rush past his chin as she sucked it in, her back arching slightly at the heat of his hand. She was wearing the amber silk with the matching lace that was so striking on her. Her hair was piled high with curls left to fall freely as they would about her face, setting off the blue of her eyes. They were moving along with everyone else to the music, but he was not dancing. He was devouring her with his eyes, impressing the feel of her upon his memory, making love to her right there on the dance floor.

She knew what he was doing. For the life of her, she did long to prolong it, yet his eyes were upon her so strongly that she was sure they were bringing notice to themselves. She wouldn't allow him to become even more of a target for Jim. Dear God, Jim. If he ever thought, even suspected . . .

Fear widened her eyes and gave her the courage to look away. Thankfully, Travers must have understood the situation for he eased his hold on her, putting more distance between them. She sighed with relief and when she dared to look at him again, found he was looking out at the swirling mass surrounding them. She allowed her lids to drop, her eyes closing, following the sure steps of Travers leading her through the dance. It was like floating, being in his arms. She ached to lower her head to his firm and steady shoulder, hungering for the comfort she knew could be found there. She didn't dare. She couldn't suppress the shudder of despair that wracked her body and tears stung the backs of her eyes. She pressed them even more tightly together. She had known better than to do this.

Travers felt her shudder and knew it for what it was and did not speak. He noted the tightly closed eyes with just a hint of moisture at their corners, the white face. She was in as much pain as he was. His lips tightened grimly. He should take her back to her seat. Now.

They made it to the edge of the dance floor before the music ended and ran smack into Jim.

The man was smiling, though it was not a pleasant sight. It looked pasted on, and the man was doing a good job of at least appearing pleasant when the vein throbbing in his neck appeared ready to burst. Sam Bailey stood just to the man's left, his lips also pulled into a nasty smile. Bailey, Travers noted, was wearing a gun. The only man here who was. Travers eased to where he stood between Maggie and Bailey.

Turning his own humorless smile upon Jim Bowers, he said "Seems you've got a habit of forgetting your husbandly duties, Bowers. What must Maggie think of you, leaving her alone the way you do? I do believe that this is the third social function we've had where you've neglected to escort her properly. Manners, boy. Did no one ever teach you?"

The smirk that Travers sent the man was full of disdain, and at the insult, Bowers' face exploded into scarlet. Maggie cringed and clutched at Travers, hoping he would leave it at that. Travers ignored her, waiting for the lout's reply.

The man impressively pulled himself under control, though the urge to kill nearly choked him. He noted the panicked look on his wife's face as she tried to get the doctor to back off. A deadly coldness settled over him. He had seen the two of them dancing, seen the looks that had passed between the two of them. Fortunately for his wife, no one else had seemed to take notice, or she would be paying dearly tonight. He pasted the smile back on.

"My *wife* understands that, unfortunately, business does call at the most inopportune times. However, it appears that she'll never lack for an escort as long as you are around, Dr. Gage."

Travers smiled. Seemed Bowers had a few barbs of his own to fling.

"One does what he must when it comes to decorum. But then, I see I've erred again." The implication that Bowers lacked in manners and decorum was not lost on Bowers. Everyone in town knew that Bowers had come from the hill country of Arkansas, a place as backward as could be when it came to social cues. If he thought his money could make him a gentleman, he sadly lacked in brains. The man was as crass as a tin plate, with no manners, no education, and no social class. His money had bought him only the power of one to be feared simply because he surrounded himself with killers and land. If anything, his status in class had sunk lower with his shady dealing in Gold City. The dig was deep, and this time Travers got the response he was looking for.

"You've got a lot of nerve Dr. Gage, to talk about decorum when you dance with my wife the way you just did. Perhaps now would be a good time to perform my husbandly duty and call you on it." The coldness in the man's voice was like granite. The gauntlet was thrown.

Maggie gasped and came to stand between the two men who were glaring at each other. Both looked fit to kill. The throbbing was back in Jim's neck, and Travers' jaw was set like a vice.

"That's enough, from the both of you. This is a dance, remember. We're here to have a good time, not brawl."

Bailey's hand had settled on his belt, mere inches from his gun. Travers suspected his palm was itching mighty bad about now. He gave the man a long hard look, letting him know he wasn't afraid of him. He was looking to fight, but Travers was no fool. He would stand up to either of them any day, but he would not do it with Maggie so near to hand. He would not risk her getting hurt.

She eased to Jim's side, slipping her arm through his.

"I'd like to dance with my husband now." Her eyes pleaded with Travers to walk away. He could read the pain there, the fear. It sickened him to see her still seemingly so devoted to the man. He turned on his heel and stalked away.

Jim Bowers watched him go, hating him with every fiber of his being. He wanted the man dead. With the doctor around, Maggie could take flight at any moment. She had maintained that the two of them were just friends, but from the looks of the two of them tonight, he'd guess that there was far more to their relationship now. The little wench had played him. She had professed her undying love for him when he had proposed to her in Georgia. He had believed that she would be true to him because her Aunt Netta had been from the old school. A southern woman always held herself to a certain standard. They kept their word and their honor intact. Watching the two of them tonight, Jim was no longer so sure.

Doctor Gage was no man's fool, he was sure of that, and he was hell on wheels with a gun. Jim had seen him in action too many times and knew in a straight up fight, there wasn't a chance in hell of taking him. But his kind could be taken. There were ways. Silently, of course. With that consolation, he turned and offered his wife a genuine smile.

"Shall we?" he asked and without waiting for a reply, whisked her away into the swirling masses.

Maggie gave a massive sigh of relief. She was certain the two of them would have come to blows if she hadn't stepped in. Travers would have to understand. Jim was her husband. Even though they had taken up separate living quarters, they were still legally man and wife. Marriage to Jim was not what she had dreamed it would be. Nothing could have prepared her for what she had been forced to face. She had always had an idea of what marriage would be like, her dreams always including Travers. When he had failed to enter her life again, she had settled for Jim Bowers and gotten a monster. He had ceased trying to bed her. Thank God. He had chosen to take his frustrations out on her physically and mentally. She was drained. When she had come to town to live, Jim had allowed her to stay, seeing she would not go without a fight. He still demanded that they be seen in public together. It was his idea to tell people that it was his decision that she move to town simply because it had become too dangerous at the ranch because of the Indian situation. Everyone knew the truth. He gave her an allowance to keep her in style and allow her to have a bit of freedom about town. She had everything she needed to be happy. Except for the man she loved. No earthly possession could make up for that fact. The love she had once felt for her husband had vanished long ago. He knew it as well. But she was honor bound to stay true to her vows. She was a lady, properly raised. It didn't matter that she was abused. A wife didn't tell. She put on the dutiful wife act for the public and for Jim, knowing he demanded it of her. Somehow, she knew if the pretense stopped, her life would change drastically for the worse.

So she smiled at her husband as they danced across the floor, appearing ever the happy couple. He returned it full measure, his own thoughts keeping his spirits high. They danced as though they had not a care in the world, each of them plotting a course of action, or inaction, unknown to the other.

Travers stomped over to the punch table hoping to hell someone had spiked the stuff. Laura was there serving the drink, and her raised eyebrows told him that she had witnessed the episode with Jim and Maggie Bowers. He just glowered at her, taking the cup she offered and downed it in one gulp. It burned going down, and he offered a silent prayer of thanks that someone had answered his prayer before presenting the cup back to Laura for a refill.

She opened her mouth to speak. Travers stopped her before she could give him a piece of her mind.

"Not one word."

Taking the cup she had refilled, he simply turned and walked away.

PART III

FULL CIRCLE

FIFTY-TWO

Maggie was furious. Jim had dragged her back to the ranch just this morning like some wayward calf that had slipped its leash. She had fretted about the house all day, waiting for his return. The hour grew late, and still, he didn't come home. An hour or so ago, she had seen several of the men ride in the direction of town. She had stepped out onto the porch to catch the breeze now coming in across the plains. There were no stars out, and she could smell the scent of rain. It was heavy on the air, but it held off, even as the wind picked up. Maggie hugged herself against the wind, though it wasn't cool at all. She couldn't seem to help herself. She shivered and rubbed her arms to warm herself. Stepping back inside she went and poured herself a stiff drink, thinking that would chase away the chill that had settled over her. Turning, she found she was not alone. . . .

The land officer cringed before the boiling rage emanating from the man before him. His employer was not happy, and that did not bode well for his own sorry hide. Just this morning, Ates had opened the office to find that someone had been there in the night. The back door was cracked open just the slightest bit, and Ates knew he had locked the place up tight. Scrambling, scouring, as best he could tell, nothing was missing. Nothing seemed to have been disturbed, and he found that odd. Very odd indeed. Whoever had been there during the night had covered his tracks well, but something was definitely amiss. He knew it, and Bowers knew it, and that was the reason for his ire.

"Damn it, Ates, I thought you said this place was impenetrable!" Bowers hissed at the man behind the counter.

"I thought it was! Whoever came in that back door is damn good. That lock has been rusted for years. Can barely turn the key in it myself."

Bowers sighed, aggravated.

"And you're sure nothing is missing?"

Ates spread his hand before him. "Not a thing. Everything is here."

Bowers leaned against the counter, flapping his hat against his thigh, his face drawn into a studious frown.

"You would think the culprit would have made off with *something*. This is strange, I tell you." Ignoring Ates' nod of agreement, he added, "I've a theory, however, that maybe we should leave well enough alone." His eyes took on a sly gleam as he looked at the little man he paid so well to keep his secrets.

"Sir?" Where was Bowers going with this?

"We'll say nothing of this to anyone. If we don't make waves, the culprit is bound to get bold and pay us another visit, perhaps too bold, so as to become careless."

"Ahhh . . ." Ates understood. Bowers was a sly fox for certain. He had not gotten rich on his own, however. He had himself to thank for that and Ates was making him pay through the nose. He had a nice stash of funds, and it was growing daily. Soon he would have enough to make that move to parts unknown and leave this pathetic little town behind. He tried to focus on what Bowers was yammering about.

"Tonight I think you should leave something lying about. Nothing too damning, mind you. Just a morsel for our mouse. Think you can handle that, Mr. Ates?"

The squat man straightened. "Of course, sir. Leave everything to me."

Bowers looked at the little man, a feral smile spreading across his face.

"All right, then."

❖

Sam Bailey had come silently into the parlor and watched her. He had a slimy grin on his face, with positively evil intent. She simply froze for a moment, unable to move. Remembering the last thing that Jim had said before he left.

"I'm sick to death of your insubordination. I think it's high time you learned just what being my wife really means. Tonight, I think you'll understand that you have crossed me in public the last and final time."

She had scoffed again at his departing back. "Oh, really? Are you honestly going to try to play husband again, Jim? When are you going to give up?"

Now, standing here facing Sam Bailey, the look on his face told her all she needed to know. He was here to break her, and he was going to enjoy every minute of it. She backed away from him slowly, trying to negotiate her way to the door. He stalked her like a rabid wolf after his prey, his eyes shining ferally in the dim light of the parlor. She was terrified and very much alone. Jim would have seen to that. The only compassionate soul she had ever met at this place had been the cook, and he had vanished long ago. Jim had made a big show of howling and fussing, claiming the man had run off during the night. Maggie had seen through him. Slim, that was his name, had been her only ally, albeit a reluctant one. Maggie had known he wouldn't last long. Jim couldn't afford a weak link in his army of killers lest his own men turn against him.

The foreman licked his lips as he advanced. She was a purty thing. He had been waiting for this moment a long time. Her with her uppity ways. Well, Sam Bailey would show her. No woman looked down her nose at him. He couldn't believe his luck when Mr. Bowers had told him his wife needed a lesson in humility. He had given him a meaningful look that spoke volumes and Sam was an avid teacher of just such lessons. This was one lesson he was really going to enjoy.

Maggie suddenly found her back against the wall, and before she could speak, plead for mercy, he was upon her. She fought like a tiger, her nails raking down the side of his face, causing him to jerk back and scream.

"You bitch! You'll pay for that." He slapped her hard across the face with the back of his hand, sending her reeling to the floor. She lay there stunned, the pain in her jaw the only thing keeping her conscious. Taking a long-bladed knife from his belt, he slit her gown and ripped the remainder of her clothes from her body. She resumed her fight desperately now, her mind focusing only on survival. This man may succeed in what he had in mind, but he would not take her spirit, her fight. He wouldn't enjoy the ride. Her struggles only escalated the abuse she received. He straddled her naked form and punched her in the face several times, hitting her in the torso as well until she finally lay quietly, semi-conscious. He grunted his satisfaction with his handiwork. The little chit wouldn't be so purty anymore. He chuckled aloud at the thought.

He grabbed a handful of her now tangled hair and leaned close so she could hear every word.

"Compliments of your husband, ma'am."

She had known. The words just confirmed it. And in that instant, Maggie knew that she would kill her husband. For this act alone he deserved to die. She would kill him for the families whose lives he had turned upside down, for all the children left orphans, for all the wives left widows. But first, she had to get out of this mess she now found herself in. She came alive, fighting the man who pinned her beneath his crushing flab and meaty fists. He rained blow upon blow down on her, even as she fought against the pain to the point of insanity.

He somehow managed to get his pants down and pry her hands above her head. She spit in his face then, only to have him spit back at her, the stringy wetness running down into her mouth making her gag. She couldn't move, she couldn't do anything but kick feebly with her feet as he held her pinned just so he could take her. She felt his invasion and strained away from him, screaming into his ear before trying to bite it off. He head-butted her right in the mouth, shredding her lips against her teeth. Her head lolled dizzily back and forth, her mouth filling with blood.

She closed her eyes against the pain, and the humiliation she knew was to come. She prayed for mercy, for a release, for it to be over quickly. She prayed for strength to get through it. She prayed for death. Her prayers were answered, but not in the way she would ever have suspected. The door crashed open, and suddenly *he* was there. She cried tears of joy and lost herself in the euphoria of it. She could rest now. She could sleep. Her eyes closed and she knew no more.

FIFTY-THREE

There was a storm brewing. A big one. Travers was racing through the dark trying to beat it and get to Maggie on time. Damn it, if she would only have listened to him in the first place. But this wasn't her fault. This was *not* her fault. She had been fooled just like everyone else. The man should be dead. Would be dead if he ever got his hands on him. But first, he was going to pay for everything he'd ever done to Maggie and the people of this town. Jim Bowers had a lot to answer for, damn his black soul to hell. Travers was not a man bent on hate or revenge, but Bowers pushed his luck with the doctor every day.

Travers had been at his clinic when he had heard a light tap at the back door. At first, he had not checked it out, thinking it was perhaps the wind until he had heard the voice whisper his name.

"Doc? Are you there?"

He had started to open the door.

"No! Don't open it. I had to sneak over here. If they see me, they're likely to kill me."

"What—"

"No time for small talk. It's me, Tandy. The Bowers crew's over to the Velvet Rose. Something bad's happenin' at the ranch tonight. I heard mention of Sam Bailey and Mrs. Margaret. They out there alone, Doc. One of the boys let slip that he's to teach her a lesson she won't soon forget."

Travers wasted no time. "Thank you, Tandy. You go on back before they catch you gone. I'll head out there now." That had seemed an hour ago. Lightning flashed, and Travers steeled himself against it, even as the ground shook beneath Cirrus' pounding hooves as he raced like a maniac blindly through the tempest as he drew closer to the Bowers ranch.

There was no one about when he rode into the yard. The place seemed deserted except for a horse tied in front of the house. He dismounted and secured his horse, palming and cocking his gun as he did so. He had just mounted the steps when the scream stopped him in his tracks. Maggie. He was through the front door in seconds, his eyes darting, searching, his gun sweeping the room before him. They were in the parlor. Bailey was on top and, oh, God, Maggie . . . She saw him and smiled, tears running down her badly swollen face.

Rage like he had never known before kicked in. He strode

over and grabbed Bailey by the hair, jerking him off and away from Maggie. He lay the gun calmly down on the mantle, fully prepared to kill the man with his bare hands. Travers pounded the man's face and body, his knuckles soon bloodied and aching themselves and still he pounded, the desire to give this animal a taste of what it was like to be beaten and broken a thirst he couldn't seem to quench. His eyes held an eerie glow, and for the first time in his life, Travers thought he would know what it was like to enjoy killing a man. After several more blows, the man collapsed in an unconscious heap, his face a bloody, mangled pulp. Travers stepped away from him, forcing himself to breathe deeply, slowly, calming himself, trying to regain a sense of composure. Satisfied that Bailey wasn't going anywhere, he turned to Maggie.

He was beside her in two strides, sinking to his knees before her. For a brief moment he thought she was dead, but he found a weak pulse. She was covered in horrible bruises already and unconscious. He took an afghan from the settee and covered her battered body gently. Holstering his gun, he raced upstairs to gather a few of her things into a valise he found in her room already half packed. She would need personal things and clothes once she started to heal but he could supply all that. He got the bare necessities because he knew he would be unable to leave her for several days as she was in desperate shape. Downstairs, he pondered on how to move her. Taking a wagon or carriage would be chancy, but more convenient. He wanted no one to be able to track them. The storm brewing out there would soon wipe out horse tracks, but might not be enough to wipe out wagon or buggy tracks. It appeared she had broken ribs and putting her on a horse might be dangerous as well. Travers had never felt so torn.

Above the howling wind, he heard the sound of a rider coming in. He palmed his gun and stepped to the window, looking out into the inky night. A tall, slim form eased himself gingerly out of the saddle and haltingly climbed the steps. A grizzled face poked hesitantly through the open front door.

"Mrs. Bowers?" the stranger called softly. Travers stepped out of the shadows, his gun trained on the man.

"That's far enough, stranger."

The man halted just inside the door. Travers noted that he walked with a pronounced limp. He was tall and thin to the point of emaciation. But his eyes held a fire that set Travers back.

"You gonna use that, you best get on with it," he said, pointing at the gun Travers had aimed at him.

"I reckon you'd best state your business." Travers was not familiar with this man. He didn't know if he was one of Bowers' goons or an ally and he wasn't leaving anything to chance.

The grizzled man looked around the room and saw Bailey lying on the floor. Noting the man's unconscious state, his eyes flew back to Travers.

"What done happened here? Is he dead?" he asked gesturing at the man's crumpled form.

"Not yet," Travers told him, implying that he could very well be soon. A mean gleam entered the old man's eyes, and he said, "Good. Then I won't be denied the pleasure." He walked over and spat on Bailey, cursing violently at him. He spied Maggie's broken body at the same moment, and he froze, his mouth open, his eyes sorrowful. He took off his hat and held it to his chest, his eyes never leaving the sorry sight before him.

"Is . . . is she . . ." He couldn't bring himself to finish the question.

The man seemed to be genuinely concerned for Maggie. Shaken was a good word for it. Travers put away his gun. "She's alive. Barely."

The thin man looked Travers over. "You that doctor from town, ain't cha? The one Bowers has it in for."

Travers saw no reason to lie.

"I am."

The man scratched his head for a moment, put his hat back on and told him, "You'd best get her out of here now. Those toughs of Bowers'll be back soon. They find Bailey dead there'll be hell to pay."

Travers gave the stranger a hard look. "Bailey isn't dead."

The stranger pulled a wicked looking knife from his boot. "He will be soon enough," he said as he stroked the blade. "That sorry sack of manure left me for dead. Stuck a knife in my gut, he did. Seems Mr. Bowers didn't appreciate the fact that I showed his wife the proper respect."

The old man rubbed his hand across his face, and he appeared to age another ten years before Travers' eyes. The man had lived a rough life.

"They call me Slim. I was Mr. Bowers' cook. I came on not long after the marriage. I held my peace about the beatings until I couldn't anymore and stood up to him. Hell, she had nobody." He raised a pained face to Travers. "I ain't no saint. Never said I was. I done my share of wrong. But that—" he said pointing to Maggie, "that ain't right. Now, you best git on out of here while you still can. That storm ain't a'gonna wait for nobody."

A loud crash of thunder shook the house. Travers crossed to the window and saw the storm was almost upon them. There was no time for a wagon now. With Slim's help, he bound her ribs tightly, certain she had several broken ones. Modesty was forgotten as they got Maggie up and tried to wrap her securely in the blanket, but they were having a time getting it to stay closed. The old man went outside and came back carrying his slicker.

"Here. Put this on her. It will stay on and cover her head too. Take the blanket, though. Roll it up under her to sit on, to cushion her. Name's Slim, by the way." He followed Travers outside where he helped them get situated on the horse. Maggie moaned softly but didn't wake up. When they got her as comfortable as possible, Slim handed the reins to Travers and said

"There's an old cabin about nine miles north of here. That's where I been holed up. It's been abandoned for a while now. Not many folks know it's even there. It's hid under a stand of trees. Bowers and his crew don't know about it, or if they do, they don't frequent it. It's not on his land, so they more than likely won't even think to look for you there."

Travers gathered the reins and nodded to Slim. "Much obliged for your help."

The old man just waved it away. Think nothin' of it. You go on now. I'll take care of things here. I plan on leaving Bowers a message he won't soon forget."

At that, Travers clicked to the horse, and they headed off into the night. Whatever Slim had planned, he was certain would not be pleasant and he wanted no part of it. The man might be old, but he had the looks of a rough character about him. He had survived being left for dead. He was a survivor.

They had not gone far when the rain hit. It was cold and stinging, not too heavy at first, but became torrential. Maggie began to moan and soon awoke to the pelting she was taking. The coolness of the rain, though it was beating her in the face, remarkably seemed to help ease the swelling in her mouth and cheeks. She tried to open her eyes and found she couldn't. Both were swollen shut.

She hurt. God, she hurt.

The bouncing motion of the horse seemed to jar her insides and pain shot through her like a red-hot poker. She tried to hold her breath against the pain, and she still produced a whimper that Travers heard above the storm.

"Maggie?" He looked down into her brutalized face, wishing he had killed Sam Bailey.

"Travers, it hurts," she moaned.

"I know, sweetheart, I know. We'll be out of this rain soon. There's a cabin just up ahead. Slim told me where to find it."

He was wrong. "Slim's dead."

"No, Maggie. He's alive. They left him for dead, but he is very much alive."

Maggie swallowed against the lump in her throat. If Travers was right, she was glad. Slim had been kind to her. It was several minutes before she responded. "He's the only one who ever showed concern for me. I'm glad he's alive."

"You hush now. Rest. We've got a piece to go before we get to that cabin. The weather's taking a turn. We gotta hurry. You up to hard riding?"

"I'll make it, Travers. As long as I'm with you, I'm all right." She turned her face into his chest and tried to doze. It was impossible. She endured in silence. Lightning seemed to crack the sky wide open, and her terror grew. She could see it even through her badly swollen eyelids. It seemed they rode hours before Travers brought the horse to a stop. Gingerly, he eased from the saddle and pulled her down into his arms. The cabin was there all right. Travers had almost missed it. The door hung loosely on one hinge, and the glow of embers in the makeshift fireplace shed enough light for Travers to see a cot in the corner. He lay Maggie gently on the rough mattress and went outside to tend the horse. The lean-to porch would have to suffice as a shelter for poor Cirrus for the night. He removed the sodden blanket and saddle and set them just inside the dilapidated door. He shed his rain gear then and stepped back to Maggie's side. She seemed to be resting easier now.

He decided to build up the fire and found a bit of kindling near the fireplace. He stirred it, and it lit up readily. Getting a better look at the cabin and its contents, he could see where Slim got his name. There was the bare minimum of provisions. Canned beans, a few candles, a plate, a spoon and a jug of whiskey. Slim picking, if he'd ever seen it. But then again, during the war, Travers had survived for days on less than that.

Maggie moaned in her sleep, and he knew she was in for several bad days. She had fought like a tiger against Bailey, inflicting a bit of damage herself. He had taken note of the jagged tears across the man's face where she had nailed him good at least once. The man was a brute. It was surprising that she had even managed to inflict that little bit of damage. Travers shuddered, remembering the instant he had walked through the door and seen her, the look on her face. Closing his eyes against the memory, he once again considered that if he'd only done what he had wanted to, to begin with, run away with her before she could marry Bowers, then none of this would have happened. He had always tried to do the right thing. It seemed like they were both doomed to suffer for it. This was his fault just as her brother's death was, just as sending her away to be raised by her family was, family she didn't even know. He reached for the jug of whiskey and downed a good size swallow. It burned all the way down, causing Travers to grit his teeth. It was ironic. For years, he had thought of taking Maggie and just disappearing with her and now he actually had. Not for the reason he originally intended, however, but he had her all to himself now, at least for a considerable amount of time as it would take her a while to heal. He frowned, knowing that he would have to examine her. The man Bailey had raped her. Of that, he had no doubt. He had seen the evidence with his own eyes. The point to ponder was whether or not he should examine her while she was unconscious or while she was conscious. He knew it had to be soon. He moved to sit next to her and ran his hand through her tangled hair, smoothing it back. His hand brushed against the slicker, and he realized she would be more comfortable with it off. He managed to slide it up and over her, though it took a bit of work to keep from disturbing her too much, but once he finally had it free, he covered her with the blanket he had brought along from the house. The softness of the blanket against her skin caused Maggie to smile in her sleep. Travers saw it and wondered how she could smile at anything given her current condition. She seemed deeply asleep now. He weighed the idea of the examination again and decided to go ahead and do it. It would be easier on both of them, he figured. Thirty minutes later, he had assessed that she had four broken ribs, a wrenched arm, badly bruised torso and she was covered in bruises. He also found traces of old bruises giving credence to Slim's statement to the effect that she had been beaten before. Travers had not known. It made sense now, the laudanum she always needed for headaches. Perhaps she had suffered from headaches, but Travers was sure the laudanum had been serving a dual purpose. Escape from the pain of the beatings and escape from her own painful reality. She had been too proud to ask for help. Or too afraid.

And now, she had been raped as well. The body would heal. The mind and spirit was another matter. Maggie was a strong woman. Her strength of will was part of what had gotten her into this mess. She would survive. And she would eventually forget the pain if not the actual attack. Travers studied her face in the flickering firelight, wondering if he ever would.

✦

Slim made it to the shack just before daybreak. He was soaked to the bone, and the clothes plastered to his skin made him appear more skeletal than he had before. Travers poured him a cup of coffee that he had just made. Unable to stomach the heavy stuff this early in the morning, Travers had scrounged in his saddlebags, remembering that he usually kept some coffee for just such emergencies stowed there. He had felt like a kid at Christmas upon finding he still had some. Slim took the coffee and poured a sizable amount of the liquor from his flask into it, swirling it in the cup and blowing on the hot brew. "Where'd you find this?"

"Had a bit in my saddlebags. You sure drinking that sour mash this early is wise?"

"Man, that's what keeps the worms out. You ought to try it." He tried to hand the flask to Travers, but he put up his hands.

"I have tried it. That stuff is a bit more than I'm used to. I'll pass, thanks."

Slim grunted. "City boy," he said under his breath. He eased to a low bench beside the fire that was now mere embers. With a nod to Maggie, he asked, "How is she?"

Travers sighed. "She slept most of the night. She's got some broken ribs. Lots of bruising. She's going to be laid up for a while." He didn't tell the man she'd been raped. He didn't have to.

Slim nodded. 'Ms. Bowers is a strong woman. She'll pull through this. May take some time, but she will. And when she does, you best watch her. She just may go gunnin' for Bowers herself."

Travers hadn't thought of that. All he could see was Bowers dead from a bullet he'd put in him. Maggie wasn't the vengeful sort. But after what she'd been put through, Travers wasn't so sure. The man's suggestion had merit. He wanted to question Slim about the beatings Maggie had taken from Bowers but held off. He didn't know if he was prepared to hear about that right now. The night had been mind-warping enough as it was. But he would ask later, while Maggie slept.

By mutual understanding, neither mentioned Sam Bailey again. Slim never told Travers what had transpired at the ranch after they had left him there with the foreman and Travers never asked. It protected them both. Travers didn't want to know. He could guess, and that was good enough for him. Whatever the man got, he deserved. He hoped he rotted in hell.

Jim Bowers came home to a grizzly sight two days later. Expecting a contrite wife who showed a little bit more respect for her husband, he was greeted by buzzards and the smell of death. They were everywhere. The smell was nauseating as he rode into the front yard. He fought the urge to retch and withdrew his scented handkerchief to cover his nose and mouth. It did little to camouflage the stench. A vulture dove at his head and he panicked, pulling his gun and fired it into the air, hoping to scatter the huge winged creatures. Several of them flew a short distance away. Four or five of them remained, plucking away at the feast they were consuming. He fired again, this time aiming at the largest bird on the object on the ground. The creature dropped instantly and the rest scattered to light in the branches of the tree nearby. Moving closer, he caught his first glimpse of the package left for him.

Sam Bailey sat tied to the hitching post, spread eagle. His eyes had been effectively removed from their sockets by the vultures that still hovered hungrily nearby. He appeared to have been beaten severely before his death, and long furrows ran the length of his face, long washed clean by the rain last night. He was already bloated and stinking beyond imaginable, but something about him looked odd. Jim Bowers sidled closer, knowing that there was a message here somewhere for him. On closer examination, the man's throat had been slit and gaped open to reveal his neck bone. And there was something in his mouth. Curiosity got the better of him, and he reached to pull it out. It was wrapped in a bit of oilcloth, and as he unrolled it, the shock made him drop it. Shuddering, he wiped his hand vigorously on his pants leg over and over, before finally giving in to the need to retch. Lying on the ground before him was the man's male member, nicely severed from his body. On the oilcloth, a note written in the man's blood, dry now, having been protected from the rain.

One by one, Bowers. Death finds us all.

FIFTY-FOUR

Bailey's death had rattled Bowers, but he attempted to shake it off. He had business to attend to today. He and Ates had spent the night before holed up, literally in a dark closet with a knothole punched out of the door for spying on their little mouse. He had arrived in town the night before and visited Celia as he so often did before and after his trips to Dodge. Then he had pretended to leave town, backtracking and hiding with Ates in the closet. The darkness and closeness of the place had almost done him in when they were finally rewarded with a visit from their prowler. Ever so cautiously, ever so stealthily, the figure had moved about the office with an ease of familiarity. Moving to the window, moonlight caught the culprit in full form, and Jim had almost crowed aloud with satisfaction as he had watched the slight figure copy feverishly from a ledger drawn from a file that was always locked safely away from prying eyes. There was the sound of a muffled sneeze, and the figure went still, straining, listening, eyes darting to the dark recesses of the place. Bowers could have burned Ates alive, his glare was so intense that even in the dark it could be felt. When Bowers turned back to the knothole, the intruder was gone, having taken the ledger along in their haste to quit the office.

* * *

Flora was uneasy, though she tried to appear her usual charming self. That was difficult, given the fact that the man before her was a ruthless, cold-blooded murderer. She had been about to dress to go next door to the saloon when she turned and found him in her sitting room. She was certain the door had been closed, and she had not heard it open. She felt a sliver of fear run her backbone. What was he doing in her quarters? His eyes said he was up to no good. Nothing this man done was ever good. Thank God Maggie had seen fit to hatch such an elaborate plan to expose him. When Bowers was brought down, he wouldn't know what hit him or what direction it had come from. He was smiling at her, and a chill inched its way along her backbone before ending at the tips of her toes. He was up to something. Surely he didn't suspect . . . wracking her brain, she frantically tried to recall any mistake, any misstep on her part, all the while returning his smile with a forced one of her own.

"I don't recall inviting you here, Mr. Bowers. These are my

private quarters. I do not entertain men here. You'll have to leave. Now."

He just smiled benignly at her. Bowers was a man who got down to business quickly, and he would do so presently. First, he had plans for this little tart. He knew about the records that she had filched from the land office. He and Ates had watched her through a secret knothole they had craftily removed from the seemingly boarded up closet. He raised his hand to run his forefinger and thumb almost caressingly along his goateed chin, looking her up and down as if he were purchasing a piece of merchandise. The smile widened as he moved to the small bar where he took the liberty of pouring himself a drink. Swirling the whiskey in the glass, he told her, "You know, Celia is a lively bit of fluff, but I've always preferred redheads myself. They always have such fiery dispositions. Don't you agree?" he asked, raising a brow at her.

Flora's brow rose as well. "And you like that in a woman? Fire over fluff? I'd have thought just the opposite. You married Margaret after all. She's anything but fiery from what I've seen."

Jim's brows snapped together as he contemplated the amber liquid in the heavy, ornately cut piece of crystal. "Yes, well, Margaret, I have come to realize was a dreadful mistake. And unfortunately, has," "he paused for effect, sighing dramatically, "disappeared."

Bowers knew that last would really hit the redhead between the eyes. Maggie *had* disappeared. He could care less about her actual wellbeing. But he knew that Gage was involved. His need to know her whereabouts was simply for self-preservation. He needed to know what she had said about him. What she really did know about him. Who she had said it to. Then he could cheerfully let her—disappear. It would be so simple. It would not be the first time he had eliminated—opposition was as good a term as any. And tonight was no exception. He smiled to himself at the look of growing terror on the madam's face.

The chill Flora had felt earlier was replaced now with a full-fledged chunk of ice. The look on his face let her know that he was not lying. Dear God, no. Not Maggie.

"Disappeared?" Her voice was barely a whisper.

"Yes. And slit the throat of my foreman, no less." The smile he gave her was humorless. "I'm afraid the poor chit has lost her mind. Why she even left me a note written in the poor man's blood."

"Oh?" Flora was feeling sick.

Bowers downed the fiery liquid and gritted his teeth against the burn. "Ummm. 'You're next,' it said. I tell you, gave me the shivers, it did. Can you imagine, a woman looking to do in her own husband?"

Flora held her breath, not believing a word she was hearing. Maggie, she was certain, had disappeared. Bowers had most likely seen to that himself. Before she knew it, he was standing close, too close. His finger traced the line of her face, pausing to rub across her bottom lip, his eyes locked with hers.

"You are one beautiful woman." He said it so sincerely that she believed him. "Such a shame, really."

"Shame?" She backed a step away from him.

"Yes. Unfortunately, you and I have some unpleasant business to attend to." His hand had now entangled itself in her hair, loosely of course, for the moment.

"I don't think I understand. What business could you possibly have with me?"

"Oh, come now. I know you have the records from the land office. I'll take them now." His hand began to tighten in her hair even as she tried to deny his accusation.

"There's really no use in trying to deny it. I saw you with my own eyes. Mr. Ates did as well." He jerked her closer, his sickly voice sweet near her ear. "The records, love."

Flora was paralyzed with fear, the pain in her scalp threatening to send scalding tears down her cheeks. She wouldn't give the bastard the satisfaction of showing weakness. She fought the pain and forced her anger to the surface, careful to let it simmer beneath the surface. Above all, she must keep her wits about her. Her life depended on it.

"They're upstairs—in my bedroom," she managed to gasp through the pain. He smiled warmly into her eyes then, and as if speaking to a child, said, "Good girl." Without releasing his hold on her hair, he shoved her towards the stairs. He took his time mounting them, finding Flora's state of undress too much temptation to pass up. He jerked the sash of her robe off and exposed her to his hungry eyes. She could feel his scalding gaze with such force it had the same effect as if he had touched her. She raised a hand with the intent to claw his face, only to have him twist it behind her back. He bit her then, deeply on the shoulder, making her cry out in pain. She began to fight back in earnest now, kicking and lashing out, trying to butt him with her head. It only seemed to excite him. She remembered then, what Celia had told her. Fear aroused him. He had found that that was the only thing that did. Flora drew on every ounce of reserve she had in her body and forced herself to endure the pain he was inflicting. She became pliant in his arms, and he noticed the change instantly.

Raising his head, he said mockingly, "My dear, let's not spoil the fun before it's truly begun." He jerked her up the stairs and down the hall, straight to her bedroom door, much to her amazement. Apparently, the man had been doing some snooping of his own on his visits to Celia, for she never made a point of entertaining in her quarters when the girls were present with paying customers. Unfortunately for her, they were all at the saloon at this precise moment. There was a cattle drive in town, and the Cowboys were getting their drunk on before carousing with the women. They wouldn't be back for some time. Flora allowed herself to be led into the room, her resolve to remain calm no matter what strained to the limit. He tightened his hold on her, his arms cutting her air off, crushing her ribs.

"Now. Let's have those papers, love. The papers *and* the ledger. I know you took them both. I have to admit, you truly amazed me with how diligently you copied everything so meticulously by hand. But the ledger was just too much temptation wasn't it? I told Ates you wouldn't be able to resist. Just like a mouse to catch herself in our little trap. The question is, how did you know about the records? What gave me away? Or rather *who* gave me away?"

Flora struggled to breathe against the hold he had on her. She knew what he was after. He hoped she'd point the finger at Margaret. If he hadn't already killed her, he would certainly do so now. Flora was no fool. She wouldn't give him the satisfaction. She wouldn't rat out her friend. Maggie had lost so much already because of this man, her future, her love for Travers. Travers had no idea what the two women had cooked up to pin Bowers' hide to the wall. If he did, he would have hogtied them both and locked them away somewhere. She would not betray Maggie to this man, husband or not.

"You gave yourself away, Bowers. You got careless. I watched you. You and Ates weren't very good at hiding your association from knowing eyes. I know a con when I see one. You thought you were going to get away with it all, didn't you? You may think so, but I know what you did. I have copies of everything you forged."

"Where are they?"

"There, in my mattress." She prayed he'd let her go so she could go and get them herself. She was beginning to feel light-headed like her corset had suddenly shrunk. She needed to be able to breathe to think. He eased the pressure on her ribs, but he didn't let her go. He pinned her arms behind her back and shoved her along before him until they were before her bed. Instead of allowing her to get them, he shoved her face first into the covers and taking his knife, slashed the mattress wildly, ripping at the material, removing its innards until there was nothing left of it but shreds. He sheathed his knife and ran his hands inside the ruined lump of straw and cloth. He finally found the tightly bound sheaf of papers and book. He stuffed them into his vest and eased away from her, releasing her arm. She struggled up for air, her arm held in front of her, rubbing at the painful needles coursing through it. "You've got what you came after. Now go. I want you out of my sight."

Bowers just smiled at her. The poor little woman had no idea. But she would. There was no way in hell that he was going to leave her alive after knowing what she knew. She'd never let him rest. She could make his life a living hell. No, it was better just to take care of the matter now. Unfortunately, Bailey had gotten himself killed. He missed the man. He had been so good at doing the dirty work for him. But this time the blood would be on his hands. It couldn't be helped.

"Oh, I'm going, love. I understand that you are having company tonight for dinner. Your friend, the schoolteacher? I think we should cook a little something special for him tonight. An evening he won't soon forget, don't you agree? You do so deserve each other." Bowers was rambling it seemed, totally off the subject of why he was here. Flora didn't quite know what to make of it. Why was he bringing Daniel into this?

"My social life is none of your concern. I'll thank you to leave Daniel out of this. He has no beef with you. He knows nothing about what I did."

"Well, then, he'll be doubly surprised when he discovers what a horrid little snoop you've been and devastated when he finds that you are the type who's here today and gone tomorrow. I think a barbecue is the ticket." Jim Bowers had made his way to the door of her bedroom. He made a ridiculous show of tipping his hat to her before adding, "You have a lovely evening."

He was out the door and gone, closing it behind him. Flora sat there for a moment, a frown furrowing her brow. He was acting so strange. She had figured that he would kill her in some way. She was still alive. She breathed a sigh of relief. She rose and went to the door, hoping to go find Travers. The door refused to open. She frowned, jiggling the handle. It wouldn't open. What on earth?

It was stuck tight. Bowers must have jammed it shut in some way, but why? She went to the window and looked out, finding him on the street below, mounting his horse. He looked up at her window, grinned evilly, touched his finger to his hat and rode away. He never looked back.

Flora inhaled sharply, glad to see the last of him. The scent of smoke froze on her lungs. She knew the scent of burning pine. She ran to the door again, frantically pulling on the knob, twisting it, turning it, praying for it to open. It would not budge.

The window. She ran to it, clawing at the wood, only to find that it had been nailed shut from the outside. The bastard. He had set the place afire with her in it. He meant to kill her after all. The smell of smoke grew stronger, and she could see the flames beginning to lick at the door. She banged on the window, screaming for someone, anyone to hear her. The small, thin panes of glass broke with the pounding of her fists, but she didn't seem to notice. Her hands were cut all the way up past her wrists, blood running like crimson colored ribbons down her arms. Terror seized her, and her screams rose above the now roaring flames that were quickly eating up the wooden house that she had built years before with her own hard earned money. Praying with all her might, she continued to bang on the now paneless window, that someone would smell the smoke and come before it was too late.

The fire was noticed almost immediately by Deke, who was crossing the street from the hotel to the schoolhouse for his lesson with Daniel. He limped inside and told Daniel,

"Appears you might have to eat out tonight. Looks like Miss Flora's burning your supper. Better come take a look." Daniel stepped to the door, grinning, and looked in the direction of Flora's and froze. Smoke was indeed coming out of the place but not the kitchen. That was when he saw her at the window, screaming, heard her screams of terror and barreled past Deke, his heart in his throat as he raced towards the now flaming inferno. Deke jogged along behind, unable to keep pace with him, yelling "Fire!" even as he did so. By the time Daniel got to the house, the fire had spread to the point where there was no possibility of entrance. Travers appeared with a growing crowd and swore when he saw the flames licking up the sides of the house and the sight of Flora at the window. Men ran to help, and the women watched in horror as they tried to get near the house. The heat was so intense that Travers ran to the boarding house and got quilts that he and Daniel doused in the troughs outside of the saloon and put over themselves to climb a ladder that someone had produced in order to try to reach Flora. Her screams had stopped, and Daniel's heart dropped to his feet as they climbed, the heat of the fire blistering them even under the heavy wetness of the quilts. They somehow knocked through the wooden frame of the window and Daniel grabbed at the now limp figure of Flora just below him, somehow managing to get her outside. Between the two of them, he and Travers got her safely to the ground and away from the house. Moments later the whole place collapsed. They had moved a safe distance away from the fire and placed Flora on one of the quilts, which was now dry. One look at her told Travers it was hopeless. Her hair was burned off in places, her skin charred black and red, her arms burned down to the meat. Fortunately, most of her nerve endings had been destroyed, causing her pain to be less severe. Shock would set in soon, and even though she was unconscious, the rasp in her throat signaled that she had inhaled a mountain of smoke. Travers did not like what he saw at all. He knew Daniel was waiting for him to tell him that she was going to be all right, but he couldn't. He had seen cases like this before. It was rare for someone to survive such burns and inhaling so much smoke. She was gray, a sure sign that she had been deprived of oxygen for too long and her burns were too severe.

"Trav?" Daniel's eyes implored him. Travers just shook his head, unable to look at his friend.

"Let's get her to the clinic." Travers hoped to afford them some privacy for their goodbyes, for he knew it would be soon in coming. Daniel gathered her in his arms and bore her down the street and inside the privacy of the clinic with Laura, Sheriff Tate and Louella close on their heels. Travers made Flora as comfortable as possible, administrating a dose of morphine for the pain, as she had begun to stir and cry out. Tears streamed down the schoolteacher's face as he locked eyes on the woman's face, the woman he had come to love more than life itself.

He had realized it too late.

Flora's eyes opened briefly, and she tried to speak. Daniel shushed her and gathered her in his arms. She struggled, trying to say what must be said. She had to tell them. Tell them about Bowers. "I have to—have to tell—" A spell of coughing seized her and she tensed against the rain of fire that ran through her lungs. She had to tell them.

"Bowers. He has the land deeds . . . he did it." Her voice was a mere whisper.

Travers stopped Daniel when he would have gathered her to him once again.

"What are you saying, Flora?"

"Bow—Bowers set the fire," she rasped. "Took the proof. I had it. He set it up—caught me." She collapsed in a fit of coughing, blood appearing on her lips. Daniel tenderly wiped them clean with a handkerchief he pulled from his pocket.

"What are you talking about? What proof? Why would Bowers want you dead?" Travers had to know.

Travers felt a coldness settling over him. If what she was saying was true. . .

"Flora, I need you to relax and concentrate, this is important. What did you have on Bowers?

She grabbed his arm and pulled him closer. "He doctored the land deeds. Ates helped. He didn't buy half of that land he claimed he did. Ates forged papers that he was an authorized bank officer handling those transactions. The only money that ever exchanged hands was between Bowers and Ates. Somehow Ates got the debts wiped off the bank records. I got the proof. He knew and cornered me. I was too smart for my own good." She gave a harsh, wispy laugh. "He doesn't even realize his own wife set him up." The coughing came again, and this time the blood flowed more freely.

Daniel pulled back from Travers' restraining hand, his face set. "No more. Let her be, Travers. She's suffering so. Just let her be."

Travers knew he was right. And they should have the chance to say goodbye. He leaned in himself and kissed her tenderly on the forehead. "Sweet, sweet Flora. You rest now. I'll be nearby if you need me."

Flora could feel the strength leaving her. She knew she had little time and looked at the three of them. They were all so precious to her. Travers was a breath away from knowing what Bowers was truly capable of and having proof that could put him away for life. Laura. . . her dear sweet, strong friend who'd seen her through some very dark times. Daniel. Dear God, she didn't know how she was going to say goodbye. But she had to. Things needed to be said. She made her choice. She was a fighter, and she struggled not to fight what she knew was upon her.

She struggled to be brave. "Sweet, Daniel. I love you so. It's too soon. I thought we had so much time." She smiled weakly up at him. Daniel took her hand in his and kissed the back of it where it was not so damaged, and she palmed his cheek. "If only we'd met a lifetime ago." She couldn't help the tear that rolled down her cheek.

"Hush, sweet. No point in what ifs. I love you, Red. You rest now, don't try to talk."

She just shook her head. "It's no use. I'm dying. We both know it. I have some things to say to you. Like how you took my breath away that first day I saw you when you arrived in town. I knew you were for me even then. You were a stubborn fool. I wish things had turned out better for us. You deserve better—deserve to be happy."

Daniel shushed her again, trying to get her to save her breath, her strength. It did no good. She was beginning to lose her grip on him, and he felt her leaving.

"Flora! Don't go! I love you, sweetheart. Oh God!"

She smiled faintly at him before her eyes closed, her body relaxing fully into his arms, her breath easing out in a final exhalation. Daniel held her, weeping openly, uncaring of those who saw him. Laura stood there beside Travers, her eyes on the body of her friend, her hand covering her mouth in horror and grief. Travers gathered her into his arms, and she sagged into him, her body shaking with silent sobs. Sheriff Tate stepped outside to indicate her passing and the men shuffled on their feet, their hat in their hands and the women wept unabashedly for the woman who had helped the town survive through so many crises. She would be sorely missed. A madam that even the women of the town admired. Such an oddity. She had given the town its flair. A ray of sunshine forever dimmed.

Travers stood looking at the woman he had learned to call a friend. God, he would miss her. She had done so much for him. She had given her life to see a killer brought to justice. He felt a chill as he recalled her words. Bowers had killed her to silence her. She had gotten the proof and Maggie had made it happen. Dear God, Maggie. He had to make certain that he kept her safe. He could not lose her, too. He clasped Laura tightly, seeking comfort as well as giving it.

FIFTY-FIVE

They buried Flora on a Wednesday. After the fire, the weather had turned severe with torrential rains and lightning forcing everyone to remain indoors for days. When the sun came out, they had had to let the ground dry out enough to dig her grave. The following Wednesday after her death had dawned bright and sunny, blindingly so, the sun bouncing off the windows of the church in arcs of brilliant color. Daniel had decided on a simple graveside service, knowing it was what she would have wanted. Flora was no hypocrite, and although she and her tenants all attended church on Sundays, a church funeral would have been out of line with her character.

Reverend Joice seemed humbled to be given the task of committing her body to the ground and her soul to the Lord. For several long minutes there, Travers wondered if he was even going to speak, the silence stretched so. When he did speak, his voice trembled slightly, as he began to speak of Flora and her life before her journey to Gold City. She had led a hard one; Travers had known some of it, but the reverend expounded on how, through unfortunate circumstances, she had been led to the life of prostitution. He never condemned her, but instead made her life an object lesson of how one must never judge a book by its cover. For Flora had turned her life around, making a difference in the lives of the people of Gold City, the lives of children, whom she loved so very much, and the men and women she had helped to nurse during the epidemics that had swept through their town. Her giving came from her heart, never expecting anything in return. Her heart was as big as the plains, and for her, no sacrifice was too great. Flora was a remarkable woman, and she would be missed and irreplaceable as a citizen of their community. Reverend Joice finished his intonation by saying that he believed God would judge her fairly, no matter her previous sins against the flesh, for she had proven that people could change. He then asked the congregation to join him in singing *Amazing Grace*. It had been Flora's favorite hymn.

Travers glanced around at the crowd, thinking the whole town had to be here as their voices rose to a swell of song. One by the one, the children from the school brought forth flowers to lay on her casket, as Daniel looked on, tears glistening in his eyes. The little Mason girl, Hannah, of whom Flora had been so fond, stopped before Daniel, and through her own tears, presented him with a single daisy. Her simple act of kindness sent him to his knees, and he gathered her close, touched by the child's thoughtfulness. Somewhere, he knew that Flora was smiling at the scene.

She would have been surprised at the turnout. From what he had seen, most of the town was here to pay their respects, including many folks from neighboring ranches nearby. That pleased Daniel, for he had come to understand why so many people respected her. It was amazing. A madam leaving such a mark on a community the way she had. He rose then, and Hannah ran to join her parents once more. Daniel was greeted by the mourners as they began to leave the graveside. It took a while. Finally, Travers, Laura, Sheriff and Louella Tate were left, along with the men who eased Flora back into the earth from which she came. Daniel strode forward and took a handful of earth and sprinkled it on her casket as he watched it sink lower into the ground. In his mind's eye, he saw her smiling face turned up to his, her eyes dancing with some devilish delight only to be replaced by Jim Bowers. He closed his eyes against the man and vowed that he would kill him for what he had done to Flora.

Travers came to stand beside his friend, seeing his dark thoughts. He clamped his jaw against the pain he was feeling as well. Daniel sensed him draw near and opened his eyes.

"We'll get him, Daniel. He got careless this time. Careless enough for Flora to catch on. He may have taken and hidden the evidence but I have a hunch there's more. But we'll find it. And then pay, he will."

Travers' frustration was mounting concerning Bowers. Erasmus had arrested him after Flora had died, with Travers and Clayton there in case he gave them any trouble. He had come along obligingly enough, professing his innocence to one and all. It had been Clayton who had cocked his shotgun, pointed it at him, and said, "Not one more word." Bowers had shut up at that and had muttered under his breath when Ras locked him up. His only request was for a wire to some lawyer up north.

Daniel didn't turn to look at Travers. He couldn't take his eyes away from the gaping hole that Flora now lay in. "You told me I was being a fool where she was concerned. You were right, Travers. I should have listened to you. Then maybe none of this would have happened. She would still be with us."

"Now, see here. There was no way you could have predicted this. And don't you go blaming yourself for something you couldn't have prevented. She may be gone in body, but she's with us still. She's free, Daniel, free of this mortal flesh that binds us so often. I figure she's flitting around up there somewhere, wondering what's taking us so long to get the ball rolling and nailing this guy. And giving God a hard time, to boot!"

There was a smile in Travers' voice as he told the last to Daniel and the schoolteacher burst out laughing, unable to help himself. "You probably just hit that one square on the head, Trav. I can just hear her now." Travers clamped him on the shoulder, and they turned away to see the others watching them uncertainly. When they joined them, Laura said, "I thought it was a lovely service. The reverend was so earnest in his sermon. And, why, I don't think I've ever seen such a crowd at a funeral before."

Ras and the others agreed. "Well, the hearing is in the morning. Bowers lawyered up with some feller from Chicago. Unless we find proof that ties Bowers to this crime, the charges will be dropped according to the judge." Tate looked from Daniel to Travers, shaking his head at the idea.

"Well, according to Flora, Bowers took whatever proof she had against him the day he set the fire. If we go snooping around his house, he's likely to shoot us all. Then we'd be back to square one. And I think Flora would want us to get it right when we do bring him down."

Travers knew that Bowers was going to walk on this one. A judge wasn't going to allow charges to stand merely on hearsay even if the person doing the saying was now dead. Besides, he had an ace up his sleeve he wasn't ready to reveal just yet. He hoped to turn their thoughts towards finding evidence applicable to the case at hand, not just to the big picture.

"I say we do this nice and quiet like. No use in barging in over there. Bowers knows the noose is tightening around his neck. He's not crazy enough to run just yet. He's going to linger and make it look like he's the one getting the short end of justice and milk it for all he's worth. When the grease in the frying pan gets too hot, that's when he'll bail. I don't recall seeing Loyd Ates at the funeral. Anybody else see him?"

No one had seen the land officer that day or for the last several days, now that they thought about it. On a hunch, Travers suggested that the men go in search of him. Laura invited Louella back to the boarding house for tea, and the men headed to the land office. It was situated two doors down from the hotel, on Flora's end of town, near the saloon and the Velvet Rose. No wonder she had gotten suspicious. She could see everything on the street from her window upstairs. She had had a bird's eye view of the town, the comings, and goings of the place. When they reached the office, the place was locked up. Travers shielded his eyes against the sun, peering into the window. There was no sign of Ates, the place dark. Sheriff Tate stepped next door to the saddle shop and greeted the leather smith, Norris Hogan. In a few minutes, he was back, a concerned look on his face.

"According to Norris, he ain't seen Ates in three, maybe four days. I think our man's skipped town, gents." They went back down the street to the hotel where Ates stayed and confirmed their suspicions. Three days before, the maid reported that Ates had apparently left during the night.

His room key had been left on the nightstand. The room had appeared tossed, but nothing was broken nor seemed suspicious. Travers asked if they could see the room. "Sure," said the clerk, before turning and locating the key. Leading them up the stairs, he paused in front of a room at the end of the hall. Opening the door, he told them he would be downstairs if they needed him and to be sure to lock it back when they finished.

Daniel thanked the man as he left, Travers already looking through drawers on the chest. The place was clean. They looked over every square inch until they assured themselves that there was nothing to find. Ates had left nothing behind. The place had been cleaned thoroughly by the maid. If he had left anything, any clue, it was long gone. They headed back to the boarding house.

On the street, just outside the hotel, they ran into the lawyer that Bowers had hired. Sheriff Tate introduced him as Mr. Hanchette. He tipped his hat to them.

"A pleasure, I'm sure. I was just coming in search of you, Sheriff. I would like a word with you about my client. It seems he has yet to be released from jail."

"That's right, sir. He will remain in jail until the judge orders him released."

"Are you saying he was denied bond?"

"That's exactly what I'm saying. Your client is suspected in more murders than the one of Flora McDonough. Murder suspects don't get bail in these parts. It's safer that way."

The little man narrowed his eyes. "Safer?"

"Yes, sir. His kind tend to get strung up purty fast if the townsfolk get wind they's a walkin' free and clear. This here ain't Chicago. We got frontier justice out here. And yore slick talkin' ways won't hold a lot of water with these folks. Bowers is guiltier than a fox caught in a hen house. We'll see what the judge has to say in the mornin'."

Travers had watched the little peacock as Tate had given him the one-two on Bowers' situation. The baleful eyes let him know that this was a man used to winning at all costs. In true Bowers style. He eased between the sheriff and Hanchette, his eyes cold as steel and let him know immediately that they meant business.

"Let me clarify something for you right now, Mr. Hanchette. If your client walks and the proof surfaces that he was indeed responsible for the fire that killed Miss McDonough, you will be charged as well as your client, as an accessory after the fact. Aiding and abetting will be the charges against you, and you will hang right along with your client. You better make sure that your client is squeaky clean before you go in there defending him tomorrow. Else, you may find yourself neck deep in a noose."

The lawyer stood there staring at Travers as if he had suddenly grown two heads. They were practically nose to nose, and the clarity of the man's words pounded him between the eyes. Hanchette knew in a moment that he was a dead man. He had hesitated when Bowers had wired him in Chicago. Briefly. The sum of money mentioned at the end of the wire had sent him packing immediately. He was already making plans to retire from his practice, and this would be a nice little nest egg to retire on. He knew his client was guilty the moment he met him. He was too smug, too arrogant, and had an evil gleam in his eye. Hanchette had represented many criminals before, but none of Bowers' caliber or wealth. His time in this town would be short. Bowers would walk because he was a man who left no evidence. There was no proof that there had been a crime committed. Except for a woman's word. A woman who was now dead. Tipping his hat to the men, he excused himself and headed straight to his hotel room where he packed his bags. He intended to be on the first stage out of town after the trial. And he would leave no forwarding address in case Bowers got a hankering to search him out. Bowers would have to fend for himself when the time came for him to face the music.

Daniel, Travers, and Tate watched the little man hurry away. Daniel shook his head. "There goes a crook if I ever seen one. He didn't like that little speech you gave him, Travers. If the proof is found, can we really try him alongside of Bowers?"

Travers sighed. "I don't know. But it put the fear of God in him, didn't it? Five dollars says he went straight to his room and packed his bags. Bowers may walk tomorrow, but he won't go far. He has too much invested in that ranch of his. And he hasn't found Maggie yet. That must be rusting his nail, the not knowing. If what Flora said was true, that she set it up, the scheme to frame Jim, then her life is in danger as well. We'll have to watch his movements, hope he doesn't find her."

Daniel grunted. "Maggie's smart. She'll stay hidden until she feels it's safe to come out of hiding."

Travers shook his head. "I don't know. I think she'll try something rash when she finds out about Flora. I just pray that we nail the bastard. Soon."

FIFTY-SIX

He dreaded telling her. It hurt bad enough just thinking about it. Their good friend was gone, buried already. He had waited to tell Maggie until she was strong enough to handle it. She was still so weak, but he dared not wait longer, or she would never forgive him. After supper that evening, Slim made himself scarce, Travers already having told him what had happened and what he had to do tonight. Slim had just hung his head in dismay, thinking he'd been a damn fool for working for that butcher Bowers. He gave Maggie and Travers their privacy and finding shelter in the branches of a nearby tree as a lookout, he began to make some plans. He had an idea. He planned to bring that sum' bitch to his knees.

———◆———

Travers had cleared away the remains of the meal and had settled in on the bed behind Maggie, his back against the rough wood of the shack. She lay in the cradle of his arms and legs, a contented smile on her pale face. It would not last long.

"Maggie?"

"Um?" She shifted slightly in his embrace, her eyes gazing into the fire. His hand absently stroked her bare arm.

"I have some bad news. Real bad." His voice was thick with the pain he tried to fight, knowing this was not going to be easy. Maggie sensed that he was hurting and turned to get a better look at him. She paled when she saw his face.

"Tell me," she said, her hand clutching his.

A shudder passed through him, and he forced himself to look her in the eye.

"There was a fire in town several nights ago. At Flora's place."

"A fire! Was anyone hurt?"

"There was no one there—except—" His throat closed on him, unable to say her name when the time had come. Maggie squeezed the hand she already held so tightly.

"Except—who, Travers?"

"The bastard locked her in her room. It burned so fast. By the time we got to her—Daniel and I had to bust through her window. It had been nailed shut. She couldn't get out and panicked. She cut herself badly, banging on the window trying to get out. By the time we got her out, she had already suffered from too much smoke inhalation and had been burned severe-ly. There was nothing we could do. She's gone, Maggie. Flora's gone." His voice trailed off into a whisper.

Maggie sat up, her back straight as a board, her horror-stricken eyes seeing the truth in his. Her head began to shake from side to side, slowly at first, then frantically. Travers fought to pull her into the circle of his arms, but she struggled against his grasping hands.

"No! Oh God, no!" She began to wail, and her struggles gradually ceased allowing Travers to pull her tightly to him. He felt the deep shudders of her pain rippling through her and knew the feeling well. Flora had come to mean so much to all of them. She had been such a vivacious creature. It was hard to believe that he would never see her lovely face again. He thought of the pain Daniel had been enduring and could only imagine the torment he must be feeling. He couldn't imagine a life without Maggie. Even as Bowers' wife she had still been a part of his life. Now that she had severed all ties to the man, they could be together. The thought of losing her now was soul shattering.

He let her mourn for a while and then told her what had happened.

"We got her out before she was burned alive and she lived for about a half hour. She lived long enough to finger Bowers, Maggie. He set the fire. Flora also said that he took proof she had against him concerning other matters. He was arrested and brought before Judge Lane on the charges of arson and mur-der. Since the only witness was dead, the charges were dropped. There was no proof to convict him. Jim Bowers is a free man. Once again he gets away with murder."

The grim reality was so bitter tasting. He hated to even men-tion the man's name, but Maggie must know about her husband.

When Maggie heard that, she turned to face Travers. "We have to nail his hide, Travers. He can't be allowed to do this any-more. Too many innocent people have suffered because of him. I wish he were dead."

Travers studied the stone like mask that had come over her face.

"Well, Flora said that you set him up. What did she mean by that, Maggie?"

Maggie sighed. "I listened in on a conversation between Loyd Ates and Jim one evening. They were talking about land deeds. I couldn't make out what they were saying, but I knew something sounded fishy. I was quite under the influence of laudanum at the time, but I distinctly heard Jim say that he had to cover his tracks about the last land he supposedly purchased. I figured Flora could get to the truth as inconspicuously as anyone. She had a finesse that I lacked. Besides, Jim would have suspected me immediately. She couldn't believe that I had asked her for help. She was more than willing to do it, to be the one to put the screws to him. And now she's dead, and it's my fault. I never should have dragged her into this mess." The tears came again, silently this time, and she closed her eyes against the image of Flora rising before her. She would never be able to forgive herself for Flora's death.

"I think I need to be alone for a while, Travers, if you don't mind."

He nodded and eased from around her and stretched. "Don't you blame yourself for this, Maggie. Flora chose to go down that path. She could have said no, but she didn't. The only person to blame here is Bowers. And we will get him. We'll find a way."

Maggie waited until he shut the door behind him before turning her face to the wall and giving in to silently weeping once more. Flora was dead. And Daniel, poor Daniel must be suffering so. She didn't know how she would ever face any of them again. It should have been her instead.

———◆———

Outside, the sun had set, and the orange glow on the horizon made it look like the world was on fire. Travers sighed deeply, breathing in the fresh air, grateful to be shed of the task he had so dreaded. It had not been easy, but she had taken it better than he could have hoped. He tried to shake off the gloom that seemed to hover over him and looked around for Slim. He found him parked up a tree nearby, his eyes scanning the countryside like a hawk's. He had a chew of tobacco the size of Texas in his jaw and was quickly recreating the Nueces with a river of spit below him. Travers just shook his head at the scrawny man. His love for whiskey and tobacco was unlike anything he had ever seen. Slim leaned over to spit and almost nailed Travers. When he saw him, he clamored down from his perch.

"She gonna be all right?"

"I think so. It's such a shock to all of us. They had become close this last year."

Slim nodded. "I think it's time we took the man down. I been doing a bit of thinking and I think I've got just the thing."

Travers knew the man before him had a quick mind and education beyond his apparent Southern backwardness. He noted the light in his eye and wondered what the man could have in mind.

"Let's hear it."

"Well," Slim said, giving his scruffy jaw a scratch, "I figure that if Bowers is harassed just enough by the ghosts of his victims, he'll break."

That raised Travers' eyebrows. "Ghosts?"

"Yeah. The man is superstitious as hell. He was always throwing salt over his shoulder and stuff like that. Pretty weird for a man of his caliber to be that way. Usually, a sign that they got something to hide. Maybe we need to remind him that the dead can speak without saying a word."

A smile slowly spread across Travers' face. He liked the idea. "And just how do you plan to accomplish such a feat? Wouldn't it be better to find the actual bodies of the men he killed? We still require proof, and they would be the nail in his coffin, so to speak. Besides, how exactly do you propose to get his attention using ghosts?"

"Well, as far as the bodies go, I've got me an idea where to look for them. Sam Bailey was a creature of habit if nothing else. And he frequented the area where he so unceremoniously dumped me. And as far as getting the man's attention, there's lots o' things I'm capable of, Doc. Lots of things. I know how to break him."

Travers frowned. "And what if he's stronger mentally than we suspect?"

Slim grunted. "Well, then you can always just call the bastard out and have done with it."

FIFTY-SEVEN

Travers smelled him long before he saw him. He had just seen to it that Maggie laid down for a nap when a scent tickled his nostrils. A bad scent. Really bad. Instead of passing, the scent grew stronger, and Travers stepped outside the shanty to get a look around. A half a mile away he could make out a wagon making its way towards him. He felt a shiver run along his backbone. If he weren't expecting Slim, he'd think that death himself had come to call. He raised his hands against the glare of the white-hot orb above him and saw that sure enough, it was Slim. The man pulled the wagon to a stop about a hundred yards away from the shack, and Travers felt his gut wrench. Before he could stop himself, his feet were walking away with him, towards that dreaded stench, his stomach reaching back to grab him by the neck even as he did so.

Slim was waiting for him. He had liberally doused his kerchief with whiskey and was applying it to his lips as Travers walked up. It didn't help the horrid smell one bit, but it kept the man from losing his lunch. He figured putting Jim Bowers in jail was worth a few rotting corpses. He had tried not to dwell on the grisly task he had performed earlier, the chore of unearthing them. His mind had been consumed with righting the wrongs that devil Bowers had committed against the good people of this town.

When Travers reached him, Slim noted the pale skin instantly.

"A'right, Doc. Now ain't the time to go gettin' sickly on me."

Travers swallowed and immediately wished he hadn't, trying to breathe as shallowly as possible this near the scent.

"I can't believe you actually did it, that you found them."

Slim squinted at him, then spat a stream of tobacco juice. "Well, it shore ain't a job to be envied, but it's an end to a means."

"Yeah, well, you've a taste for the macabre, my friend. How on earth did we come up with such an idea?"

Slim, unable to stand it anymore, reached into his pocket and withdrew a flask, turning it up with a hand that shook. After a sizable swallow, he leveled his eyes at Travers.

"You said you needed the bodies as proof. I figure it only fitting that we play a little game of cat and mouse with ol' Bowers before we reel him in, seein' as how he'd had his way around here so long. Time we turned the tables. I wanna see that bastard squirm."

Travers nodded his agreement. Knowing he had a sickening job before him, he said, "Let's get my part done." Slim hopped from the wagon and walked with Travers to the rear. It took him a while, and several sips from Slim's flask as the bodies were in various stages of decomposition, but by the time he was finished, Travers had four of the five missing men from the town accounted for. Their families would now have closure. It had been far too long in coming.

Travers and Slim eased back to the front of the wagon in an attempt to put the sight of the dead men from their thoughts. Neither was successful. Slim eased back onto the wagon seat and sipped from the flask again before stowing it in his pocket.

"You be careful out there. And take it easy on that whiskey. Tends to dull the senses. You're going to need your wits about you."

"Ain't dulled 'em yet," the lanky man muttered under his breath, his eyes now watering profusely from the smell of rotting flesh.

If Travers hadn't been so nauseated himself, he would have laughed. Instead, his stomach just sort of flopped over as the wagon pulled away. Travers watched him go, knowing that if he hadn't stumbled upon Slim the night Maggie was raped, Bowers might never be caught. But the big man was in for a hard, hard fall. He didn't know what Slim had in store for his former boss, and wanted no part of it, but as he had said. It was an end to a means. That was all Travers was worried about. As long as Bowers paid for his crimes, he would let Slim dish out all the terror he wanted on Bowers. If he had the man figured right, Bowers was in for hell.

Back inside the shack, he saw that Maggie still slept, though fitfully, frowning and squirming. Eventually, she eased into a deeper sleep, and Travers knew that she had merely been reacting to the smell of death. It was amazing, he thought, as he sat there watching her sleep, how even the unconscious are disturbed by death.

————◆————

It had been so very easy getting into the house. Slim had sat hidden in the tree all day, watching, listening, learning their routines He needed complete concentration for what he was planning to do. For all of Bowers' paid thugs, none of them seemed to be around much. Four of them rode off to town in search of whores around mid-afternoon. There was no guard posted at the house. Apparently, the man had never replaced him as a cook, and as soon as he was confident enough that the house was empty, he was inside. It took him all of an hour to accomplish what he had set out to do. Jim Bowers would never know what hit him until it was too late.

FIFTY-EIGHT

Jim Bowers had a funny feeling before he ever set foot in his house that evening. Something told him that he would be in for a long night. He had a bad feeling, deep down in his gut that this was going to be a bad night. He headed straight for his bar and poured himself a stiff bracer of whiskey, downing the glass full in one gulp. The burning in his throat only intensified his anger. He savored it, allowing it to burn hotter and heaped insult upon injury.

He had failed to find Margaret.

Damn the woman! She seemed to have fallen off the face of the earth. An impossibility for sure. No one in town or the surrounding areas had seen her, or they had blatantly lied to his face at even the prospect of being paid for the information. He had been generous with his bribes to no avail. She was gone. Wherever she had fled to, she had covered her trail very well. Or someone had. Even Travers Gage seemed to be clueless about where she could be. The doctor had threatened Bowers that if 'Maggie' were hurt in any way, he would kill him. He had been quite convincing that he did not know where the man's wife was. Bowers believed him. He didn't disappear for days at a time, which might imply he had someone hid away somewhere. He made his regular rounds and seemed to forever be in town.

He swallowed another glassful of whiskey and in disgust, threw the crystal snifter against the fireplace in his study. Jim fumed, thinking what a terrible waste of money, for the crystal was quite expensive, but the release of anger made him feel somewhat better. He reached for another glass and noted that there seemed to be an odd odor to the house this evening. He poured himself another glass of the amber liquid and went in search of the source of the lingering smell. He couldn't put his finger on it, but it smelled as if an animal had crawled under the house and died. He went outside and looked under the house, finding nothing that would produce such a smell.

Odd, but the smell seemed to come from inside. A field rat had most likely gotten into the kitchen supplies. He headed there and checked the barrels and bags. Nothing. The scent still lingered. The animal must have gotten into the wall somehow and died. It must have been a big joker, for the stench was nigh unbearable now. He went back to his study and sat at his desk, the bottle of whiskey before him. He contemplated what his next move would be concerning his wife. She had to be found. Bailey couldn't be counted on for this. Poor soul had gone and gotten his throat slit. He found himself wondering if Margaret had done that herself. Was she *capable* of doing that? The very thought sent a shudder down his spine. He didn't think so, but who else could have known about what they had in store for Margaret that night? He felt that Travers was worried all right. Worried because he was just as in the dark concerning Maggie as Bowers was. No, the man knew nothing. Bowers was sure of it. He shifted uneasily in his chair, the smell emanating nearer. What on earth was that smell? He uncapped the bottle and turned it up to his lips, this time not bothering with a glass.

He felt his lids grow heavy and closed his eyes for a few moments. He needed to relax a few minutes before heading out to the range to check on his men. When he opened his eyes again, there was a large dark shape before him. The shadows were deep in the room, and at first, he wasn't quite sure what he was seeing. But there was something there, something extremely disturbing. He closed his eyes and rubbed them. When he opened them again, the figure was gone. He shook his head, trying to clear the cobwebs from his sight. There was nothing there. A figment of his imagination. He was so stressed with all that was going on that now he was apparently hallucinating.

It was no wonder with everything that had been going on. He had managed to escape the noose where Flora McDonough was concerned. There had been no witnesses and no proof that the blaze had been set by him. The folks had fairly run him out of town on a rail when the judge had dismissed the charges. Travers had had to physically hold Daniel McCullough to keep him from attacking the rancher. The lawyer he had hired had scooted quickly out of town, demanding his money the morning before the trial. He had counted his money twice to be sure it was all there. Jim's hackles had risen at that. He might not be a model citizen, but when it came down to defending his life, his money was just as good as that of anybody else's.

Rising, he went outside and mounted his horse, heading to the west pasture. He had not gone very far when he got the idea that he was being followed. He stopped his horse and listened, shifting uneasily in his saddle, looking back over his shoulder, seeing nothing, but sensing something, someone was out there. The darkness swallowed everything up out here. It was a cloudy night, with only a few stars scattered here and there. His horse seemed to be a bit spooked as well. He didn't seem to want to go when Jim spurred him forward. He resisted, and Jim nudged him again, turning him. The horse reared up, his eyes rolling. It was then that Jim smelled it: the scent of death and decay. The smell that had permeated his home could now be smelled out here. He shuddered. Thinking the smell must have gotten into his clothes, he shrugged it off and tried to get the horse moving. The animal sidestepped and shied away from something in the dark. Briefly, the clouds parted to allow a bit of moonlight to shine through. In the same breath that Jim thanked God for small miracles, he cursed. Just ahead, there was a spectral figure, a dark form that Jim had seen before at the house. He jerked the reins and turned the horse, sending him into a full gallop. The horse didn't need much persuading. Jim didn't know what the hell was going on, but he couldn't shake the feeling of dread settling on him. The men would have to do without him tonight. He was headed back home. No matter that the house smelled of death. Right now he needed the comfort and security that those four walls could afford him. Glancing back, he found that the black figure was nowhere in sight. He felt his body relax just the tiniest bit.

He needed another good stiff drink. And sleep. He had not slept in two days. He needed rest because he was sure his mind was playing tricks on him. He was seeing things now that just weren't there. He grabbed the bottle from the desk in his study and watched the flame in the lamp flicker out. He was surrounded by darkness. Funny, no breeze could have blown the lamp out, and there was still plenty of oil in it. He turned to his humidor and opened it, feeling for a match. Finding one, he lit the lamp again. The flame flickered uncertainly but finally held. He concentrated on the flame and reaching into the humidor, pulled a cigar from it, holding it to the lamp's flame to light it. He shrieked in shock, dropping the object that now smoldered. It was a finger. Badly decayed, shriveled, and black, the nail grew long, the bones of the knuckle pronounced against the thin tissue skin that still clung to it. The smell of rot was intense now, and Jim felt his stomach roll at the smell. He reached for the bottle of whiskey and poured it on his hands, hoping to kill the scent, unmindful of the liquid splashing onto the desk and floor. He turned the bottle to his lips again, gulping the fiery liquid. He hoped it would numb his senses enough to let him sleep. The night was getting stranger by the second. He was not staring at a decayed finger on his desk. He wasn't. Was he? He checked his humidor and found that there were no more fingers inside it. He knew that it had to be his mind playing tricks on him. He made his way to his room and lay down on the bed, not bothering to disrobe. He didn't know what the night may hold, and he may have to leave in a hurry. Jim was a careful man. He left nothing to chance. If his imagination *were* working overtime, he would get a good laugh about it in the morning. For now, he desperately needed sleep. He went to sleep with a fresh bottle and a prayer that he was not losing his mind.

The black-robed figure had melded into the shadows, awaiting the opportune time to strike. There was no hurry. Death could wait another day for Jim Bowers.

FIFTY-NINE

Travers got to the shack late that evening and found Maggie literally climbing the walls. She nearly cried with relief when he walked through the dilapidated door.

"Thank God! Finally someone to talk to! I was just about to go mad!"

He offered a smile. "Slim not much for conversation?"

"How would I know? He hasn't been here for three days now. He slips in during the wee hours of the morning, and he's gone before I wake up every day. I know because he's got coffee made for me when I get up. I don't know how he survives on so little sleep, Travers. What is he up to? What are the two of you up to?"

Travers took her hand and pulled her to sit beside him on the cot. She was looking frazzled, concern over the situation leaving dark circles under her eyes.

"Slim is taking care of some unpleasant business. He knows that you're safe out here. Otherwise, he wouldn't leave you alone. Besides, he's trying to tie up some loose ends so that we can get you back to civilization."

She looked at him with eyes that dug, trying to see deeper than his words.

"He's set out to get Jim."

Travers didn't answer. He hedged, thinking maybe he should tell her, then thought better of it. Maggie wanted her husband to pay for his crimes. He just wasn't sure how badly.

"I can't rightly say," he finally admitted. "But whatever he's up to, you can be sure he'll do it right."

Maggie let that settle in her mind. Slim could do lots of things. She had heard him once, singing as he cooked one afternoon. He had a surprising voice as if he were classically trained. She had slipped further to the door so she could hear a little better and recognized it as part of the Verdi opera *Il Trovatore*. How on earth would Slim know such beautiful music? The man she had come to know as Slim was a multifaceted man. His grungy appearance hid much, she had come to realize. Hid. Perhaps he was hiding. From what? From whom? It didn't really matter. He had been kind to her with no question of payment in return. Whatever Slim was doing in this part of the country, she would not attempt to hazard a guess. Everyone had secrets. His would go with her to the grave. She owed him that much.

"I miss having him around. I miss having *you* around. I thought you were coming last night."

"Jim came to town. He's watching, hoping for some indication that I know where you are. I couldn't slip away without him noticing."

"I see. How are Daniel and Laura?" She had to know how her friends were doing. It had been a month since Flora's death, and she had yet to see either of them.

Travers leaned back against the folded blanket Maggie had taken to using as a pillow. "They are—making it. Hanging in there. It gets rough, but we somehow manage."

"Do they know where I am?"

"No. No one knows where you are. Everyone believes that you ran off. I've been pretty convincing that I haven't a clue as to your whereabouts."

"Won't they be angry when they find out you knew all along?"

"That's just a chance we're going to have to take. Right now your safety is the priority, not hurting people's feelings. Bowers has already killed one woman. He won't hesitate to do the same if he finds you. You don't honestly think he's searching for you out of concern for your well-being?"

"No. You're right." Maggie released a sigh of resignation. She would be so glad when all of this was over. She needed privacy, privacy that these four walls couldn't give her. She tried to shake off the worry that niggled at the back of her mind and curled up beside Travers who wrapped his arms around her. She felt so safe there in the circle of his arms. He hadn't attempted to kiss her or touch her intimately since the attack. She longed for him to. Wished he would so it would wipe her memories of that man touching her, hurting her. As the days passed, she decided that he wasn't going to. He was waiting for her to make the first move. And still, she hesitated. She wanted to so desperately, but she held back. Intimacy was the farthest thing from her mind right now. There were issues yet to deal with, and she had to keep a clear head about her. She spent the remainder of the evening listening to Travers talk about what had been happening in town, the wagon train from South Carolina that had the dance troupe headed to San Francisco. She had listened and given obliging nods and answers when expected. All too soon they faded into sleep.

Travers awoke to the sound of a horse outside. He slipped free of Maggie's embrace and eased to the door, his gun already cocked. It was Slim. He slipped inside like a wraith and eased his saddle to the floor by the hearth, careful not to wake Maggie. Travers stepped from behind the door, and the man near jumped out of his skin.

"Dang it all! Don't kill me a'fore I can nail Bowers, man."

Travers gave a low chuckle. "You seem a mite spooked. Just what have you been up to, old man?"

"Well, when you go playin' at bein' a spook, surrounded by death and all that entails, one tends to get a mite jumpy. And our friend Bowers is jumpy. I think we've got him on the run now. He's convinced he's hallucinating." He paused to wipe a handkerchief across his face and motioned to Maggie who still slept peacefully on the cot. "How she makin' it?"

"Well, she's put out with you. Seems she's getting a bit claustrophobic being here alone all the time. What is that on your handkerchief?" Travers couldn't help asking when he saw the black stains that had come off of the man's face and onto the square of cloth.

"That is pure panic with a punch. Been worth its weight in gold these last few nights. Ol' Jim is a squirmin'. He's convinced the devil is after him. And he sure as hell is. He bought his ticket to hell a while ago. I'm just makin' sure he hops the right stage in gettin' there."

"How are you still going, man? Maggie says you come in after she goes to sleep at night and you're gone before she gets up every morning."

"Well, dang it, she sleeps ten hours at a time! I never knew a body could sleep so long without it being ill. But I guess she is still healing. She's a mite better than she was this time weeks ago. That man left bruises that I'm afraid won't ever heal."

Travers knew he was talking about the beatings that Maggie had endured at her husband's hands. He got the courage up to ask him.

"I let it pass before, but I'd like to know what happened in that house, Slim. You said that he had beat her. What happened?"

Slim tossed the square cloth he'd been using to wipe his face clean into the basin to be rinsed later.

"He hit her with his fist, Doc. Caught her smack in the stomach, and backhanded her, splitting her lip. She shut herself up in her room 'til he broke the door again. He used to just go off on her. He couldn't make her submit otherwise. He couldn't stand that he couldn't control her, that he couldn't control himself where she was concerned. You knew he couldn't get it up for her, didn't you? He took his anger out on her. She learned quickly that fear was the key to getting his motor goin'. She wasn't havin' any. She braved it out, actually laughed at him on occasion. Boy, that really fried his fritter. Ms. Maggie is tough as a cob, but he cut her to the core. Broke her heart. I think she really loved him in the beginning and tried to make it work. Whatever she might have felt for him, though, died the minute he took his hand to her."

Travers felt his stomach coil in pain, thinking how Maggie must have suffered at the hands of her husband. Yet she had never come to him. She had approached him about laudanum, complaining of headaches and he had not seen the depths of her pain. He had gotten rid of her as soon as possible, careful not to look her in the eye. Her eyes always could hypnotize him. And they revealed so much of herself. The one time that he should have paid careful attention, he had not, and once again failed her. That brought a frown to his face. He was finished with being a failure where Maggie was concerned. This time Bowers would pay for what he had done to her.

"How much longer you think this is going to take?"

"Oh, I figure another day or so. Bowers ain't goin' nowhere. He's convinced that if he goes outside the devil's a'gonna get him. He's got garlic and salt and all kinds of paraphernalia hanging from around his neck trying to ward off evil spirits."

"You better watch out. He's liable to figure you out and take his gun to you."

"Let him try. I've got that figured out, too."

"So, if I wanted to take Maggie into town in the next day or two, it'd be safe?"

"Give me one more day just to be on the safe side. Then you haul tail."

They continued to speak of things in lowered voices, and the woman on the bed continued to pretend to be asleep. She couldn't hear them as well now, and that irked her. She had known that Slim was after Jim. She had felt Travers slip away from her and had awakened instantly. She had feigned sleep, hoping they wouldn't be able to tell she was awake in the low glow of the firelight. She had cringed when Slim had told Travers of Jim's abusing her, but she couldn't bring herself to stop him. It was something Travers should have heard from her. She just hadn't been able to bear the thought of telling him. Some things were just better left unsaid. Travers didn't need any more reason to want the man dead. He already had plenty. She had known Slim would stand by her. He had apparently stood up to Jim after she left and he had nearly gotten himself killed for it. Slim had a bit of payback he was ready to dish out as well. She would love to know what the old codger had up his sleeve.

SIXTY

That old codger had a lot up his sleeve, and he was putting all his talents and skills so carefully hidden until now to good use. His face was painted black and gray with a few streaks of white, giving him a skeletal effect. His hands had been given the same treatment, and they looked quite convincing in the dimness of the house that Jim had practically barricaded himself in. He wore a long hooded cloak that covered him from head to toe, his face shadowed deeply by the hood. Last night, he had succeeded in getting one of the dead bodies to cooperate. He had hoped to use them throughout the house, making it seem that they were the ghosts of the dead men. The first one he had used had fallen to the floor with a horrific thump, causing Slim to cringe, sure that Jim Bowers would see through his little game. Fortunately, the man had consumed so much of the alcohol laced with peyote that he passed completely out the moment the poor dead soul hit the floor. Unlucky for Slim, for the poor body on the floor took quite a beating when it fell, as decomposed as it was. Slim couldn't be sure exactly which one of the men he was, but he couldn't help but think, that somewhere, the souls of these dead men were getting a kick out of giving it to Bowers. He had considered whether or not this was a sacrilege, using the bodies this way, but living in the house with Bowers had given him a keen insight into the man. He was a superstitious, paranoid man. That was what had given Slim the idea.

Last night things had worked just fine. He had managed to make it appear that the man was walking about of his own strength. He had come better prepared this time, bringing his gloves just in case the same thing happened again. After handling the bodies so much, they now tended to have the consistency of cottage cheese. Slim had a stomach of steel, or so he thought, but he was ready to retch after cleaning up the mess the night before. But the thrill of watching his plan come to fruition definitely had its rewards. Bowers had cowered like a baby against the wall, his seemingly never empty bottle of whiskey clutched tightly to his chest. Slim had managed to switch the bottles when Jim had ventured out earlier in the day. He never stayed gone too long at a time. The landowner was convinced, though, that the ghosts would escape and reveal themselves to others and point out Bowers as their killer. He had become quite delusional, the mixture of peyote and alcohol doing the trick. Slim wanted

Bowers ranting and raving by the time he was ready to take him into town. He wanted the man to admit to anyone and everyone that he was being haunted by the men he had killed.

He was so close.

Jim had stumbled in an hour or so ago, already good and soused. His clothes were rumpled, having not changed in three days now. And Slim could smell him, even above the decay that surrounded them in the house. His hair was lank and grimy, his face unshaved. Bowers had definitely begun to slip. He was whispering to himself as well.

"You're not real. None of you are. You're dead. All of you are dead. Bailey killed you and buried you."

Slim hissed snake like his eyes turning into slits in beneath the hood.

"Oh, they're real. Just like I'm real. And you'll be joining us very soon. They called to me from the grave, unable to rest. They led me to you, demanding your life for theirs. Soon, Bowers. Soon."

Bowers wiped his hands across his face, unable to bear the words he was hearing. He began to sob, great, heaving sobs. He wasn't ready to die yet. He had to find Margaret. He had to settle things with her. He shook his head.

"No. I won't go. You can't have me yet."

"You have no choice, murderer. You gave these men no choice. You snuffed out their lives disregarding the fact that they had loved ones who desperately needed them. And for what? A bit of earth that you hoped to see plowed across by some engine of steam? Your greed has gotten you killed, just as you have killed for it."

Bowers screeched a loud, "No!" His body shook with fear, and he launched himself at the black-robed creature before him, his gait particularly unsteady. Slim easily sidestepped him, his hand darting out and depositing a small pistol, unseen, on the table nearby. Slim laughed uproariously, his voice echoing in the house. He turned a chair to face Bowers, who brought himself up short when he found himself facing another corpse. He backed away and staggered against the table. His hands went to steady himself, and they closed over the gun. He held it before him, frowning, examining it carefully, unsure just where it had come from. He checked it and found it loaded. A sly grin climbed onto his face. He whipped around and pointed the gun at the specter, finally feeling a bit triumphant. The specter simply laughed again and headed straight for him. Bowers pulled the trigger, expecting to see the figure of death fall at his feet. It didn't. Bowers' eyes grew as did his fear, for he had believed he had gained the upper hand. He fired again with the same effect and in desperation, threw the pistol at the apparent apparition coming towards him. It was swatted away with a wave of the billowing robe that covered what Bowers had come to know as the very face of death.

"It's time to meet your maker. Perhaps you can buy a ticket into heaven. You always did believe money could buy anything."

Jim cowered away from the raspy voice. "No! It's not my time!"

"Oh, but it is! Come!" The skeletal hands reached for the man, gesturing, a finger beckoning.

"Come!" The voice was more forceful as it drew ever nearer the trembling man who suddenly couldn't seem to move.

"Your judgment awaits! Come!" The hands made to close about the neck of Jim Bowers, hoping to render him unconscious so he could get him bound and transported to town.

Just before he touched the man, he collapsed at his feet. Slim stood there a moment in wonderment. The ordeal had apparently been more than the man could handle, for he had dropped to the floor in a dead faint. He stared down at the pitiful excuse of a man before shaking his head and wiping his brow, which had begun to perspire heavily under the woolen robe he wore. He took no note of the paint that came off on his hand. From somewhere in the folds of the robe, he produced a length of rope and proceeded to tie the prone figure up nice and tidy. A chuckle escaped him. He had not expected it to be so easy.

———◆———

The sun was high overhead when Bowers awoke with a jolt and bounce that sent him tumbling about the back of a wagon. Trying to right himself, he found he couldn't, his hands tied securely in front of him and attached to a short length of rope that bound his feet together as well. He was hogtied. The rope was also looped around his neck and any struggling he did managed to cut off his air supply significantly. Another jostle and he flung himself into a sitting position. He was loosely gagged, and he worked the bit of cloth with his tongue as he studied on his situation. The black-robed, hooded figure that had tormented him for the last several nights was at the reins, but it made no sound. In fact, it never turned around once to see what all the grunting and flopping about in the wagon had produced. Bowers' chest was heaving with exertion and fear, not quite believing that death had come to take him to hell. The landscape would be drastically different, he figured, and all he could see was an ocean of grass. He slumped against a roll of something behind him, then quickly sat up again, nearly vomiting at the smell. Getting himself under control lest he lose his lunch and die gagging on his own vomit, he studied the spongy, log-like thing he had at his back, only to recoil suddenly in horror, his breath tearing out of his lungs in muffled screams. He was trussed up like a Christmas turkey with four very dead men, and death itself carrying him off to God knew where. Even though each was in varying states of decay, he recognized them as his handiwork After his initial contact with the first corpse, he watched in horror as a very corpulent maggot wormed its way out of a putrefied eyeball, causing what had apparently been a delectable meal to crumble in upon itself. He began to shiver at the sight, unable to help himself. Trussed up as he was, bound so tight that he could no longer feel his hands and feet, panic turned to sheer terror, and that, to plain insanity, once he realized that his traveling companions were well and truly dead.

Somewhere along the ride into town, Jim Bowers lost touch with reality. His moans and screams, though muffled against the gag held a vibrato that sent shivers down Slim's spine. Bowers' eyes became glassy, the terror that this was for real being too much. He screamed for nearly a half hour before either fear or exhaustion claimed him and eased him into the darkest of voids.

Slim sighed with relief, his head aching from all the racket his captive had made earlier. He pulled his handkerchief from the folds of the robe and swiped at the paint that was beginning to run down his face like smutty rain. The paint was barely a fine sheen now, but he still couldn't take the chance of Bowers seeing his face. Not yet. Slim let out a long, satisfied breath. Yes, it had been a lot easier than he had thought it was going to be. He had staked out the place well before putting his plan into motion. Bowers had been so confident that he hadn't even posted guards. That was brass, to think that one was so above the law that no one would come after him on his own land. Hiding out in the attic had made things easier for sure. The fool had not even considered looking there when the 'mysterious things' had started happening. A grim smile took his face. It was a good thing no one hereabouts knew that he had theatrical experience for it had stood him in good stead the last few weeks.

But, durn it, it was hot as Hades in the garb he wore. And the stench, well, gut-wrenching was the only word for it. He pulled the bottle from underneath the seat, uncorked it and gulped heavily from it. If he kept this up, he was going to be sodden by the time they got to town, and he didn't want to miss that for the world. Replacing the bottle under the seat, he clicked to the horses, urging them along.

SIXTY-ONE

They were lining the streets to see the spectacle winding its way through the town, most of them with their hands covering the lower half of their faces, either from shock or the horrific stench. Though all of their eyes rounded to see the man perched atop the grisly contents of the wagon being driven by a gaunt, lanky character that could have been Death itself. That was his intention exactly. The man in the wagon was hog-tied and seemed to have lost his mind. He was screaming obscenities one minute, then blubbering and pleading for mercy the next. Anyone watching the procession could well imagine the man's horror for he was sitting amid the decaying remains of four men. But it wasn't the dead men so much that held their attention. It was the man raising such a ruckus—Jim Bowers.

Upstairs at the hotel, Travers and Laura had just gotten Maggie settled in when they heard the commotion outside. Going to the window, Travers had a clear view of what he feared would soon turn into a lynch mob if someone didn't intervene quickly. He turned to Maggie and Laura who had come up behind him and said, "We did it, ladies. We've got him. Ol' Slim pulled it off."

Maggie seemed to sag with relief and Laura eased her down into the rocking chair that sat nearby. Concern creased his brow as Travers asked her softly, "Are you alright?"

"Yes, I'm fine. You go on. You're needed out there."

He nodded and hesitated the merest of seconds before turning on his heel and disappearing out the door. He was not about to miss this. Jim Bowers had been brought down. But justice had to be served, and it was best served cold. The crowd outside didn't seem to cater to that idea.

After he had gone, Laura turned to Maggie.

"Are you sure you're all right? You seem so pale."

"I'm more than all right. I only regret that I don't get to kill the bastard myself," she said, raising tired eyes to her friend. Laura gave the woman a consoling pat on the arm, thinking if anyone deserved that privilege it was most definitely Maggie Bowers.

Sure enough, by the time Travers got through to where Slim and Sheriff Tate and Bowers were, the crowd had turned into a mob. A rope had been produced, and several angry men were making their intentions known.

"Come on! Let us have him. We'll show that bastard what happens to his kind around here."

"Hangin's too good for the man. Let's let the injuns have their way with him!"

"I say we just shoot the bastard right now. That way we'll all know and be witnesses that justice was served. He done escaped the noose once. Cain't let it happen again!"

Travers mounted the wagon and held up his hands for quiet.

"All right, folks. Let's all just calm down," he implored the crowd. They eventually began to cease the murmuring and appeared willing to listen.

"Now look," he said, "I know that all of you want to see justice administered swiftly to this man and you have good reason. So do I. But we have to do it right. Let the law have its way."

The crowd burst into angry shouts at that, and one man separated himself from the crowd.

"Law, my ass! He can afford to pay off any official! All he would get is another slap on the wrist. That sum'bitch ain't gettin' off so easy this time, even if I have to kill him myself!"

Travers recognized the man as a brother-in-law to one of the dead men in the wagon.

"Carter, isn't it?"

"That's right. That lowlife killed my sister's husband." He jabbed the air towards Bowers angrily. Travers ran his hand through his hair, nodding.

"I know. And you have a right to feel the way you do. All of us do. But as citizens of this town, we have a responsibility to uphold the law, and that means due process for this—man." He had hesitated to call him a man, thinking the word snake was more suitable. There was also a very important point he needed to make.

"I crave justice just as much as any man here. I've believed for some time that Jim Bowers was the man responsible for the deaths of the men from this town. But until now, we had no proof. Today, we have the proof! No judge in his right mind will dismiss multiple murder charges against a man, no matter how wealthy he is when there is so much evidence against him. We have four bodies here, Carter, including the body of your brother-in-law, to prove that Bowers was involved in their deaths. We have Sam Bailey's gun and knife and Bower's gun as well. We simply have to connect the dots. Match bullets to guns. The bodies were all buried on Bowers' property, in separate graves. True, this man is a murderer, and he deserves to die, but if you take matters into your own hands, then you become what he is, a murderer as well. And I don't believe that any of you want that for yourselves or your families. Believe me, that is a feeling that you never want to experience."

The murmuring quieted again. Carter asked, "And if he still manages to walk? What will you do then, Doc?"

"He won't."

"But if he—"

"Then I'll handle the matter personally." Dead silence fell. Several long minutes ticked by before Carter said, "All right. But if he—It's on your head then." Carter pointed up at Travers, his frustration evident. Travers understood. They had all thought that they had Bowers when Flora died. The man's weasel of a lawyer had gotten the charges dismissed due to lack of evidence before he promptly disappeared, apparently taking Travers' threat to heart. This time, Travers vowed, there would be no escape for the man, just justice, swift and sure.

"All of you go on home. Let us do our jobs here. Carter, get a few of the men to help get these bodies unloaded at the undertakers. They need proper burial. I'll be over to gather the evidence momentarily."

The crowd finally began to disperse, one by one, then by twos and threes. Carter rounded up three other men to help him with the corpses. Throughout all of this, Daniel had stood there like a stone, his eyes locked on Bowers who was desperately try-ing to shrink into himself. The big schoolteacher waited until the street cleared before he moved and then with measured steps, he strode to the wagon and drove his fist into the man's face, driv-ing him back to lay atop his own grisly handiwork. The bound man didn't move. Travers bent and felt for a pulse.

"Well, Daniel, you've knocked his lights out. He'll wake up with a helluv'a headache."

Daniel clenched his fists. "A pity, too."

Travers cocked his head. What is?"

Daniel didn't take his eyes off Bowers' prone form as Carter, and the men drug the unconscious man from the wagon and followed Sheriff Tate into the jail with him.

"The fact that he will wake up."

SIXTY-TWO

Judge Cahill came around ten days later. He was a barrel-chested man, tall and portly, his demeanor stern and precise. He didn't beat around the bush when it came to serving up sentences. Travers had gotten his bullets from the bodies of the dead men, though it had taken some doing, for they were in such bad shape he hated to even touch them. It was bad enough that these men had suffered so horribly at the hands of Jim Bowers, they were drug around by Slim and then cut upon by Travers. He prayed for their souls and for God to forgive them for desecrating the graves of these men. They had promptly reburied them, giving them Christian burials this time, their families finally having closure.

It was as if the town all gave a sigh of relief. Bowers was behind bars, and it seemed certain that this time he would not escape justice. Slim had still not shown himself to Bowers and would not until the trial. He had taken a room at the hotel next to Maggie's and had made it his job to see that she was taken care of. He had become her shadow. Bowers did not know his wife was in town. It would make no difference. She would not lift a finger to help him.

Bowers was treated as any other criminal was. He was fed and treated with decency by Tate and Travers who made it a point to visit several times a day. He was surprised to find that the man seemed to have coiled into himself. He had little to say, a remarkable change, as he was ever talking about himself. He didn't mention the ranch once, his hands seemed to have scattered to the winds after Bailey died as they had no one to ride herd on them. A few of the men from a neighboring ranch had ridden out to check on things, finding the house ransacked and the cattle scattered. Not a soul was in sight.

But Travers worried. He had been watching Bowers, noted the darting eyes, the quiet mumbling to himself, and feared that the man might be judged insane. If that was the case, Bowers just might walk free once again.

***

The trial got underway at ten that morning. Every man, woman, and child in the town and even the surrounding ranches came to this one. They wanted to see just what Judge Cahill was made of. Sheriff Tate read the charges and produced the evidence collected by Travers. He produced the weapon used by Bailey and called a star witness. Slim walked through the doors of the schoolhouse. The crowd fell silent as they watched his careful, measured steps to take the witness stand.

Jim Bowers could not believe his eyes. He gaped at the man who was supposed to be dead. The cook he had Bailey kill because he had let Margaret walk away from their marriage. He knew his fate was sealed the moment he walked through the door. Slim had known about the other men he'd had Bailey kill. Not that he had told him anything about them right out, but he and Bailey had talked in front of the man. The cook had heard about where the foreman had buried the bodies or dumped them. Bowers had not been concerned. He had believed the man dead. Until now. He closed his eyes in resignation.

The judge directed his question to Slim.

"State your name for the record."

"Pierre Thibideaux. I am known as Slim to folks round about."

"And what is your association with the accused, sir?"

"I was employed by Jim Bowers to be his cook."

"I see. And did you at any time have knowledge or were you involved in the deaths of these men?"

"I became aware of the situation during a conversation that my employer had with his then foreman Sam Bailey one afternoon. They were discussing a particular incident where Bailey had buried the body of a man he had killed. Mr. Bowers did not seem too pleased with the location he had chosen as he felt it might be found by cowhands from a nearby ranch. I was never asked to do murder for Mr. Bowers, no."

The judge looked severely at Slim, his mind ticking.

"And why did you not come forward to report this matter to the sheriff immediately?"

"There were more pressing matters."

"Such as?"

"Protecting Mrs. Bowers, sir."

That brought the judge's head up. His eyebrow raised.

"There is a Mrs. Bowers?"

"Yes, sir."

"Where is she now?"

"Safe."

"I believe the question was 'Where is she now'?"

"Safe."

"Now, see here —"

"With all due respect, your honor, Mrs. Bowers is recovering from a horrible incident involving a—rabid animal and is unable to attend. She was severely ill for some time and is still recovering. That is all I'm afraid that I am going to say on the matter."

Judge Cahill studied the man. He could sense a lie a mile away, but he sensed that this man was doing so to protect this Mrs. Bowers. He didn't normally allow for such behavior on the witness stand, but something told him to let it go. The accused, the woman's husband, had numerous charges against him. Including murder. It would stand to reason that a man with a violent streak could very well have harmed his own wife. He would let that subject drop for now.

"And how did you manage to leave the employ of Mr. Bowers?

"Well, sir. Mrs. Bowers packed her bags and left one afternoon. I was cooking supper when the boss got home. He wants to know where his wife is. I tell him she left. He wants to know why didn't I stop her. I tell him she did right to leave him after all he put her through. He was a cruel man to her, judge. I tried to protect her as much as I could. She had no one else. Mr. Bowers took issue with my stance and had his man knife me. He took me by horseback away from the ranch and tossed me into a wash along the river. Left me for dead."

The judge sat back, his arms crossed. Murder and attempted murder. If what Slim was indicating were true, he had also severely mistreated his wife. He decided to move the questioning along to this Dr. Travers Gage.

"You may step down, sir."

Slim eased from the chair and left the building. The judge called for Travers to take the stand.

"Please state your name and occupation, sir."

"Dr. Travers Gage, medical doctor, and surgeon."

"And how long have you been practicing medicine, sir?"

"Fifteen years."

"And what is your relationship to the defendant?"

"I am a close friend of Mrs. Bowers."

"How so?"

"I knew her when she was a child. She and her brother helped me around my clinic back in Virginia before the war."

"And where is her brother?"

"Dead, sir. He died of cholera last winter."

The judge went on and on, gathering information that he thought might be relevant to the case. Travers thought he never would get to the point. They discussed his tour of duty in the war and his qualifications as a doctor. They moved to his association with Bowers and how the man had been surrounded by suspicion ever since his arrival in town. Travers told of the men who turned up missing, and the one found hung. The bullets were produced to match to the gun that Bailey had used in carrying out the murders. The local gunsmith confirmed that the gun belonged to Bailey as he had been the one to sell it to him just after Bowers hired him. The judge called a recess until two in the afternoon.

At two o'clock, Jim Bowers would take the stand in his own defense.

SIXTY-THREE

The crowd pressed in to see this one. There was hardly enough room to breathe in the church, let alone move, so packed in the place they were. Jim Bowers sat on the witness stand, his eyes darting back and forth, taking in the crowd. They all wanted him dead. They had been against him from the beginning, ever since his arrival in this town years ago. They wanted his blood, and he feared the judge did as well. But he would show them. Jim Bowers feared no man. He stiffened his spine in the chair, his body going ramrod straight to the point of aching, but he held himself aloof. They would not break him.

Judge Cahill was speaking.

"Please state your name for the record."

"James Allen Bowers."

"And your occupation?"

"Rancher."

"I understand that you own a considerable amount of land."

"Yes, sir."

"How many acres, Mr. Bowers do you own?"

"Six thousand acres."

"That's sizable. Must take a lot of men to run a ranch that large."

"It does."

Judge Cahill frowned. He was dead curious to have some answers to some pressing questions. He didn't care if this line of questioning was out of the ordinary.

"How did you come into your money, Mr. Bowers, the money you used to purchase the initial fifteen hundred acres? It is my understanding that you came to Gold City penniless and suddenly was the wealthiest man around. How did you manage such a feat?"

"I inherited a sizable portion from my family."

"I was under the impression that you had no family."

"You are correct, sir."

"Which leads me back to the question, who did you inherit from?"

"My brother, Charles. He died shortly before I came to Gold City."

Murmuring began to rise. Charles. Charles Who?

"And what did your brother do that you inherited such a large sum of money from him, large enough to buy such a parcel of land?"

"He was an officer at a bank."

Travers had been holding his breath. He let it ease out. The man and Maggie's uncle were brothers. Somehow, Jim had managed to keep that secret to himself. And he would bet his bottom dollar that Charles Pritchard had kept that his own little secret as well. And that had to mean that Netta Pritchard was right in believing that Jim Bowers was behind her husband's death. Maggie must be dying inside, he thought as he looked back at her, where she sat white-faced beside Laura, still as stone, her eyes glued to the man on the witness stand.

"I see." The judge clamped his mouth shut, thinking he had satisfied his own curiosity enough to know that the money was legit. He turned the subject to the men who had just been placed properly into the ground once and for all.

"I want you to tell me what happened that you ended up with the land that these four men and those not yet recovered once had in their possession."

Jim Bowers shifted to ease the strain on his back. The silence was so deafening that the creaking of his chair sounded like thunder in the room.

"It is my understanding that the men ran off and deserted their families, sir. I simply purchased the notes from the land office when the families left in the lurch could not pay."

"And you have records of these transactions?"

"Why, yes, sir."

"Can you produce them?"

That brought a stammer. "Well, I don't have them on me, no."

"Where is the land officer who oversaw the transactions? Surely he could produce them for us in a timely manner."

"I'm sure he could, your honor. But I'm afraid I don't know the whereabouts of the man. He seems to have up and run off as well."

That knotted the judge's brow. He turned to Sheriff Tate.

"Is that true, Sheriff?"

Tate stood and held his hat before him. "That is right, judge. We have failed to locate the man to date. And it seems that all the records have either been destroyed or stolen as well."

The judge pinned Bowers with a grim stare even as Tate took his seat.

"There seems to be a lot of men *disappearing* around here. A man doesn't just fall off the face of the earth. He usually has to have a bit of help to do such a thing. Now, let's get something straight. From all accounts, it appears that there is lots of speculation concerning your involvement in the disappearances of these men. I have to admit, that I think you are either the smartest man I know or the dumbest. A smart man would have walked away after the first man *disappeared*. You, on the other hand, got greedy, it seems. And unfortunately, greed and murder have a nasty habit of going hand in hand. You have a lot of evidence against you, sir. You'd do well to think on that tonight in your jail cell. You can tell the truth and hope for leniency or lie and surely get death. We'll break for the day. Trial will resume tomorrow at ten in the morning." He sounded the gavel and rose, and realized he couldn't get out of the door, so he made his way over to where Sheriff Tate and Travers sat just beyond Jim Bowers. The crowd began to disperse, slowly as there were so many of them. Jim watched as the three men conversed, straining to hear what they were saying. He couldn't hear them above the din that was rising inside the church. He gritted his teeth and waited for Tate to come take him back to jail.

"Well, how do you think it's a goin'?" Tate asked Travers.

"Surprisingly well. I can't believe Bowers managed to keep the fact he was Charles Pritchard's brother a secret from Maggie. I wonder what the real story is there, but I doubt we'll ever know. He's wound tighter than a bowstring. Better keep an eye on him. He's liable to try something now that his back is against the wall."

When the judge reached them, they shook hands and spoke of things other than the trial. The judge could stand it no more. He had to ask.

"Is the lady sitting with Mr. Thibideaux the accused's wife?"

"Yes, sir," Travers said. "Why?"

"I take it she has recovered from her ordeal with this—animal?"

"She has recovered to a certain extent, your honor. But she is by no means fully healed. An attack like that could take years to recover from."

"Am I right in assuming this animal was of the two-legged variety?" The judge's brows were drawn severely over his eyes.

Travers looked from him to Sheriff Tate and back to where Maggie still sat with Slim right beside her. She was still so pale, but she had assured him that she was fine.

"You may assume whatever you like, your honor. I'm afraid I can't divulge a client's medical history in any shape or form."

"Even if it means an attacker goes free?"

"He didn't."

That got raised eyebrows. "Is that a fact?"

"It is."

"Anything I need to know?"

"No, sir. Not a thing." His tone brooked no argument.

The judge looked from Travers to Sheriff Tate and shook his head. "Well, fellers, I'm going to get some supper. I will see you back here in the morning." He left them then, knowing the doctor was watching him as he left.

When Travers turned his attention back to Maggie, he saw her in a heated conversation with Slim. He made his way to them.

"What's wrong, Maggie?"

She clamped her mouth shut. That wasn't a good sign.

"Slim?"

Slim rose to stand beside Travers. "She wants to see him." He could barely get the words out.

"See who?"

"Bowers."

Travers looked at Maggie's pinched face.

"You know that is out of the question."

"Why? Why is it out of the question? Am I not still his wife, legally? I do still have rights."

"Have you suddenly taken leave of your senses? You know that any interaction with him could jeopardize this trial."

Maggie bit her lip and looked at her hands clasped so tightly in her lap that her knuckles were white.

"Travers, I *need* to see him. We have unfinished business."

"Unfinished—un—, You've got to be kidding me. The two of you were finished the day he took his hand to you. And by God, if you so much as attempt to see him alone, I'll lock you up and throw away the key!" Travers didn't know what she had in mind, but he was taking no chances this time. True, Maggie did still have rights as the man's wife, but she was asking for too much. If the people of the town got wind that she had visited the man, she was liable to be strung up right beside him. That was not a chance he was willing to take.

"Travers, Jim knows that the end is near. We have the proof, the witness, the literal smoking gun. What we don't have is a confession. I can get you that confession. All I need is to talk to him. Please."

Sheriff Tate pulled Travers aside when he saw that he was going to protest further. Tate was not one to mince words, and he knew that Maggie had a valid point.

"Now, see here. I don't see the real harm in letting her see him. He *is* still her husband. If she can get him to confess, then we will know once and for all the reason behind his madness."

"Ras, I don't even want to consid—"

"Well, you'd better, cause I for one am wantin' to know his

reasonin' behind these killin's."

Tate looked back at the now dispersed crowd and told Travers, "I have to get this vulture back behind bars. You two discuss this some more. Deep down, you know you'd like to know the truth as well."

Tate and Daniel moved to Bowers who stood awkwardly and walked stiffly between the two of them out the front door. He was glad they had finally conducted their business with the doctor and judge. Jim Bowers longed for the comfort of the cot in his cell. He was stiff from sitting on the witness stand, his hands bound tightly in irons. And he was starving. He found his mouth watering at the idea of a nice slab of beef and a good drought of whiskey. He hoped they fed him steak tonight.

Travers, Maggie, and Slim remained in the church, neither wanting to give an inch.

"And just what are you going to gain by talking to him, Maggie? The man is insane. I doubt if he could clearly express any reasoning whatsoever as to why he did what he did."

"I need to face him, for myself. For what he did to me if only to show him that I'm a survivor. That he didn't break me the way, he intended. That need alone surpasses the need to know why he singled these men out for death. They are dead. Those men aren't coming back. We may never know why they had to die. But *he* needs to know that he failed at *something*."

Travers admitted she had a valid point there. He hated to admit it, but she was right.

"I agree that you have that right, but I don't like the idea of you confronting him alone. If we do allow this, I *will* be present for the meeting. Understood?"

She nodded, knowing that there was no way Travers would let her see Jim alone. But see him, she must.

"I want to go now. The sooner, the better."

Travers started to argue, then thought better of it. Hell, there was no harm in getting it over with, he figured. As she said, the sooner, the better. He scratched his head a second before telling them, "Hold up here and let me check with Ras, make sure he's got him settled behind bars first. I want to be sure the bastard can't pull a fast one and disappear."

He went down the street and found Sheriff Tate just settling Bowers behind bars, the lock clicking resoundingly with a sharp snap. He had not taken the shackles off of him. The man seemed to mutter to himself distractedly, looking around the cell as if searching for something. He had the look of one who was fast losing his mind. Disoriented, the muttering to himself. . . Travers was sure he was on the verge of going insane. He prayed the man stayed lucid long enough to pay for his crimes.

The law frowned on putting killers to death who showed signs of insanity. Mere hours could be telling in Bowers' case. They had to get him convicted.

Ras tossed his hat onto the coatrack nailed to the back of the door after Travers shut it behind him, easing down into the chair behind his desk.

"I figured you'd be gettin' Maggie back to the hotel."

"She wants to see him. Now."

Ras' eyebrow shot up. "And you said okay?" He didn't quite expect Travers to allow it and was surprised when he said yes.

"Well, his supper will be here shortly. I say we go ahead and get her in here. He can wait to eat."

"I'll go get her." Travers disappeared out the door.

Within minutes the three of them were there, Maggie, Travers, and Slim. The two men were not letting her out of their sights. And Ras made it plain that he would be present as well for the encounter. No way was he going to miss it.

They went down the hall where Jim Bowers was reclined on his cot, his back propped against the wall, his head turning in a twitching manner, his eyes darting here and there. When he saw the four of them, he seemed to visibly relax, actually smiling at Maggie. For a second, his countenance was free of stress, free of fear, free of the ravages of the last few days. He actually looked like the man Maggie had fallen in love with. It rattled her to know that the man before her had been her husband. This man had killed, beaten her, attempted to rape her and when he had failed, had his foreman do the job for him. At the moment, he didn't look sick, but Maggie knew that only someone deeply deranged could do the things that he had done.

"Margaret. I was hoping to see you. I hope the folks here are treating you better than they are me. I'm afraid I don't like the accommodations very much at all."

"Really? What a shame. I believe I warned you that you wouldn't like the view. I like mine very much, thank you. I'm in my old room at the hotel. Everyone has been more than accommodating to me."

He bobbed his head. "That's good, that's real good. You haven't been out to the ranch, have you? I can't seem to find Bailey to let him know I won't be back for a while, leastways not until all this sordid mess is straightened out."

Maggie looked at Travers, a frown marring her brow.

"Jim, Bailey is—gone. Don't you remember?"

"Gone? Where? I don't remember sending him anywhere."

Travers put his hand on Maggie's shoulder, a silent message to let her know she should change the subject. She took his cue.

"Jim, do you understand why you are here?"

"They say I killed someone. Laughable, isn't it? I mean," his voice turned conspiratorial, "you know they are out to get me. All of them."

"Who?"

"Everyone. The sheriff, the doctor. Especially Gage. He won't rest until he sees me hang. Yes, he's always wanted this."

"Why, Jim? Why do you think Dr. Gage wants you dead?"

The man's eyes went hard then, revealing the old Jim. "Because he wants you, wife. He always has. Always wanted what he couldn't have. You belong to me. Ain't no Yankee lovin' blue belly goin' to take what's mine. Ever." The slimy grin that Maggie had come to associate with her husband crawled across his face and lodged itself there. Maggie felt her skin crawl at the sight.

"Why did you kill those men, Jim?"

"Margaret, there you go listening to rubbish about me. I didn't kill anyone."

"No? Not even Flora? We know that you killed her and why. She had the records that you forged with Loyd Ates. You stole them back from her that day that you set fire to her place. But there was one thing that you hadn't counted on, Jim."

"What's that?" He looked bemused.

"She gave me part of the evidence."

He went pale. "What?" His voice was a mere whisper.

"Flora was no fool. She knew that you would come after her if you ever got wind what she was up to. She made sure that the evidence fell into the right hands all along. After all, it was I who told her where to look."

Bowers stiffened like a porcupine bristling. The change that came over him was noticeable to all who saw him. He was on a low boil.

"You're lying. You have nothing." He gave a short, rattled laugh. "Why are you doing this to me?"

Maggie snorted. "To you? What about what you did to me, your wife, Jim? What did I ever do to you that I had to pay such a high price? Tell me, Jim. Was it worth it? Was it worth your life to get a little extra acre of land here or there? Was it worth it to send your man Sam Bailey to beat and rape your own wife? Were the deaths of those men you had killed to silence them and Flora worth it? What? No answer? I guess we'll see when you're swinging from the gallows that I will personally finance the construction of."

Her tone was as flat and solid as a pine board. Her face was devoid of expression, but Jim Bowers' wasn't. He was beginning to come unglued at her little diatribe. How dare she.

"You bitch. I always knew that you were no better than a

whore. If you associate with whores, you become one. Flora got what she bargained for. She knew the consequences of messing with me. It seems I underestimated you, however. You set me up. You set it up so that all these charges would be leveled against me. You wanted me out of the way so you and Gage could be together. I should have killed you myself. I should have just done the deed myself instead of letting Bailey have a go at you. How was that, by the way? Sam always was good at breakin' in fillies."

Maggie took an angry step forward, controlled by the restraining hand of Travers who was having a hard time keeping his own temper in check. It was Slim who answered.

"He never got to finish the ride. I'm afraid that he got a little full of himself."

The irony of the words struck Jim as funny as he had found Bailey with his penis severed and shoved down his throat. He began to laugh.

"I never remember you being so funny, Slim. If I had known, I'd have waited to let Bailey knife you. Kept you around a while longer just for the entertainment."

Slim just backed away, knowing if he didn't he was liable to have a go at him even though bars separated them. Travers stepped forward then.

"Well, I for one would like to know the why of it all, Bowers. I can understand the greed for land, but why me? You've had it in for me from the day you arrived in town. I had never met you before to my knowledge. You hated me before you ever knew Maggie and I knew one another. Why?"

The man behind bars looked at Travers hard, his eyes boring into the man he had come to hate. This man had come to represent all that Bowers resented, despised and envied. This man was responsible for the failure of his marriage. And he wanted to know why?

"You really don't know, do you?"

Travers looked at the expression on Bowers' face, seeing nothing there that would reveal the reasoning behind the vendetta against him.

"You always were one mighty high on yourself. I know all about the big hero at Gettysburg, how you saved that Union general. I saw it first-hand. I was there."

"You were there?" Travers was puzzled. He couldn't place Bowers at the battle of Gettysburg. Then again, there were so many people going through his sights at that time, he probably wouldn't have recognized anyone through the haze he had been in at the time.

"I was there. I was captured by the blue bellies. I was wounded, taken to your tent to be treated. But you, you worked on that damned Yankee general for so long that you passed out. You never got around to me. Seems you let a lot of us Southern men suffer rather than see to us properly. Some claimed you were wounded. I figure you just wanted to stick it to us 'cause we was bad enough to stand up for our rights. It don't matter no more. The simple fact is, you treated that Yankee before your own countrymen and that is just not to be borne."

"Bowers, I was wounded, severely. I passed out from loss of blood. I can't help the fact that you didn't get proper treatment. There was another doctor there. He didn't see to you and the others?"

"I nearly died of pneumonia because of you. The other doctor came around and looked us over, took a swig from his bottle and left us bleedin' and dyin'. He never came back."

Travers shook his head. He had known Morgan was no good, and this news solidified what he had long suspected. An alcoholic and a bigot. Bowers and the other prisoners must have suffered terribly, and he did feel partially to blame. After all, Morgan had been working on him.

"I'm sorry that you weren't treated properly, Bowers. Morgan and I had had words concerning his ethics with even our own men. It wasn't just Southern men he neglected. He was a drunk, and he just didn't give a damn. The color of the uniform had nothing to do with it."

Bowers grunted. "Don't make no difference now. You came out of the war smellin' like roses. You had a name, a name that carried weight. A man fast with a gun. Everywhere you went, you got respect and a handshake. You gunned down your fellow man and got a damn medal for it. Where is the logic in that?"

Travers just sighed. "There is no logic in it, Bowers. War is war. Killing is all a part of it. I tried to avoid it when possible. Luck wasn't on my side that day. Nor yours either, apparently."

"Apparently not. Hatin', you has been almost as rewarding as killing those men. Satisfaction does come to those who wait patiently. My only regret is that, when I realized I didn't stand a chance in hell against you man to man, I couldn't find a man who could. I thought I had you when that darkie took you on, but you still wouldn't die. I don't guess you ever will."

His voice held a bittersweet note. He was sad, disheartened and tired. He wanted them to leave. He was hungry, and they were wearing on his frayed nerves. Turning to the sheriff who had stood by quietly listening, he said ever so politely, "I'd like to be alone now."

Sheriff Tate cleared his throat, and Travers knew it was time to go. They had gotten what they come for. He had confessed to killing them all, perhaps without even realizing it. Maggie had faced him down, though perhaps not to her complete liking but it was enough, and she was satisfied. She didn't protest as Travers led her out the door with Slim close on their heels. As they left, she turned and caught a glimpse of Jim staring out the barred window, his lips moving silently.

It was the last time she would see him alive.

———•———

Early the next morning, Sheriff Tate found Jim Bowers hanging from the top row of bars in his cell by his belt. He had taken his own life. He had left a note, having asked the night before for a pencil and paper from the sheriff after his visitors had left. Tate had to go in search of the items, and while he did so, Bowers had eaten his supper with relish, even though the steak and potatoes had grown cold. Then he had put his plate aside and written what he had to say on the paper he would leave for whoever found him.

I do not ask for forgiveness save one: my wife, Margaret.
I do know the pain of loss for it haunts me daily.
I care not to be judged by man, but by my Creator.
I wash your hands of my blood.

Sheriff Tate gave the note to Maggie, thinking perhaps she would like to keep it. She stared at it, hollow-eyed, not knowing how to react. Travers had pronounced Jim dead and allowed her to see him. In death, he finally had peace. His hatred, envy, and greed had eroded his mind to all that was right and just. That was the only reasoning that Maggie could come up with concerning why he had done such unspeakable things. She had loved him, though not the way she loved Travers. Jim was really gone, and the knowledge of that lightened her head so that she fainted, causing Travers to put her to bed in the clinic. She stayed there most of the day before he allowed her to leave. It took a great deal of convincing on her part that she was fine before he let her go back to her room at the hotel.

Maggie Bowers was now a widow.

SIXTY-FOUR

The world seemed to tilt slightly on its axis, causing every-thing to seem out of balance. Travers had never known true fear in his life—until now. His gut wrenched convulsively, and he felt the urge to wretch but managed to keep himself under control.

She was leaving.

After all, they had been through, she was standing before him now telling him that she had to go away, that she could no longer stay here. The one hope he had ever had in the world was walking out of his life. For the third time. The first time, he had sent her away. The second time, she had chosen marriage to a killer. And now she chose to simply walk away, leaving on her own accord.

He didn't know how much more of this his nerves could take.

He simply was not believing this. She was a widow now. She was free. They could marry. But she was leaving. For the third time in his life, he felt his world shattering into splinters of ir-replaceable moments in time. Panic seized him.

"Maggie, don't do this." Every fiber of his being told him to grab her and run lock her up in his room at the boardinghouse.

Maggie forced down the lump in her throat, determined to do this as quickly and as painlessly as possible. She'd had every intention of skipping town and not saying goodbye. The idea of telling Travers goodbye had hurt so badly that she didn't have the heart to approach him to tell him the news herself. He had seen her preparing to board the stagecoach and had wasted no time crossing the street.

"Travers, I *am* leaving. On *that* stage," she said and pointed the few feet to the coach that waited nearby. She looked him squarely in the eye and paused for the merest of moments be-fore adding, "If you ever cared for me at all, you will not inter-fere. This is something I have to do. Alone." Her eyes pleaded for his understanding.

Travers forced himself to breathe, his head feeling light of a sudden, his chest tightening in pain.

"Maggie," he took a step towards her only to be stopped by her upraised hand and a determined look in her eyes.

"No! Please don't make this any harder than it has to be." She stood there memorizing his face, pale as it was from the anguish so openly displayed.

"Where will you go?" he finally managed to ask quietly.

"I'm not sure. I'll let you know when I've settled somewhere. I may travel for a while. Try a few places on for size." She grinned a little, trying to lighten the heaviness hanging between them.

Travers simply nodded, lowering his head, studying the mail he had just picked up, his eyes not comprehending a single written word on any of it. His head felt full of fuzz. Nothing made sense anymore.

The lump in Maggie's throat had grown to the size of an ostrich egg. She couldn't bear to see the pain on his face any longer. She had to wrap this up quickly.

"Take care of yourself, Travers. Don't worry about me. I'll be fine." Her voice was hoarse as she quickly picked up the valise beside her and turned away to board the stage.

"Maggie."

She stopped, and half turned to face him. He simply stared at her for the longest and with a deep breath told her, "Take care of yourself, Margaret."

Maggie smiled tremulously and turned to be helped into the stage. She refused to look out the window lest he see the tears streaming down her face. She had done it. She had severed the ties and feared that this time there would be no mending them. She prayed that she was doing the right thing. It had been hell itself to see the pain her leaving had caused him. Hurting him was the last thing she ever wanted to do. With a sudden realization that chilled her, she recalled how he had called her Margaret. Travers had never called her that. He had always used his pet name for her, Maggie. That told her how severe the breach between them had now become. In her mind's eye, she could see him literally washing his hands of her. She couldn't blame him. She had brought him nothing but pain. The significance of that usage of her name closed her eyes against anything but what lay ahead for her. She had to steel herself for what lay ahead.

From her vantage point a few feet away, Laura watched the scene unfold with a heavy heart. Travers may not understand why Maggie was doing this, but she did. And she also knew what this was costing Maggie. She had seen Maggie's face when she had turned away from Travers. She had worn that look before herself and knew the chance Maggie was willing to take.

She ached for those two. They never seemed to be able to get it right. It was so obvious to everyone that they belonged together. She stood and watched Travers follow the stagecoach with his eyes until it disappeared from sight. And still, he remained there, staring down the road it had taken, willing it to reappear. His face had smoothed into a marble-like frieze, an attempt to hide the anguish but his eyes told the story.

Laura walked the few feet that separated them and just stood quietly beside him. He noticed her after several minutes, looking her in the eye before turning and hurrying briskly away. She let him go. When the time was right, she would talk to him. Right now the last thing he needed was company.

A week passed with no news from Maggie. Travers was in his room staring out the window, seeing nothing as he debated what to do. He had conducted business as usual at the clinic, but things had been slow, so he had elected to stay in today. The town's folk knew where to find him if they should need him. He looked as if he had aged ten years. His hair was tousled, and his clothes were rumpled, not in keeping with his usual very tidy appearance. He had slept little this week, and his eyes were showing it.

Travers knew that Laura was itching to say something but to her credit had kept her peace so far. He didn't need a lecture from her. He wanted Maggie to come back, but a part of him prayed that he never see her again. He loved her so much, but that had not been enough to make her stay. She was destroying him. She hovered there in his dreams, causing him to toss restlessly in a bed made hard as stone with her leaving. He saw her everywhere, at the clinic, at the general store. She haunted him day and night. Yet again, she had chosen a life without him. It was more than he could bear.

Laura hesitated outside his door. A week she had given him to deal with Maggie's leaving. It was time. He needed a release of his anger and pain and if that meant being his chopping block, so be it. She could stand it no longer.

Taking a deep breath, she twisted the doorknob that she had somehow known would not be locked, the door opening easily. He was standing at the window, one arm raised bracing himself against the frame and staring out at nothing in particular. It took him a moment to acknowledge her presence, and when he did, his response was expected.

"Go away," he said quietly, his eyes never leaving the view out the window.

"No. I'm here as your friend, Travers." Laura stepped into the room and closed the door. Propriety be damned. She had never professed to be proper. She strode over and taking his hand, led him away from the window to the rocking chair that she promptly pushed him into. Kneeling in front of him, she paused a moment before she spoke, hoping she was doing, saying the right thing.

"Travers, I am so sorry about this. I know that you don't want to hear this, but I'm gonna say it anyhow. Maggie had to do this."

Travers sighed heavily, closing his eyes and rubbed his weary lids with the tips of his fingers. He sat slumped, dejectedly with his legs on either side of Laura.

"You're right. I don't want to hear this."

Laura put a hand on his knee.

"Look at me, Travers. I know her leaving sent you for a spin, but Maggie has issues to deal with that have nothing to do with you."

"Laura, anything involving Maggie has everything to do with me."

Laura heaved a huge sigh to get control of her frustration at this man.

"Now you listen to me, Travers Gage. To be such an intelligent man, you've got to be one of the most obsessive, stubborn, pig-headed, and—" she bit off the tirade, seeing his eyes flash angrily.

"What I am trying to say is, Maggie has been through hell. Most women I know would have folded before now from just the memory of such an attack. It's remarkable that she even survived and you well know it."

Travers sat forward. "There! That's just it. Maggie has always been strong. And stubborn. Why is she so determined to reject me at every turn? I can help her through this. I love her, and I know she loves me. She told me so!"

"Travers put yourself in her place. She was raped, for Christ's sakes! As soon as she recovered physically, she was forced to deal with the trial. She never faced her attack, never dealt with it. You have no idea what that does to a woman!" Laura rose and paced before him in agitation. "It's like falling into your worst nightmare the second that monster touches you and purgatory afterward. You spend your days, if you're lucky enough to survive, wondering if it was your fault. You cringe at the thought of intimacy with another man. Even a man you know in your heart would never hurt you or mistreat you. You live in a world of fear: fear of rejection once you've overcome your own demons. Fear that friends will turn their backs on you because they think maybe you *did* do something to deserve what you got."

Laura had wandered over to the window and glanced out at the activity on the street below, but the world outside this room held little interest for her at the moment. She was reliving her own private hell.

"Laura, Maggie knows that I would never hurt her. My God, I love her more than life itself!"

Travers rose to stand beside her at the window. Laura just shook her head at him.

"Travers, she knows that! This is not about you! She has to know for herself that she can learn to trust again. That she is worthy of your love. You cannot convince her of that no matter how hard you try. She has to remind herself, and she can't do that with you constantly begging for her to love you!"

She let go a frustrated sigh and turned to the window again.

"A woman has a hard enough time of it out here, Travers. A woman has to prove herself. In Maggie's eyes, she lost her 'worthiness' as a lady the moment he touched her. It doesn't matter why it happened or that it wasn't her fault. But it's up to her to come to terms with it. 'Cause sooner or later, some lunatic will throw that tragic day in her life right in her face, and she has to be strong enough to withstand it."

Travers let that soak in. He knew what Laura was saying was true. Yet he didn't see why she had to leave town to heal. Maybe he had been putting too much pressure on her. He had just automatically assumed that she would bounce back from this because she was so strong. And Laura was right. As soon as he had gotten Maggie back to town, they had had to deal with Jim's trial. It made sense. Explained why she had been so hesitant to see him. And Laura spoke with such authority on the matter that he knew in his gut that she had endured the same horrible ordeal that Maggie had.

They stood side by side in companionable silence for a while before he brought it up.

"When did it happen?"

Laura looked at him with tormented eyes, her bottom lip trembling slightly. She tried to cover it with a weak smile.

"Nine years ago. Before I moved here. It's why I moved here."

"To escape the demons?"

"Yes."

"Was he ever caught? Punished?"

She gave a bitter laugh. "Ha! Now there's the crux of the matter right there. See the townsfolk felt that I somehow deserved it seeing as how I was a known prostitute. It went with the job. All in a day's work."

Travers' eyebrows rose in surprise. He shouldn't have been surprised, but he was. Somehow he had never pictured Laura in that line of work. It did, however, explain the friendship with Flora.

"You were a prostitute?"

Laura noted the raised eyebrows and nodded.

"Yes, I was. My paw died when I was thirteen. Maw had died

when I was ten, so it was just Paw and me for a while. He drank profusely after Maw died. Never could climb out of the hole he fell into after she died. He loved her, but when she died, he just fell apart. He hardly ever noticed me. But other men did. We scratched out a living by selling the few vegetables I managed to grow in our garden to the local grocer. When Paw died, I lost the place and had nowhere to go. The madam in town needed someone to clean up after hours, so I took the job she offered. The pay was decent even if the atmosphere wasn't and pretty soon I was promoted so to speak."

Travers frowned. "I'm sorry, Laura."

She gave a shrug. "Don't be. I've recovered. I wouldn't be the person I am today if I hadn't had to go through that. I've let it go. I can't change the past. It changed the course of my life. For the better, I'd like to think. If it hadn't happened, I'd probably still be making my living on my back. Life gave me lemons, and I made lemonade." Her face softened into a smile.

Travers reached and drew her against him. "And so you have. You are a special woman, Laura Murphy. Don't ever let anyone tell you otherwise."

"Oh, I wouldn't consider myself special, Trav, just older and wiser. You live your life, make mistakes and move on. If you lay down and die out of choice, what have you accomplished? I chose to fight, to regain my self-respect. I never had much, to begin with, but when you go through what I did, it makes you realize 'I deserve better than this.' Only you can know the value you have to this world. It made me realize that there are people out there just like me, suffering the same atrocious injustices and it sickened me to think that I had nothing of value to give to society. I'm more than a pretty face or a warm body to give a man a few fleeting moments of pleasure. I *matter*. I matter, whether or not anyone else thinks I do or not."

"How right you are, Laura. How right you are." He pulled her tighter, his arms going around her hugging her, and he felt the tension in her begin to melt away. He knew from the great release of breath that came from her that this had been something she had never told another soul. He was glad that she had chosen to share it with him.

What he would never know was that she had suffered greatly from the rape. She had been horrified to learn that she was pregnant from the attack. For months she had fought against the idea that she was carrying the bastard's child. It had nearly driven her insane. She had left town, wandering aimlessly about the countryside after the sheriff in the town had refused to press charges against her attacker for what he considered was just a case of rough sex. She had nowhere to go. She had packed her things and had left. For months she seemed to live in a dream world of denial, camping under the stars. She ate little and slept even less. One day, when she was fairly lucid, it hit her that the child she carried had no choice in the matter just as she had had no choice in the attack. The child she was carrying deserved better. It deserved a life. She had struggled to get hold of herself, taking one day at a time, hoping the fear and disgust would dissipate as time went by. She had stumbled upon a farmhouse and the lady who lived there, weak and seven months along. She was barely alive. The woman took her in and nursed her back to health, but unfortunately had been unable to save the child. Laura cried for months, knowing that if only she had stepped up when she had first realized her predicament that the child would have survived. She would have had a daughter to care for. A beautiful black haired angel to call her own. It had no longer mattered who the baby's father was. When she had seen the frail, tiny little body of her child, she had known instantly what she would have named her—Camille. She had been perfectly formed, but so tiny. There was nothing either of them could do for her, for she was stillborn. They had wrapped the child in a shawl and buried it out back in the woman's flower garden. Laura had stayed with her while she recovered, and the two had become close. Travers would never know that the woman who had helped her through that difficult time was Flora. Flora had helped her to regain her sanity, her strength, and her will to live. And it was Laura who had talked Flora into moving to Gold City. And now she was gone. Her best friend in the world was dead and buried because of another maniac who needed to be stopped.

And Maggie Bowers had every reason in the world to leave town, Laura figured. If her guess was right, Maggie was well on her way to finding out what hell was really all about.

SIXTY-FIVE

There was silence. Such a stillness that it seemed as if the town was captured in one of those oil paintings of Rance's. The creak of Travers' rocker broke the oppressive silence with a sharpness that surprised both he and Laura, sounding like the crack of a gunshot. Bad weather was no laughing matter out here. There was a pressure in the air that Travers knew could only mean trouble. Laura sensed it too.

"Storm's moving in. A bad one."

"Yeah," Travers nodded. "We're in for a rough night, I think."

Even as they spoke, a rumble of thunder shook the ground followed by a torrent of rain. Both stood and went inside, settling into the parlor for the duration of the storm.

An hour away, a lone carriage was making its way through the torrential rain. Maggie Bowers was headed home to Gold City. She had been released to travel by her doctor just two days prior, and she had waited until she thought it was safe for little Tanner to travel. Her son. Travers' son. Was he ever going to be in shock when he laid eyes on the boy? There was no denying the child was his. Not that she thought he would, but her earlier doubts about his conception could come to worry Travers. It was why she had left in the first place. Travers had never known she was pregnant. She had chosen to go through her ordeal alone, telling only Laura so that she would understand. When Tanner had finally arrived, she had fairly floated with relief. She had been unable to wait a moment longer. She had been on the road about forty-five minutes when it struck. The fierceness of the storm rattled her. Lightning cracked nearby, sending a rain of sparks and bark from the damaged tree it had targeted. Her horse bolted, and she fought for control, praying and cursing within the same breath. The normally gentle horse was terrified, and she was becoming so as well. They needed to find shelter fast. The carriage offered little protection from the drenching rain and Tanner began to wail as he quickly became soaked.

Maggie finally managed to get control of the horse just as the rain was beginning to let up. The clouds seemed to lift just a bit, and the wind died. For a few minutes, everything stilled, and Maggie could hardly breathe. Then a sound like nothing she had ever heard before seemed to crash about her. It sounded like a hundred trains rumbling, and she looked up in horror, her heart in her throat, to see a funnel-shaped cloud bearing down upon her from the ever darkening sky.

Miles away, Frank and Jesse were caught in the deluge. They were still a mile or so away from their hideout, and the rain was coming in such sheets they could not see where they were going. They struggled against the rain and let the horses have their heads as it seemed they had an instinct of where they were going. Finally, they reached their underground covey and took the horses inside with them. They heard the roar in the distance and knew a certain sense of relief that they were, at last, safe and out of the storm.

After about an hour, the fury passed, and the brothers stepped outside the shelter to relieve themselves and take their horses out as well. Frank was gazing in wonder at the now cloudless, starry sky when he heard a faint wail that he knew belonged to an infant.

"You hear that?" he asked Jesse who had wandered back up after hobbling the horses nearby.

"Hear what?"

"Listen." Frank listened intently for a moment, and the sound came again.

"There. Someone's out there. A baby. That's a baby crying."

Jesse couldn't hear it. "It's just the wind, Frank."

"No." Frank shook his head. "There's a child out here. Alone."

Jesse let out a sigh. "Now how do you know that?"

"I just do." Frank glared at his brother. "I'm going out there."

Jesse just threw up his hands. "Fine. We'll both go. I still say it's just the wind."

They rode for about a quarter mile in the direction Frank had heard the noise. They could make out what looked like the twisted remains of what used to be a carriage. They pulled up short, assessing the situation. Traps had been laid for them before, and they were leery of even the most innocent looking setups. The carriage was a crumpled mess and the horse that had pulled it was nowhere to be found. The wail was clearer now, sharper and there was no responding sound of another person anywhere in the vicinity. Frank and Jesse eased forward cautiously, their guns drawn and ready. Indians were known to mimic the sound of crying babies to lure people to their deaths, but this wail had too much pure terror to be a hoax. Dismounting, Frank took the lead and eased around the carriage. A woman lay face down, trapped beneath the heavy rig but the child was nowhere to be seen. Frank put away his gun and checked the woman for a pulse, finding a very faint hint of life. Her hair covered her face, and he carefully moved the tangled wet mass to draw back in alarm.

"Help me, Jesse!" he called to his brother who was still searching the area.

Jesse came, and they heaved the broken coach up and onto its collapsed wheels, freeing the woman. Frank ran his hands down her body, checking her for broken bones. His assessment didn't bring him the hope he thought might exist. She was critical.

"We've got to find that baby. And get this woman help fast."

Hearing the urgency in his brother's voice, Jesse circled the area once again and this time returned with the baby cradled against his chest. It was a boy, about two months old with the clearest silver-blue eyes he had only seen on one other person.

"Damn!"

They were going to have to work fast.

SIXTY-SIX

The elderly couple had just sat down to supper when a knock came at the door. Maw Thames went to answer it, grumbling all the way, wondering who on earth would be traveling in this kind of weather. It had started raining again, and the scene she opened the door to was a soggy damp mess. Two men stood before her, and one held a squalling infant in his arms under the protection of his slicker.

"Evening ma'am. Sorry to intrude, but we're in desperate need of help. This baby and his mother were caught in the storm and the lady's hurt really bad."

Maw Thames squinted hard at them, seeing earnest, weary faces. They seemed to be honest young men. The tall one with piercing eyes stepped forward.

"Ma'am, there's no getting around the fact that me and my brother here are wanted, men. I just wanted to be upfront about that with you. But even if you refuse us entrance, please, can you find it in your heart to help these folks?"

Maw Thames pushed her spectacles up her nose to get a better look at the two.

"Who you be?" she demanded.

"Frank and Jesse James, ma'am."

The old woman chortled. "Glory be! Come on in out of that weather. The dampness ain't good for the baby."

The men stepped inside, and Jesse handed the baby to the old woman who bundled him close.

Without bothering to see what the old woman would do with the now squalling infant, they headed back into the darkness and within a matter of seconds returned carrying a makeshift stretcher draped with a rain slicker. Maw Thames told them to follow her to the kitchen where she surprised Paw, who was still sitting there eating his dinner. She shooed him away from the table.

"Help me clear the table, Paw. This here woman needs medical attention."

Paw didn't stop to question, just busied himself and they had the table cleared in no time. Frank and Jesse placed Maggie stretcher and all on the table. Removing the slicker, Frank saw that Maggie's eyes were open.

"Ms. Margaret?"

Maggie blinked, looking up at Frank with pain filled eyes for several seconds.

"I'm not dead?" The words were barely a whisper.

"No, ma'am."

"I thought I was dead. It was so dark." Her eyes grew alarmed then. "My baby!"

Frank put his hand on her arm to prevent her from trying to rise.

"He's fine, Ms. Margaret. He's safe, right here, see?" He motioned for Maw to bring the child near so she could see for herself. He was now sleeping soundly in the old woman's arms, his lips making a slight sucking motion. Maggie smiled and tried to reach out to touch him, finding her arms too heavy to lift. She frowned weakly up at Frank.

"I'm so tired."

Frank shushed her, telling her to rest. Her eyes closed gladly, the strength seeming to have left her body. Pulling Jesse aside, he told him quietly. "You've got to go get Travers. Now."

Jesse noted the urgency in Frank's eyes. He nodded and placing his hat back on his head, headed for the door.

"Jesse, be careful out there."

Jesse stopped and tipped his hat to his brother and disappeared out into the mist-filled darkness. Frank watched him go, thinking that this was not going to be a good reunion. He turned to Maw and said, "I'm going to need your help." He shed his slicker, short jacket, and hat and rolled his shirt sleeves up, instructing her to bring blankets and set some water boiling. Paw was standing around watching the flurry of activity that had burst in on him so suddenly, trying to figure out what the heck had happened. Maw saw him and said "Paw, don't dawdle. Fetch my laundry basket so's I can lay this little one down." Glad to have something to do, the man hurried to the next room to do her bidding. Once the babe was made comfortable on a soft throw placed in the basket, she got busy gathering blankets and such to help Frank. She turned to give more orders.

"Paw, you go see to this man's horse. Poor thing's still out in this weather."

The old man sauntered to the door, pausing to turn to Frank. "You be needin' anything off'n him?"

"Bring my saddlebags inside, if you will."

The old man nodded and went to take care of his business.

Maw produced a pair of scissors for Frank so he could cut away Maggie's ruined clothes. He had already eased her shoes and stocking off, finding her toes blue and ice cold to the touch. She had not moved her feet at all, not even responding to his touch to the arch of her foot. It wasn't a good sign.

Maggie had opened her eyes again, and Frank had eased to

where she could see him.

"Ms. Margaret, I'm going to cut your dress away so I can examine you. I'm afraid it's already ruined, anyway."

Maggie looked at the warm, caring eyes that had known so much pain in their lifetime, eyes that tried to reassure her although she already knew she probably wouldn't make it through the night. She felt like mush inside. She offered a smile to the man who had brought her in out of the storm.

"There's no need."

Frank realized that she was trying to tell him that she knew there was little hope, but he was adamant.

"I'm going to examine you, Ms. Margaret. Travers will have my head if there was something I could have done for you."

Her eyes brightened at the mention of his name. "He's not so bad, once you get behind the steel in his eyes. You should know that by now."

Frank gave a curt nod. "Yes, ma'am. He's a good man. One of the best friends I've ever had."

"He cares for you, like a brother. When he found out that you were the one who helped him after he was wounded, he gave Daniel such a tongue-lashing like he'd never heard. It killed Travers to know that we had placed you in such danger by bringing you into that situation. He would never have done that— knowingly place you in danger."

"Well, he had no choice in the matter. I owed him, many times over. Friendship is a priceless thing out here. True friendship, anyway. Now let's get that dress off of you." He turned and instructed Maw Thames to warm a blanket by the fire as he cut away the sodden mess from Maggie. She set one over a chair by the fire and came to hold Maggie's hand as he began to probe and prod. Maggie tried to be silent during the ordeal, but couldn't help moan in pain when he contacted broken ribs and bones. Below the waist, however, was a different story. She felt nothing. Frank had suspected as much.

Maw's eyes met Frank's knowing ones as they placed the heated blanket over her chilled body. He shook his head sadly at her and the old woman's eyes teared up. She turned away and went to sit beside the woman's sleeping baby.

Frank sighed, knowing this would be difficult. It had to be done. At this point, they were beyond being formal.

"Maggie, you . . . you have a lot of broken bones and internal injuries. And Maggie, I believe your back is broken."

She smiled sadly up at him. "I could have told you that."

Frank leaned his hands on the table beside her and lowered his head, his eyes closed in regret.

"I'm sorry, Maggie." He shook his head at the helplessness

he felt.

"It's not your fault. I should have stayed in town another day, but I was so eager to get back to Gold City, to Travers. I thought the storm had passed. It happened so fast. One minute I was going down the road, rain pouring in on me and the next, I was flying through the air."

"The wind picked you up?" Frank asked her.

"Yes. It suddenly stopped raining, and the sky turned a funny color. The next thing I know I'm spinning through the air. The force was so great I could hardly breathe. I was so afraid we were going to die. And Travers would never get to meet his son."

Frank smiled at that. "He's a fine boy, Maggie. Just like his father. Travers will be so proud of him. You rest now. Jesse has gone to fetch Travers. He may be awhile. Save your strength for him. And hold on, Maggie. Just hold on."

Maggie smiled up at him, the knowledge that Travers was on his way giving her joy and courage to fight the coldness settling in on her. She closed her eyes to rest, if only for a little while. She eased into a deep sleep. Frank noted her slowed breathing and frowned, checking her pulse. He hoped Jesse hurried back with Travers soon. She didn't have a lot of time.

SIXTY-SEVEN

The fury of the storm had passed, and a gentle breeze had replaced the sweltering heat that had consumed the town before the storm. Travers had gone outside to stand on the porch to catch the breeze that was like a healing balm. He had discarded his vest earlier, and his tailored white shirt was unbuttoned farther than propriety normally allowed due to the heat earlier. The wind caressed his hair, lifting it, parting it, and he inhaled deeply, allowing the cool dampness it carried to flow through his system and refresh before exhaling with a great sigh. He cut a fine figure as he stood there, his head thrown back, eyes closed in rapture as the breeze caressed him, his shirt billowing in the breeze.

Laura stood poised just inside the door, unnoticed by the doctor. She was observing him, thinking how funny it was, life. Laura had known Travers was handsome, but it had never really struck her until now just how much. She loved him, she realized, though not in the way that makes a woman weak and unable to think for herself. She loved him like she would a brother. Or would have if she'd had a brother. Maybe that was why she had been immune to his manly charms. She knew Flora had been utterly attracted to him. Could understand why now. Laura had been alone all of her life it seemed. She was not looking for love. She had always hungered for companionship, a family of sorts, but had never been willing to go that extra mile to secure a husband and start a family of her own. Travers had been a perfect fit from day one. They had both been loners and had gravitated to each other out of loneliness. Now, looking at him, she could well understand why the women of the town seemed to swoon in his presence. He was a fine looking man. And a decent man. The combination of both in one serving of male perfection. She smiled. Stepping out into the breeze he was enjoying, she held out a glass of lemonade.

"Care for a drink?"

Travers turned, grinning at her. "Sure," he said and took the offered glass. He downed half of it almost immediately. "Man, that's good." Laura moved to the rail beside him and looked up at the stars now shining brightly in the cleared sky.

"Aren't they beautiful tonight?"

"Yes, they are. I never get tired of seeing them. Back in Virginia, there never seemed to be as many. I suppose it's just that it is so open out here."

As one, they moved to the rocking chairs on the porch. They sat and rocked and savored the cool drink, enjoying the companionable silence for a while, making small talk and enjoying the breeze coming in off the plains.

The creak of the loose floorboard in the hallway alerted Travers to the fact that they were no longer alone. A shadow appeared at the door but didn't step out onto the porch, careful to stay in the darkness of the hall. Travers had stopped rocking at the first indication that they were not alone but said nothing, listening, waiting for further sound. Laura had not heard anything, but had seen Travers tense up, and knew his instincts told him something was wrong. The voice, when it came, was low.

"Doc."

Travers eased around to peer into the darkness to try to get a better look at the man.

"I'm Dr. Gage."

"Well, hell, I know that. I was sent to fetch you. You're needed at the Thames place pronto." Travers stood and stepped through the open door to face the intruder.

"Jesse?"

The man tipped his hat. "Frank says you best come quick."

"He get himself shot again? I told him—"

"Stop yore yammerin'. This ain't about Frank. That Bowers woman's hurt real bad. We found her and her baby out on the prairie. They got caught in the storm. Wind-tossed the carriage onto her."

Travers' eyes widened, fear eating his insides. He had stopped hearing past Maggie being hurt.

"Laura! Get my medical bag. I'm going to get our horses! Move, dammit!"

Laura sprang into action, running up the stairs to get his satchel and stopped to get their rain gear lest they need it as well. That seemingly clear sky could disappear at any moment. She had not heard the conversation in the hallway, but by the sound of Travers' voice, this was a matter of urgency. She didn't even notice the man in the hall hiding in the shadows until she had come back downstairs to wait for Travers. He wasn't a tall man, and he looked vaguely familiar. She stepped closer, offering her hand.

"Hello. I'm Laura Murphy."

The man doffed his hat, a scrunched looking excuse for one at that and shook the hand she extended to him.

"Jesse."

"Jesse. . ." she encouraged.

He just shook his head and chuckled. "Well, ma'am, I've found it's better to have a little mystery in one's life. Sometimes a name can mean the difference between life and death."

Laura's right eyebrow slowly arched itself. She liked this man. Didn't know why, but she did.

"Is that a fact?"

Jesse grinned back at her, cramming his hat back on his head. That's a fact, ma'am. That surely is a fact."

Travers chose that moment to appear with their horses, and he and Laura mounted up, Travers taking the time to secure his satchel before he did so.

"I'll meet the two of you out by the cemetery," Jesse said and melted into the darkness again.

Laura looked at Travers. "What's happened? What's wrong?"

Travers sucked in his breath to steady his nerves. A vein throbbed in his temple, belying his stress level. "Maggie's been hurt."

Laura felt the breath leave her. "Oh, no!"

Travers put the spur to his horse and leaped away leaving Laura to follow behind. The rain that had stopped earlier now seemed eager to fall again. It did just as they met Jesse at the cemetery but they pushed on, knowing it was imperative that they reach Maggie. Jesse was a veteran at traveling in the worst of conditions, so Travers put his trust in the man. He had to. Maggie was waiting for him.

SIXTY-EIGHT

Maw Thames had brushed and dried Maggie's hair and washed the mud and grass from her arms and face. Maggie had thanked her, grateful that she would at least look presentable when Travers arrived. She hoped he wouldn't be too angry with her risking the life of their child to get to him, to come home. But she hoped above all else that he arrived soon. She knew she was slipping away. Could feel it in the marrow of her bones. She asked to see her baby, and Maw Thames brought the sleeping boy and laid him on her breast. Maggie drank in the sight of him, praying silently for God to protect this child of hers. He would need all the love and care he could get since she was not going to be around to raise him. Travers would be a good father, she knew, but her son would need a mother's touch from time to time, and she kept wondering how Laura would treat Tanner. The two of them were like family now. She wanted Tanner to grow up knowing what family meant. Tears welled up in her eyes as she imagined her son at the ages five, ten, fifteen. He would be a smaller version of his father, she knew, as devastatingly handsome and just as intelligent. She had so wanted them to be a family. The pain of knowing it was not to be seared through her conscience. The pain came in waves, mixed with the pain of regret. Her eyes closed and she slept again.

Frank and Maw were keeping vigil, by Maggie and by the window.

"I sure hope that man of hers gets here soon." Maw fretted, gnawing her bottom lip. "Who did you call him?"

Frank moved away from the window to pour himself a cup of coffee that Maw had brewed earlier.

"His name is Travers Gage. He's the doctor over at Gold City."

"Ah. Think I've heard of him. Supposed to be purty good, I hear." Maw had moved to take a seat near the fire, needing to warm her old bones. Paw had fallen asleep in the rocker across from her, and she had left him there in the case that he may be needed.

"He's the best around here by far. The best I've ever met."

Maw looked at Frank closely. "You seem to know the man well."

"He's a good friend. We met before the war. He's an honorable man. His kind is few and far between out here."

Taking a sip of his coffee, he eased to check on Maggie and the baby again. Both slept soundly. He resumed his vigil then beside the window.

Almost another hour passed before the sound of hooves slapping mud brought Frank and Maw to their feet. Boots thumped heavily on the porch, and the door opened to reveal the tired, wet threesome. Travers tossed his hat and slicker into a corner, not caring that it missed the chair he had aimed for. His eyes roamed the room for Maggie. Through the open door of the kitchen, he could see her lying still as death upon the table. Frank put his hand to his friend's chest when he started forward.

"Travers, there's nothing you can do," he told his friend softly. Blue eyes locked with dark ones.

"Tell me."

Frank sighed heavily. "She's been crushed inside. The carriage fell on her. And," he paused, "her back is broken. To be honest, I don't know how she's lived this long."

Any hope that Travers had entertained crumbled in that one moment. If Frank spoke the truth, and he knew he did, they would lose Maggie tonight. He looked past Frank to where she lay on the kitchen table, a child cradled against her chest. He couldn't reach her fast enough.

Laura had come in and was in the middle of shedding her slicker when she heard the stranger's words to Travers. Oh, God. Not Maggie. Not now. It was too devastating a blow after all these two had been through. She started to follow Travers, but the stranger held her back.

"No," he told her.

"Let go of me. They need me right now." She flung back over her shoulder at him, finding herself oddly captivated by his dark eyes.

"They need privacy right now, and that's exactly what they are gonna get." He ushered her back into the other room with Maw Thames following close behind. Jesse had just come inside from putting the horses in the barn.

"How is she?" he asked Frank.

"Bad. Real bad." He hated it. He hated it for Travers who deserved to be happy.

So did Jesse. The only words he could think of fit the situation to a tee.

"Damn. Damn, damn, damn."

SIXTY-NINE

He eased to her side, having closed the double doors behind him. Her eyes were closed, and her lips were tinged with blue. His eyes raked her, noting the misshapen shape of her body, even covered with the blanket, it was obvious that she was in a bad way.

"Maggie?" Travers reached and lightly traced the curve of her cheek with his finger. She was so deathly pale that he feared she had already passed. "Maggie?"

Her blue eyes opened to reveal eyes tinged with death. They no longer held that sheen that he had come to know as her sparkle. She smiled weakly when she saw him hovering over her.

"Travers. You did make it. I was so worried you wouldn't." Her breath was little more than a whisper.

"I'm here now, Maggie. My God, I didn't want to believe Jesse when he showed up in town. . ." His voice broke, unable to finish.

"I'm sorry, Travers. I should have waited, but I was so eager to come home. I was trying to get home—to you."

He shook his head. "It's all right, Maggie. It's not your fault. It's nobody's fault. Don't go blaming yourself for this."

She shook her head and smiled in regret, though it looked more grimace than smile.

"I was trying to come home to you. So you could meet your son." She looked down at the child who had begun to squirm on her chest. "This is Tanner. Tanner Rance Gage." She eased the blanket away from his face so Travers could get a better look at him.

Travers turned his attention to the child, at last, his hand going to softly cradle his little head. He saw a bundle of joy, noting his coloring, so like his own, with a head full of dark hair. He had his mother's hair. Maggie watched the emotions pass across Travers' face as he touched his child, thankful that she had got the chance to see this exchange. "When I realized I was pregnant, I knew I had to leave. It was never about you, Travers. I knew that I had to be alone to deal with the idea that this child might have been conceived of rape. All I could think about was this child might not be yours, that maybe it belonged to that awful man. I don't think I could have faced you knowing that it was his child. I had to know for myself. I had to resign myself to that fact."

Travers let go a long, heavy, frustrated sigh. "Maggie, it wouldn't have mattered to me. I would still have loved him as my own."

Maggie's eyes closed briefly, and she looked away in shame. "But I don't know if I could have, Travers. That's why I had to leave. I didn't know if I would be strong enough to keep him and raise him, knowing how he had been conceived. I was so afraid."

Travers picked the child up and cradled him high on his chest. Noting the petal softness of his skin, he touched his finger to his son's cheek. The boy opened his eyes to see who had disturbed him from his rest and in doing so revealed the same silver-gray eyes of the man who held him so tenderly.

"He's got my eyes," he said laughing suddenly, thrilled, knowing why Maggie had been so desperate to come home to him. She had known the child could only belong to Travers when he had been born with the odd silver eyes instead of the usual blue.

"Yes. He came into this world with those eyes and I wept for joy. You have no idea the relief that his birth brought me."

Travers bounced the baby lightly in his arms, making funny faces at him. The tyke was not amused, just looked at his father with the oddest expression, before fussing a bit and finally found his fist with his mouth, sucking noisily on it.

"Was it a difficult birth?"

"I lost a lot of blood. The doctor kept me in bed a month. He had just released me to travel last week."

He looked from Maggie to the baby. "He's beautiful, Maggie. Thank you for my son," he said and bending over, kissed her softly on the lips. She muttered something unintelligible and her eyes closed. Panicked, Travers felt for her pulse. It was there still, but so very faint. He turned and walked into the parlor, startling everyone there. The four of them had been silently lost in their own thoughts, all dreading the time they knew was near. Coming to stand in front of Laura, he handed his son over to her and instructed her to tend him while he went back to the kitchen to spend what little time he had left with Maggie alone. Closing the door securely behind him once more, he took a chair and placed it as near her as he could, noting she was beginning to struggle for breath. In a few moments, her eyes opened again.

"Travers?"

"I'm here, Maggie," he said, slipping his hand into hers.

"Tanner?" Her eyes questioned.

"I took him to Laura for a while. He's fine. Sleeping again."

Her face visibly relaxed. "I want him raised in a family, Travers. Laura would make you a good wife, I think."

Travers stumbled on that one. "Well, she will definitely make someone a good wife, but I'm afraid it won't be me, Maggie. Laura and I are like brother and sister. I'm sure she'd be pleased as punch to be Aunt Laura."

Maggie frowned. "He'll need a mother. A woman's touch."

"Maggie, stop fretting. Laura is more than capable of tending to our son. We're all the family that boy needs. Stop talking about it as if you won't be around to see him grow up."

"But I won't be. And we both know it. I'm leaving my son. I wanted to be his mother, to watch him grow up to be the image of his father." Maggie's tears fell freely now. Travers edged closer, his arms going around her, trying to offer what comfort he could given the situation.

"Hush sweetheart. Don't you fret? That boy of ours will grow up in the most loving home possible. Laura and I will make sure that we stick around to raise him proper. And we will teach him all about his mother and how very much she loved him." The grip in her hand upon his arm was growing weaker. Travers began to lose his reserve, tears beginning to trek down his cheeks. He attempted to hide them in her hair, his face buried in the fragrant tresses he always acquainted with orange and vanilla.

"I wanted to be his mother, Travers. I was going to be Mrs. Travers Gage, and we were going to live happily ever after . . . a wonderful life." She smiled weakly through her tears, knowing he felt her pain as deeply as she. "I was a fool to dream such things."

Travers pulled back slightly, his eyes fierce on hers. "Don't say that, Maggie. No one could have known things would turn out like this for us."

She managed another rueful smile. "We've had so little time together. I seem to have brought you nothing but pain all these years. And still, you fought for me. For us. You believed in us even when I didn't any longer. Promise me you'll not let this destroy you—my—passing. You have our son to care for. He will need you, your guidance, patience, and levelheadedness." Her voice was beginning to fade. "And your strength, just as I need it now. I need your strength now, Travers. I'm so afraid." Her voice caught on a sob, and a weak shudder passed through her. The time was upon her. "Kiss me, Travers. I need to feel your lips on mine, just once more."

Travers gathered her tenderly in his arms and pressed the gentlest of kisses to her pale lips.

"I love you, Maggie," he told her, brokenly, the tears flowing freely, unheeded down his face.

"My love, my life. . ." she whispered, her eyes locked with his, and then, the light faded in them.

Travers knew the instant she left. There was no struggle, just a soft exhalation of air, a gentle breeze that caressed his face. He stood there for a long time just holding her, trying to memorize the contours of her face, her lovely blue eyes that now stared lifelessly at him. He eased her lids down, unable to handle seeing the light gone from her eyes a moment longer.

It was as if a dam had burst. His body shuddered in silent grief as huge sobs wracked his body. He was in agony, his heart felt as if it were being crushed by a giant vice. It hurt, damn it, it hurt so bad! It was not supposed to end this way for them. They were ever at odds with one another. He had lived a nightmarish reality when she had married Jim Bowers. He had suffered the fates of the damned, watching from afar, trying to move on with his life. Fate had taken a wicked turn, thrusting them together in one night of unspeakable, undeniable passion, only later to be thrust into a nightmare of rape and murder. He had thought that with Jim dead, they could start a life together now that the nightmare was over. Then Maggie had left town, leaving him to endure his own private hell once again. He had not known she carried his child.

It was a while before he got hold of himself long enough to ease her body back to the table and take his seat again beside her. He cradled her soft hand between the two of his. He studied it as he had her face, memorizing. The softness of her skin, so different from the child of thirteen. The roughness had been replaced by a petal softness that Travers would never have believed. He had known the strength behind her facade, and that had made him love her even more. She'd had to be strong as a child for her family, for herself. She had endured poverty, beatings, and cruelty from her husband. Still, she retained her pride, her spine, her inner strength. But even she had limits. There was no way that she could have survived the beating her body had taken in the storm. Travers consoled himself with that knowledge. It had been an act of nature that had taken Maggie. Nothing any doctor on the face of the earth could have done for her. And she was right. He would not let her death destroy him. Yet he couldn't begin to conceive of saying goodbye to her, let alone place her in the ground, a hole where the worms and bugs would return her to that from which she was made. But he wouldn't think about that right now. He would sit with her for as long as he could, just as long as he could still touch her, no matter that she had long grown cold.

SEVENTY

Hours had passed, and the people gathered in the parlor had paced and dozed and paced again. Frank and Laura had struck up a hesitant friendship after his curtness to her earlier. They had spoken quietly amongst each other, admiring the child that Travers had told them was named Tanner. Laura could see Travers written all over him already and knew he would be a handful to raise. So far he had been a good child, sleeping fitfully, waking once, only to be lulled back to sleep by a lullaby that Laura made up. That had brought a titter of laughter from Frank, as the words didn't rhyme and had no noticeable tune. Frank had remarked that the child had to be tone deaf to appreciate that pitiful excuse for a song. He had laughingly joked that the child was probably feigning sleep to get her to stop singing. At the moment, Tanner was asleep, safely tucked into his makeshift bed in the laundry basket pulled a safe distance from the fire. The others were catching up on some shut-eye.

Laura had stared at the kitchen door for so long her eyes felt crossed. She could stand it no longer, the silence from within revealing nothing. She eased to the door and listened, straining to hear. Silence greeted her. She eased the door open and found Travers gazing into the fire of the stone fireplace, his hand still clutching Maggie's. She slipped inside and closed the door, pausing a few steps behind him. If he heard her, he didn't show it.

"Travers?"

For a long time, she stood there, met by silence. She hesitated to speak again, the mood so solemn, so heavy. For a long time, there was silence. When he did speak, he only confirmed what she suspected, his voice barely audible above the crackling of the fire.

"She's gone."

Laura stepped closer, her hand going to his shoulder, feeling the tension in his frame.

"She went peacefully, in my arms. She just . . . faded away."

His shoulders shuddered yet he made no sound. Laura's arms went around him, holding him tightly to her and his hand came up to grasp hers as if she was his only anchor in a sea of insanity. She held him, and he held her, drawing comfort from her embrace as only she could give.

He had sat there for the longest, wondering what he was going to do without Maggie. He couldn't imagine life without her.

For so long she had been a part of his life, from just a child of eleven years old, she had left him at thirteen, yet he had carried her with him throughout the war and after. Reentering his life a grown woman had been a shattering experience for him. Even though she had never really been his, she had always been just a heartbeat away. Very much like an elusive dream, a dream that had become a nightmare. His heart ached as never before. Not Maggie. They had lost Flora less than a year ago. Now Maggie was gone as well. He didn't know if he was strong enough to take her loss. He tried to be strong. He tried not to break down.

He tried so hard.

He lost the struggle and gave in to the sobs that spilled forth. Laura held on tightly, knowing his world had just been shattered, his hopes and dreams for the future scattered like ashes in the wind.

"I'm here, Travers. I'm right here. You just hold on to me and let it all out. We'll get through this somehow. We will do it because we have to. We have to, Travers. She loved you so very much, and she gave you a beautiful child. You have a son who needs you, Travers. He needs his father to be able to raise him proper. So you just let all the grief out now. There may not be time for it later."

He heard her through the fog of his grief. He wasn't loud or overly dramatic with his sorrow, but it wrenched his gut so that he felt tied into a thousand knots. He understood what she was trying to tell him, understood her perfectly. He would grieve now and forever, but this was his chance to get it out of his system. He would always grieve for Maggie, for what might have been between them. Tanner was his future, Maggie's future. He would not, could not let her down.

EPILOGUE

Time flies raising a child. In the beginning, time seems to drag, the washing of diapers, the long nights of colic. Flared tempers and frayed nerves when nothing seems to quiet a cranky infant. The utter frustration of not knowing what to do, what to say, how to soothe. The anger, the heartache, the laughter, and yes, the tears. The heartstrings that bind tighter than shackles. Time seems to get away from one when life gets back on track and order overtakes chaos. The early years pass so quickly that in reflection, it takes a powerful memory to recall certain aspects of past birthdays and holidays, milestones that should never be forgotten, but seem to fade somehow with time. A child's first steps, first tooth, first curl and haircut, first puppy. That one had been a near catastrophe! The memory brought a twinkle to his eyes as he sat there watching his child scamper across the rug in the parlor, recalling the black long-haired creature that had struggled so desperately to get shed of the child's grasping hands. Travers had thought it funny until he had seen the white warning stripe just seconds too late. His boy. He had a head full of black hair, as silky and shiny as his mother's. His features were his father's, his eyes like glass pools. Travers found the boy studying him on occasion, just a curious look on his face. He often wondered what went through that little head of his.

It had been three years. It seemed like yesterday. He had made peace with it, her passing. They had buried her in the town cemetery on a bright sunny day, not far from Flora. She had not been buried beside her dead husband. That would have been a sacrilege and Travers would not have it. Daniel had been there for him, though he was little comfort, having to deal with his own grief of losing Flora. For a year he had seemed to drift mechanically through the routine of living day to day. He had realized almost too late what he was doing to himself and to his child. Tanner had clung to Laura, not finding love in the arms of the one person who should have been giving him the most. Then they had almost lost him. He had contacted a fever that would not go away. Travers could not determine its cause and desperately fought to save his child. *His and Maggie's* child. His thoughts had been consumed with the fact that he had always seemed to let her down. He had let her mother die, then Rance, and he had been unable to save her as well. He had to save Tanner, not just for her, but for him. He fought the fever with every bit of book knowledge he had, and then some. He conferred with shamans from several of the nearby Indians tribes. All of them had not a clue. It came to him in a dream one night. Maggie had appeared to him and told him the healing was not in his hand but in his heart. He had not understood at first, but then he realized how severely he had neglected Tanner with his own grief for Maggie. From that night on, he talked to Tanner about his mother, her love for him and his love for her. He told him stories of her childhood and their life together. The fever began to dissipate, and the child woke up. Travers could not believe the change. Tanner had begun to warm to him and was now his shadow. 'Travers in miniature' is what Laura called him. She had been there through the difficult times, and the good. She had been the mother that Maggie had so desired for her son. Laura had been a godsend. She seemed to come alive as never before caring for Tanner. Tanner had even taken to calling her MeMe, his form of 'mother.'

At that moment she happened upon the two of them in the parlor, both in the middle of the floor, giggling and tussling.

"What are you two characters doing? I thought we could go on a picnic. It's such a perfect day out."

"I think that is a wonderful idea! How about you, kiddo? Want to go on a picnic with your Paw and MeMe?"

The toddler clapped his hands joyfully. "Pi'nic!" He squealed, giggling with delight.

They had been on four in the last few months, and they seemed to have caught fever with it. It gave Travers much needed one on one with his son away from the town. The town had grown so much in the last year that he stayed busy at all hours. When he was away, people were less likely to bother him. And Laura had enjoyed the quiet respite as well. She had time to write, a hobby she had taken up of late. The open prairie offered a quietness and serenity that could not be found back in town. And she had begun to see Frank on a regular basis. Of course, he waited outside of town for her at the Thames place. The Thames' had taken the James boys under their wing after the ordeal with Maggie. So far they had not been bothered, but Laura knew it was just a matter of time before word got out that they frequented the area. But she would not think about that right now. Today she wanted to celebrate life with two of the most important people in her life. She scooped Tanner up and swung him high. The boy giggled delightedly.

"I say we blow this joint," Travers said, grinning at the picture the two of them made and rose to stand beside them.

As one, they moved to the door and Tanner gurgled something unintelligible, his eyes on the painting above the fireplace.

They paused before the portrait of the raven-haired woman as the child blew a kiss to her, and said in the sweetest of voices as clearly as day, "Wait wight heah, pwetty wady! We'll be wight back!"

Travers ruffled the boy's hair, tears forming a lump in his throat, even as Laura hugged the child closer, his head falling securely to the comfort of her shoulder. Seeing the love between the two of them, and knowing that even in death, Maggie would always be a living presence in his heart, and in their son, he knew that he had come full circle in his journey to happiness. He may not have gotten to spend his life with Maggie, but she had given him something so very precious—her heart—in every sense of the word, and it lay within their child. His blood. His son. Lawrence Sharpe had commented to him long ago on a distant piece of forever hallowed ground, that sometimes blood is all that saves us. He had been in a desperate situation at the time, his very life in the hands of the doctor who had come to his aide, on the field of battle and off. The general had been referring to the men Travers had been forced to kill to save him, that sometimes blood had to be shed to save lives. But now, Travers saw just how loaded a statement that was. In taking life, he had saved the general's. In creating life, he had saved his own. His son, *his blood*, had saved him, helped him rise above the pain of loss, failure, and doubt. More than that, he had brought him peace. A piece of Maggie and a piece of himself. Travers smiled past his tears, and after Laura exited the room with his son, he turned to the portrait and blew the woman on the canvas a kiss as well.

"We're fine now, Maggie. Thank you for our son."

With those words, he walked out into the sunshine, where his family waited, to find a bit of peace.

THE END

Afterwards

Most of my research came from the Internet. It is a wonderful source of almost inexhaustible information on any subject you care to know anything about. Wikipedia has an anthology called

"Legends of America" that was of considerable value. "The Forsyth Scouts" by Lee Zion was good reading to get an idea of the movements and activities of troops between forts in that time frame. A detailed timeline of Kansas events came in handy. This is a compilation of various authors – Louise Barry, Richard J. Bowe, William G. Cutler, David Dary, Kenneth S. Davis, Matt Dennis, Dorothy L. Galway, Charles R. Green, Kurt Parsons, John Rydjord, and Midwest Research Institute all compiled and managed by George Laughead, Jr.

My list would not be complete without mentioning Frederick Boling's "A Tribute to the Frontier Doctor." His article confirmed a lot of what I had known and suspected concerning medical practice at that time. Other sources contributed but perhaps none so important as this one.

I cannot tell you how many books or articles I have read on the American Indian. Better yet, I won't even attempt to credit any as they are so numerous. I believe I must have been one in another life. My earliest recollections of childhood play had me as the feared red man. I never wanted to be the cowboy. I wanted to be the first one into battle and the one with the peace pipe.

My heart aches for these people. They have lost so much and gained so little over the years. They are indeed, for the most part, a defeated people. In my opinion, no western is complete without an Indian, for they *are* the west, and always will be.